# HUNTER KILLER

GEOFFREY JENKINS was born in Port Elizabeth, South Africa and educated in the Transvaal, where he wrote his first book – a local history – at the age of seventeen. After leaving school he worked as a sub-editor in Rhodesia, later becoming a newspaperman in both Britain and South Africa.

His first novel, *A Twist of Sand*, was published in 1959 and immediately became a best-seller; it was later filmed. Since then he has written seven more successful novels which sold over five million copies in twenty-three different languages.

Geoffrey Jenkins is now working on a new adventure story and also, with his wife Eve Palmer – also an author – *The Companion Guide to South Africa*. They live near Pretoria.

GEOFFREY JENKINS

# Hunter-Killer

FONTANA / Collins

First published in 1966 by William Collins Sons & Co Ltd
First issued in Fontana Books 1968
Sixteenth Impression May 1983

© 1966 Geoffrey Jenkins

Made and printed in Great Britain by
William Collins Sons & Co Ltd, Glasgow

# CONTENTS

# 1 COMMANDER GEOFFREY PEACE R.N.

Geoffrey Peace was dead.

I could not believe it. For three days, ever since a naval officer had enquired 'Mr. John Garland?' and handed me that agonizing message from the flagship, I had not believed it. Even when the ominous shape, covered by a tarpaulin, had been brought alongside in a launch by a naval party, my mind rejected the thought. But now there could be no doubt: I stood looking through the glass trap in the coffin lid into the hard face of the man who had been so much a part of my life: Commander Geoffrey Peace, Royal Navy, D.S.O. and two Bars.

Death had not softened the clean-shaven face; the strong jaw with the cruel line of the mouth was held shut by the black rubber diving-cap he had worn at the time of his death. They had dressed the body again in the underwater suit. Its cowled effect brought no feeling of sanctity but rather one of evil, or—I told myself in hurried excuse for the dead—the desperate rejection of any hope of afterlife, like the wild keen of a piper's lament in the Outer Isles.

Geoffrey Peace should not have died like this, I thought angrily—to be hauled from a few feet of water with heart failure. Automatically my eyes sought the hands which had sent so many other men to their deaths, but they were hidden. All the Peaces had died hard. A strange resentment welled inside me that this one should have met his end so tamely after so violent a life. Simon Peace, his grandfather, had gone to meet his Maker with the cry of the sea and England on his lips; old Sir John Peace, his piratical ancestor who had terrorized the Indian Ocean, had been cut in half on his own quarterdeck by a triple-shotted broadside. But Geoffrey Peace, who was in the full glare of the public spotlight in Britain and America because of his part in the controversial American Navy missile project, had died no more excitingly than an overfed businessman who drops dead after a dip at Ramsgate.

Now he lay 'slung atween the roundshot'—not old Sir John's way, perhaps, but as near as they could get to it in this age when men had already stepped on to the moon; for Geoffrey Peace's wasn't an ordinary coffin at all. The coffin at which I looked was steel, fashioned like a cylinder: it might have been a section of torpedo-tube or, more likely, a length of discarded missile-casing from a cruiser in the bay. No, it couldn't be that, I realized, bending closer. The metal was riveted, not welded, and a missile needs a smooth bore. I ran my fingers unseeingly along the line of grey-painted metal studs. Perhaps if the sight of my dead comrade-in-arms had not affected me so greatly, I might then have suspected something of the secret which was to shock the world and the United States in particular.

The sound of a powerful jet engine overhead jerked my attention away from the dead man's face. Here were the top brass coming to pay their last tribute to Geoffrey Peace. The plane circled the anchorage. Peace was ' lying in state ' aboard his own luxury motor-yacht, *Bellatrix*. In the bay, backed by palm-fringed islets, I could see the American Seventh Fleet, a magnificent array of fighting ships. Among them were two of the new Shenandoah-class nuclear subs, replacing the first Polaris-firing George Washington class, which had become obsolete in the early 1970's. To the north-east lay the Royal Navy's new Limuria Squadron, a crack task-force which had again raised the Navy's battle ensign of glory after the long starved years of the 'fifties and 'sixties. It did my sailor's heart good to see the lean, deadly silhouette of two Loch-class cruisers, *Loch Vennachar* and *Loch Torridon*. Complementing the American submarines were the British Devastation-class nuclear subs.

*Bellatrix* was at anchor in Port Victoria, Mahé Island, largest of the Seychelles group in the northern Indian Ocean. The Seychelles, a 5,000-square mile agglomeration of islands, atolls, cays and coral reefs, lie about one-third of the way between East Africa and India. This group stands at the head of another immense chain stretching away boomerang-shape for over 1,000 miles to the south-east. The northern pivot is Mahé and the southern Mauritius. These islands—often no more than a fringe of coconut palms round a strip of sand a few feet above water-level—have been named collectively Limuria. They are inhabited by fewer than 2,000 people spread over tens of thousands of square miles of sea. The islands are believed to be the last visible peaks of a drowned continent which once lay between Africa and Australia. The inhabitants—descendants of pirates, natives and slaves—speak Creole, a tongue which has mutated as far from its original French as have the strange animals of Limuria from their African homologues. Limuria is a never-never land of soft tropical islands and languor, a surfeit of sweetness among the endless palms, lagoons of breath-taking loveliness at dawn and sunset. Here, some years ago, Britain had established her big missile base.

I screwed up my eyes against the afternoon sun and watched the big jet bank round Mount Howard, Mahé's northern tip, and circle over the densely wooded ravines and peaks which back Port Victoria. I lost it momentarily, then it reappeared from behind Morne Seychellois, the highest peak in the island, to make its landing approach. I turned away from it, sick at heart, dreading it for what it represented: the publicity ordeal of Peace's funeral, with myself as the chief mourner.

What secret did that hard face hold below the glass, the secret which he had summoned me to tell and yet, for reasons which had died with him, had held back for one week, a week which was to prove his last on earth? My eyes searched the dead face, tried almost to get beyond the half-closed lids, to find out. What was it all about, I kept asking myself, as I had done while we had raced towards the Seychelles from Mauritius, where we had met. I had sought the answer then, but in life Peace was not the man to be approached—not even by his closest friend—if he did not want to be approached. I saw now that his tense, highly nervous state in the days preceeding his death was not, as I thought, due to the weight of his secret, but was caused by the shadow of the heart-attack which had killed him.

The superficial explanation he had given for asking me to come all the way to Mauritius from South Africa was, of course, a blind. That was clear to me soon after our meeting. I had left the Royal Navy to take charge (thanks to my knowledge of navigation) of the head office of NACCAM, an advanced commercial air and sea navigational system, in Johannesburg. Under my supervision, we had installed navigational aids for ships and aircraft round the southern, strategic tip of Africa. Peace had cabled me asking if I would meet him to discuss the installation of a similar system in the islands of the Indian Ocean. He had suggested Mauritius as the rendezvous, since the island is only six hours by jet from Johannesburg. Peace's message came as a surprise to me, for I had been out of touch with him for several years, although his work in connection with the British missile mission to America had kept his name constantly in the news.

For months before his death, Peace had been the centre of a bitter controversy over an Anglo-American missile. British scientists had developed a small light-weight nuclear power plant for missiles and satellites. The newspapers nicknamed it SNAP—System for Nuclear Auxiliary Power. The motor,

9

according to the papers, was considerably in advance of anything in America or Russia. Peace had led a British technical mission to the United States, offering the Americans the new motor as a co-operative effort in space exploration. Britain made no secret of her pride in her invention, and SNAP was equally well received in the United States. Its merits were endorsed by no less a man than Marvin K. Green, the brilliant young American astronaut and scientist who had become Vice-President. MKG, as he was popularly known, had turned that rather stultifying office to splendid account as the representative of the new technocratic society which had sprung into being in the United States. He had assumed the chairmanship of Special Projects—an independent body answerable to the President only—whose function was the development of special American missiles. Special Projects was enthusiastic about SNAP, MKG and Peace formed a close friendship, and it seemed that a new bond in Anglo-American relations was about to be forged.

Then—success struck. The Americans launched two men, Davis and Acton to the moon. Using a land-based Air Force Sirius rocket staged from a space-station orbiting round the earth, these astronauts reached the moon but failed to return, and were cremated in a shallow orbit round the earth.

The great American success—a skyport was established on the moon itself by Davis and Acton—killed the new Anglo-American project. Against the wishes of the President, an economy-minded Congress scrapped it. What point had it, they argued, now that there had been a successful landing on the moon?

Peace—and to a lesser extent MKG—had been publicly outspoken against the dropping of the project and Peace's forthright views had made him the storm centre of the controversy in the United States.

I had thought Peace to be in England when his cable arrived. Glad to go and eager to see my old friend, I had been shocked at his tenseness when he met me at Mauritius as the South Africa—Australia jet landed. He had hurried me aboard his luxury yacht *Bellatrix*—another surprise for me—and persuaded me that the place for the discussion with unspecified persons over the NACCAM installation was the Seychelles. We had sailed from Mauritius within a few hours on the four-day trip. Apart from his tenseness, the first indication I had of the impending shadow over Peace was a diversion to a remote island group 250 miles north-north-east of Mauritius known as St Brandon, or Cargados Carajos. St Brandon is nothing more than a hellish group of islets and coral rocks with one tiny port on Raphael Island. Peace's excuse was that his ancestor, Sir John Peace, had used St Brandon in the reign of Charles II as a base for piratical forays against shipping in the Indian Ocean. Peace made much of the fact that Sir John had been the first Englishman to chart the group. To my astonishment, he had insisted on spending days in an island boat charting the risky seaward passages of St Brandon's great 25-mile coral barrier reef. When I protested, and pointed out that I had joined him to discuss a big business proposition, he became withdrawn and angry. I got no more out of him until we reached the Seychelles, where, instead of going ashore at Port Victoria to discuss what I had irritably ceased to regard as a deal, he decided to go spear-fishing.

When Peace announced that he intended to take *Bellatrix* to a cluster of islets centering on Frigate Island, 25 miles east of Mahé, I exploded. If he wanted me, I told him angrily, he would find me ashore at the hotel—if I hadn't left on the next plane for South Africa. MacFadden, the tough Scots engineer who had been with us on the Skeleton Coast of South-West Africa in earlier years, had gone on a bender ashore immediately we arrived. I sympathized with him. I had no wish to go wandering aimlessly about the islands under the pretext of a business deal in the offing.

My irritation with the whole affair increased when I found that I would have to stage back to Johannesburg via East Africa, and that the aircraft was an old flying-boat which only made the leisurely trip once a week. That meant a further delay of three days in the Seychelles. I cursed the soft languor of Limuria.

Peace had seemed animated, less tense, when I announced my intention of going ashore. He didn't try to stop me. For a moment I thought he was about to say something, but then he shrugged as if he had changed his mind.

As I sat at dinner at the hotel that evening, a naval officer came to my table and saluted.

'Mr. John Garland?'

I nodded, wondering if my anger had provoked somebody to do something about discussing the deal.

He handed me a note, which I took more in irritation than anticipation. It said: 'I have to inform you that the body of Commander Geoffrey Peace was taken from the water at Noddy Rock, half a mile northward of Frigate Island, at approx. 1330 hours today by a boat's crew from H.M.S. *Loch Vennachar*, operating in that area. Artificial respiration was applied without success. Commander Peace was taken aboard *Loch Vennachar*, where he was pronounced dead by the Senior Naval Surgeon. The body will, at the direction of the Commander-in-Chief, Limuria Command, be held aboard *Loch Vennachar* until suitable arrangements have been made . . .'

I hadn't seen the room after that. All I saw was an indelible vignette from the past; Peace at the periscope of a submarine, Peace going in for the kill . . .

The sub-lieutenant was dutifully sympathetic. 'You were his friend, sir, weren't you? They say he was the greatest skipper that ever took a submarine to sea . . .'

I had my own memories of that. I cut him short. The manner of our parting ate into me like acid, now. 'Can I see him?'

'Afraid not, sir.'

I got up. I *had* to see Geoffrey Peace—only once again. Not the way we had parted, with a flare of anger and a shrug.

'By whose orders?' I demanded.

'Commander-in-Chief's, sir. No one allowed to see the body. As a serving officer . . .'

I must have raised my voice, for several of the diners turned. 'Take me to *Loch Vennachar*.'

The sub-lieutenant had obviously been chosen for the job. 'Sorry, sir, no civilians allowed aboard missile cruisers. Security and all that.'

'Civilian!' I exploded. 'I'm no bloody civilian, man— I'm a reserve captain in the Royal Navy! Ask! Ask!'

He was cool and sure of himself. 'Ask—who, sir? Perhaps we could discuss this . . . ah . . . away from . . .' he gestured at the staring diners. He led the way outside. I demanded again to see Peace's body, the C-in-C, the Senior Naval Officer ashore. The most I could wring out of the young sub-lieutenant—whom I heartily detested by now—was that he would try and establish my *bona fides*.

I walked down to the pierhead. I do not know how long I stood and stared at the lights of the fleet. He could not end like this, I told myself over and over—not Geoffrey Peace. I had to talk to someone. I spent the next few hours looking for MacFadden among the pubs and joints. There was no sign of him. I tried to telephone the SNO, but the naval exchange was adamant. For the next two days I fretted and fumed. Then the sub-lieutenant came to the hotel and reported that *Bellatrix* was back in port. I could go aboard, I was informed politely, but must not leave harbour. I tried again to find MacFadden, but he must have holed up somewhere.

12

If, however, the body of Peace was being concealed, the news of his death was not. The morning after his death, the BBC gave it a high place in its early bulletins. The evening newscast contained a tribute from the Prime Minister to Peace's part in the development of the SNAP motor and his mission to the United States.

Other bulletins stated that Peace would be buried at sea with full naval honours by the Limuria squadron and the U.S. Seventh Fleet. This seemed to me a belated attempt at recognition of what, on the face of it, might have been a highly successful joint space effort between the two nations. The British Defence Minister would fly to Mahé to attend, as well as senior naval officers from Allied countries, it was stated. This, I took it, was because of Peace's famous wartime exploits. I was interviewed by long-distance telephone from London about Peace. A television news crew arrived and the hotel foyer looked like a studio. Through all this I was denied access to the C-in-C.

I went aboard *Bellatrix*—still no MacFadden. Then came the awful moment when the naval party arrived with the body and my realization that the face below the glass was indeed dead. There was also a message to say that the C-in-C would be pleased to discuss the funeral arrangements with me at my convenience. The funeral was to be delayed, I was informed, pending the arrival by plane of more VIPs.

The big jet came round once again, flaps hard down for the landing. Perhaps this was a plane-load of them. If I could have had my way, it would have been a quiet committal to the sea from the deck of *Bellatrix* . . .

Had the soft thump on the hull come a few minutes earlier, it would have been lost in the roar of the jet. Its very gentleness made it sinister. A boat makes its own particular noise against the hull of a bigger vessel. This was the thump of— a body.

I slipped over to the opposite porthole, and crouched down with my ear against the sycamore panelling. There it was! The slow slide of a body pulling itself up to the deck, with great caution. Had this suspicious approach something to do with the secret Peace never told me? I glanced round the cabin hurriedly and then ducked behind the bar-counter in the corner.

Whoever it was made no sound on deck. I waited.

Then the after door of the cabin began to open slowly. Out of sight, I would have to rely on sounds from now onwards in order not to be seen.

Silence.

I risked a quick sideways glance round the bottom of the bar.

Back towards me, a man, wet, naked except for swimming trunks, was kneeling at the side of Peace's coffin. His head was cocked to one side and a rubber tube led from his head to the steel cylinder. A stethoscope! Like a veterinary surgeon sounding the heart of some strange creature, the man placed the stethoscope against the metal. I could almost hear his breathing. As if the instrument were not functioning properly, he slipped the earplugs off and put his ear—face sideways to me—against the coffin. Still not satisfied, he went to the head and listened again. I heard the faint hiss of his breath. I craned round the bar. It could not have been his breath, for the man was standing, every nerve alert, looking down at the coffin. He was muscular, sun-tanned, and I saw thrust into his belt, the walnut butt striking against the whiteness of his belly, a Colt .38 Detective Special. He moved slightly and the gun clunked faintly against the steel. He must have been as taut as I was, for he wheeled round on the empty room. I jerked my head back. Colt Special! That was the gun used by American police, the FBI and detectives, a beautiful little weapon with a stubby barrel and a lethal strike. I had seen, too, something that alarmed me—the hammer of the Colt had been hocked, to enable a quick draw from a shoulder-holster. Whoever it was knew his way around with guns.

I peered out from behind the bar. The man had dropped the stethoscope and now leant with his chest across the glass window. I heard his rapid breath as he thrust down on a screwdriver. He was unscrewing the panel to get at the corpse!

Loyalty to Peace, devotion, admiration, grief at our unhappy parting, made me blind. That anyone should desecrate Peace's body in front of my eyes . . .

I was on his back, my hands reaching for his throat, before he heard me, even. As he swung and grappled, dropping the screwdriver, I knew I had been a fool. This man was skilled at in-fighting. There was no blind panic in his actions, simply a swift muscular reflex to offset the ground he knew he had lost in that split-second of my surprise attack. I dodged the swift kick to the groin and hung on to his throat. There was no fear, only a hint of acknowledgment of a worthy enemy in his grey-green eyes. He feinted with a knee to try and prise loose my grip on his throat, and then, with a spasm of strength, jerked me over his head. My spine crashed sickeningly against the top of the coffin. My grip eased and he struck me savagely across the heart with a flat blow from his forearm. My scream of pain died from lack of air in my lungs. He eased back, drew in a deep controlled breath like a swimmer, and his hand went to the Colt. I lay spread-eagled across the coffin, my face to the ceiling. The swift, cool actions of my unknown enemy were those of a professional. I lurched forward as his hand clutched the butt and struck a karate blow to the carotid artery with my left hand. It wasn't a heavy blow, for I was completely off balance and it was my left hand—a blow like that can kill when administered with the right. I saw the face go blank with pain and semi-consciousness. The Colt came up, though. He was a foot from me. Then, as if from nowhere, a bottle smashed down on his head and he fell half across me, showering me with whisky and glass splinters. His face hit the steel side of the coffin and he slid slowly to the floor.

Mac stood looking at the label of the broken bottle in his hand. 'Glenfiddich!' was all he said. 'Waste of t' best whusky in t' world.'

The unconscious man lay grotesquely on the thick carpet, blood and whisky about his head. Mac walked over and looked through the glass trap. He drew back a little and the dry sob which shook him was the most terrible thing I have ever heard.

'Geoffrey . . .' I began.

'I heard about it,' he rasped. 'Whusky!'

I went over to the bar and pulled out another bottle while Mac simply stood there. I handed him the unopened bottle. He tried to pluck off the foil and unscrew the cap, but his hands shook so uncontrollably that he could not. With an oath, he smashed the neck across the coffin and the amber liquid flowed across the glass, blurring the face below. He threw back his head and gulped some of the spirit, drinking from the broken edge. A trickle of blood ran from his lips, but I do not think he noticed.

'Mac!' I said sharply. 'Mac!' He stared unseeingly at the dead face. I shook him roughly by the shoulder. He took another strong drag from the ragged edge of the bottle. 'Aye,' he said quietly, under control now. 'Aye, nothing.'

I broke the silence. I nodded at the unconscious man. 'Thanks for that . . . he was going for his gun.'

Mac said uncertainly, 'He was?'

I told him briefly about the stethoscope and the screw-driver. Mac picked them up and we rolled the intruder over.

15

'He won't die,' said Mac with the ghost of a grin. 'I hit him hard enough just to break the glass.'

I knelt down and tried to find something to identify him. Except for the Colt, there was nothing visible. The numbers had been filed off the weapon. I emptied the shells. The trigger was hair-light.

'Nothin',' said Mac in disgust. 'Not even any clothes . . .'

I bent down again and threw back the man's limp left arm. I pointed to the back of the armpit. The skin was chafed and rougher than the rest.

'Shoulder-holster,' I remarked to Mac. But that wasn't what I was looking for. I stretched the arm out so that the skin of the inner arm was visible.

On it, grouped in a triangle, were three small brown dots, like small moles. It was enough.

I rose, balanced the Colt. 'Central Intelligence Agency. American.'

Mac peered and shook his head. 'All I see are three brown moles.'

'Take a close look and you'll see they're not pigmented,' I said shortly. 'It's the secret mark of the CIA's agents. It's how they identify each other.'

Mac examined the 'moles' closely and gave a soft whistle. 'Tattoo.'

He looked admiringly at me. 'Where didyer pick up that one?'

I shrugged. 'I worked a long time with Geoffrey Peace. And Peace worked with Naval Intelligence.'

Mac looked thoughtfully at the muscular figure. 'What did he want with——?' He nodded, leaving the name unsaid, as if he couldn't bring himself to speak it. Mac was closer to Peace than even I had been; it was a blind, headlong devotion backed by a cunning and ruthlessness learned in the gutters of Glasgow. I knew Mac's past; I also knew there was nothing he would not have done for Peace. Perhaps it was only because he was still suffering from his bender that he hadn't killed the CIA man with the jagged whisky bottle. He looked dangerous enough now he knew who the intruder was.

'What did he say to you?' he asked hoarsely.

'Not a word,' I replied. 'He came at me as silently as a snake.'

An order was shouted from outside and an engine went into reverse. I felt the launch come expertly alongside. Another order, and heavy feet on the deck.

'Quick!' I said to Mac. 'That's the Navy.'

'Engine-room,' he replied. 'Help me with him—just as far as the companionway.'

We half-carried, half-dragged the limp figure from the cabin as several pairs of boots fell into step on the planking above. I snapped the door shut behind Mac and tried to straighten my clothes in the bar mirror, but before I had run a comb through my hair a man in admiral's uniform, with two officers behind, stood in the doorway. He came forward, stopped at the sight of me, the broken bottle, and the stench of whisky. He stretched out his hand.

'Mr. John Garland? I am Admiral Sir William Irvine.'

The C-in-C himself! I was not in any mood for him, or any of the others who were staging a Roman Holiday out of Peace's death. I was still short of breath from the fight.

'I have been trying to get hold of you for three days.'

One of the officers looked shocked at my abruptness. Irvine remained bland. 'You'll appreciate that in view of the high public esteem in which Commander Peace was held, it was not possible to rush through the arrangements.'

'Arrangements be damned,' I retorted. 'If Peace had had his way, he would have asked to be thrown over the side with some old iron at his feet to take him down.'

'Commander Peace was very unorthodox, we know,' he replied thinly. He frowned at the whisky-blurred glass and the broken bottle. 'It appears that his friends are, too.'

'Mac the engineer and I were saying goodbye to him in our own way,' I snapped back. 'We broke a bottle of whisky over his face. It's the sort of thing that would have appealed to him.'

The admiral looked pointedly at my dishevelled appearance. 'May we sit down and discuss the arrangements?'

He and the officers found themselves chairs and one of them smoothed out a typewritten sheet.

'Ackroyd?'

The officer went into action with the smooth competence of a computer. He read: 'Funeral arrangements for the late Commander Geoffrey Peace. The body will lie in state aboard the yacht *Bellatrix* for three days . . .'

'Three days!' I exclaimed. 'You mean this sideshow—' I gestured at the coffin—'is to go on for three days just to satisfy the ghoulish whims of a lot of sightseers?'

The admiral dropped his blandness. 'I think you should moderate your tone, Mr. Garland. It is not a sideshow, as you choose to call it. Commander Peace is a national hero—an internationally known figure—and he will be accorded the recognition due to him. A naval guard of honour will stand

17

watch over the coffin. I am afraid we must ask you to leave *Bellatrix* until after the funeral . . .'

I scarcely heard him. My mind was on that strange figure listening at the coffin, trying to get in. Had he taken a chance in broad daylight because he knew there would be a naval guard after that?

' . . . following the lying-in-state, the body will be conveyed aboard *Loch Vennachar*,' droned on Ackroyd. 'Limuria Squadron will put to sea at 0900 hours, using the North Entrance. The u.s. Seventh Fleet will also proceed to sea and take up station in line ahead two miles northward of Récif Islet, bearing 155 degrees, while Limuria Squadron will be stationed in line ahead approximately three miles south of Renommée Rock.'

'We are burying Commander Peace as near to the area where he was drowned as we can,' consoled the admiral. 'Frigate Island is a bit tricky for the big ships, particularly if we get a squall from the north-west.'

Ackroyd resumed. 'A fighter escort over the fleet will be provided jointly from h.m.s. *Teaser* and u.s.n. Springfield.'

The more I thought about the grand display, the less I liked it.

'The mourning party will be abroad *Loch Vennachar*,' intoned Ackroyd. 'Launch for the chief mourner to be at Victoria pierhead at 0830 . . .'

'That means me,' I said.

The C-in-C was patient. 'The Admiralty has informed me that no relatives of the late Commander Peace could be traced. As his close friend, the honour falls to you.'

Honour! At heart I felt like Mac—I wanted to smash something.

Ackroyd went on. 'The official naval party——'

The admiral broke in sharply. 'What about the DNI?'

'The Director of Naval Intelligence, sir? No invitation was sent . . .'

The C-in-C smiled apologetically. 'Not the current DNI. No, the Old Man himself—just retired——'

I felt a thrill go through me. How often had Peace spoken of him, although I had never met that legendary figure of British Naval Intelligence! I said off-handedly, 'There's no call for the DNI to come all the way from England for this circus.'

The C-in-C's glance contained something I did not understand. 'He does not have to come from England—he lives here—in the Seychelles.'

He watched me closely, too closely. First, the CIA man

18

and now the head of British Naval Intelligence himself, when I had thought him to be living in a country cottage in England, or sailing a yacht at Cowes. Stranger still that Peace had not mentioned him in the week we had been together; he must have known he was in the Seychelles. Where did Peace's secret come in? I was in deep waters.

'Didn't you know?' asked the C-in-C. 'He's living here at Mahé—retired and came straight to the Seychelles. He'll be aboard *Loch Vennachar* for the funeral. You can renew acquaintance.'

'I never met him,' I replied.

'Strange,' he murmured, watching me still. The tenseness seemed to go out of him with my last remark, however. Mac and I would have to find out more from our faceless stranger, even if Mac had to rough him up a little in the process. The odd coffin began to look odder still as my suspicions mounted.

Ackroyd cleared his throat and broke the tight silence. At least the funeral arrangements were neutral ground.

'The committal service will be conducted by the Reverend Miles Sands, Fleet Chaplain. The customary salute will take the form of a salvo fired from the main armament of *Loch Vennachar* . . .'

The bizarre ceremony took shape in my mind's eye—the double row of British and American ships stopped for the committal, the ramp over the cruiser's side, the weighted body tipped as the padre intoned ' . . . we therefore commit his body to the deep . . .' the uptilt of the ramp . . . the faraway splash as the object hit the water . . .

' . . . following which a wreath will be dropped over the spot by helicopter flying from H.M.S. *Teaser*.'

I had to be aboard that helicopter! Only if I saw Peace's body sink into the depths would it allay the crowd of doubts and questions which clamoured now in my mind.

'I'd like to fly in that helicopter,' I said quickly.

The C-in-C froze. His reply confirmed my suspicions. 'I'll consider it.'

'Consider!' I retorted. 'You don't have to consider! You can okay my request here and now.'

He said steadily, 'I said, I'll consider it. I'll inform you of my decision in good time. I can, however, promise that if you wish the pilot to drop a personal floral tribute——'

'Personal floral tribute!' I laughed in his face. The reek of whisky was in my nostrils. Mac's 'personal tribute' was raw from the heart and it could stay at that, for my part. The mystery remained, larger than before.

'Forget it,' I muttered.

Ackroyd had been well trained. He glided on, trying to reduce the tension. 'The fleet will then make half-speed to a position east-north-east of Récif Islet, to bear 220 degrees . . .'

My sharpened mental reflexes jerked at the mistake in the orders.

'The fleet's stopped for the committal,' I snapped.

There was a flash of anger, but also amusement, in the C-in-C's eyes. Ackroyd dutifully fell silent. My eyes followed his steady stare at the coffin. I saw, too—the thing weighed a ton! I'd been thinking in terms of a body sewn in canvas. How would they get that heavy object over a ship's side?

'The fleet will not heave-to,' replied the C-in-C evenly.

'If you get it overboard it'll foul the cruiser's screws!' I expostulated.

'Cruiser?' echoed the C-in-C, playing with me. 'Who said the ceremony was to be from *Loch Vennachar*?'

I half rose, but he waved me down.

'I think you should get the picture clear in your mind. Commander Peace will not be buried in the ordinary way. The method might have pleased his own macabre taste. No, the British and American fleets will steam in line ahead, the mourning party being on *Loch Vennachar*'s bridge. The fleet destroyer H.M.S. *Amirante* will detach and proceed at full speed between the lines of ships. *Amirante* will carry Commander Peace's body, while the chaplain conducts the service from *Loch Vennachar*. It will be relayed by radio to the other ships.' He turned to Ackroyd. 'What is *Amirante*'s speed?'

'Thirty-five knots, sir.'

I was revolted at the thought of the Hollywood-type spectacle to please millions of television viewers (there was to be a hook-up via Telstar satellites) which would also massage the egos of the British and American naval commanders. The press, radio and television ballyhoo had also been deliberately engineered.

My anger flared. 'Thirty-five knots! Don't be bloody silly, man—you can't drop a body overboard at thirty-five knots!'

'Who said we intended to drop him overboard?'

I rose to my feet in incredulity.

'Not drop—fire.'

'Fire?'

'Yes,' said the C-in-C evenly. 'We are going to fire Peace into his grave from a depth-charge mortar.'

20

# 2 MORTAR-RIDE FOR A CORPSE

I could not believe that he was serious. It sounded like a circus display to me.

The C-in-C went on. 'You must have wondered about the special coffin—I think *Loch Vennachar*'s engineering shop did a fine rush job.'

'You sound like a professional undertaker,' I grated.

He shrugged. 'Commander Peace's burial demanded special arrangements. You must have wondered why your request to see the body was not granted.'

'I don't wonder any longer. Whose bloody-fool idea was all this?'

'Mine.'

'I won't have any part in it,' I retorted. 'You and your—your arrangements can go to hell.'

I did not seem to get through to him. 'It would look rather strange, would it not,' he went on blandly, 'if John Garland, Peace's friend and comrade-in-arms, sulked while the hero was given the honours and recognition due to him?'

'Honours and recognition be——! There is still time to call off this whole silly farce.'

'Is there?' He was cool, sure of himself. 'Tell the Defence Minister not to come? Tell the top representatives of the Limuria Grand Alliance that John Garland claims the exclusive right to bury his friend as he—and no one else—thinks fit? Reverse the chain of communications now in motion to relay the ceremony? Tell millions of television viewers . . .'

I cursed myself for not having broken through the obstructions when I first heard of Peace's death. Now it seemed too late.

'Don't you wish Commander Peace to be honoured?'

'Not in this way.'

'How, then, if I may ask?'

'I . . . I . . . all I know is that he should have been buried quietly at sea . . .' My voice trailed off.

The C-in-C rose to go. 'You have not made any of the constructive suggestions I had hoped for from someone so close to Commander Peace.' Bloody hypocritical bastard, I thought. 'I think we may take it that the present arrangements will stand. Ackroyd will keep in touch with you. Can you have your things packed in, say, an hour? I must ask you not to come aboard *Bellatrix* except during the formal lying-in-state hours. Naval guards will be posted with orders.' He shrugged slightly. ' I hope you will not embarrass either me or yourself. I suggest you be as accommodating as possible, Mr. Garland.'

' Captain Garland,' I reminded him.

He smiled, the iron hand in the velvet glove. ' To me, mister. Had you fallen under my orders—well, this interview might have proceeded somewhat differently.'

His remote, formal air was impenetrable. He picked up his cap and ground out his gold-tipped Benson and Hedges cigarette: The two officers matched his actions. A formal salute, and he was gone.

The steel coffin creaked gently under *Bellatrix*'s quiet lift. What had an American Intelligence agent sought to find out with that stethoscope? Had he suspected that Peace might not be dead? I didn't want to look at the dead face again, but the tumult of questions hammering in my brain drew me to the coffin itself. Those heavy rivets! I fingered them. Had *Loch Vennachar*'s engineers indeed fabricated the strange contraption? *Could* they have made it in a brief two or three days?

I was drawn to the glass trap. What secret big enough for the CIA to be interested in lay behind the closed eyes framed by the monkish cap? I had not noticed previously that Peace's head was pillowed on foam rubber. I wiped away the last of the whisky. The glass still wasn't clear. There seemed some condensation inside, but the humid climate would account for that. They must have embalmed the body for it to lie another three days ' in state '—six in all since his death. Then I noticed that the entire interior was of foam rubber.

I took the stethoscope, adjusted the plugs in my ears, and listened. Nothing. That layer of foam rubber would have damped any sound, however. Although the admiral had said Peace was to be fired from a depth-charge mortar, the body did not seem to be strapped in. I calculated the width of Peace's shoulders against the size of the cylinder and recalled his height. Strange! The coffin was much longer and wider than necessary. I explored the foot. There was a heavy flange. I ran my fingers over it. The metal was rough and painted, but I felt something. I looked round for some instrument, then went and fetched an ice-pick from the bar. With it I scratched and found lettering. It read: ' Cammell-Laird, Ltd., Shipbuilders, Liverpool.'

I reflected grimly that the key might well lie with the

unconscious CIA man. Mac and I would have to make him talk. As far as Cammell-Laird's were concerned, the coffin was probably a stray section of casing or tubing from a submarine bearing their imprint. That would account for its shape and size. The C-in-C had been very much on the defensive with me, but he had warmed a little when he had spoken of the DNI.

The thought of the DNI decided me. I would go and visit the man whose fame behind the scenes was matched only by his anonymity outside the Service. He was, of course, Peace's friend. The C-in-C had said he had settled recently in Mahé. It would not be difficult to track him down in a small place like Port Victoria. Even at this late moment, I thought, he might be able to have some of the undignified extroversion of the funeral modified. He might also know Peace's secret.

I started towards the engine-room, and as I did so I heard the naval guard of honour coming alongside.

Mac was wry. 'The bastard's still out. Nothing to be had from him for hours.' He looked down at his oil-stained hands. 'We may have softened him up a little, though.'

'We've got to be off *Bellatrix* soon,' I reminded him, looking at the muscular figure lying on the gratings. Mac had patched up the wound on his head and he looked corpse-like with the blood cleaned away.

'We can't carry an unconscious man past the guard.' I pointed out. 'We'll lock him up and come back in an hour or two on the pretext that we've forgotten something.'

Mac's voice was savage. 'And—question him.'

I nodded. 'He'll be tough, though. The CIA boys aren't given to shooting off their mouths, least of all to a couple of amateurs like ourselves.'

Mac said coldly: 'He tried to get at the skipper. That's enough for me. He'll talk—or else.' He picked the man up under the armpits and half-pushed, half-threw him into one of the steel lockers. It had a latch, but no lock. It was the best we could do, with the guard already aboard.

I pocketed the Colt and went to the cabin. The naval party had grouped themselves with reversed arms round the coffin. The officer-in-charge frowned to see Mac and me still there. I packed quickly, leaving some of my things as security to be allowed back aboard. From my locker I took the cherished yachting cap I had worn with Peace on the Skeleton Coast. I decided to carry the old cap at the funeral as a token of sentiment, despite the fact that I would be in civilian clothes.

A boat was summoned to take us ashore. Before it arrived, I went and stood at Peace's head. A long shaft of sun struck down over Morne Seychellois, enriching the sycamore panelling of the cabin. The curtains over the portholes shifted in the land breeze. It was all sunshine, softness and light: the bizarre grey coffin was as out of place as a Viking hand-axe on a silk cushion.

This was goodbye, yet I felt nothing. I would never look on Geoffrey Peace's face again. I tried to concentrate my thoughts on that square foot of rather dirty glass, but they kept wandering out across the gentle anchorage, listening to the sounds of the fleet, to the raucous note of a patrol-boat's loud-hailer keeping the curious at bay. I abandoned my silent farewell, telling myself that we'd looked death in the face together so often that now, when it had come in such common-place fashion, all I could do was to recognize the fact.

Ashore at the hotel, I traced the DNI easily, though the English receptionist had been a little stiff, saying merely that he lived in a cottage with a companion. She didn't elaborate. Now I walked beyond the town up a valley towards the mountains. They were striking the Union Jack at Signal Hill, at the northern end of the red-soiled valley. It wasn't far.

The high casuarina tree screen, with its tangled, lush undermat of plumbago, golden allamanda and hibiscus in which Creole *négrillons* played hide-and-seek, thinned to show me my objective. Here, indeed, were roses better than the DNI's in Kent, but there the resemblance ended. The cottage was topped by palm-leaf thatch and the slabs of pink coral of which it was built still held some of their underwater colour in the dying sun. My eye did not linger on its beauties. The object of the *négrillons'* interest was a Royal Navy petty officer with a sub-machine-gun at the gate. In the garden were more men with .45 Smith and Wessons and a walkie-talkie.

The petty officer looked severely at me. 'Sorry, sir. No admittance. Orders.'

'Tell the DNI it's John Garland—Commander Peace's friend. He'll understand.'

The man's voice held a new respect, but he remained adamant. 'Nothing I can do about it, sir. It isn't for the DNI to say who comes and goes. I have a list here—' he tapped his pocket—'and you aren't on it.'

Anger and frustration boiled inside me. 'What the devil is all this?' I demanded. The *négrillons*, sensing a diversion, crept closer, chattering like monkeys. 'What's going on that an armed guard has to be thrown round the home of a harmless old man?'

'I wouldn't say that—'e's very spry still.' The petty officer gave a quick glance round and dropped his voice. 'Maybe she keeps 'im young, sir,' he leered.

'What do you mean?'

'Young lady in there.' He grinned. 'Now wot's 'e got that I ain't?'

My concept of the DNI was shaken. Peace had spoken of the dedicated aesthete; here was a sailor leching over an old man and his trollop. In St Brandon the islanders will tell you how the women who come from the Seychelles have corrupted the men. And, certainly, to see a *sega* danced on neighbouring Agalega is to understand how easy it is to obtain a ' poultry-keeper '—trial bride or sleeping partner, as you wish. Agalega pioneered the system of a husband selecting from among his friends several to share his wife under a gentleman's agreement that the right man is at the right place on the right night. And Agalegans, who consider themselves moral, point accusing fingers at Seychelles women! No wonder the receptionist had been prim when I had asked about the DNI!

He was likely to be useless in the present crisis. My wish to see him left me. 'It's nothing important,' I said.

The petty officer reacted to my tone. 'We all 'eard about Commander Peace—you was 'is mate, wasn't you?'

'Yes—yes, you could call it that.'

He went on: 'Did you 'ear the radio today, sir? BBC? We aint s'posed t'listen except on our own wavelength, but we did—was 'e really like that, sir?'

An iron band seemed to constrict round my head. If I didn't break free of this publicity build-up and sloppy patriotism, I should.

'He was a brave, cruel, heartless, determined, ruthless bastard who killed more men than he could remember,' I grated. 'But if I had thought he would have had to endure this bloody rubbish when he died, I would have killed him long ago with my own hands.'

The petty officer gave a gasp. I swung on my heel and stalked down towards the town. I found Mac and, in a savage mood, I rowed out to *Bellatrix*. I rode rough-shod over the officer of the guard and Mac and I went to the engine-room. He let out an oath at the sight of the empty locker. An open porthole told its own tale. Either the intruder had been foxing us, or he had come round sooner than we had expected. Silent, angry, we returned to the port.

The morning of the funeral broke crystal clear, as had done a million other mornings in Limuria. I had been awake since first light due to the clump and clatter of the television crews moving out their equipment. I dressed and looked out.

From seawards came the heavy revving of British and American jet carrier planes. *Bellatrix* looked forlorn, guarded only by a small naval launch. The prying small craft were missing. The reason was on the radio. The BBC said: 'Last night the body of Commander Peace, the British naval hero who is to be buried today with full honours at sea in the Seychelles Islands, was conveyed aboard H.M.S. *Amirante*. As listeners already know, Commander Peace will be committed to his final resting-place by the unusual method of firing his coffin from a destroyer's depth-charge mortar. Television cameramen have been stationed aboard the destroyer *Amirante* and, by courtesy of the Admiralty, viewers in many countries will be able to see the actual moment of firing . . .'

With an oath I switched off. Cap under my arm, I strode down to the pierhead to the launch taking me to *Loch Vennachar*. They hadn't expected me early and I had the bridge to myself. A few cables' length away was *Amirante*. Cameramen, reporters, news commentators and TV crews clustered round the stern depth-charge throwers. Peace's coffin was lashed to one of them, shrouded by a tarpaulin. I tried to watch the fleet, but my eyes always went back to that.

Two hours later I still stood alone on the bridge wing, as chief mourner who couldn't mourn. I had been treated by the C-in-C's staff as a sort of pariah, set apart by being Peace's friend, but without the status of a relative. The Defence Minister and naval officers stood together in reverent silence as the Fleet Chaplain intoned the well-known words into a microphone. Black cassock and white surplice blew in the wind, a foil to naval blue and gold braid and black formal coats. The fleet steamed slow ahead. For miles ahead and astern was a superb array of missile cruisers, aircraft carriers, fleet destroyers and corvettes. In the centre, near *Loch Vennachar*, were the tall sails or conning-towers of six nuclear submarines. This was Britain's crack Limuria Squadron. Parallel, a mile distant, was the American Seventh Fleet—the same ships in line ahead, but instead of six submarines, they had ten. Keeping precision station almost under my feet was *Amirante*, with Peace's body lashed to her mortars.

At the chaplain's wind-blown words, ' . . . Thou hast showed us terrible things and the wonders of the deep . . .' an officer stepped over and raised his hand to *Amirante*. If I disagreed with the C-in-C's publicity methods, I could not fault his ships. *Amirante*'s engine-room bells rang. There was a quick thresh of water as her screws went full ahead. Simultaneously, the tarpaulin was jerked from the coffin.

I looked for the last time towards Geoffrey Peace's body. Only then did I feel the surge of my pent-up emotions at the sight of the armada of fighting ships, the long swell rolling in on the south-easter, the throb of powerful marine engines, the scream of carrier jets trailing wing-tip smoke.

' . . . Thou sufferedst men to ride over our heads: we went through fire and water . . .'

A dollop of sea creamed over the destroyer's stern, inundating the depth-charge throwers. *Amirante* raced down the line of ships. Récif Islet, a white, cuspate, guano-stained rock, fell astern and, fine on the starboard bow, was Frigate Island, where Peace had died. A flock of frigate birds circled over it, like a squadron of planes protecting a fleet. The swell was increasing—we were getting into the cyclone season—and the coral reefs and cays where Peace had spent his last hours were white. *Amirante* reached the head of the fleet, swung towards the American side and came round in a dramatic, full-ahead turn—a bone in her teeth, a splendid, unforgettable sight.

The destroyer reached us. Her timing—and the chaplain's —were split-second. As he spoke the sonorous last words, *Amirante* was alongside.

' . . . we therefore commit his body to the deep . . .'

There was a sharp explosion, a puff of smoke at *Amirante*'s stern. The ungainly coffin cartwheeled high into the air. Cameras locked on the grey object as it hurtled upwards and news commentators, hanging on to the stern rails with one hand and with microphone in the other, gave their word pictures. Slowly the thing rose up and up. It arced downwards. I thought almost I heard the splash above the destroyer's engines.

The C-in-C allowed the raw drama to sink in. The chaplain was silent, too, before the Benediction. An officer pressed a button at the rear of *Loch Vennachar*'s bridge. The deck trembled and shook. Four missiles leapt from the cruiser's launchers in a flurry of flame. Four others rose from an American cruiser. There seemed scarcely any time between the launch and a thunderous detonation overhead. Then a helicopter was over Peace's grave and a huge wreath floated down at the end of a parachute.

As it hit the sea, I felt a sudden impulse. Something of Peace for Peace's end. I reached out my hand——

'I wouldn't waste a good cap,' said a prim voice.

Peace had spoken of that voice a thousand times: didactic, precise. The DNI stood next to me, screwing up his eyes at the water. Like me, he was not in uniform.

I held my cap—the Skeleton Coast cap—uncertainly.

'*Ny anivon riaka,*' he said, articulating the words with a slight forward throw of the lips, like an actor. He smiled. 'My Creole isn't the best, but it means, "that which is in the midst of the moving waters." Mam'zelle Adèle says Creole was once a French patois, but no longer. Everything in Limuria seems to undergo a sea-change.'

Could this indeed be the man whose influence over Peace had been so great? I could not equate his blathering about an obscure language in an obscure ocean with his knowledge of submarines and underwater strategy, which, Peace claimed, was greater than that of anyone living.

He went on, 'You would not think that so scattered a community as the Limurian islanders could have a language with the subtletly of expression which Creole has. It's as diverse as their *brede* dishes—in South Africa there is almost the same word, *bredie*, which means rice with things like peppers and tomatoes. There are any number of nuances for *bredes*: *brede giraumon*, with pumpkin leaves; *brede martin*; *brede malabar*——'

No wonder Peace admired the DNI—they were equally heartless.

'You feel all this is appropriate to——?' I nodded towards the swiftly disappearing patch where Peace had been fired.

He seemed amused. 'You yourself wanted to give him his own sort of farewell—from what I hear—but now you object to anything but formal funeral conversation about the departed hero.'

'Departed hero! If a sneer is all Peace could expect . . .'

He remained smiling, and gestured with his hand. It seemed wrong, too, that he should be smoking. 'I think you've missed your moment with that cap.'

Annoyed, thrown off-balance, I went to the dodger. The mocking and ironical words followed me. I raised the cap to throw it.

'The camera crews are working hard to record the last dramatic gesture of Peace's comrade-in-arms.'

I looked down—into a battery of cameras and telephoto lenses aboard *Amirante*.

'It would be a futile gesture, anyway,' went on the cool voice. 'During our conversation we gathered speed and I doubt if anyone could locate the spot now where they fired our hero.'

I saw the reason now for his small-talk—he had saved me from contributing one more of the kind of histrionic gestures which I had so deplored.

'Thanks,' I said. 'Thanks very much.'

The clear grey-green eyes were expressionless. He said, with an almost conspiratorial air, 'Come on—let's give it to them—a smart double salute from two old comrades.' He flicked the cigarette-stub into the water. 'There's a fag-end for friend Peace—it's all right. don't look so startled, we're not being broadcast. Now!' He jumped smartly to attention and pistoned a salute which would have been the envy of a stars-in-the-eyes midshipman. I saluted too.

'Well, that's that,' said the DNI. 'Wish we could get a Pink Plymouth in the wardroom. but I don't suppose everyone is as broadminded as to pour Glenfiddich into a dead man's face.'

I went cold. Glenfiddich! Only Mac and I had been there. Had the DNI heard from the CIA agent? What was the tie-up?

I turned from watching the two fleets' complicated manœuvre to bring them back to port to find the DNI's eyes on me, unsmiling, hard. 'You came to see me a couple of evenings ago?'

It was a statement, a demand.

'Yes.'

'Why come to me?'

'I wanted you to help stop this silly charade.'

'I? A retired naval officer living quietly among the back-blocks of the sea?'

'Yes. You still carry a good deal of weight in high places.'

'My dear boy, you overrate me.'

'I don't think so.'

He said quietly: 'The petty officer underrated Mam'zelle Adèle.'

'You mean to say——?'

'Oh, come, Garland!' He was impatient, but pleased at his minor triumph in disconcerting me. 'I naturally heard all the petty officer said about myself and my young lady—I had him dismissed from the guard.'

'How?'

'You can't live all your life surrounded by cloak-and-dagger listening devices without taking some into retirement,' he replied. 'I had an ultra-sensitive mike in the post-box which recorded everything the petty officer said. There are others in the garden, too.' He was pedantic. 'Your outburst and character delineation of the late Commander Peace was apt, penetrating and very touching. You must hear the tape. I regret that the petty officer's Eliza Doolittle exclamation is a little blurred. But I was delighted to have the *négrillons'* patois—a patois within a patois, as it were. Mam'zelle Adèle says the language is perfect.'

The petty officer didn't seem so very far off the mark, the way he enthused about his Mam'zelle Adèle. She must be a cut above the ordinary Seychelles good-time girl. though. A teacher of languages—well, that was as good a cover as any, even though it didn't deceive the locals.

He watched me closely. 'I couldn't make out why you suddenly went back without pressing your desire to see me.'

I could not tell him why. I improvised something about his being part of Peace's funeral circus, but I could tell he was not deceived.

The fleet split up for the difficult North Passage past St Anne's into the main harbour. The lush green hills of Mahé were so close that I could pick out the DNI's cottage.

'Come and have a drink with me tonight.' said the DNI, with the peculiar type of authority the experienced clubman conveys with an invitation not to be refused 'A drink and some dinner. I have some excellent turtle steaks from Agalega—the real thing, not the sort of mush they pass off as turtle in Mahé. *Varra-varra* to start with—I've never seen a fish look more like copper. Mam'zelle Adèle will be delighted.'

## 3 MAM'ZELLE ADELE

Mam'zelle Adèle's smile was welcoming. but her eyes were shadowed. It seemed almost as if a light had been deliberately dimmed above the high cheek-bones and it gave to the sensitive, volatile face and expressive lips a strangeness which, in the unusual tropical half-light before the dark, set my pulses racing. She answered my knock at the DNI's cottage door and stood holding it open for me to enter. With her was a Limuria creature as strange and elegant as she was—a small pale-grey ring-tailed lemur. I was later to know him as

Nossi Bé. He rubbed himself gently against her unstockinged legs, watchful, friendly, but with reservations, like Mam'zelle Adèle herself. She could not have been thirty and the pinkish cotton dress—a flushed coral colour favoured by the islanders—did nothing to hide her exquisite figure. She wore coconut fibre sandals. Her face was tanned, her light hair sun-bleached. That perfect vignette of her standing at the door in the half-dusk is with me yet.

'You're staring.' She smiled. As she said it, I knew that it was important for me to remember every detail about her. Her voice had a strange, dammed-up quality, like a current race through a reef passage. When I did not reply, there was a touch of light somewhere in the back of those shadowed eyes, like sun striking on the flash of a frigate bird's wing.

'You'll be John Garland, Commander Peace's friend.'

Somehow the voice had drawn a subtle distinction between myself and Peace by using his title. I was glad of it.

'Yes,' I said, at a loss under her scrutiny. 'Yes, that's right.'

A silence fell between us and she said, 'I'm Mam'zelle Adèle.'

'Not Adèle someone or other but—just Mam'zelle Adèle?'

She laughed a quiet, easy laugh which met my query half-way.

'In the Grands Carreaux—those are the big fishing-grounds north of St Brandon—there's a poison-fish which they call Mam'zelle Adèle. So it's difficult for anyone in these parts to say simply, Adèle—they must add Mam'zelle.' She looked hard at me. 'A title gives status, you know.'

Was she perhaps trying to explain her relationship with the DNI? I didn't want to discuss it, looking at that unusual face.

'St Brandon—I like that better than the Portuguese Cargados Carajos.'

Before she could reply, there was a soft tap-tap from inside the bungalow, like a blind person's cane.

'My father—I'm French, you know—held the oil *jouissance* for St Brandon.'

'*Jouissance*?'

'Concession.' She gave a soft value to the syllables, like a pirogue's keel on sand.

She added, 'St Brandon has a ring about it.'

I shared her warmth, remembering a grey old ruined abbey on the Atlantic shore of Ireland, where once I had made a pilgrimage to St Brendan's grave. When the squadrons of clouds come to obscure the mountains above the saint's grave, they will tell you in the soft Connemara tongue that it is St

Brendan's angels bringing him safely home across the sea from America 800 years before Columbus. I wanted to tell her. The soft tap-tap came to my ears again. It reminded me of the intruder's stethoscope against Peace's coffin. It broke the chain. She sensed it.

Tap-tap. Tap-tap.

'You've been there, then?' Her voice was flat, as if she already knew the answer.

'Commander Peace and I called there on our way from Mauritius here,' I replied. 'An ancestor of his, Sir John Peace was the first Englishman there. He charted it. Peace thought it might be fun to do the same.'

'A bit of fun!' she exclaimed ironically. 'Yes, that is what Commander Peace would have said.'

So Peace *had* been in touch with the DNI. The shadow of his death lay between us.

Tap-tap. Tap-tap.

She looked at me, a little puzzled, then said formally, 'Sir George is expecting you.'

Sir George!—the DNI to me. I wondered less now that I saw her why he had set up with Mam'zelle Adèle, but it left me with an inexplicable resentment, nevertheless.

She led the way into the fair-sized bungalow. Pressure-lamps gave a comforting sizzle.

Tap-tap. Tap-tap.

Steel against steel. Mam'zelle Adèle opened a door.

Tap-tap. Tap-tap.

The toughened steel punch was against the white bone. He was tapping it with a tiny hammer: tap-tap, tap-tap. The skull lay on a cushion, surrounded by blue-grey chips. The DNI did not look up but tap-tapped again. A flake came away and the bone stood out, dirty-white.

'Got it!' he exclaimed with satisfaction. He blew the chips away. 'Isn't he a beauty? Scarcely distorted at all—look at those teeth.'

The skull was the size of a horse's, but the teeth were predatory—as long as a man's finger—and hooked. Above the eye-sockets its shape broadened like an aeroplane's tail.

'If he's not an Aulacephalodon, I'll eat blue shale,' the DNI remarked.

I drew closer to the grotesque thing on the cushion. Much of the bone was free of its stone matrix.

'Aulacephalodon?' I queried.

'This chap was a reptile which wandered about Africa two hundred million years ago. Up to now specimens have been confined to the semi-desert Karoo region of South Africa—

never found anywhere else. Now I'll rock them—here's blue Karoo shale among the corals of the Saya de Malha Bank.'

Peace and I had skirted Saya de Malha after St Brandon on our way to the Seychelles. It is a vast collection of shoals, atolls and cays scarcely above water-level, extending over thousands of square miles in the Sea of Limuria.

'You're talking Greek to Captain Garland and me,' Mam'zelle Adèle chided him gently.

The DNI laughed. 'Why yes, I am—Aulacephalodon is Greek for a winged head: look at the winged formation of the back of his skull.'

Mam'zelle Adèle was reproving. 'I think we all need a drink, don't you, Sir George?'

'Usual, please.'

I asked for whisky, wondering at his commanding tone. Well, he'd been used to ordering people around all his life. He got up and sat on the edge of the table, swinging a leg.

He asked didactically, 'You realize what this means?'

'I'm afraid I don't.'

'The Karoo,' he said with a schoolmasterish air, 'is a unique semi-desert area of South Africa which is the richest repository of reptile fossils in the world. Man, of course, had not yet appeared on the scene when they lived.' He looked at me penetratingly. 'Man is still young in the scheme of things—only a million years, maybe—and some of these creatures were adaptable enough to survive for sixty million. But in man's short stay on the face of the earth he has evinced one characteristic which may cause him to survive longer than any other creature—there has never been a killer like him. There is nothing man will not kill, has not killed. He knows the lesson these creatures never learned—kill first, have the best weapon, and you live.' His voice was precise, prim. 'Man must kill in order to survive.'

'Geoffrey Peace's philosophy,' I replied. But before the words were out, I knew I was wrong: Peace had learnt his killer-philosophy from this man.

I looked away. The room commanded a panorama of the fleet anchorage, the isles, and the sea beyond. There was still enough light to see the white tip of Récif where we had buried Peace. The full-width glass doors were closed against the sea-breeze and below them stretched lawn and flower-beds. Was it coincidence that the DNI was in the Seychelles for the mighty resurgence of British naval power, the Limuria Squadron? What had been his part in restoring the Royal Navy's power and prestige?

Mam'zelle Adèle's arrival with the drinks broke the spell.

'You see what this means?' he repeated. Although the didacticism was there, the fervour had gone from his voice.

I sipped the whisky. 'No.'

'It contradicts all previous theories that Saya de Malha was due to subsidence, not upsurge, of the land mass underneath.' I winced at the academic sophistries.

Mam'zelle Adèle said, with that odd pitch to her tone, 'He's trying to say, the Karoo and Saya de Malha are related.'

What did it matter to me whether the Karoo was or was not related to a bank in the Indian Ocean? At that moment I was more interested in Mam'zelle Adèle.

'Where do you figure in this?' I asked her.

The DNI replied before she could answer. 'Mam'zelle Adèle knows the islands. She speaks Creole like a native. She is my guide on my fossil-hunting expeditions. St Brandon . . .'

She sipped a cloudy drink. It wasn't alcohol but her own mixture of fruit juice and the nectar of coconut-flowers.

The silence was oppressive.

The DNI went on, 'You find these fossil reptiles only in blue shale. This piece was overgrown by coral at Saya de Malha. It had enormous implications.'

I waited politely. If it had not been for that flash of his while Mam'zelle Adèle was fetching the drinks, I would have been bored stiff.

'Implications?'

'Why, yes—it means I have definitely proved the existence of Limuria.'

'I'm afraid I'm not with you.'

He sat swinging a leg. 'The presence of blue shale in mid-ocean thousands of miles away from the Karoo itself proves the existence of a common tie hundreds of millions of years ago. Here I've found a Karoo creature in Limuria.' He tapped the skull. 'It shows that Africa was once linked to Limuria—by land. It is not fantastic now to speak of Limuria as an Indian Ocean Atlantis. Of course, there's a great deal yet to be done, but I am inclined to think the same upheaval which threw up the Karoo mountains was the one which drowned Limuria under the sea.'

'Very interesting,' I murmured.

He went off at a tangent, speaking rapidly to Mam'zelle Adèle, asking if dinner was nearly ready, offering me another drink.

She took my glass. There was a lot in her eyes I wanted to understand.

34

'What were we talking about?' he asked when she had gone.

Here was my cue. The clear eyes watched me intently.

'Killers,' I replied. 'Man the killer.'

'Good,' he said. 'Good.'

There had been a message and I had got it. The voice became more precise, and I knew I was in deep waters.

'All man's long tale of killing—' he tapped the grotesque skull—'from this fellow onwards has one short moral: kill, first—' he tapped the hooked fangs with a finger-nail— 'have bigger and better teeth.'

'Or—' I said it very slowly—'the weapon to end all weapons.'

The voice was gentle, almost prim. 'The ultimate weapon— yes.' The words came from deep inside the man. The soft tones belied the steel beneath.

I put the sixty-four-thousand-dollar question. 'In this age?'

The clear eyes probed me, assessed. Then he walked over to the glass door. It was dark now and the lights of the fleet stood out. The DNI jerked his head towards them.

'In this age.'

A cold thrill went through me, for Peace had spoken of that slightly world-weary, compassionate tone which the DNI was given to use in times of great crisis.

I joined him. We stood, saying nothing.

Then he sighed, glanced at his watch, and threw open the doors.

'A lovely night! I wonder if one gets nights like these anywhere else in the world except South Africa?'

I did not hear Mam'zelle Adèle in her soft sandals. She handed us new drinks. The DNI stood looking. No one spoke. Then he said, 'Turn out that light, will you, John—it rather spoils the effect.'

It was an order, not a request. John, not Garland, or Captain Garland, but John. For him to address me like that, I knew I had surmounted some obstacle he had laid in my path. I was surprised to see Mam'zelle Adèle put out a bottle of Glenfiddich and a glass. I turned out the pressure-lamp. My eyes were blinded by its closeness. A soft arm was slipped through mine and Mam'zelle Adèle said, 'Let me guide you.'

She was close. I smelt the sun-smell of her and was glad I had come. I stumbled to the doorway, still half-dazzled.

I didn't see him, only the gleam of the knife.

I jerked aside, dragging Mam'zelle Adèle with me. I can-

35

noned into the door-frame. Then, as he laughed, I froze. *It was Geoffrey Peace.*

He pulled off the black rubber cap and grinned at the DNI. 'Nothing much wrong with John's reflexes, is there?'

I blinked in disbelief. Peace stood on the terrace in the same black rubber suit in which I had seen him in his coffin. A long diving-knife was in his hand. I tried to speak, but the words would not come.

Peace said ruefully. 'Next time you want an arse-over-elbow stunt, you'd better give me some astronaut training beforehand. I thought the bloody thing would never stop cartwheeling.'

The DNI laughed too. 'You went up a lot higher than I expected.'

Peace said, 'I'm black and blue, despite the foam rubber.'

'The ejector gear work all right?' asked the DNI.

Peace laughed again. 'If it hadn't, I wouldn't be here now.'

The DNI said, 'Get inside, will you, Geoffrey? Nobody saw you?'

Peace shook his head.

I gasped, 'Geoffrey!'

'Pour me a whisky, boy, will you, if there's such a thing in the house? Christ, to watch that bloody MacFadden pour the stuff all over my face and I dying for a drink!'

Mam'zelle Adèle was still on my arm. Peace's greeting to her was level, comradely. 'Hello, Mam'zelle Adèle.'

She detached herself. 'Good evening, Commander. Was it a good trip?'

'Get me a drink and I'll tell you,' he replied.

'Geoffrey——' I started again.

He cut me short. 'The funeral act must have been pretty convincing, judging from your reactions then—and now.'

The DNI locked the glass doors and drew the thick coconut-matting sunblinds. He relit the lamp.

Peace glanced at the bottle. 'Hmmmm, Glenfiddich for the returning prodigal.'

My hands shook so that the drink slopped. 'What is all this about?'

'Later,' Peace grinned. 'What I need is whisky, food, and lack of adulation—in that order.' He swallowed the smooth spirit at a gulp.

'Your clothes are in your room,' said Mam'zelle Adèle.

'What's to eat?' he demanded.

'*Varra-varra,*' replied the DNI. '*Varra-varra* and turtle steak.'

'Excellent! You want to live on those bloody spaceman pills inside a steel coffin for days to appreciate what a square meal means. If I'd been one of those blokes who first got up on to the moon, I'd have come back to earth just for a decent meal.' He laughed and added, 'I nearly indulged in an old Limuria remedy—drink a pint of turtle's blood to restore your own.'

I felt the amused twitch of Mam'zelle Adèle's lips was meant for me, as she said, 'I should have kept some of to-night's dinner gravy for you, then, rather than Scotch—it's turtle steak.'

Peace dropped his gay mood and turned to me. 'Don't look so damned serious, John—the whole thing was a hoax. The DNI and I engineered it. I breathed air from Scuba bottles they stacked in the bottom of the coffin. When you mourners weren't grieving over the dear departed, I took a whiff through my face-mask.'

I remembered the sharp hiss I had heard while hiding behind the bar. The CIA man had heard it, too.

Peace swung on me as if he were reading my thoughts. 'Thanks—for that other business.'

'Other business?' The DNI was sharp.

I pulled out the Colt with the hocked hammer and held it in my palm. Peace gave a low whistle. The DNI took it while I explained about the intruder. I realized from his reaction that it was not the intruder who had told him about Mac and the Glenfiddich. Adèle's eyes never left my face.

The DNI and Peace stared at one another. Peace's face was bleak, which always spelled trouble for somebody; the DNI's impassive, cold.

The DNI addressed himself to Peace. 'This puts a different complexion on—a lot of arrangements.'

'How are you sure he was a CIA man?' asked Peace abruptly.

I told them about the three smalls 'moles' under the armpit. The DNI permitted himself the ghost of a smile. 'This is the man we want, Geoffrey.'

I told them about the man's disappearance from the engine-room.

Peace pursed his lips. 'No other identification?'

'Nothing except—' I nodded at the weapon—'that.'

The DNI sniffed the barrel. 'High-velocity powder. Been fired recently, too. Undoubtedly——' He stopped, looking at Peace for confirmation.

'Hand-load,' he replied. 'Therefore probably American. Bears out what John says about the CIA marks.'

The tense silence fell again. I had not yet recovered from the shock of Peace's return. I remembered the die-cut lettering on the ' coffin '.

' It seems to me far too many people were on the inside of this hoax—the C-in-C, for example.'

Peace became uneasy. ' What makes you say that, John?'

I told them about the Cammell-Laird nameplate. The DNI frowned. ' Too many loose ends, it seems, Geoffrey—especially when a man like John smells a rat. No, the C-in-C was not in our confidence.'

' Nor am I,' I retorted.

' *Touché*,' replied the DNI, inclining his head. ' The coffin was built specially for the job, in England. It was—ah—insinuated in the right place at the right time.'

I looked at the three. It was clear that Mam'zelle Adèle knew all about it, too. I remembered the strange undertones in the DNI's voice earlier.

' You're not a couple of schoolboys to play a practical joke —let's take it from there,' I snapped.

Mam'zelle Adèle started to withdraw. ' My dinner is spoiling,' she excused herself.

The DNI did not give me the chance for further questions when she had gone. He said to Peace, ' Was the pirogue in the right place, Geoffrey? No other leaks? No one in sight?'

' We had an island boat waiting in a cove at Récif for me,' Peace explained to me. ' I paddled here under cover of darkness. The coffin had an ejector device. I pulled the chain and it shot me clear. There wasn't anyone around.'

' How deep were you?' I asked.

' Sixty, seventy feet.'

' It seemed fishy to me that the C-in-C refused me a ride in the helicopter.'

' He had his orders,' replied the DNI in his precise voice.

Peace went on, ' I had to get out tonight. Tomorrow there was a chance that someone might have taken a boat o'er the grave where our hero was buried. They would have seen the coffin half-submerged.'

I took the Colt from the DNI. ' The owner of this, for example.'

' How much did he suspect?' Peace demanded.

' I didn't give him much of a chance. But we both heard the hiss of air escaping from the coffin. I don't like the idea of that coffin still floating around.'

The DNI shook his head. ' No. It was loaded with two explosive charges, one for Geoffrey's ejector seat, and the

38

other for a demolition charge. Geoffrey Peace is at the bottom of the sea, to the best of everyone's knowledge.'

Mam'zelle Adèle came back. 'Dinner in ten minutes, whether you're changed or not changed.'

Her arrival broke the tension. Peace and the DNI went off. I stood silent, an avalanche of questions in my mind. Nossi Bé rubbed himself softly and affectionately against me.

Adèle said, 'Another drink—John?'

Her eyes were level, unsmiling. I started to say yes, but stopped. Peace might drink whisky like that, but not me if I wanted to catch the undercurrents—there were plenty—of the DNI's words and Adèle's.

She paused fractionally at my refusal, then picked up the elegant lemur and put him on the table. She was relaxed, easy. 'Come, my lovely one,' she said. 'Shake hands with our tough fellow-conspirator.'

Nossi Bé extended a jet-black paw. He was as much a creature of Limuria as Mam'zelle Adèle—strange, lovely, sun-warmed, gentle. The creature's action momentarily stilled the tumult in my mind.

I scratched his chin. 'It's sheer magic.'

The eyes warmed above the high cheek-bones. 'Magic?'

'Less than a fortnight ago I was sitting in an air-conditioned skyscraper office in Johannesburg,' I replied. 'My whole world revolved round NACCAM and its affairs. A touch of the button and——'

She smiled. 'A man under authority.'

I sounded a little unreal to myself.

'And now?' she prompted, when I fell silent.

'Nossi Bé,' I replied. 'Limuria. Mam'zelle Adèle.'

'The languid charm of the islands,' she teased. Then that odd quality of light round her eyes dimmed. 'You underrate yourself,' she said quietly. 'I'd add, a man who half-kills another with a karate blow to the throat and is quite prepared to rough up a semi-conscious man to extort information from him. The chosen companion-in-arms of Commander Geoffrey Peace.'

The suddenness of it took me aback. She picked up Nossi Bé, who was grumbling under his breath.

'There are things about you which also don't add up,' I said. 'You're French, for example, yet your English is impeccable.'

She knelt, putting Nossi Bé on the floor, and looked up into my face. The V of her breasts under the slight cotton sent the blood into my ears.

'I act as the DNI's interpreter,' she replied evenly. 'He told you so himself. I speak Creole—well.'

'But your English——'

She shrugged. 'I went to school in England. I learned my trade there.'

'Trade?' I echoed, but she stood up and turned away. There were as many questions I wanted to ask her as I wanted to ask Peace and the DNI. Then, with an odd little gesture, she swung back and slipped her arm through mine and led me in to dinner.

Her dinner was a masterpiece, but my preoccupation prevented my enjoying it fully. The *varra-varra* was served with a *beurre vert* in tiny flat wicker baskets on a bed of fern-like *langue de vache*: the turtle steaks were sweated in butter with a thickish sauce of coconut flour flavoured with sherry. The wine was a favourite of Peace's, a superb South African Bellingham Grand Crû served in an 'ice-bucket' made from the famous double coconut-shells of the Seychelles.

Mam'zelle Adèle sat at the head and the DNI at the foot. I faced Peace. We had just finished the *varra-varra* and I reached forward for the wine. The Colt fell, like a reminder, on the table. Mam'zelle Adèle picked it up and handed it back to me.

'The Colt Python's better,' she remarked. 'A sort of Cadillac among hand-guns.

I saw Peace stiffen. He stared at her. His eyes were deadly cold and his mouth hard. The DNI caught the look. From that moment the meal seemed to go dead. The DNI's voice became more precise and he talked palæontology. Peace was withdrawn. My conversation, I felt, fell flat. Mam'zelle Adèle alone seemed unaffected, though she must have sensed the tension. She was gay, beautiful in her strange way as Nossi Bé, who jumped on to her chair and curled his long tail round her neck in imitation of a fur. A frozen lemon sherbet rounded off the meal. We went back into the big room overlooking the harbour. Mam'zelle Adèle brought coffee and cognac. The silence was intense.

The DNI swirled his Napoleon brandy round in its balloon glass. He said to me, 'You must be asking yourself what this is all about?'

His glance went over the rim of his glass to Peace, then to Mam'zelle Adèle, and back to me. The prim voice was slightly defensive. 'I had to convince—ah—a number of people that Geoffrey Peace was dead.'

'Including John Garland,' I rejoined.

He went on, ' " The deep damnation of his taking off " had to be spectacular, something everyone could see for themselves.'

'At least the CIA man had his doubts.'

Peace stirred in his deep cane chair. 'I wonder if you didn't overdo the business of the depth-charge mortar?'

'There was that risk,' replied the DNI. 'But everyone had to *see* Geoffrey Peace go to his grave.'

'It all looked very real and decorous on TV,' interjected Mam'zelle Adèle.

'Was the glass hatch a calculated part of the display?' I asked.

The DNI nodded. 'It was armour-plated, of course. Did you see anything publicly in the set-up to make you think it might be a fake?'

'Nothing, except your flippant attitude on *Loch Vennachar*'s bridge.'

He frowned at my tone. 'You're on the inside of this.'

'I wasn't then—I'm not sure now.'

'Now,' he went on, 'having publicly disposed of Geoffrey Peace, I bring him back because I——'

I interrupted him. 'It strikes me as peculiar the way you keep saying "I". You're retired. You're spending your declining days messing around with reptile fossil and learning Creole.'

I froze when I saw his eyes. 'I'm doing neither.'

He looked at me thoughtfully, calculating. It was the most frightening glance I have ever had directed at me. It struck me that he was assessing how, if he had to kill me, he would have done it. The gentle, slightly weary voice lent high drama to his words. Mam'zelle Adèle sat very upright and still. Peace no longer lolled in his chair. Maybe he was remembering his own excoriation by that same gentle, deadly voice.

The DNI rose and sat on the arm of his chair. 'I, of course, have a secret. Geoffrey, of course, has a mission.'

'And some hellish weapon is involved,' I added grimly.

His smile was wintry. 'Ultimate—it softens the concept, somehow. A small handful of people share this secret. They include the Prime Minister of England and the President and Vice-President of the United States.'

I shot a glance at Mam'zelle Adèle. The skin was stretched tight across her cheek-bones, as if someone had put hands over her ears and pulled it back. She pushed Nossi Bé absently from her knee.

There was a long pause. The only sound was the swish of the trade wind through the broad leaves of the latanier trees.

The DNI placed the tips of his fingers together. In my heightened state of mind I saw the gesture as akin to the crablike pincers of the cannibal centipede of the islands when it throttles its victim. Their rasp was in his voice, too.

'We are going to launch the Vice-President of the United States into space.'


## 4 LITTLE BEAR

Like the curtain suddenly going up on a startling and un-familiar stage-set, the DNI's words seemed to bring un-reality with them. The room itself now looked unreal to me, like looking through the wrong end of a telescope. I felt almost clinically detached from the group—the lovely woman, the silver-haired Intelligence chief, the submarine ace, tough and alert as if he had undergone a resurrection rather than an immersion.

I repeated the Vice-President's name for want of anything better to say. 'Marvin K. Green!'

'MKG,' corrected the DNI. 'Better get used to calling him that. You're to see a good deal of the man shortly.'

I looked at Peace, for it was with MKG that he had worked on the SNAP nuclear motor project.

'He's a regular guy, as they say,' he replied.

The DNI's precise voice cut in. 'You and Geoffrey will see him launched safely into space. That is your assignment.'

Mam'zelle Adèle spoke for the first time, more to me than to the others. 'I'm part of the assignment, too.'

I banged down my glass. 'This sounds like science fiction.'

'On the contrary,' replied the DNI. 'There is no fiction. The Prime Minister has guaranteed to the President our full co-operation in launching MKG.'

MKG had emerged as product and leader of the American technocratic society which had grown up round nuclear science and missilery. He had graduated from the famous Naval Research Laboratory and, as the nation's top scientist, had been picked for the Vice-Presidency. As a result, an aura of glamour had developed round this office, which in the past had been regarded as rather a backwater, consonant with America's lead in the space race and MKG's not inconsiderable part in it. The United States—and the world—had watched the youthful MKG (in his thirties) train as an astronaut and set the seal on his devotion to space exploration by actually making a trial orbit and splash-down. From that moment he was the darling of the nation. In brief, MKG personified the rule of science in the space age.

Peace said, as if following my line of thought, 'MKG is a Navy man, through and through. He has what the U.S. Navy calls "in-house capability". But this isn't a simple orbiting job, like he has done before. It's the big thing. MKG will space-liaise and land on Santa Fe.'

The Americans had christened their principal skyport for Davis and Acton's moon-shot after the great trail of the Old West, which certainly sounded more homey than the official designation: Space Logistics, Maintenance and Rescue Spacecraft.

Without my asking, Mam'zelle Adèle took my glass and poured me a stiff shot from the brandy decanter. Peace also splashed more liquor into his rummer. He was very tense. All the world knew that Peace, a nuclear submarine commander and one of the bright stars of Britain's new Navy, had headed the top-flight SNAP team to the United States. After meeting Peace and the British team, MKG had been sold on the SNAP miniature power plant for missiles, and by virtue of his scientific status, had been designated by the President to head the maze of committees handling atomic energy projects. With MKG's endorsement of SNAP, it looked as though the world was to benefit from a highly-successful Anglo-American space project.

Then Davis and Acton reached the moon in a Sirius, an Air Force liquid-fuelled rocket. The Americans went crazy over Sirius, despite the fact that it was hinted, although not officially admitted, that its failure to return safely to earth had been due to the erratic behaviour of the capsule's solar-powered batteries. The two astronauts had been unable, because of power failures, to re-enter the earth's atmosphere, and had been burned up with their space-ship. The built-in genius of SNAP, averred MKG and Peace, would prevent any similar recurrence in future.

A bitter controversy had arisen and the British public then became aware of the complicated system of checks and balances which operated in the American atomic programme. They learned that overall control of the atom in the United States was vested in the Atomic Energy Commission, a civilian body of five appointed by the President, but that the budget and legislative side was handled by the Joint Congressional Committee on Atomic Energy, whose eighteen members, divided equally between the Senate and the House, were policy-makers and watchdogs. The Commission also relied on the advice of its own body of nuclear experts. This body, despite pressure by MKG and the President—who was known to favour SNAP—threw out the British project.

The British public became aware, at the same time, of a revival of the old rivalries between the American Services. MKG and SNAP stood for the Navy, Sirius for the Air Force. The Air Force rightly pointed to the successful moon landing and countered the Navy's claims by insisting that SNAP had never been tested in space, whereas Sirius had, and, moreover, SNAP was a non-American motor which should give way to American enterprise.

Peace had made himself very unpopular in the United States because of his outspoken criticism of the dropping of SNAP. His remark that Sirius was no more than a land-based missile of little advanced strategic value had aroused a storm of resentment amongst the American populace, blinded by the success of their two astronauts in reaching the moon first. Peace had returned with the SNAP team to England, licking his wounds, still a target for American criticism.

Now he and the DNI were talking of launching MKG himself into space.

I got to my feet and faced Peace. 'Are you really serious about this incredible idea of shanghai-ing America's top scientist in order to launch him into space to prove the value of SNAP?'

'We are not shanghai-ing him. MKG wants to go.'

I turned to the DNI, but he ignored me and picked up his tiny punch and hammer.

Tap-tap. Tap-tap.

The DNI prised loose a chip of shale. 'I should have made it clear. This is not a kidnapping job. It is more than that.'

'If Geoffrey got the publicity works for his so-called funeral, imagine,' I said, 'what MKG's launching will be like: a round-by-round, second-by-second commentary by every radio and television station in the world.'

Tap-tap. Tap-tap. The DNI let my words fall dead. Peace stared into his brandy.

I was conscious of Mam'zelle Adèle's eyes on me.

Then the DNI looked up and hooked his thumb into the eye-socket of the fossil. He said, 'MKG goes alone. No publicity. You, John, and Geoffrey, and Mam'zelle Adèle—apart from a handful of experts—will be the only people present at the launch.'

Sirius's send-off from Cape Kennedy with the two American moon astronauts aboard had been one of the most spectacular shows the world had seen to date. Now the DNI was talking of a secret launch of the Vice-President with a handful of men and one woman!

'You're talking in riddles,' I said shortly.

Peace inclined his head slightly towards the DNI as if he, master-brainwasher that he was, should explain. The measure of rapport between them was plain to see.

'You see,' began the DNI, 'MKG is a Navy man . . .'

I realized—the sea! The DNI had moulded the great new Royal Navy with Peace as its star; MKG was the Navy-graduated supreme technocrat of the space age. The common bond which held them together was the sea.

'Man is the sea,' the pedantic voice said softly. He tapped the fossil skull. 'This creature was the remote ancestor of Old Fourlegs, the coelacanth fish that science asserted had been extinct in these very waters of Limuria for millions of years. Today the coelacanth still swims among the drowned peaks of Limuria. Man came from the sea. He must find his salvation again—in the sea. The ultimate weapon in his hand must be—from the sea.'

Peace saw what I was thinking. 'SNAP was to power the ultimate weapon.'

'That is what MKG and his team had been working on,' observed the DNI. 'The ultimate weapon. It was to be fired from the sea.'

'And,' I said slowly. 'Congress threw it out.'

There was a rasp in his voice. 'The Pentagon has a Military Liaison Committee which works with the Atomic Energy Commission. They were all for it. But it was the Joint Congressional Committee on Atomic Energy, drawn from the Senate and the House, which put paid to it. They, like their experts, were blinded by the moon landing. They hold the purse-strings. It wasn't Congress, but this joint committee which killed it. They threw away the ultimate weapon which MKG and his team had developed in favour of a modified Sirius rocket. SNAP—a small, magnificently ingenious machine, was to have provided the power for the new weapon. The power plant was the one thing in which American genius had not quite succeeded. SNAP, the Briton, was to be married to the American, Little Bear.'

'Little Bear!'

The DNI smiled thinly. 'Yes, that's its name—Little Bear. You would have thought the Americans would have learned from their past experience over the nuclear submarine and

45

the Polaris missile, both of which in a previous epoch nearly underwent the same fate as Little Bear. The most under-rated and under-publicized breakthrough in the whole history of modern armaments was the Polaris missile. The Americans, for all their publicity-consciousness, did it less than justice. The first crude Polaris, fired from a submarine submerged hundreds of feet down, introduced a completely new concept into war.' The voice became schoolmasterish. 'Up to then, all war had been a battle of refinements. But Polaris was the untraceable missile fired from an untraceable source, a submerged submarine, a minute pinpoint in the ocean deeps beyond the power of any tracking device to locate! Polaris was crude, but the concept was right.'

'Crude!' I exclaimed. 'Jesus Christ!' I gulped down my brandy.

'I don't mean the weapon itself,' went on the DNI. 'There were fantastic refinements of guidance, pioneer work on solid fuel, blast-off in the confined space of a sub's hull— I mean the principle was crude. Polaris was dependent on extraneous factors: the vulnerability and complexity of the submarine, the human factor of the men in her—no, the concept needed simplifying to be fully effective.'

'The Sirius rocket——' I began.

The DNI picked up his punch and tiny hammer and inched it round a sliver of bone.

Tap-tap. Tap-tap. It was as inexorable as Chinese water-torture.

The DNI became more emphatic. 'Sirius, a liquid-fuelled rocket, put two men on the moon. It is useless for anything else. It has no strategic concept. Tactical, yes. But it is simply an old artillery-piece, super-refined.'

I looked at Peace as the DNI returned to his tapping.

Peace said, 'About two years ago we—that is, the SNAP team—evolved what we considered a first-class miniaturized power plant for missiles. I naturally informed the DNI. I then went to Washington where I met MKG for the first time.'

I knew Geoffrey Peace. 'That would be fertile soil for a friendship.'

He smiled, easing the tension, and Adèle flicked a grateful look at me.

'When MKG heard about SNAP, he indicated that they themselves were working on an exciting new weapon.'

'I, too, met MKG in the United States—a very remarkable man,' said the DNI. 'At our first meeting I had the temerity to suggest that Polaris—the new Polaris as I conceived it—would rule the world. With me, it was purely an idea, but MKG revealed that he and his team were, in fact, working in a practical way on just such an ultimate weapon. I offered them SNAP. From that moment there was no question but that we would go along with them. You know, the President has delegated so much of his authority in all things atomic to MKG—and rightly so—that the say-so is virtually his in the maze of committees clustered round all nuclear projects.'

'Except,' Peace put in, 'in the Joint Congressional Committee on Atomic Energy.'

The DNI frowned and went on, 'MKG's missile had only a code number, but we three, MKG, Geoffrey and I, decided to keep the generic name Polaris. So we called the new weapon Little Bear, for Polaris, the Pole Star, is the brightest star of Ursa Minor, the Little Bear constellation.' He smiled with grim satisfaction. 'Little Bear is all hell.'

I felt the DNI had been carried away. I shrugged. 'Little Bear is still only a refined Polaris, fired from a nuclear submarine.'

'It is not fired from a submarine,' he replied. 'Little Bear is completely self-contained. It is like a big submersible mine —the missile proper fits inside a casing. It is sunk hundreds of feet beneath the sea and is virtually untraceable, since its radio antenna sticks up only a foot or two. It is fired by ultra long-wave radio from thousands of miles away. Like Polaris, though, a shot of compressed air lifts it to the surface, after which the solid-fuel motor takes over.'

'The ultimate weapon—almost,' I conceded. 'But it's still not wholly independent.'

'Little Bear's inertial guidance system is pre-set on its target,' continued the DNI. 'Once the missile is down, it cannot be changed until the whole thing is brought to the surface again. It's enough, though—Little Bear is fully independent of gantries, crews, tracker teams and all the complicated paraphernalia of the Sirius moon-rocket. It guides itself like the old Polaris. Little Bear is compact, reliable— a killer in the truest sense.'

'The Prime Minister promised full British support for the Little Bear project,' said Peace. 'You can see what it means to the Navy. It puts us up alongside the Americans.'

'Both of you talk as if Little Bear were a fact. I thought you said Little Bear was killed; dead, finished!' I pointed out.

The DNI started his unnerving tapping again. Mam'zelle Adèle's long fingers tattooed on Nossi Bé's head in sympathy. Hers looked like the long fingers of an artist, or a pianist. Where did she fit into this strange project?

'No,' replied the DNI. 'On paper, Little Bear *is* finished. But MKG believes, as we do, that Little Bear is the ultimate weapon which puts the West way out ahead. Officially, Little Bear cannot be revived. But MKG, to prove its worth, will rocket to Santa Fe in Little Bear.'

'Think,' added Mam'zelle Adèle, 'the Vice-President of the United States.'

'The nation's darling,' said Peace.

'What about Cape Kennedy . . . ?' I started to say.

'How?' asked the DNI. 'How could he use the facilities there for a project which has been axed?'

I shook my head.

Peace went on. 'Little Bear was practically complete when the axe fell. It was tested in secret. There are just a few Little Bear prototypes in existence. The one which MKG will use to Santa Fe will be readied by a small team—four or five American experts—under Dr Boz Blair, another genius from the Naval Research Laboratory at Anacostia, who is coming to Limuria for the launch. From our side, it will be us and Captain Trevor-Davis, the top British missileman who was with Geoffrey in Washington on the SNAP project. Our mission is, simply, to get MKG safely into space. The American experts will come out in a freighter carrying the missile, and MKG in the Navy's latest sub, U.S.N. *Willowtrack*.'

My mind went back to the intruder. 'With so many people in the know, it is easy to see why the CIA became suspicious.'

The DNI looked uneasy, but retorted, 'No one could undertake a project of this magnitude without outside help. The U.S. Navy's in the know because they appreciate, as we do, the enormous implications of this ultimate of weapons. The Navy was quite willing, for the sake of a man of MKG's status and prestige, to detach a nuclear sub to bring him to Limuria. The Navy also feels pretty sore about the Sirius rocket—you must realize how bitter inter-Service rivalries are in the United States. The Air Force is now completely cock-a-hoop about Sirius and billions are coming its way for future moon-shots. The Navy is solid behind MKG.'

'The Vice-President isn't only a man, he's a vital cog in the American constitutional system,' I objected. 'I don't see a Vice-President simply chucking everything overboard in order to be shot off secretly into space. Any man who acted so irresponsibly wouldn't be fit to hold the office of Vice-President.'

'It was a big decision to take,' replied the DNI thoughtfully, 'and it could not have been done without the full—unofficial—endorsement of the President. The President, like

MKG and ourselves, appreciates the value of Little Bear. America will be supreme in a military sense for at least a decade by virtue of Little Bear. The President is taking a calculated risk. He's deputed *Willowtrack* with an S special Gold Crew to bring MKG out. Her skipper is Revs Tyler, and you know what that means.'

Revs Tyler was the man who rose to fame and earned his nickname by taking a nuclear sub 1,000 feet under the ice of the South Pole to prove to the sceptics that a deep-water channel existed between the two halves of the Antarctic continent, cut by a seasonal warm current. Tyler made the run at full speed, dodging ice projections the size of a skyscraper at 40 knots, knowing that one touch would have sent him and his crew to instant death. More revolutions, he demanded throughout this amazing voyage, always more revs.

' Is Revs in on the secret too?' I asked.

' Up to a point only,' replied Peace. 'He and his crew naturally know they have the Vice-President aboard, but they believe he is to conduct firing tests on a new secret missile. After all, there's nothing unusual in that, except that it's so far away from home. Don't forget, either, that MKG's a trained astronaut.'

'There's a sword of Damocles over this whole mission,' said the DNI gravely. 'It's something you must not lose sight of.'

I watched Peace's mouth go taut as the DNI said it and the cruel, ruthless lines assert themselves. Little Bear was not only a personal matter with him; the future of the new Royal Navy depended on it.

' *Willowtrack* has orders to make the voyage submerged,' went on the DNI. 'But both the President and MKG were adamant that there should be a daily signal from *Willowtrack* to the White House in code.' He smiled slightly. ' I suggested twilight every evening—as the U-boats used to do, when the light makes it the most difficult time of day to spot a sub on the surface.'

' A nuclear sub doesn't have to surface,' I said.

' I know, I know,' he replied impatiently. 'But it is a good time. *Willowtrack* will simply stick up a radio antenna and signal the White House. In order to preserve maximum security, no other signals or reception will be permitted. And if Revs Tyler's in command, he'll keep to that—he won't even listen to a newscast.'

Peace's face was bleak. ' I wanted full radio silence.'

The DNI went on: ' If, for any reason whatever in the intricate complex of the American political system, it is

49

necessary for MKG to return to the United States, the mission will be called off. MKG's first duty is to the American nation, not to Little Bear, the Royal Navy, or ourselves.' He turned on Peace, his voice very quiet. 'Do I make myself clear?'

Peace said nothing.

The DNI picked up the hammer and punch.

Tap-tap.

The prim voice was in deadly earnest. 'Unless I have a categorical undertaking from you, Geoffrey, the Little Bear mission is off—now.'

Peace looked down at his hands, the hands which had sent so many men to their deaths, turned the palms inwards and the knuckles outwards again, a strange, sinister gesture. He nodded.

Adèle's face was pale. Like me, she realized what it must have cost Peace to put a halter and bridle on a mission so close to his heart.

The DNI went on quickly, trying to obliterate the tension. 'The original plan called for Geoffrey to go to St Brandon in H.M.S. *Devastation*, our newest nuclear sub, and rendezvous there with *Willowtrack* and MKG. The two subs would then go to a remote island called Love-Apple Crossing. *Willowtrack* would receive her onward briefing at St Brandon. Tyler doesn't know where the test-fire is scheduled from. As an additional security measure, we chartered a French freighter called the *Semittanté*, trading to these waters, to carry Little Bear. Boz Blair and the scientists are signed on as ordinary members of *Semittanté*'s crew.'

'*Semittanté*—that was the name of one of Napoleon's frigates,' Mam'zelle Adèle exclaimed.

Peace smiled for the first time. 'Not this *Semittanté*—just an old battered tramp grown rusty humping guano and coconuts from Limuria to whoever wants them anywhere in the world.'

I said to Peace, 'I wondered why you took *Bellatrix* past Love-Apple Crossing on our way to the Seychelles.'

Mam'zelle Adèle smiled her strange smile. 'Another strange name!'

Love-Apple Crossing is a speck on the map (and most maps of Limuria are old) about 50 miles east of the beautiful twin island of Agalega, which is situated almost exactly halfway between St Brandon and the Seychelles. From Mahé it was about 400 miles. East again of Love-Apple Crossing is a great collection of shoals and shallow banks, over 10,000 square miles each in extent, where the ancient peaks of Limuria project above the sea.

'You say, original plan—what is the new one?' I asked.

Peace glanced across at the DNI. 'The news of the firing of Little Bear has leaked out.'

The DNI added quickly, 'A partial leak only.'

I looked from one to the other. 'The CIA man at the coffin?'

'It proved what we suspected,' said the DNI, 'and it doesn't make us any easier in our minds. Somebody in the United States has been asking what MKG is up to. The President considered that it would be quite safe for him to be missing from the public scene on the grounds that he was carrying out secret work. He's a bachelor, as you know, so we don't have to worry about home security. But how would your mind work, if you were in the CIA or connected with it, or had confided in it, if suddenly both MKG and Peace were missing?'

'Where Peace was, MKG might be,' I replied.

'We made no secret about Geoffrey coming to the Seychelles—after all, it's the biggest missile launch site outside the United States. You don't have to be a genius to work out that MKG might be here, too—if you had the right clue to start with. Therefore,' the DNI went on quickly, 'I—we—had to convince the world that Geoffrey Peace was dead. All suspicions had to be stifled. They had to *see* him go to his grave. Hence the funeral build-up.'

'Remember that stethoscope,' I said. 'The CIA wasn't one hundred per cent convinced. I'm glad I didn't give him time enough to find out you were alive in the coffin, Geoffrey.'

Peace said warmly, 'We owe you a big debt of gratitude for that, John. I always could count on you in a tough spot.'

'It worries me that he went free,' said the DNI. 'Maybe we should change the plan again——'

'Not now,' broke in Peace. 'John, we want your navigational skill.'

'How?' I asked.

'I've said, the original plan was for *Willowtrack* and *Devastation* to meet at St Brandon and go together to the firing-point at Love-Apple Crossing. Actually, it's not the island itself, but a spot at sea near by. Using a nuclear sub's gadgets, you can't go wrong in pinpointing a minute spot like that. Now we've had to change all that. We feel certain that any unusual movement of subs in these waters is being watched. Love-Apple Crossing is right in the middle of the missile firing-range. Nuclear subs give off electrical emissions. Two and two make——'

'Little Bear,' said Mam'zelle Adèle.

'The plan for the two subs to rendezvous at St Brandon still stands,' said the DNI, taking up Peace's explanation. '*Willowtrack*'s daily sunset signal is to and from the White House only. It's at a fixed time and as brief as they can make it, for obvious reasons. But we've decided to change the whole plan from the St Brandon rendezvous onwards.

'You, John, will take *Bellatrix* to St Brandon. Geoffrey goes to *Devastation*. Bob Peters, *Devastation*'s Number One, is in the plot, and the officers know no more than that Peace is not dead but involved in some hush-hush British-American experimental missile-firing project. They're all top men, they won't talk. Little Bear is being carried in *Semittanté* under the guise of a new coconut-oil plant for the islands.'

Mam'zelle Adèle smiled. 'The two, main exports of Limuria are coconut oil and rugged individualism.'

'*Semittanté* is bound for Love-Apple Crossing from New Orleans. She was just too glad to get a load to take her half-way across the world. You'll rendezvous with her there.'

Peace prowled about uneasily. I could see that the incident of the CIA man was eating into him as the DNI elaborated the launching programme.

'There is an exact firing schedule to be met,' continued the DNI. 'You don't simply point a missile at Sante Fe and blast off. Trajectories, orbits, what have you—Boz Blair and MKG have them all taped. As far as we are concerned, all we have to know is that Little Bear's instrumentation has been set to coincide with the optimum position of the earth relative to the space station Sante Fe. Tomorrow is February 1st. On February 16th Sante Fe will be at its best orbital position for Little Bear to rendezvous—space-liaise—with it. The missile has a computer-compensated docking device which will guide it in to Sante Fe. Little Bear must be fired at nine o'clock on the morning of February 16th. 0900 hours on February 16th.'

'Local Limuria time?'

'Yes.'

'Eight o'clock is no good, nor is seven. It must be nine,' Peace put in. Using a radio-firing device, I shall pull the plug on MKG's behalf six hundred feet down in the sea.'

'Pull the plug?'

'Fire the bloody thing!' Peace retorted. The tone of his reply betrayed his anxieties. 'The ultimate push of the button is from the surface—a small instrument tuned in to the radio antenna which Little Bear shoots to the surface when she is at the right depth. MKG does the countdown, I send the bird flying.' He suddenly swung round on me. 'I—

all of us—have been taking one big factor for granted: are you in this thing with us?'

I looked round the three faces—Peace, hard, dedicated, ruthless; the DNI with his pedagogic whims overlying the tempered blade beneath; Mam'zelle Adèle—what did I know of her?

'Yes.' I replied. 'Yes, of course. All I need is a good set of navigating instruments.'

The DNI relaxed. I felt Peace had been sure of me all along, despite his question.

'I've got the best,' he said. 'Nothing that gives off a single amp of power. It's all skill—John Garland's skill.'

'Good. I'll want to check them over.'

Peace went on speaking to the others, his tone warm. 'All this man needs is the traditional star to steer her by. He——'

I cut short his eulogy. 'We can't launch a missile without radio guidance.'

The DNI gave a short laugh. 'You're saying almost exactly what the early American land-based missileers said about the first sea-based Polaris. Admiral Red Raborn, the father of Polaris, confounded the critics. He successfully fired Polaris from a moving platform in a liquid, ever-shifting medium because he went back to that primary element at the base of all man's activity—the sea. You'll have lots of technicalities thrown at you in the next few weeks, but SINS is the heart of it all. Tell him, Geoffrey.'

'Ships Inertial Navigation System,' he explained. 'Raborn put his guidance package *inside* Polaris. It needed no help from outside—radio guidance or the rest of it. We've done the same with Little Bear, a development of the A-4 Polaris now in service with the U.S. fleet. Our Little Bear follows the same pattern. Of course, the SINS system has now become highly sophisticated in Little Bear—the guidance package is a marvel. Boz Blair will talk for days about it. But essentially it is a self-contained missile inside its own casing, a combination of mine and torpedo-tube.'

'How big is it?' I asked.

'The missile itself is forty feet long, six feet across, and weighs twenty tons,' replied Peace. 'The casing is another fifteen feet in length. All of it is highly streamlined. The casing is, so to speak, the gun-barrel.'

'It seems so involved, and yet so simple. Can a handful of men really get a thing like that to a launch-point at sea?'

'It's highly streamlined,' replied the DNI. 'Has to be. Goes through water, air, space . . .'

'It's a piece of cake for *Bellatrix* to tow it to sea,' Peace replied. 'You could do it with an outboard motor.'

'What about the submersion?'

'It's got ballast tanks like a sub to take it down. It is kept at a constant firing angle by two mated gyroscopes. If you want to hear all about accelerometers, earth rate and coriolis computers, automatic precision fathometers and all the rest of it, Boz Blair will oblige with the greatest pleasure. Our job is to get Little Bear in position to fire when sequencer starts an hour before blast-off?'

'Sequencer, what's that?'

'Countdown,' he replied. 'We've got to have MKG in position one hundred fathoms down before eight o'clock. I suggest we pull rods at dawn and have Little Bear hot to trot by seven-thirty.'

I looked helplessly at Mam'zelle Adèle. 'I'm as foxed as you are,' she said.

Peace smiled. 'All the terms, like those of the nuclear subs are American—rightly so. After all, they pioneered the damn' things. Translated, we must get the SNAP nuclear reactor operating by dawn so that Little Bear is ready to be launched from seven-thirty onwards. Countdown to begin an hour before blast-off. You don't have to know any of this—Boz Blair and MKG have the most detailed schedules and technicalities written down—pages and pages of it. There's a firing checklist as long as your arm, too.'

The DNI broke in. 'The Americans are great on code names. We looked for one. When the Little Bear project was under way originally, it went under the code name Brickbat Zero One—highest priority, top secret, most urgent, the lot. We've kept that—Brickbat Zero One.'

I turned away from technicalities to something close at hand.

'And where does Mam'zelle Adèle come into all this?'

'Code and cipher expert,' said the DNI briefly. 'My best girl. Break anything wide open.'

'I thought she was an islander . . .'

'I am.' She smiled, making a gesture as if to lay her hand on my arm. 'Adèle Dauguet. My father did hold a *jouissance* at St Brandon, and it covered Love-Apple Crossing. What Sir George didn't say was that there's only one landing-place on Love-Apple Crossing and it's called Vingt-Cinq Coups—twenty-five lashes.'

Something cold seemed to come into the conversation as she said it.

'Love-Apple Crossing was a solitary confinement cell for the Agalega plantations in the slavery days,' she explained. 'Vingt-Cinq Coups means exactly what it says—twenty-five lashes. You can still see the remains of the flogging grating there.'

Peace was watching her calculatingly, as he had done at dinner. Both she and the DNI sensed his scrutiny.

The DNI said: 'Adèle was one of my girls in London and when this project first blew up, what more perfect cover than a girl from the islands teaching Creole to an old dodderer of a naval officer in retirement!'

She blushed slightly. 'I don't think that's the way the locals look at it.'

'It was necessary,' retorted the DNI crisply. 'A whiff of scandal only gave credence to it.'

'So,' I said slowly to the DNI, 'you aren't even retired?'

'Officially,' he smiled. 'But the Prime Minister and I remain in close touch.' He turned to Peace. 'I wonder if we couldn't risk taking Maude along too?'

'Another woman!' I burst out.

Adèle gave a low laugh. 'MAUDE—short for Morse Automatic Decoder!'

Peace grinned too. 'I think Maude can stay at home—her power system might give the game away. From what you say, Adèle's quite good enough.'

The DNI was conspiratorial. 'One of my men smuggled the new U.S. Navy code-book to me. We can read anything the U.S. Navy sends.' Peace whistled. 'Offence punishable with——'

The DNI nodded. 'Adèle's been swotting up on it. MKG also sent me—this!' He took from his pocket what looked like a magnetic tape casset and switched on the radiogram's tape recorder.

'I want you both to memorize this,' he said. 'It's from the U.S. Navy's Anti-Submarine Warfare Library.'

He turned up the volume. The sound came through foggily—a jum-jum-jum noise and then a faint squeak. Then the noise blanked out, giving way to a dissipated crackling, like breaking cream crackers by the thousand; then a faint, irregular hammering. Peace's jaw was tense and his head slightly cocked. Jum-jum-jum—squeak. Crackle. Silence. Then a low droning hum, like a generator.

'Sound signature of a nuclear sub—deep,' said Peace with satisfaction. 'Not in these waters, though.'

Jum-jum-jum—squeak.

The DNI gestured. '*Willowtrack*'s sound.'

Peace whistled softly. 'This could be worth almost anything—in the wrong hands.'

I asked, 'What's the rest of it besides the main noise—fish?'

The DNI nodded. 'The crackle is shrimp. This was recorded off Greenland by—well, let us say, by an unauthorized source.'

Jum-jum-jum—squeak.

Peace said, 'Why don't they fix that circ pump? It's the biggest giveaway . . .'

'You wouldn't believe what heartache that little squeak has caused,' replied the DNI. 'It's a special seal where the drive-shaft enters the pump. Oddly, there's nothing wrong with it. The nearest the backroom boys have got to it is saying that it is caused by some sort of ultra-sonic vibration. Revs Tyler had this seal in *Willowtrack* unseal itself a thousand feet beneath the South Pole.'

Peace said grimly, 'Only Revs could have made it after that.' He turned to me. 'You'll play act about my death still, but you must, of course, tell Mac. After a couple of days, you'll give out that you're taking *Bellatrix* back to South Africa for sale, in accordance with my will. You'll let it be known that you're going back via Madagascar. Trevor-Davis will come aboard at night. Keep him out of sight when you leave port. Steer a course for a couple of hundred miles as if you really were heading towards Africa. Then double back and make for St Brandon at your best speed. We'll meet you there, MKG and I.'

'What about *Willowtrack*?' I began.

'She's due at St Brandon after thirty-six days mainly submerged from Connecticut, and if I know Revs, he'll be there to the hour,' Peace replied. He added, 'No radio, radar or other transmissions from *Bellatrix*. Better keep even the receiving radio dead until you're out of range of all the tracking equipment of the missile range.'

'You've forgotten Mam'zelle Adèle,' said the DNI. 'She goes with you, John.'

My heart lifted and she smiled back at me. Suddenly, despite the extraordinary nature of the project, life felt very good. Johannesburg, NACCAM, high-powered sales talk, all seemed a very long way away.

It was the DNI's cold voice which brought back the dangers, the realities of the mission. 'There is a complex meshing together in Brickbat Zero One of imponderables, all sorts of factors which could ruin the project—or cost someone's life,' he said. 'MKG might even find himself a victim, rather than a conqueror, of space.' The gentleness of his voice made it sound more sinister. 'The missilemen always allow an extra safety margin for the imponderables; I have tried to do the same. They also have a name for it.'

'They call it the Jesus factor,' Peace said.

## 5 NUCLEAR HIGHWAY

The black whale-backed sail rose sinisterly out of the sea half a cable's length to port. Her identification numbers had been newly painted out and above the fairwater—I still thought of it as a conning-tower—rose periscope masts, radar and radio antenna. The long shape of the nuclear sub swung and held station on *Bellatrix*.

It was our second morning at sea, two days after the meeting in the DNI's cottage. I was in the wheelhouse after breakfast. It was a perfect day. *Bellatrix*, under my command, had cleared the Seychelles Bank and was making a breath-taking eighteen knots. I could almost hear Mac singing along with the twin Rolls-Royce diesels. Captain Trevor-Davis, the Royal Navy missile expert, was checking the fuel levels below. I had taken an immediate liking to this tall, flaxen-haired Englishman when he had come aboard *Bellatrix* in Port Victoria the night before we sailed. He said little, yet there was a sense of strong competence about him. I saw why the DNI had chosen him for the job.

Out to starboard, a white line of foam announced La Perle Reef. When we had first sighted, Mam'zelle Adèle and I, from the weather-deck dinette during breakfast, she had asked me to take her up on the coachroof to see. My heart missed a beat at her unusual loveliness as the north-westerly wind blew her hair into her eyes, and I slipped my arm round her shoulders. For a thousand miles to every point of the compass, Limuria stretched away. From the submerged continent under our keel life had first sprung millions of years ago and now, from its deeps again, a man would try to make a strange, imperishable and wonderful new journey in a vehicle named after the stars. I found myself sharing my thoughts with Adèle, but when she looked gravely up into my eyes, the DNI's words hit us both—somewhere was the Jesus factor. Somehow her own presence on board threw that warning into sharper relief. Despite the mild morning, she shuddered with a sense of foreboding. Without a word,

57

she turned and went to her luxury cabin below-decks. I occupied Peace's own weather-deck cabin, which commanded an unimpaired view of the ocean.

I switched *Bellatrix*'s helm over to the Sperry auto and kept the telegraphs at full ahead. The sub kept pace effortlessly. Three figures appeared on the black bridge, minute by comparison with the rest of the structure. I focused my glasses on them. An officer picked up a microphone from its waterproof housing and looked across the stretch of sea between the two craft. The closeness of the metallic voice of the loud-hailer took me by surprise. It brought Adèle and Trevor-Davis to the wheelhouse at a run.

'*Bellatrix*! Keep course and heave to! Understood?'

It was an English voice at least.

I clicked on *Bellatrix*'s own loud-hailer.

'Who are you?'

The other voice came back, imperative. 'Do you understand?'

Trevor-Davis said quietly. '*Devastation* class. Look at the flared bow.'

'Yes,' I replied. 'Understood.'

Adèle stood next to me. 'John, this isn't part of the plan . . . ?'

Trevor-Davis said reflectively, 'The plan's only two or three days old, too.'

The metallic voice from across the water said, '*Bellatrix*! Is that Mr. Garland?'

'Yes.'

'Captain's compliments. We are sending a boat for you and—' there was the slightest pause—'Mam'zelle Adèle.'

What was Peace up to, I asked myself angrily. The DNI had ordered him explicitly to take *Devastation* to St Brandon and here he was hundreds of miles out of his way. Had Peace, after I had sailed, prevailed on the DNI to change plans again, in the light of the CIA's snoopings? I had kept rigid radio silence in *Bellatrix*, as the DNI had instructed, and had cut down the use of the electrics to the minimum.

I used the engine-room voicepipe. 'Mac—there's a big sub alongside—numbers painted out. I think it must be *Devastation*. Stop, will you?'

There was something suspiciously like a chuckle at the other end. I would never forget the moment when I told Mac that Peace was still alive. It had been worth all the glory of Limuria. Mac's allegiance to Peace, right or wrong, had never known any bounds, and since setting out in the knowledge that his beloved skipper was indeed still alive he had been less dour than I had ever known him.

'Commander Peace requests that you and the lady bring some clothes. Give you ten minutes.'

I shrugged at Adèle. 'No point in arguing—O.K.?'

'O.K.—but what about me?'

'What about you?'

'A woman aboard a nuclear submarine!'

Trevor-Davis smiled slightly. 'These new subs have every creature comfort, Mam'zelle Adèxle: hot baths, washing machines, the lot.'

She still seemed very uneasy. 'John, I thought Commander Peace would have stuck to orders . . .'

Her tension communicated itself to me. She was putting into words what I had felt from the moment the long shape had surfaced. Mac joined us before I could reply.

'What the bluidy hell is the skipper playing at?' he grumbled good-naturedly. 'I thought . . .'

The sub circled *Bellatrix*, which was now stopped.

'*Bellatrix*!' came the loud-hailer. 'Captain Trevor-Davis to assume command. MacFadden to remain. You are to steer a course of one-six-zero true, repeat, one-six-zero true. *Bellatrix* will proceed on that course at twelve knots—repeat twelve knots—until again intercepted. Is that clear?'

I turned questioningly to Trevor-Davis. He nodded.

'Not to worry,' I said. 'There's no land in any direction for six hundred miles. I marked our position on the chart not an hour ago.'

'No other ships,' he asked laconically.

'This is a prohibited area—missile range, don't forget.'

Adèle said, 'I'll get my things together.'

'Slacks,' I replied. 'Don't try to be glamorous aboard a submarine. Pants are woman's best friend for the modest negotiation of ladders, hatches, and watertight bulkheads.'

She smiled, but she was worried. 'Thanks.'

'*Bellatrix*!' called the sub. 'Have you briefed Captain Trevor-Davis and your engineer? Any problems?'

'Briefing complete,' I replied. 'What about the weather?'

'Seems good enough,' came the curt reply. 'Nothing exciting from Chagos.'

In the Chagos Archipelago south of Ceylon the Limuria Squadron maintained a big weather station. Chagos is where cyclones are born. This was the cyclone season in the Sea of Limuria.

Adèle was waiting in the wheelhouse when I returned with

my hastily-packed case. Trevor-Davis was as economical as ever with his words when I said goodbye. I resisted the temptation to call the anonymous sub's name on the loud-hailer in the traditional manner of the sea.

'Ready! Standing by for your boat.'

As we watched a topside handling party debouched on to the sub's casing deck. A rubber dinghy pulled clear of her side. I noticed that *Devastation* lay deep and air hissed round the hull like a hippo surfacing.

I helped Adèle to the dinghy as it came alongside and willing hands assisted her. The gunner's mate in charge looked up at me and winked from a dead-pan face. We pulled across to *Devastation*. A rating waited on her deck for us. Round his waist he wore a 'monkey-tail' safety-belt with a chain and traveller running on rails along the deck. Here indeed was a far cry from the days when submarines risked their lives unprotected on the casing in foul weather!

The Officer-of-the-Deck—the OOD—looked down from his high perch. He sang out. 'Control—Bridge here—blow forward group for one second.'

Air burped and the deck lifted—a Raleigh-like space-age courtesy which kept Adèle's plimsolled feet dry as she held out her hand to the monkey-tail rating. The gunner's mate lifted her under the arms and snicked a quick-release safety-belt about her. I could imagine the way this story would be told in the mess.

'Follow the tramrails, miss,' he grinned. 'Can't go wrong. First stage fare, fourpence. Mind the step.'

Our arrival crowded the tiny bridge. Its lack of instruments surprised me—merely a 7 MC set to communicate with the Control Centre in the sub's heart, a gyro repeater, a loud-hailer mike, collision and diving alarms and rudder-angle indicator, all heavily waterproofed. Behind, the radar, radio mast and twin periscopes were snugged down alongside an upward-seeing television-camera 'eye'.

'Control—Bridge—*Bellatrix* range three hundred yards, and steady.' The OOD listened. 'Aye aye, sir. Stand by to dive.' He leaned over the bridge handrail. 'At the double —boat party below.' He glanced round the horizon and pressed the diving alarm. 'Clear the bridge! Clear the bridge!' The two look-outs stood back and raced past below as the raucous sound came up—here at least was something familiar from my submarine days—the old-fashioned 'ahooga' of the alarm klaxon.

I gripped Adèle's arm and ducked through the hatch. The OOD followed, snapping it shut with a length of steel cable.

The quartermaster flattened himself to allow us to edge by. Then he spun a wheel and secured the hatch.

The compartment into which we emerged was shadowed, unreal. Infra-red light muted the faces of the eight or so men who stood about in the glow of the luminous instruments. My eyes automatically went to the nerve-centre—the periscope stand. Caught by the strange light, drops of water from a faulty packing gland seeped down the barrel. Peace stood there, his mouth tight, his whole being alert. A black sweater and matching Dacron trousers gave him the same sort of swaggering, deadly look as the great U-boat aces; it was a silhouette I would remember all my life.

The tight compactness of the Control Centre was a new-old world for me—the intricacy of valves, cables, lights and electronics. Two planesmen sat in deep red leather chairs before what might have been an aircraft's instrument panel, their hands gripping half-wheel joystick columns to dive and steer the sub. Behind them was the diving officer, one arm draped carelessly over the sail planesman's chair. The soft red glow of the compass repeater lit their faces. Its red merged into the green fluorescence of the radar a few feet away. On the ballast-control panel glowed a series of straight little red bars—submariners call it the Christmas tree. The red bars indicated, I was to learn, a 'straight board' which meant that all the openings in the sub's hull were closed. Beyond the diving-stand to starboard was the sonar-room and aft the radio-room, abutting on to the navigator's chart desk, the inertial guidance system, the fathometers and the television 'eye'.

The agglomeration of sounds in the Control Centre was new to me, intriguing: the discreet burr of the hydraulics, generators and turbines in place of the thumping diesels, fumes and stink of the old subs; a high-pitched whine from the fathometer, a lion-like purr from the sonar. Most unfamiliar was the warm, wax-like smell instead of the doggy odour of the old boats. The bright colours, too—the floor was inset with bright red vinyl blocks among discreet greys and greens. So far I had not heard a command; this was the stillness of automation.

Then the radar operator's voice came over the loud-speaker. 'Contact now bears three-zero-zero true, range opening.'

Peace drew to his mouth a microphone on a flexible cable. His orders were clipped and tight. His dark clothes merged into the shadows; he seemed disembodied.

'Shut the induction,' he ordered. His eyes rested imper-

61

sonally on me for a moment and then went round the Control Centre.

'All clear topside,' called the OOD.

'Open the vents.'

The petty officer's fingers played on the toggle switches of the ballast-control panel like an electric organ. I noticed Peace incline his body slightly as if by reflex as the water poured into the tanks. Adèle looked at me, awed by the complexity of the intricate fighting machine. From that moment, too, I think she gained a new respect for Peace.

His eyes were everywhere. 'Right full rudder, ahead full, four hundred feet smartly,' he ordered. 'Steady on course zero-nine-zero.'

One planesman reached up and turned the handle of the engine-room annunciators—in my day we called them engine-room telegraphs—to 'ahead full'. A red pointer responded.

'Answers ahead full, sir.'

Another voice said, 'Course steady on zero-nine-zero, sir.'

The sonar operator came through. 'Contact now bears two-seven-two degrees true.'

Peace nodded, satisfied. The Exec was looking across at him from his station. 'Okay, Number One?'

I grinned to myself at the familiar term—nowadays it is Exec.

The Exec replied, 'Four hundred feet, sir. Speed sixteen knots. Steady on zero-nine-zero.'

'Take over, Number One, will you?'

'Aye aye, sir.'

'How much water under her?'

The fathometer operator replied, without waiting for the direct question via the diving officer. 'Eighteen hundred and seventy-five fathoms, sir.'

Eleven thousand feet! Certainly *Devastation* was not yet over the ancient landmass of Limuria. Peace gave a quick glance at the rigged-for-dive panel and nodded to Adèle and me to follow him into the dark passageway. He strode quickly down to his cabin door and flung it open, not waiting for us. We stepped into a small, compact room, L-shaped, with a pull-down bunk littered with papers. There was also a small folding desk, a safe, steel locker, cocktail-bar type stools, a fold-up washbasin snugged into the wall and no fewer than three telephones and two intercoms. By the foot of the bunk in the steel wall were a gyro repeater, fathometer repeater and speed indicator. I saw that this section of the wall was, in fact, a door leading to a pint-sized shower and toilet cubicle. Here indeed was luxury for a submariner! I found myself blinding in the cheerful white light reflecting off the eau-de-nil colour scheme, red floor, green shellbacked rubber matting and blue ceiling, pale as a Limuria dawn.

'Pansy, isn't it?' said Peace abruptly, scrabbling among the papers on the bunk. 'Psycho boffins say it's good for morale, but give me battleship grey any time.'

As he spoke, Peace's eyes strayed to the gyro compass repeater. Mine followed. Only then did the significance of the new course he had given in the Control Centre strike me. Zero-nine-zero—a ninety-degree turn away from *Bellatrix*! We had turned away from the rendezvous at St Brandon.

I gestured at the compass. 'Geoffrey—what the devil! This submarine is heading away from its course to meet MKG. It's heading for Saya de Malha!'

A glance at Adèle was enough to show that she was equally puzzled.

The bleak, trouble-erupting look was in Peace's hard face. 'Yes,' he said curtly. 'I'm heading for Saya de Malha.'

'Why?' I demanded. I'd sailed with Peace long enough to respect his sea-foxiness, but his intended break-in into thousands of square miles of shoals, coral-heads, innumerable sea-deeps and unmapped islets seemed madness.

There was a pause for a moment. The only sound in the tiny cabin was the distant hum of turbines. Adèle made a tiny gesture of helplessness with one hand.

Then Peace said, 'Your intruder—he was back.'

'The cottage?'

Peace nodded in grudging admiration. 'Yes. He got past the guard, which was pretty smart. But he hadn't reckoned with the DNI. Every room was wired with its own independent alarm-system working off a separate circuit. The CIA man craftily immobilized the first one, which worked off the mains. That in itself must have taken some doing. But he walked into the second like a fly into a spider's web.'

'Who was he?' asked Adèle.

'My one and only glimpse of him was sprinting across the lawn. Tall, well-built, plenty of muscle——'

'That's him.'

'I kept out of the way,' added Peace. 'It was a hell of a temptation to go out and mix it with him, but in that case he would have got what he came for, a sight of me. I had to content myself with a long shot as he ran.'

'Any luck?'

He shrugged. 'Maybe, maybe not. He stumbled, but it

could have been a blind. But one thing it told him: for a house to be protected like that meant it had a big secret somewhere. The DNI and I decided to change the plan then and there. That's why I intercepted *Bellatrix*. I couldn't signal you because of your radio silence. Moreover, it might have given the show away.'

I jerked my head upwards. 'Identification numbers painted out.'

'That's the least of it,' he said.

'And you're still going ahead with Little Bear?'

His determined look answered me. 'My first duty is to this mission. It means more to me even than it will mean in terms of balance of power between West and East. SNAP is mine; Little Bear *is* supreme power at sea for whoever has it.' No wonder he had jibbed when the DNI had pressed him to agree that MKG's first duty was to the American nation!

'Assume,' he went on slowly, 'that the CIA only suspected *Devastation* was on her way—what then? All the nuclear subs based in the Seychelles take the milk-run route through deep water to St Brandon. At any time experts could pinpoint *Devastation* down-range within a few miles. But—' he added grimly—'not in the Saya de Malha.'

'What about the rendezvous?' interrupted Adèle, drawing closer to me.

'I intend to keep the rendezvous,' he replied. 'Red Indians used to cut branches and brush out their trail; I'm brushing out *Devastation*'s trail, just in case. Once in the Saya de Malha, the tracking stations in the Seychelles and Chagos will never find this sub.'

He let the words fall dead, and then said sombrely, 'This is a top-secret mission and I intend it to remain so. I think I know a new nuclear highway through the drowned land of Limuria.'

I gave an involuntary shudder. On the map Saya de Malha looks like a Disney elephant's head with a sawn-off trunk blowing bubble-gum. The bubble is the small northern sector. The head is the south. Between is a gap of fifteen to twenty miles—no one knows exactly—and through this Peace would have to dive. The depths were vague. But the overall picture was clear: as cruel a collection of shoals as any sailor could hope to miss.

'And after Saya de Malha?' I asked.

'A deep dive between the Saya de Malha and the Nazareth Bank. Then St Brandon.'

I shook my head. Peace was laying his ship open to the gravest risk, making a 50-mile corkscrew through shoal waters which have a traditionally evil reputation among sailors rather than following a straight course to the rendez-vous.

I started to object, but he shrugged off my words and said to Adèle, 'You'll take this cabin.' He opened the door which led into the shower, decorated with gay, flame-proof curtains. 'Toilet. Shower. John and I will shack down on the other side, in Bob Peters's cabin. We share the facilities. He'll have to hot-bunk somewhere.' He swept the coverlet from the bunk as he gathered up some papers. 'Looks like a damn' geisha's kimono,' he snapped.

There was a knock at the door and a rating handed Peace a signal. He read it through quickly and dismissed the man, who looked grey with fatigue. Adèle glanced at me and said. 'Commander Peace, that signalman looked dead on his feet——'

'This is a secret mission,' he replied curtly. 'Twenty-four hour shifts. Too bad if he can't stand up to it.'

'It's my field, code and communications,' she went on impulsively. 'I'll gladly take a shift——'

Peace's reaction astounded me. 'You'll stay right here,' he snapped. 'Don't fiddle with the phones—you might cause a crisis. You'll be quite comfortable. You may not go beyond the Control Centre without my express permission.'

The colour flushed her face and she turned to me, hurt, puzzled, wanting my support. Peace turned away and picked up a phone, dialling 'O'. I reached out and touched her arm. Despite my anger at his harshness, I almost blessed Peace for that momentary unmasking of her heart.

'OOD?' asked Peace. 'Commander here. All calls to me in future to be directed to the Exec's cabin.' He laughed shortly. 'Yes, *your* cabin, Bob—John and I are taking it over. What's the score'

I heard Peter's formal reply, distorted through the instrument. 'Very deep, sir. We've crossed the eighteen-hundred-fathom curve. Sounding is now nineteen-hundred-fifty fathoms corrected.'

Peace raised his eyebrows to me. 'Very well. Plane down to six hundred feet. Echo range and take soundings continuously. Where do you reckon we'll cross the continental shelf?'

'Can't rightly say, sir, but NAVDAC estimates about eighteen hundred GMT.'

'Call me at sixteen hundred. Earlier, if there's anything.'

'Aye aye, sir.'

'What's NAVDAC?' I queried.

'Navigational Data Assimilation Centre. It's a very sophisticated device to pinpoint our position—the sort of thing we would have used for finding Little Bear's blast-off position had we followed the original plan—we've got three SINS computers and we flood the bloody things with their readings, plus data from the radio direction finders, the star trackers and the "magic box", which is really a radio telescope in miniature.' He smiled. 'I brought you along to match all that with your skill.'

I relaxed slightly. He picked up the blue-bound U.S. Navy Code, and said: 'Ultra-top-secret. The DNI's parting gift.'

Adèle was about to speak, then bit her lip and turned away.

I wondered whether Peace even noticed. 'I'm sacking down,' he said. 'Been up all night. Come on.'

He led the way to Peters's cabin on the other side of the bathroom without a look at Adèle. The cabin was a replica of his own, except that it had two bunks. I remained silent. Away from Adèle, the hurt to her seemed magnified in my mind.

Peace lit a cigarette. He seemed eager to talk. 'Smoke? The carbon dioxide scrubbers and gas analyser take care of all that here. We make our own fresh air from sea-water.'

I took one and lit it up, not replying.

Peace paced three steps each way. He stopped in front of me. 'What's eating you, John?'

I met his eyes. 'Was the brush-off to Adèle really necessary, Geoffrey? She's a code and cipher expert—you have the DNI's word for it.'

He blew a smoke-ring with careful deliberation. 'She was just too keen, that's all.'

'What in hell do you mean?'

'Nice girl, very affectionate.'

I felt slightly embarrassed.

'At dinner that night at the DNI's,' he went on. 'Remember what she said about guns?'

'Yes,' I replied. 'I remember clearly. She said a Colt Python was better than a .38 Detective Special.'

He looked hard at me. 'Hand-guns, not guns, she said. Colt Python. Cadillac among guns. No one but an American speaks of hand-guns. In England they're pistols, revolvers, small arms, but never hand-guns. Her entire metaphor was—American.'

The implication of what Peace said knocked me back.

'You're suggesting she's a double agent?' I said slowly.

'I don't know,' he replied carefully. 'I'm just careful, with so much CIA around. And then—so soon after finding out that I intend making for the Saya de Malha she volunteers for radio duty. Radio—whom?'

'I don't believe it,' I retorted emphatically. 'I don't believe Adèle is tied up with the CIA intruder!'

He came and clapped me gently on the shoulder. 'I hope for your sake not. But there's such a thing as softening up the opposition, you know.' He grinned lop-sidedly. 'You're a man who takes some softening up, too. Adèle is another good reason for the Saya de Malha.'

He did not give me time to reply, but started pacing up and down the tiny cabin again.

His uneasiness communicated itself to me. 'What's up, Geoffrey?'

'This ship is an electronic marvel,' he said, choosing his words carefully. 'Every marvel aboard her has a back-up marvel—in other words, there are two of everything, in case one goes wrong. There are not, on our assignment.' He crushed out his cigarette impatiently. 'It is—was—all too bloody tailor-made: take one nuclear sub and meet another eight hundred miles away, one that's been practically out of touch with everything for over a month under the sea. Cruise down a well-charted ocean highway. Pick up the Vice-President of the United States. Rendezvous with *Semittanté*, an old tramp which has been at sea for God knows how long out of New Orleans. Shoot off the bastard in super-missile, practically untried, untested. Mission accomplished.'

'It's already out of gear,' I observed dryly.

'The sea, John, the sea! That's the great imponderable!'

'The Jesus factor,' I added.

He nodded. 'We haven't allowed for the safety margin of the sea. You know it, I know it. The DNI—he doesn't know what it is to love a hunk of metal filled with machines, computers and other electrical wonders, something that takes you and brings you out on the other side. He's cold. For him, *Devastation*, *Willowtrack*, Little Bear are all expendable.'

'Us, too.'

'Us, too,' he echoed sombrely. He swung on his toes and started to pull the sweater over his head, the muscles apparent in his chest and arms.

'Like to see the ship?' he asked. 'Get a dosimeter from the hospital orderly to check your exposure to radio-activity —but I can tell you now, there's less aboard *Devastation* than you get every day in London or New York.'

'I'd like to see the missiles,' I ventured.

He held up a small key which hung on a gold chain round his neck. 'I could start a nuclear war with this. It unlocks

*Devastation*'s Polaris A-4's. You're free to go into Sherwood Forest.' He made an expressive loop with his arms. 'Big seven-foot steel tubes from keel to deck, like trees—Polaris silos. Our Little Bear is experimental, but these Polaris missiles are operational. Better get Bob to take you round. Only officers and operating ratings are allowed in Sherwood Forest.'

Sherwood Forest itself was a disappointment. I felt my heart quicken as Bob Peters—a short, cheerful, sandy-haired man with quiet, shrewd eyes—unlocked the main door. The compartment consisted merely of double columns of circular tubes wrapped in canvas, painted an artistic green. There was nothing to show that these were the deadliest missiles afloat.

In the keel's 'mushroom factory' at the base of the missiles, I had the same feeling of clinicism rather than power. Under each Polaris A-4 was a big steel ball like an enclosed, outsized kaffir-pot. These were the compressed-air flasks which tossed the deadly birds to the surface. The same sort of thing was built into the casing of Little Bear for the initial take-off.

Peters took me for'ard through the crew's quarters to the torpedo-compartments in the bows. Through a low steel door I saw a heavy bronze tube running out of sight into the bulkhead above. Set into it was a hatch, like an outsize oven door. Peters explained that this was an escape route for the crew if the sub should be flooded. It worked on the principle that when the air pressure inside the tube equalled that of the ocean outside, all the five or six men in the bronze tube need do was to rise to the surface . . .

A telephone buzzed. A rating answered and automatically jumped to attention. He handed the instrument to Peters.

'For you, sir!'

Peters listened for a moment and slammed it down.

'Quick!' he said. 'Control Centre!'

He raced through the ship with me at his heels and reached the Control Centre breathless.

The OOD said quickly, 'Sonar reports contact bearing zero-nine-zero true, twelve miles.'

Peters took a quick glance at the fathometer, whose stylus was clicking and chuckling, as he asked: 'All round?'

'Aye aye, sir. Something massive is blocking our way.'

# 6 SAYA DE MALHA

Peters snatched up an intercom. 'Captain in the control-room, sir!'

In a moment Peace, pulling on a shirt, joined us at the diving-stand. The sleep seemed to have evaporated from his eyes in the few short moments it took him to get from his cabin to the Control Centre.

Peters explained the situation briefly. Peace nodded.

'Ahead one-third,' he ordered.

'Six hundred feet,' chanted the diving officer.

'Bring her up—four hundred feet, handsomely,' went on Peace.

The strong sound of the pumps—the diving officer was careful not to blow the vents for a too rapid rise through water of unknown salinity and temperature—filled the Control Centre.

'Sonar?'

'Contact now bears zero-nine-zero true, confused background echoes.'

'Is it moving?'

'No, sir. Steady range and bearing.'

'Come right to one-two-zero,' ordered Peace. He swung *Devastation*'s bows away to point at an oblique angle.

The sonar-man said in his flat voice, 'Contact steady on zero-six-zero. Confused background noises.'

'What the hell is it?' I asked Peace.

'These are seas with coral formations,' he replied. 'Theoretically, there should be a gradual shelving approach towards land, or shoals like the Saya de Malha.' He swung round. 'Depth?'

'Four hundred.'

The fathometer sounding read 1800 fathoms under our keel, and on Peace's orders *Devastation* lost way, hanging in mid-ocean. The diving officer stood with his eyes glued to the ballast-control panel, trimming, adjusting, holding her delicate balance.

The sonar-man reported, 'Contact now bears zero-five-seven, ten miles.'

Without warning, *Devastation* rocketed upwards, caught by some formidable power combination of current and salinity.

'Flood her down—emergency!' roared Peace. My ears

clicked and clacked as scores of tons of high-pressure water poured into the tanks.

Then—*Devastation* plunged downwards in the opposite direction. The men in the Control Centre hung on to the trolley-straps.

'Blow negative to the mark!' rapped the diving officer.

With a roar like an express train, high-pressure air creaked against the cork insulation lining the control-room dome.

'Blow secured, negative at the mark!' came the answer.

'Shut the flood, vent negative, pump auxiliaries to sea!'

My stomach righted itself as we pulled out of the unexpected dive. Beads of sweat stood out under Peters's eyes. Peace, at the raised periscope stand, glanced round with narrowed eyes. There was an indefinable atmosphere of fear.

'John, it can't be coral,' said Peace.

Limuria! I saw it so clearly that I could have laughed. Limuria had died a million years ago, not by volcanic upsurge—which would have meant customary coral formations —but by subsidence, by falling into the sea! The huge obstacle barring our way—was it the high rim, the ancient boundary of Limuria, a giant rock soup-plate resting on the ocean bed, the inside of it being the Saya de Malha? My idea would account for the lack of shelving and the shallow, unknown, broken waters extending over 12,000 square miles of treacherous ocean.

I told Peace quickly what was in my mind. Before I had finished he ordered, 'Make your depth two hundred feet.'

I was becoming more accustomed to the swift, deft responses of the planesmen and the ballast control.

'By God, John!' Peace exclaimed, after giving the order. 'The only person with the guts to run these shoals was old Surcouf, the French corsair.'

'Surcouf logged an island two hundred years ago somewhere off the northern extremity of Saya de Malha. He named it Roquepiz. Today it's supposed not to exist.' I indicated the fathometer. 'But Surcouf didn't run like a bull at a gate at his shoals.'

In my mind's eye I saw the picture, straight ahead the drowned land of Limuria, a giant rim, probably volcanic, the wall of a vast plateau on which the ancient continent had stood. Our sonar showed that the rim lay in a broad arc across our bows. Inside that rim—what? Few except some eighteenth-century pirates had ever ventured to Saya de Malha on the surface; beneath the ocean, we were the first. What was under that narrow slot, shown on the charts as lying between the main mass of Saya de Malha and my Disney elephant's head?

'Captain, sir!' It was the sonar-man.

Peace and I joined him for'ard.

'Listen to this doppler effect, sir.'

The operator turned up the sonarscope volume on the sound reproducer. Even with the primitive instruments I had been schooled in, I had been able to recognize the change in pitch of the echo which comes back to a listening sub from a target or underwater obstacle. *Devastation*'s sonar was sophistication itself. The doppler effect was clear through the transducer. We were converging on a solid object in our path.

The searching sound went out as a long purr-purr impulse, but it returned with a faint break in it.

'Land?' Peace, too, was puzzled.

'Aye aye, sir—but more—seems something solid is standing out, sort of, from the land.'

'Hill?'

'No, sir. You can hear yourself. Regular, all round the clock. Waves, too, sir.'

I caught the faint crunch of water on the transducer.

Peace shook his head. 'Water, not waves.'

'Could be, sir,' replied the sonar-man. 'Tide-race against these—unidentified objects.'

My mind was out in front, in *Devastation*'s sonardrome, where hyper-sensitive instruments probed ahead through water where sunlight never penetrated, parallelling the dark dreadful night of the spirit when all is lost. I shuddered. We were deeper than man had ever been before over the detritus of a once-great continent which had fallen victim to the sea. I was afraid.

Peace's voice broke the oppressive silence. 'Navigator! What is our position?'

Without waiting for a reply, he strode over to a glass-topped table under which moved a needlepoint of light, striking up through a chart folded over it. The navigator marked its path towards the opening between the two great banks of Saya de Malha. He gestured, unspeaking.

The sonar-man chanted formally. 'Contact evaluated as land, with confused echoes, may be surf.'

Peace watched 'the bug', as the needlepoint of light is called, move across the dead-reckoning tracer. Then he went to another instrument console to watch the nervous whip of the precision depth-recorder stylus on its sensitized paper, sketching, with frantic haste, it seemed, every sea-bed undulation. He walked slowly back to his raised stool at the periscope stand, glancing half-left beyond the attack periscope to the depth-gauge and course-indicator. The crew were tense, over-attentive to every sound. This sort of waiting game is the test of the submariner.

Peace said softly to me, 'There's a temperature or salinity barrier blocking the sonar return—I think.' He paused. 'I don't think it's land.'

Then, as if ashamed of his confession of uncertainty, he ordered: 'Left fifteen degrees rudder. Come left to course zero-four-five. Decrease speed to ahead one-third.'

Peace had swung *Devastation*'s nose in towards the barrier. Would he dare go in at this depth? Unconsciously, I turned to the person next to me. It was Adèle. I whispered: 'Keep quiet!'

'Ease her up—two-fifty feet,' said Peace.

I breathed again. With his deadly instinct, **Peace was easing** up on his target—whatever it might be.

'Rig for ultra-quiet!'

A pall of silence fell on all, on every machine not vital to the running of the sub. From the sonar-repeater came a curious, fogged thump like the sound of a distant diesel. Peters's eyes were wide with anxiety. The thump was followed by a sharp whining swish and a noise like brown paper being crumpled.

'Possible goblin contact bearing one-zero-zero,' came the sonar-man's chant.

Goblin! Only a hostile submarine is called a goblin. Cat-and-mouse—but *Devastation* had the edge, for she had gone ultra-quiet first.

The disembodied voice went on. 'Range twelve thousand yards. Approximate course zero-two-zero degrees, speed fifteen knots.'

A cold thrill of excitement passed through me as I watched Peace's hand reach out for the general alarm-button. He unhooked his command microphone with the other.

An unidentified submarine was passing across our bows at less than seven miles! We knew there were no friendly subs in the area.

Then came a faintly apologetic note in the sonar-man's voice. 'Contact now evaluated as giant ray.' He said to Peace, 'Sorry, sir, at first I thought it might be a one-thirty r.p.m. fish, but there was that extra something I couldn't account for.'

Fish are a sonar-man's nightmare. The brown paper crumpling noise we had heard was probably a school of small fish and the sonar-man could be forgiven for being ultra-cautious.

The operator went on, 'That doppler effect is still there, sir.'

It was clearer now, a curious sort of measured echo coming back to the transducer. The precision depth-recorder showed a steep shelf leading to the entrance slot.

Peace committed *Devastation*.

The ship was still rigged for ultra-quiet. Peters whispered, 'Bottom shallowing rapidly, sir.'

Peace went to the precision depth-recorder. I saw the twitch of his jaw muscles and his look of surprise. 'John, come over here, will you!'

The stylus had given up its St Vitus' Dance movements. Instead, it was moving up, across, down, up, across, in regular patterns.

'It's packed up,' I said briefly. 'No sea-bed ever looked like that.'

Peace shook his head. 'No. There are other instruments monitoring this one. It's okay.'

I peered closer. Traced on sensitized paper were a number of small rectangular blocks, followed by an intersection, and then the small blocks began again. When the stylus came opposite the next intersecting line, Peace gave an order and *Devastation* swung along the course of the plainly demarcated line. The stylus traced it straight, unfalteringly.

We had 600 feet of water under our keel.

Peace then reversed course, and *Devastation* glided over the straight line being traced by the stylus. Then the precision depth-recorder started to rise vertically.

'All stop! Rudder amidships!'

'Speed zero,' reported the navigator.

The needlepoint of light under the chart was still. The planesmen sat quiescent in their red leather-backed bucket seats. There was a faint splash of water down the leaking periscope gland. All eyes were on Peace. At the ballast-control panel, the petty officer might have been a statue, hands extended to the multiplicity of switches in front of him.

'Bring her up to five hundred feet—handsomely,' commanded Peace. 'Slowly, now. Stop her there.' The first mechanical noise I seemed to have heard in hours brought reassurance—the purr of a ballast pump. Like a Navy dirigible hanging over a suspect contact, *Devastation* drifted slowly upwards. Twenty feet, thirty feet. The stylus levelled off.

'Secure!' said Peace.

*Devastation* hung, a masterly example of touch-and-go.

Whatever it was, was right under our keel. The pointer outlined a big flat slab.

'Ahead one-third, one minute!'

The 15-foot propeller bit, turned, slowed. The stylus fell away, showing a gully, or way, about 25 feet in depth. The pattern on the sensitized paper was now one of big rectangular blocks divided by channels some 50 feet wide.

'Ease her down. Take it very easy.'

Again the quick purr of the pump, and a slight thump as *Devastation* settled on the sea-bed.

Peace went to the periscope. His face was strained. By his skill he had already undertaken a manœuvre so delicate and so dangerous that few men afloat could have matched it. I remained at the precision depth-recorder. What could those rectangular blocks be? They looked like fashioned pieces of concrete used for building breakwaters, except that they were ten times the size. Among the rectangles were bigger and smaller ones; only a few were square.

'Up periscope!'

The periscope jockey flicked the control-lever and with a hiss like a spitting cat the long tube rose up, slowly, lethargically, thrusting against the outside sea-pressure. The leaky gland gave a spurt. The eyepiece with its double wooden handles emerged from the well. With the gesture I knew so well, Peace snapped down the handles and fiddled with the focus-lever. He gestured to me.

I put my face to the soft rubber eyepiece. I swung round. Darkness. Nothing.

At my elbow, Peace ordered, 'Turn on the sail floodlight. Active television eye.'

I was still at the instrument. Automatically I put my eyes to the periscope.

I looked straight into the carving of a ship.

It lay, in sharp focus, in the middle of a carved pediment. The spotlight illuminated a small area. Carved pediment—building—a city!

I knew then. I was looking at the ancient drowned city of Limuria.

The rectangular blocks were buildings, some big, some small. The channels between were streets.

Limuria!

My thoughts raced to something which had stuck in my mind from Mauritius. The Mauritius Institute recorded that when the first explorers set foot on the island—the Portuguese, about 450 years ago—they had found carved tablets in wax, inscribed with lettering which they thought to be Greek. Hands trembling, I swung the eyepiece round. Above the dim ship outline—could it be lettering?

I snapped up the handles and turned to Peace. The TV screen showed nothing beyond a murk of water. 'A city . . .' All eyes in the control room were on me. How could one tell? I gestured silently to Peace. He went to the eyepiece, looked and withdrew. Our eyes met. There, lying on the steep rim of the slot, was what must once have been a harbour and, with the cataclysmic collapse of the ancient continent, it had half-slid down the steep side of the undersea mountain plateau.

'We'll plot this,' said Peace in a quiet voice. 'This was perhaps what was meant by "The Flood".'

'Down periscope!'

The sleek tube hissed into the well. 'Secure from ultra-quiet.' There was a subdued whispering among the officers. Peace picked up the control-stand microphone.

'Captain here. We have just made what may be a major ocean-floor discovery. I am about to carry out a grid-search.' He clicked off the instrument. 'Bring her up to four hundred feet, handsomely. Grid pattern search. Ahead one-third.'

The resumption of conversation eased the tension.

'Call the depths,' commanded Peace.

'Five-twenty,' chanted the diving officer. 'Five hundred.' We were now 50 feet above the level of the ancient city.

'Take a sweep round,' Peace told the sonar operator.

Without warning, the precision depth-recorder stylus gave a jerk and plummeted to 2,000 fathoms. There was a gigantic hole under *Devastation*! The patterned line of the houses and buildings fell away into abysmal depths.

The sound reproducer of the sonarscope, still fully switched up, which a few minutes ago had dominated everybody, now was relegated to the background by the steady flow of orders and the comforting hustle of machinery. *Devastation* was changed from the stealthy killer of the deeps to a ship under way and her men were human again, not hyper-tense listeners on whose acuity of hearing depended their salvation.

Then the sonar beam swung round. Something hit me like an express train.

Deafening, pulsating, terrifying sound blanketed the control room—high-pitched, screaming, grinding, like a giant pencil being scratched across a giant slate. I saw Peace shouting an order, but his words were lost in the crescendo. *Devastation* shuddered under an immense crash. I was thrown sideways across the Control Centre. The lights went out.

I and several others lay in a heap. A torch snapped on and I saw Peace, bleeding from a cut above the eye, crawl towards the diving-stand.

'Emergency circuits!' he shouted.

The emergency lights flickered, disappeared in a flash of blue sparks. I dragged myself towards Peace.

'Battle lanterns!' he rasped. 'Break out the battle lanterns, for God's sake!'

As the first dim light came on, I grabbed Adèle and put my arm firmly round her shoulders.

The floor of the control-room canted sharply downwards. The fathometer spun. We were racing for the bottom!

'Eight hundred feet!' I yelled.

Men were crawling up the inclined deck to their stations—stunned, bewildered, but training and discipline brought them back to their posts.

Peace snatched up the engine-room intercom. I heard his muttered 'Thank God!' as the emergency circuit came alive. The control-room became dimly, eerily lit as one 'battle lantern' after another—battery-operated lighting independent of the main circuit—came on.

'Eight-fifty,' I called. *Devastation* fell as if through air.

'Chief——' Peace started to say, but his voice was drowned. The sonar screamed like a madman in his dreams.

Peace said, fear in his voice, 'She's still under power!'

'Nine hundred!' responded the diving officer. He was back on the job, all right.

'Christ!' panted Peace. 'She's going for the bottom!'

'Bottom is twelve thousand feet!' I exclaimed. *Devastation* was designed to reach one thousand.

Bob Peters returned, hanging, as I was, on to one of the overhead grab straps. *Devastation* spiralled down, twisting like an aircraft in a spin. Peace crouched, jammed with one shoulder against the periscope operating gear.

*Devastation* was completely out of control.

'Blow all ballast!' roared Peace. The burst of high-pressure air made me swallow hard and my eyes watered. 'Emergency! Ahead flank! Left fifteen degrees rudder!'

A planesman brushed a trickle of blood out of his eyes and yanked the control-stick. Peace was giving him every ounce of horsepower he could to get the planes on the sail to bite and pull her out of her death-dive.

'Sounding!'

'Nine-fifty feet: falling fast.'

'Blow all main ballast—blow again!'

Again the roar of air.

'Sounding!'

'One thousand feet.'

There was fear in Bob Peters's voice. For the first time in *Devastation*, I smelled the smell of men who were afraid—desperately afraid. The faulty packing gland on the periscope gave a vicious spurt.

Peace snapped: 'Ahead flank—emergency!'

The planesman's reply was mildly reproachful. 'Answers, ahead flank, emergency, sir!'

'Then what the hell——'

As if in answer, the long mournful wail of the oversteam alarm burst through.

'Blow main ballast tanks! Again!'

Again the desperate rush of high-pressure air.

'Sounding!'

'Eleven hundred feet!'

There was a crack in the planesman's even voice. 'Can't hold her, sir!'

*Devastation*'s nose pointed twenty degrees down.

Peters called, 'Eleven hundred and fifty! Slowing!'

I saw the prickle of sweat on Peace's upper lip. In my heart I blessed whoever had built that extra two hundred into her. The hull gave an ominous creak. A fountain spurted down the periscope barrel under the immense sea pressure. Peace had given the planes their chance to save us. They had failed. Now, the engines. But even if we pulled out now, there would be the 'mushing' effect of a full-power down-angle nose-dive, which would mean we would travel another 100 feet deeper. *Devastation*'s hull was already past the point of no return.

'Blow secured, negative at the mark!' reported ballast control. We had blown every ounce of sea-water out of her —still we went down.

'Trim her a little, for God's sake!' urged Peace.

Then he addressed himself to the planesman, as if he were the only person there. He spoke slowly and distinctly. 'All stop! Back emergency!'

The planesman leaned forward and turned the engine-room annunciator.

He said quietly, 'Answers, all stop, back emergency, sir!'

Suddenly the floor tilted almost horizontal, a further sickening movement, and *Devastation* was on an even keel.

The diving officer's face was grey. 'Something—something turned us like that, sir! It wasn't us.'

'Something!' I exclaimed.

'Sounding!'

I felt the massive power-bite of the screw racing astern. The oversteam alarm whooped and bayed like hounds of death.

'Inclinometer reads zero,' said Peters.

*Devastation* hung in her death-dive, held against the massive downward force by the reverse thrust of her screw. Now it was as dangerous to break loose as it was to be forced down, for if released the sub would shoot to the surface like a cork.

Peace spoke into the engine-room intercom. 'Chief . . .' He paused. 'Main circuit shorting, blowing every time? Can something—' he glanced round—' be outside?'

The thunder of water racing past the cracking hull matched the braying of the alarms.

Adèle was close to me. 'Is it very bad?'

'We're holding our own—just. The hull may go at any moment.'

'Eleven seventy-five,' reported Peters. We had gained 25 feet!

Adèle said, 'I think it's a devil-fish.'

Peace, half-hearing above the din, extended the trolley-strap to the full to join us.

'What did you say?'

'Devil-fish,' she repeated loudly. 'The fishermen of Agalega think of them as gods. At night you see them glowing hundreds of feet down.'

'The electrics!' murmured Peace. 'That explains the short-circuits. What size is this thing?'

'Very big. The fishermen say, like an islet. The biggest of all big rays.'

'What else do you know?'

'Island cutters—big ships—have been pulled down by them. They are from deep—deep.'

'Eleven hundred!'

'You won't hold her if she frees, Geoffrey!'

Peace's face became set over the strong line of his jaw. 'I'm going to try something,' he said. 'If this is a devil-fish, it may be a natural depth. I'll flood her to regain trim, and try to shake it off.'

I gestured hopelessly. He slid back along the trolley-strap to the control-stand.

'Stop all! Rig for ultra-quiet.' He turned informally to

the petty officer who had remained so stoically at the ballast-control panel. 'Trim her as best you can, will you? If she shakes free, flood her down, see?'

'Flood her down, aye aye, sir!'

The ghastly cacophony of braying alarms stopped. With a sick feeling in the pit of my stomach I felt the strong backward thrust of our propeller cease. The silence was as ominous as the previous racket.

*Devastation* hung suspended between life and death at 1,100 feet below the surface, nose down.

The second planesman, stunned in the first violent dive, rose and staggered to his seat. He automatically felt the control. He turned to his companion. There was a note of hysteria in his voice.

'This bitch has got lead in her tits.'

The other laughed. 'Lead! Christ! It's broken right through her flippin' bra!'

A sharp hissing, like water on a fire, came from outside the hull. The angle of the deck changed.

The planesman jiggled the control column.

'Answers now, sir!'

The sonar shrieked momentarily as it was turned up. 'Contact not evaluated,' said the operator laconically.

In the tomb-like silence of ultra-quiet, every face was turned towards Peace. What would—could—he do? Tons of weight lay across our forward topside casing and bows. Could Peace take the risk of startling the creature to clamp itself again across the controls? Could he risk another massive electrical discharge like an outsize electric eel?

Again, the sharp sizzling hiss. The monster moved slightly —placated by the silence, perhaps.

Peace must make the captain's decision—a decision which would take a hundred men to a bottomless ocean grave, or back to life in Limuria's soft air. He reached for the microphone.

'Rig ship for hydrobatics!' he rasped. 'Right full rudder! Ahead flank! Six hundred feet smartly!'

Hands clutched the trolley-straps in anticipation of the violent movements to follow. In terms of aircraft, Peace meant to go stunt flying, to shake the creature free.

The planesman turned the dial. The diving officer's knuckles were white on the back of his seat.

'Answers, ahead flank!'

'Secure from ultra-quiet!'

Peace knew there was no reason now to keep silent. He had cast the die.

The propeller bit full thrust. The control-column went hard over. I gasped and hung on. *Devastation* swung into a snap roll and her bow came up. Another sharp slithering hiss. *Devastation* gave a wild lurch and her bow came up, but the weight held it from the swift movement which would shake the creature free.

'Depth?'

'Eight hundred!'

The bow dipped. Would she dive, never to come up again? Peace said, 'Man battle stations torpedo!'

The heavy alarm for general quarters pulsed through the ship, striking at my chest like a drum. Peace would lighten *Devastation* by firing her bow torpedoes!

Men hung on, trying to get some sort of attack discipline. He ordered, 'We will fire six. Speed high. Depth maximum.'

'Speed high—depth maximum.'

'Make ready tubes 1, 2, 3, 4, 5 and 6. Open outer doors.'

'Torpedo-room—tubes 1, 2, 3, 4, 5 and 6 ready in all respects! Outer doors open!'

'Set!'

'Shoot!' Peace stood balanced.

'Shoot,' came the repeat.

'Fire!' There was a faint jerk. A torpedo was on its way.

'One fired electrically!'

'Set!'

'Shoot!'

'Fire!'

'Two fired electrically!'

'Set!'

'Shoot!'

'Fire!'

'Three fired electrically!'

Peace said, 'Left full rudder, ahead flank, six hundred feet smartly!' He turned *Devastation* into a full-speed 30-degree-angle turn in the other direction as he emptied her torpedo-tubes.

'Set!'

'Shoot!'

'Fire!'

'Four fired electrically!'

The bow jerked upwards. Outside there was a savage hiss like steam blowing and at the same time a heavy movement.

'Blow all the main ballast—handsomely now!' commanded Peace.

The burst of high-pressure air drowned the firing orders.

As it roared into the tanks, Peace whipped out, 'Right fifteen degrees rudder! Back emergency!'

*Devastation* shook her head, like a crocodile's jaws savaging a great fish to death—a lash and whip from side to side. The propeller gripped, gathered sternway. There was a heavy rending and crackle outside.

*Devastation* leapt free.

Peace shouted: 'Hold her, Bob! Don't let her go!'

The submarine spiralled upwards, a wild angle on the floor.

'Flood her down—emergency!' roared Peace.

Again the choking burst of air pressure as tons of water boiled into the ballast tanks.

A fusillade of helm, diving and trimming orders brought the great sub on to an even keel. As if to crown our escape, the main lighting came on. Control-room routine was re-established. The turbine reduction gears and hydraulics hummed. We sauntered along, safe.

Peace climbed on to the diving-control stool.

'Sonar, any contacts?'

'He's running like a bat out of hell—beg pardon, sir!'

'Bob,' said Peace. 'I'll take the conn. You get aft and have a spot of sleep.' He added briskly to the operators: 'Keep that fathometer and precision depth-recorder going. And send me some coffee, will you?'

We went, dead with fatigue and strain. At the bulkhead door I looked back. Peace in his turtle-necked sweater, sat tireless, commanding, devoted—to what, I asked myself. I found the answer as my head touched my pillow. The sea. Peace belonged to the deep sea.


## 7 THE MAN FROM ANACOSTIA

'Up periscope!'

With a cheerful hiss, the long barrel slid up from the well of the ship. Peace snicked down the hinged handles and looked into the eyepiece.

It was three days later. We had made our rendezvous—St Brandon. Four hundred miles to the north-east lay the Saya de Malha.

'Fifty feet,' reported the diving officer.

'All stop,' ordered Peace. There were great shadows under his eyes. He seemed never to have left the Control Centre during the long plot of an ocean-bottom contour chart of

Saya de Malha. The abstruse technicalities of it had kept at bay the foreboding which grew in my mind as we approached the rendezvous. Peace still refused to allow Adèle to do a radio stint. She had been listless, almost a prisoner in the tiny cabin, but during the long hours of her company one thing was clear and I would have traded away Little Bear for it: her deep and growing affection for me.

There had been no signals from the DNI, nothing to indicate that *Willowtrack* was converging on the remote reef to meet us. The isolation of being 500 feet beneath the widest ocean in the world, completely alone, preyed on my mind, shadowing my anticipation of the coming meeting with the Vice-President and making it seem unreal.

On Peace's curt order the needlepoint of light under the glass-topped chart table slowed, halted.

It was scarcely necessary for Peace or myself to consult it, since we had drawn the chart ourselves during our trip from Mauritius to the Seychelles in his yacht. It seemed years away now. The great boomerang-shaped reef of St. Brandon, twenty-six miles long and five wide, narrows at both extremities and is broadest northwards, diminishing to less than a mile in the south. Inside its enclosing horns are 22 islands and islets, all on the western side of the main reef. The islands are ludicrously small—even Raphael, which has a permanent population of little over a hundred, is less than half a mile long and a few hundred yards wide.

'Like a look?' Peace asked.

I adjusted the focus lever, blinking at the bright sunlight. The day was brilliant. It seemed impossible to distinguish where the china-blue sky began and the china-blue sea ended. Dead ahead were two islets, no more than sandbanks, a strip of yellow sand, a few coconut palms, a millrace of water between them, back-dropped against a high misty curtain of spray which stretched out of sight westwards as far as the eye could see—the great St Brandon reef. Over this immense and awesome natural barrier the open ocean pounded and thundered, throwing spray high into the air, to be caught by the trade wind and flung far across the coral barrier.

A big shoal of fish tore for the shelter of the reef, and above it, like a tenacious carrier attack squadron, hung grey noddy birds, sooty terns, startlingly white love terns and white tropic birds. Majestic and deadly, echelons of broad-spanned frigate birds crash-dived the mass to snatch a tasty morsel. The sunlight flickered, flashed, reflected off the wheeling birds and the churned-up sea; it turned to pale pink and rose against the two islets; and then blurred into a breath-taking gauze of reds, violets, yellows, greens and blues as the sea-spray separated out the colours of the spectrum. Delicate as a water-colour, the tiny twin islands of Big Capitaine and Little Capitaine—our rendezvous-point with *Willowtrack*—stood out against the spume-filled mist.

I drew back from the exquisite scene in the periscope. Peace was at the radar repeater. Its eerie green glow reflected his face as the electronic sweep revolved.

'Anything yet?' he asked.

'No, sir. Nothing yet. Plenty of land echoes.'

'Report any moving target immediately.'

'Aye aye, sir.'

Peace glanced briefly into the eyepiece.

'No sign yet of *Willowtrack*,' he said. 'But—' glancing at his watch—'we are ahead.'

He went on, 'Let's get some fresh air. Down periscope!'

A flick of the periscope jockey's hand on the hydraulic oil control and the steel tube slid out of sight.

'Stand by to surface!'

Like a spring released, men went into action.

'All vents shut, sir, ready to surface,' reported the diving officer.

The surface alarm-klaxon sounded three times.

Peace said, 'Blow all ballast.'

'Surface, surface, surface!' said the loudspeakers.

Peace checked the control-room barometer after the low-pressure blower had taken a suction on the ship.

'Open the hatch!'

The rating spun the handles of the locking dogs and opened the vault-like cover. Peace, as was his prerogative, was first out. I waited for the bridge personnel before I squeezed out. The fresh air on the trade was moist, salty, satisfying, after the sterile dryness of *Devastation*'s interior, but with it was the fishy, deep-water smell which a submarine gathers after long submersion.

Here was the full beauty of Big Capitaine and Little Capitaine: both were miniature replicas of a hundred other islands in Limuria. Flanked by yellow and rose coral, the lagoon of each islet stood out like a green gem set in the deeper circle of the blue sea. The illusion of a ring setting which sprang into my mind was enhanced by the platinum-white reflection of the sun glancing off the restless water as it surged and plunged through the pass between the two islets. Limuria's daylight dreams; night-time and the trades breathe with a curious rise and fall through the palms and scrub thickets and in the distance is always the sea, eternally burnishing the coral for the next day's loveliness.

Peace called out, 'Take a look there, John.'

He pointed at the hull. The forward bank of stabilizers, like projecting bollards, were twisted aside.

'Devil-fish. There, too.'

Paint was stripped raw to the hull. A ragged fringe, curled and blackened along the casing, marked where the monster had lain.

Peace added, 'He took a bit of *Devastation* for a souvenir, too.'

About six feet of bridge handrail was missing.

'What do you really think it was?' I asked.

He shrugged. 'Devil-fish—that's good enough, I suppose.'

Finding it difficult to shake off my uneasiness, I said, 'These are cœlacanth waters. God knows what else they conceal.'

He looked round the gentle scene and then his eyes moved to the south, from which *Willowtrack* would come.

'From what I've heard about Tyler,' I said, 'it would have been better to have told him everything.'

'No,' retorted Peace. 'More than enough people know. Look at the leak. Look at the intruder—and this business of my funeral.'

'Are you going to tell Tyler straight from the shoulder that from St Brandon onwards his part of the mission is accomplished?'

Peace looked uncomfortable. 'I'll play it by ear when we meet.'

The metallic voice of the speaker cut in. 'Bridge—Control! Possible radar contact bearing one-six-zero degrees!'

Peace snapped the knob of the bridge command speaker. 'Control—Bridge. Keep and log ranges. Any sonar contact?'

'None, sir,' came the answer. 'The reef's in the way.'

We searched the quadrant of sea with our binoculars, but it was obstructed by the blowing spray.

'Contact now bears one-seven-zero true, moving right . . .'

'It must be *Willowtrack*,' said Peace, 'coming round the point.'

'Contact not evaluated,' droned the radar-man. 'Approximate course two-seven-five degrees. Approximate speed sixteen knots.'

'Control—Bridge,' said Peace. 'Report immediately you evaluate contact.'

'Range twelve thousand yards, closing.'

'Bridge—Control—sonar reports, probably a submarine.'

The radar-man said, 'Contact closing rapidly, course now three-five-zero degrees . . .'

'Sonar reports contact evaluated as submarine.'

'She's up!' exclaimed Peters. He became formal. 'Bridge—Control—submarine, range eight thousand yards and steady.'

'Contact now bears two-two-zero true,' droned the radar-man.

A long black shape came into sight round the reef, riding low, her sail half awash, and the identification numbers painted out.

The bridge speaker said, 'Message coming in, sir.'

'Send it up,' ordered Peace.

He glanced at it. 'Brickbat Zero One! That's *Willowtrack* all right.' He turned the slip over and scrawled a combination of code letters for transmission.

The sub rounded the point and then, as if reassured, she shook the sea clear of her casing and came swiftly across the anchorage. A churn of white at her stern, and she anchored.

Within minutes, the rubber dinghy was in the water and Peace and I were being rowed across to *Willowtrack*. Halfway, I looked back. Never had the Bay of the Two Capitaines seen such an array of naval power. The two lean black shapes offset the fairy colours of the breaking spray.

A capless figure in faded sea-going khaki looked down from *Willowtrack*'s paint-scuffed bridge. Despite the cigar clamped in the corner of his mouth, it was easy to see in those strong features where the command lay. There was about him that inherent air of anticipation, of intuition, which stamps a great sub skipper. This was the famous Revs Tyler.

'You *Devastation*?'

The question was rhetorical, but a menace underlay it, had we not been.

'Aye,' called Peace. 'No reception committee, I see.'

Tyler leaned over and grinned lopsidedly, the cigar in his teeth. I could see the ripple of muscle at the base of his neck.

'We got everything pointed at you,' he said. There was no laughter in the long-drawn vowels.

It was the sort of finger-on the trigger attitude which Peace respected. It was reflected in his voice as he called back, 'I was all ready to pull the plug if you didn't add up.'

Revs tugged the cigar from his mouth and gestured widely round the bay. 'Right on the nose with the navigation—we've split this dump in two. Now come on in.'

Tyler had a new cigar in his mouth when we reached the bridge. His handshake was like iron. 'Glad to have you

85

aboard,' he said. 'Glad to get a breath of fresh air, too—thirty-six days submerged. Nearest we got to the surface was periscope depth for the White House messages. And—' he indicated the cigar—'whatever the General Dynamics guys say, they can't make a cigar taste the same below as in the open air.' He took a large breath of the fresh, cool air. 'Boy, if anyone sleeps better than me tonight, he's drunk.'

I wondered after what we had to tell him. Still, I knew how he felt. Submarine air is like drinking distilled water—aseptic, safe. Even the cook aboard a nuclear sub falls under the whip of pure air restrictions and cannot use lard, for instance, because it gives off acrolein, which is an eye irritant. No aerosol sprays, either—because of the gas they contain.

'I'm Peace—Commander Geoffrey Peace,' Peace said. 'This is John Garland.'

The American looked at me penetratingly. It was a strong face, tough, without the cruel lines round Peace's mouth. If he had every weapon pointed at you, it flashed across my mind, he wasn't the man to jib at using them, if he thought it necessary.

Tyler inclined his head slightly. 'Hi, Geoff, hi, John.' But he still stared at me. 'The morning's pretty well shot,' he added. 'Let's get below, much as I hate to, but we can't talk up here. MKG's waiting.'

Peace nodded perfunctorily and Tyler led us below. If I had been uneasy before, I was more so now after meeting Tyler. His integrity and loyalty to the Vice-President were obvious.

Peace, too, was tense as we entered *Willowtrack*'s Control Centre. It was airier and lighter than *Devastation*'s, but that seemed about all. The steel-walled compartment, the instrument consoles, the diving-stand, the soft whirr of machinery, were all the same. But the tight groups of men, taut, alert, were not.

Peace nodded towards them. 'Action stations?'

'Relax, fellahs,' said Tyler informally. 'It's okay. Break it up.' He turned to a stocky officer. 'You have the deck and the conn, Lou. I'm going aft. We'll take time out to let these guys get some fresh air topsides. Call me if there's anything.'

With this sub skipper's time-honoured injunction on handing over, we threaded our way through to Tyler's cabin. For the first time in my life I felt a shut-in feeling in a sub; the steel walls did not seem big enough to contain our anxieties and our secret.

Tyler remained distant. He kicked the cabin door closed,

turned his back on us, picked up a phone and spoke in to it. 'MKG? The Limeys are here.' As the instrument crackled, he turned and looked hard at Peace. 'Sure, sure, he says his name is Peace. No, I dunno the guy. But the code reply was in order—Brickbat Zero One.' He put down the phone. 'The way MKG feels about Commander Geoffrey Peace, he'd give him a command in the United States Navy itself.'

His voice had a curious edge to it, and his use of the third person instead of speaking directly to Peace, left me wondering. Was the famous skipper jealous of the Vice-President's regard for the bright star of another Navy?

'I am Commander Peace,' said Peace evenly.

'Yeah, oh yeah,' said Tyler in the same tone. He paused for a moment, but neither of us spoke. Then, as if to cover up his unfriendliness, he said quickly, 'I don't as a rule hold with VIPs in my ship, but MKG is different.' He shrugged as if he realized he was just talking. 'Anyhow, you guys don't want me to give my own Vice-President the soft sell, but MKG sure has a way with him. My navigator's Chuck Wilson —MKG shares a cabin with him, wouldn't hear of taking over mine. That's the kind of guy he is. Chuck's a whiz when it comes to figures, but MKG has him beat. Somehow—don't ask me how—we began to get some drift in the gyros of the analogue computer. Who fixes it?—MKG!' He gave me an acute glance, sensing my confusion. 'You familiar with these ships?'

'No,' I said.

Again the tight scrutiny. 'I see. Well, there's seventeen thousand transistors, thirty-nine thousand diodes and forty thousand circuits in the system——'

'A dockyard job,' said Peace.

Tyler's pride was touched. 'I guess there are at least thirty-five American nuclear subs on station in all oceans of the world at this moment,' he said with a thin smile. 'The U.S. Navy doesn't care for dockyards when they can do the job at sea.'

Peace and I exchanged glances. Tyler was certainly not making it any easier for us.

'But in this case,' he went on, 'I'd say *Willowtrack* needed the whole goddam' Massachusetts Institute of Technology! But MKG fixed it and we hit St Brandon right on the barrel-head.' He gave a short laugh, the first touch of warmth that had come into his conversation. 'He and Chuck Wilson talk, but what in hell they say, don't ask me.'

I said, 'Well, he's one of the great scientists.'

Somehow, the remark seemed off-key.

'Sure, sure,' replied Tyler briefly. 'Just that.'

Our voices fell dead. In the silence we could hear the chatter of the off-duty men on the casing above.

Tyler pushed across a box of Phillies Bonanzas and Peace took one.

'*Willowtrack*'s poison,' he remarked, glancing towards the door, as if anxious that MKG should not come in on us sitting silent. 'I tried putting out the crew's smoking lamp for a week once—medical experiment. It lowered everyone's morale so much that I stopped it after three days. I must say, though, I wouldn't mind a Jack Daniels at this moment. But the urge goes, once you can't get it.'

'American ships still dry?' asked Peace noncommittally.

Tyler frowned, as if wanting to take exception to any remark. 'Sure, always have been. Always will be. Keeps the crew fit. And the fittest of all is MKG—punchball, medicine ball, Relaxicizor—the lot. You'd think he was training for the World Series.'

'Well, he's an astronaut——' I began, but the words froze as Peace glanced at me. I'd forgotten—Tyler knew nothing of the space-flight to Sante Fe! All he knew was that MKG was to test a secret weapon.

The look was not lost on Tyler.

Then the American skipper said casually, 'What's the news —topsides?'

I saw Peace's momentary hesitation—he had been in the headlines for days—and then he replied, 'Usual. Nothing you'd want to look up for reference.'

Tyler seemed to relax a little. 'Fine. You know, this past week I've been lying awake nights and thinking what if some sonofabitch had mashed the tit and started a shooting war, and here I am cruising five hundred feet under the sea not knowing a word about it?'

I felt the sweat on my palms, but Peace said levelly, 'You were in touch with the White House every day.'

'Twenty-four hours between signals,' answered Tyler. 'The whole U.S.A. could be in ruins before I knew.'

I said gravely, 'Then you'd be the only fighting unit left in the world. You'd carry the decisive factor in your Sherwood Forest.'

'Uh-huh,' Tyler replied noncommittally, looking again towards the door. MKG seemed a long time in coming. 'No news, eh? Well, that's good, because if there's anything my crew likes, it's news. News. They must have it. Normally on a deep-water mission I put up a radio antenna and tape it up. Then we play it back in the mess hall when the crew comes off watch, but on this mission—' he swung his bulk aggressively to and fro—' no dice. Strict orders. White House signal at sunset only. Not even a news flash. Nothing to fill the ship's newspaper except the same old corn, and you get pretty tired of that after a while. After all—' he seemed to be talking just to study us and our reactions—' I'm editor-in-chief. I get sick of my own corn. Just about as sick as the boys do with the same old movies. We play 'em over and over. They speak the parts, they know them so well—run 'em into the ground, funning around——'

There was a light tap at the door.

'Come in!' called Tyler.

Peace and I swung round. As the door opened, a thrill passed through me. I can still smell the acrid aroma of Tyler's cigar and see the tiny pastel-green cabin in sharp focus: the gyro repeater, speed indicator and depth gauge at the foot of the bunk; four telephones; a brace of speakers; the greenish-moon reflection off the bottom of the snicked-up Pullman washbasin; the grey metal lockers; the utilitarian desk.

MKG stood in the entrance.

He wore the same sea-going, washed-out khaki as Tyler. He was much the same build and had to stoop to enter. The face was long, the jaw badly shaven, squarer than Tyler's. It lacked the captain's rangy, weather-beaten look. But there was no mistaking its power, its determination, its command. Black hair, submarine-cut, receded slightly at the temples. As he came forward, he screwed up his eyes like a sailor viewing a far horizon. The regular line of his teeth showed as he went forward and gripped Peace's hand.

His look was questioning, though, when he shook me strongly by the hand, as if to try and place me in the Little Bear project.

'John Garland,' explained Peace. 'One of the finest navigators afloat. He's coming with us.'

'We don't need a navigator,' said Tyler curtly. 'With this ship's instruments, I can find anything, anywhere. My instrumentation's better than any Limey sub's.'

MKG said quietly, 'The inertial navigation—it's one hundred per cent now, Revs.' He, too, seemed to be seeking neutral ground. 'I checked it over. The gyros and accelerometers are just dandy now.'

He hadn't Revs's long drawl, but a quicker, shorter accent, reminding me of President Kennedy's when I had heard him broadcast.

Tyler tried to soothe the unease in the cabin. 'Coffee? It's the one thing we never run short of. Navy Nectar.' He picked up the intercom. MKG's eyes were on Peace, waiting for him to make the opening.

Tyler went on. 'They're always trying out new shapes of coffee makers to see which gives the best—we've had cylinder shapes, round, square, even a triangular one with a shot of cream from a gadget in the side.'

It was MKG himself, however, who started the ball rolling. He looked penetratingly at Peace. 'Is *Semittanté* safe, Commander?'

'Are we to start talking shop right from first base before the coffee comes?' asked Tyler.

The rapport between MKG and Peace was clear to see. I felt like a supernumerary, especially in the light of Tyler's antagonism towards me.

'*Semittanté* refuelled in Mauritius and left on schedule,' Peace replied. 'We should pick her up according to plan.'

The platitudes were not lost on Tyler. He frowned. 'See here, I got personal orders from the Secretary for the Navy himself. The Vice-President of the United States is entrusted to my special care. That cargo of mine is more explosive than a salvo of Polaris missiles. I mean to keep it that way. I don't go for cryptograms like that.'

'It happens to be my responsibility to test-fire Little Bear, Revs,' said MKG levelly. 'I don't have to remind you that you are under my orders.'

Tyler looked truculent. 'I know my orders. I have to rendezvous with the British submarine *Devastation* at St Brandon, Indian Ocean. If she answers the code signal Brickbat Zero One, she's okay. If not——' His smile was icy. 'She did. All I know is that I am to receive a new briefing from this point onwards.'

The prickly American skipper went on, as if he had been waiting to have his say: 'I can't make out why the Limeys have to come in on this mission at all. It's an American missile, a United States project and, goddam it, we've shown ourselves quite capable of looking after ourselves in two wars over seven seas.'

MKG remained unruffled at his outburst. 'Little Bear is a joint American-British effort, Revs. The motor, the key to the whole thing, is British—SNAP. It's good, or else I wouldn't be sitting here half-way across the world from the United States to prove the missile.'

'Davis and Acton——' began Tyler.

MKG's voice took on a strange resonance. 'I'm glad you mentioned them; it's just the sort of tragedy that SNAP can prevent in future. Davis and Acton could have homed okay if they hadn't lost their power at the critical moment. Here is something you and the rest of the world haven't yet heard, Revs: as you know, Davis and Acton went into a shallow orbit round the earth on their return from the moon. When the power from their solar cells started to fail, there was no chance of a space-liaise with Santa Fe and they knew it was only a matter of time before they were cremated in the earth's atmosphere. I spoke to Davis before his radio finally packed up. Know what he said? " It's not the thought that we are going to die so soon—it's pretty beautiful up here—but that we nearly made home base. We would have done, except for the power." I tried to get him again, but the radio was dead. Dead, Revs, for want of the sort of power SNAP can give the next generation of missiles.' He added slowly, ' Davis and Acton were dead, too.'

A steward tapped and came in carrying coffee in the traditional United States Navy blue-trimmed crockery. The wait while he set out the cups seemed endless. How would Peace break the news to Tyler that the operation from St Brandon onwards would exclude him?

The steward went and Tyler poured coffee. He said impatiently, ' I don't want to gripe about security arrangements, but this whole thing seems a bit lopsided to me. First, we send Little Bear out in a French freighter. The U.S. Navy is quite capable of flying it out and looking after it en route. Or I could have brought it out myself in one of Willowtrack's Polaris silos.'

' That would have meant too many others being brought into the know on the project,' said MKG. ' No, the fewer people who are aware of Little Bear, the better. This was very carefully thought out. Semittanté was the best and most unobtrusive way to transport Little Bear.'

Tyler rode the rebuke. ' I get a new briefing from St Brandon onwards. From whom? Where do we go for the test-fire?'

' MKG, I'd like a word with you alone,' said Peace.

Tyler reddened. ' This is my ship and I'm in sole command. Anything you have to say can be said in front of me. Nothing behind my back.'

Peace checked his anger. ' Very well. The plan has been changed because there has been a security leak. There is a new schedule from St Brandon onwards. MKG comes with me in Devastation.'

' The hell he does.' snapped Tyler. ' Just like that. You give me the orders. The Vice-President comes with me.'

He glared at us and thumped the table with his fist. 'I take my orders from the United States Navy. On this mission, I take 'em only from the Secretary for the Navy. I don't allow the Vice-President to go off with two Limeys who come aboard my ship and say the plan is changed, the Vice-President comes with us. Nor do I like the look of a submarine with her identification numbers painted out and her sail damaged!'

'We ran into a devil-fish in the Saya de Malha!' said Peace.

'Fish!' snorted Tyler. 'Don't give me that bull!'

'You can check——' began Peace, but Tyler would not listen. 'What happens to *Willowtrack*?'

'You go home,' said Peace roughly. 'Your job's done.'

MKG stood up between the two tough skippers. 'Sit down, both of you,' he said. There was steel beneath his quiet tones. 'Order some more coffee, Revs,' he went on. 'We all need it.'

Tyler picked up an intercom. 'Dan! Come here—damn' quick!'

'I told you to order coffee; Dan's the radio operator,' intervened MKG.

Tyler picked up one of the plastic coffee spoons which had fallen on the table. He jabbed it down on the surface. The snap of its shaft sounded like a pistol shot. He swept his hand towards the intercoms.

'I got four telephones and two speakers,' he said tightly. 'I can pick up anyone. I can signal anyone, anywhere, in the world. I can start a nuclear war with that one, see? I am the captain, a Navy captain entrusted with the responsibility of the person of the Vice-President of the United States, and I don't buck my duty. And I don't simply hand over the Vice-president to two guys who come aboard without credentials, from a suspicious ship.'

*Willowtrack*'s crew certainly knew how to jump when they heard that note in Tyler's voice, for before MKG could reply, Dan had arrived. The boy looked scared.

'Dan,' ordered Tyler. 'Send this signal——'

MKG stopped him. 'Revs, I am the Vice-President.'

'Sure, sure,' replied Revs. 'It's a responsibility I take seriously.'

'No signals whatsoever are to be sent until I authorize them,' said MKG. 'Get that, Dan?'

The boy glanced uncertainly from MKG to Tyler. 'Yes, sir, I mean, Mister Vice-President.'

'Get out!' snapped Tyler. 'Get the hell outa here!'

Dan fled.

I admired the superb command MKG had over himself. It was he who had taken over the situation, now.

'Coffee!' he ordered.

Tyler picked up a phone, never taking his eyes from MKG. In a moment, it seemed, fresh coffee was on the table. Tyler kicked the door shut.

'Now——?' said MKG, turning to Peace.

'The CIA got wind of our plan, somehow. They put a man on to tag me.' I nodded confirmation of this cryptic account. 'So the DNI decided it was safer to change the plans. I picked John up at sea, left no trail.'

'I can't accept a statement like that,' said Tyler stubbornly. 'I don't know either of you from a wave in the ocean.'

'God's truth!' exploded Peace. 'At this stage I can't go into a round-by-round explanation. You have my word for it. That's why I wanted to consult alone with MKG. He'll vouch for me.'

'I only take orders from the United States Navy,' repeated Tyler, the cigar clamped in his teeth. 'I want proof and documentation before I allow MKG to leave my ship.'

MKG glanced quickly at Peace, whose anger at Tyler had begun to flare. 'Revs,' he said, 'Little Bear is more than a mere missile project. It is the ultimate weapon which will put us—the United States and Britain—way out ahead of any other nation for a decade at least. It's so good that I am going for a space-ride in Little Bear. This mission is not a simple test-fire. I am blasting off to Santa Fe in Little Bear.'

The colour drained from Tyler's face. He rose, sat down heavily again, and started to spoon sugar into his coffee, staring into the strong liquid.

'The ultimate weapon, Revs.'

Peace gave a slight shudder. Perhaps the scar of the DNI's briefing in the blood-and-oil days of war would never heal, for him.

Tyler did not seem to hear. He stirred his coffee unseeingly.

'This thing has bucked me,' he said at last, 'I won't say it hasn't.' He looked up at MKG. 'I gotta Mark One eyeball check I'm speaking to the Vice-President, a top scientist of our age. Or else I'd think some boot seaman was razzing me with a phoney news item in the ship's newspaper. He says, I'm blasting off into space. To Santa Fe. In Little Bear. Experimental missile. Untested——'

The tough skipper stood up mechanically and sat down, automatically dumping more sugar into his coffee. MKG went over to him and put a hand on his shoulder.

Tyler jerked up, brushing aside MKG's hand and facing him. 'The Vice-President test-fire an experimental missile and go to Santa Fe! We know you got the spellout, MKG: Anacostia. Naval Research Lab. And a great guy. But no Vice-President of mine goes on a space-ride in an experimental missile—not while Revs Tyler is around. The safety of the Vice-President of the United States is my responsibility and I won't duck it.' His hand went out to the intercom.

'Revs!' The power in the controlled tones stopped Tyler. 'I ordered you not to touch that phone.'

Tyler's hand wavered uncertainly and then fell back. The four of us were so close round the tiny table that I could smell the detergent from their sea-khaki, blended with the aftermath of the pungent Phillies. It did not seem incongruous that MKG, in direct line for the Presidency, should wear drab khaki—in all the long line of Presidents there had been men in the garb of lawyers, doctor, businessmen, farmer, soldier, clergyman, artisan, and at that moment MKG symbolized our age, the space age. His was the ascetic raiment of science, the technocrat risen to the highest political rank and now seeking to set a seal on the new hierarchy by a voyage into the far-flung spaces of the heavens.

There was a curious, luminous light in the Vice-President's eyes. 'Little Bear is not only a question of justifying a supreme missile,' he told Tyler. 'It is also a question of justifying the spirit of the age—my age, the age of science.'

'I'm not with you,' muttered Tyler.

'I am the supreme representative of the new American technocratic society,' replied MKG. 'In the age of science, science's top representative and the American people have chosen me as that. Science must be at the helm; therefore *I* have to make the flight to Santa Fe!'

'In an experimental missile!' burst out Tyler.

MKG went on quickly. 'Von Braun, the father of American rocketry, had the same basic idea way back in the fifties, namely, a sea-based missile. Von Braun's was rough-and-ready—pontoons in the water, the missiles to be sown like mines round the enemy's shores. But the seed-idea was there and it ripened—' he swung on Peace—'in the brain of that remarkable old man, the DNI. Little Bear is the ultimate weapon.'

There was a pause so intense that again I could hear the

cheerful voices of the crew on the casing above as they rejoiced in the sunlight.

Tyler stood up, his eyes hard. 'I don't buy it,' he said curtly. 'Nor would the American people. The office of President—and you are part of it—is one of the three bastions on which the Constitution rests. See Revs Tyler shooting off part of his heritage into space!'

'We are only as great as we are to our inward vision,' said MKG. 'Remember that, Revs.'

Tyler raked the coal of his cigar across the ashtray and then threw it into the trash basket under the desk. He lit another as automatically. Peace sat like a coiled spring. From the casing came the shout of a swimmer and the thump of his body against *Willowtrack*'s hull.

Tyler looked from Peace to myself. 'Two Limeys—why bring them into it? Two Limeys I don't even know!'

'The motor is British—SNAP,' MKG repeated, his voice tinged with asperity. 'I don't have to explain it all again.'

Tyler wheeled on Peace and me, his face livid. 'That's what burns me up—two Limeys!' he shouted. 'It's not *your* goddam' Vice-President! What do you care if he's burnt to hell in a test-missile!'

'Sit down, shut up!' retorted Peace. He turned to MKG. 'My dinghy's waiting. Let's get aboard *Devastation*. Don't forget to bring your code so that we can signal the White House at sunset.'

Tyler grabbed Peace by the shoulder. 'Who are you to order me and MKG around, fellah?'

Peace shook himself free and MKG interjected, 'You know the set-up with Commander Peace, Revs.'

'You say you know this guy, but who in hell is this?' He indicated me. 'You didn't know him, did you, until now?'

MKG was on his feet, too, an angry light in those strange eyes. 'I know Commander Peace and anyone he vouches for I trust!'

'But I don't!' came back Tyler. 'See here, this whole thing stinks to me. And when this guy says, bring along the White House code, it stinks more!'

MKG looked dangerous. 'Revs, as Vice-President I order you——'

'I'm signalling the President direct,' replied Tyler. 'I dunno the original plan you talk about. I dunno the changes. I dunno this sonofabitch freighter's course, even. I thought all along there was something crook about a French ship carrying an American classified weapon. I don't like the look

95

of that sub across the bay. I don't like taking orders from anyone but the Secretary for the Navy, leastways this guy.'

He picked up the empty coffee-pot, tried to pour from it, and with an oath tossed it away, consoling himself with yet another cigar and glaring at us.

'The essence of this mission is secrecy,' said MKG. 'If you signal, you destroy it.'

Tyler paused and then reached across for an intercom before MKG could intercept him.

'Bridge—Captain! Clear the casing! Clear the bridge! Rig for diving!'

MKG wrenched Tyler round to face him. 'I ordered you——!'

The alarm-klaxon brayed its mournful note, a double blast, through the ship. The thudding of feet overhead and the slam of steel doors followed.

Tyler put down the phone. He was in full command. 'You said—sure. But who are these guys? I'm taking no chances. I'm a Navy captain and I know my duty, and that duty is to the person of the Vice-President and the office of President of the United States. Santa Fe! It needs no spellout what it would mean when the world heard what a sucker Revs Tyler had been!'

'You are an American officer. I order you to put me aboard *Devastation*!'

There was no wavering or hesitation about Tyler. His voice was hard, his face strained with the weight of the decision he had taken. 'My duty is to protect the Vice-President with every means at my disposal—and that means I'd even set the birds flying to start a shooting war.' He wrenched a key similar to Peace's from around his neck. 'If the Vice-President is going to Santa Fe, he is going in an all-American missile with American scientists under the eyes of the American people. *If*. That's as maybe, depending on a lot of things which ain't my concern. But it ain't gonna be this way.'

'You've talked a lot about your responsibility, now listen to mine,' said MKG. 'The condition on which I came on this mission was that during the outward leg of the voyage to St Brandon I would be in radio touch every day at sunset with the President at the White House. Anything could happen during such a long voyage. From St Brandon onwards things will be different. I'll be in friendly waters, close to the British base at Mahé. The arrangement from now on is that I'll signal regularly to the President through the DNI. It won't be the tight daily schedule because, if there is anything I should know, the President will inform the DNI, and he can be in immediate touch with me. It's safer, too, at this distance from home, to use the British land-based communications facilities than a sub's radio.'

'This is a United States sub and we're quite capable of looking after the Vice-President——' Tyler broke in angrily.

MKG ignored the interruption. 'If anything—anything—were to arise during my absence from the United States which in the opinion of the President necessitated my abandoning the Santa Fe space shot, I would drop it here and now,' he said forcefully. He underlined each word, his eyes going from Tyler to Peace in turn. 'That is a basic condition of Little Bear. I know my duty to my office and to the American people as well if not better than you, Revs. So far nothing has cropped up to reverse the original plan, but if it did, I assure you I would call it off. The President and I both believe in this ultimate new weapon and I intend to prove its worth. We have had to resort to these unorthodox ways, but we feel them justifiable because of the supreme value of Little Bear to the free world.'

Tyler looked more rangy than ever. 'I'm taking this ship down,' he said doggedly. 'I'll use your sunset time to signal the President—direct.'

'You won't!' said MKG. 'Only two people know the code —the White House and myself.'

Tyler shrugged. 'I'll send a signal *en clair*, then. I want this whole thing straight in my mind—from the President— before I allow you to go walking off with these two—two——' He glared at us in unconcealed hostility.

'As soon as this ship is ready—this is a crack Gold Crew and it takes less than three minutes—I intend to submerge to periscope depth. As a start, I'll signal Submarine Headquarters in New London.'

The loudspeaker blared metallically. 'All clear topside! The ship is rigged for dive and compensated, Captain!'

Admiration chased the anger for a moment from Peace's face. By any standards, it was some going.

An intercom buzzed. Tyler answered in monosyllables, but his face darkened. 'Bring it through Dan—damn' quick!'

He turned on Peace, his face livid. 'So you're on the level, are you, Mister Goddam' Commander Peace!—while your sub tried to jam my radio!'

It was Peace's turn to look astonished. He swung on MKG. Tyler picked up an intercom. 'Stand by to dive! Periscope depth! I'll come through and take the conn.'

Dan came and retreated quickly at the sight of our faces.

Tyler read the signal, looked round at us, unspeaking, reread it. His mouth was like iron.

He addressed MKG. 'You say you know this guy.' He jerked his head at Peace. 'Who is he?'

MKG looked puzzled. 'Of course I know him, Revs. Commander Geoffrey Peace, Royal Navy.'

Tyler spun on Peace. 'That so?'

Peace nodded.

'Then listen to this,' he replied grimly. 'It's a general signal from ComSubInd, submarine headquarters of the Seventh Fleet in the Seychelles, incomplete because it was jammed towards the end. But enough.' He quoted: '"To all subs: Admiral Thornton, commanding U.S. Seventh Fleet, has received the following message from the British Prime Minister—on behalf of the Minister of Defence and myself, I wish to thank you and the officers and men of the Seventh United States Fleet, and especially units of the nuclear submarine force based on Mahé, for their generous gesture in according the last honours at the funeral of the distinguished British submarine ace, Commander Geoffrey Peace . . ."'

## 8 BLOW AND GO

The two skippers stared at one another. Peace said nothing. His face was bleak, withdrawn. Tyler watched him as narrowly as a boxer coming out of his corner. He backed away to the intercom, facing Peace all the time, felt for the instrument, dialled. 'Hold it, Lou, I'm coming through.' His vowels grew more pronounced with tension. 'Dan, keep the radio antenna up when we submerge, see. We'll be at sixty feet—I gotta lot of signalling to do. What—again!'

He moved forward towards Peace to the length of the intercom cord. His voice was menacing. 'So you're on the level, are you, the late Commander Geoffrey Peace! Every signal of mine is being jammed at this moment.'

'Nonsense!' Peace retorted.

I was glad that Tyler had to use his hands to hold the intercom. Otherwise he might have been at Peace's throat. He listened again. 'Goddam it! Here in the bay?'

He rammed it down. His face was livid. He said slowly, 'Peace—or whatever your name is—if that goddam' sub of yours doesn't stop jamming me, I'll—I'll—sink her!'

'Revs,' MKG interposed, 'pull yourself together! I recognize Commander Peace—I know him personally. Why would a British sub jam you anyway?'

'British?' Tyler flared. 'Does a friendly sub jam another on a top-secret mission like this? You'll all stay here until I've sorted this one out.' He pushed past to the door.

'Revs!' called MKG. The tough skipper paused. 'If you go on like this, you'll live to regret it.'

There was a moment's uncertainty about Tyler, then he said curtly, 'If this guy had been who he said he was, I might . . . No! I wasn't sure, even then. Now it's the other way. I'm signalling New London. Then I'm going after *Semittanté*.'

'Will you take it upon yourself to act in direct opposition to the orders of the President? You have your orders. Obey them!' The cabin did not seem big enough to hold three such towering personalities.

Revs shook his head, as if trying to clear it. 'My orders ——'

MKG's voice was resonant, hard. 'I order you to go ahead with the mission as planned!'

Tyler jerked round, so that his face was away from MKG. He picked up the intercom. 'Dan! Get that other sub. Signal her skipper is coming on a trial evolution with *Willowtrack*. Yeah, that's what I said, trial evolution. Say he'll be away a day or two. And, if you can get past that jamming, say Commander Peace's orders are that the sub must remain here in the Bay of the Two Capitaines until—until further orders. Got that?'

Peace moved towards Tyler. The big American put down the intercom, his hands hanging ready at his sides.

'Tyler——'

'Keep back!' he replied. 'Keep away from me, Peace. You're a prisoner and you and Garland will stay so. You can't get away. Like on a plane, you can't step outside.'

Peace turned with a gesture of his hand towards MKG. Tyler spoke into another phone. 'Lou! Tell that other sub's dinghy to stand clear. Pull the plug. Sixty feet. Handsomely. Use the pumps.'

The speaker clicked on. 'Captain—Control: ship rigged for dive and compensated.'

I could see the impact of his decision upon Tyler. The tall, rangy figure seemed to sag slightly. At the door, he half reached out his hand towards MKG but, as if ashamed of the gesture, hastily plunged it into the cigar box.

'You're already smoking, Revs!' MKG's voice struck like a sjambok.

Tyler ground out the cigar savagely. 'I am, goddammit.'

'Listen for the last time, Revs,' said MKG. 'I have a date to keep with Little Bear. I mean to keep it.'

'Not this way,' repeated Tyler doggedly. 'I'll go after the freighter first. Little Bear!'

MKG's voice sharpened. 'One of the very few prototypes of Little Bear.'

'Aye,' retorted the big American. 'That's the kicker.' He glared at Peace and myself. 'I'd say this whole story is a frame-up to get a classified weapon to the Reds and to kidnap the Vice-President of the United States.'

'God's truth——' began Peace, but Tyler was gone, the door slamming behind him. Within seconds came the familiar whirr of the pumps and the rush of water as Willowtrack started to submerge. It is a delicate manœuvre to take a nuclear sub down without engines, but Tyler rightly boasted he had a Gold Crew. She went down smooth as a lift.

MKG and Peace stood silent. There was nothing we could do. We were completely in Tyler's hands.

MKG took one of Tyler's cigars and lit it, staring at the burning tip. 'It's the way we planned it or nothing,' he said at length.

I said, 'Tyler sees his duty to the office of the Vice-President as overruling all other considerations.'

'He didn't give me time even to explain about the CIA man, the leak and all the rest of it,' added Peace.

'Revs is the low man on the totem-pole,' MKG answered wryly. 'Strange, having someone else try and teach one one's duty as Vice-President. I thought his loyalty to me——'

'I don't understand the jamming of Willowtrack's radio by Devastation,' said Peace. 'I don't like it, either. I gave no orders.'

The thought struck me like a body-blow: suppose it wasn't Devastation?

'What if there's another sub in the bay?' I asked swiftly. 'What if the CIA had another United States nuclear sub shadow us?'

'No,' replied Peace. 'The U.S. Navy's too deep in this, isn't it, MKG?'

The Vice-President nodded.

'But what if it's a Red sub?' Peace continued.

'My god!' exclaimed MKG as we stared at him. 'Maybe I'll need Revs's protection after all. What makes you say that, Commander?'

Peace glanced at me. 'The girl, Adèle. What if she has homed a Red sub on to us?'

The thought left me sick.

'We'll find out—soon!' snapped Peace. 'MKG, what have you aboard this sub that you need for the Little Bear launch?'

MKG rose slowly to his feet, dropping the cigar unheedingly on the table. 'I don't get you.'

'Space-suit—instruments—anything like that?'

'No. Boz Blair's got the space-suit and other gear.' He stared, puzzled, at Peace. 'I've got a few countdown details —a few of the final stable table settings, but Boz has dupli- cates of them all. The White House code, of course.'

'Nothing heavy you need?'

'What have you got in mind, Commander?'

'Tyler said you can't simply step outside a submarine. But you can, you know. Blow and go!'

'Blow and go?'

'We must hurry, while Tyler is in the Control Centre. Every nuclear sub has three escape hatches——'

Peace's daring plan broke upon me when I remembered the escape tube Bob Peters had shown me when conducting me round *Devastation*. He had told me of the three escape routes: the usual one via the bridge and sail, and two others, one for'ard and one aft. I had seen the forward escape trunk myself. The hatches leading from these escape trunks were the only ones in the ship which were independ- ent of the main ballast-control panel. The men escaping operated them.

MKG stood transfixed at Peace's rapid explanation. 'But when they see us with escape gear . . .'

'No, no! No apparatus is needed. That's why it's called blow and go. All you have to do once you're inside the hatch is to equalize the air pressure inside the escape tube with that of the ocean outside. You allow water into the trunk until pressure is equal. Then, you just open a side hatch and step out into the water. You heard Tyler say we'll only be sixty feet down. It's a piece of cake at that depth.'

'But our lungs will burst.' MKG hesitated.

'There isn't time to explain it all now—you'll have to take my word for it. It's a well-tried and tested method—buoyant ascent, it's called. You get compressed air in your lungs in the escape tube. As you rise to the surface, the compressed air expands and blows itself out.'

'No masks?'

'No, there is no equipment at all. It takes only about six seconds to rise to the surface from sixty feet. Can you swim?'

MKG grinned. 'Let's go, fellahs!'

'*Devastation*'s dinghy won't be far,' I added.

It was unbelievably easy. MKG led. We made our way down the short passageway to the cabin which MKG shared with the SINS expert, who was at his general quarters station in the control-room. MKG flung open a suitcase, took out some documents, tied them into a plastic bag which previously had held a shirt, and thrust the parcel into his sea-khakis' pocket. He scrabbled deeper and pulled out a flat wooden case.

'You won't want a pistol,' Peace said.

'This isn't an ordinary hand-gun.' He snapped it open. There, with 100 shells banked round, was the finest weapon I had ever seen. It looked like a pistol, but it had a bolt action.

'Remington XP 100,' MKG said tersely. '221 Fire Ball shells—highest velocity ever fired by a hand-gun. Sort of holster rifle.'

Peace found another plastic shirt-cover in which he wrapped the gun, while MKG did the same to some other papers.

In the passageway I felt naked. I wanted to rush. MKG sauntered casually, talking to Peace as if he were showing him the ship.

We reached the main forward bulkhead which separates the torpedo compartment from the rest of the ship—one of the five main watertight compartments into which the hull is divided. My stomach dropped as we stepped over the high lintel. Fear of discovery vied with fear of the unknown plunge into the sea which Peace had outlined. I shut the bulkhead door behind us. The narrow passageway ahead was lined with light-alloy bunks, their Pullman-type curtains drawn. The 20-foot-long Mk 18 torpedoes, loaded with 500 lbs of TNT in the head and driven by over a ton of mixed water, alcohol and hydrogen peroxide, seemed as outmoded as a spear compared to a carbine in the deadly complexity of *Willowtrack*'s main armament. Two torpedo-men were checking the tubes. One of them paused, his hand on a big clamp. The news obviously hadn't reached them yet.

'Hi, MKG!' he called cheerfully. 'We fixed the homing gear in t'other sonofabitch. You were right on the pickle-barrel about the trouble.'

The other crewman grinned and MKG, acting magnificently, replied, 'Well, that's sure good, fellahs—the thing won't run and hit us in the ass, now.'

They all laughed. MKG said, 'You guys, I want you to meet Commander Peace, from the British sub. He's coming for a ride with us. Wants to see *Willowtrack*'s escape gear.'

'Can't leave this right now,' replied the other torpedo-man. 'But Jeez, MKG—help yourself.'

'Close t'hatch, willya—there's going to be some hammering in a moment,' added the first man.

'Sure, boys, I'll do that.'

We edged through a low steel door. Peace slammed it. In front of us was the 'trunk', a heavy bronze tube running out of sight into the bulkhead. Hung round it from the steel beams were sacks of onions for the galley. It struck a homely note. Peace flung his weight against the big locking dogs and snapped open the hatch into the tube.

'Aren't there any lights?' I asked.

Peace's voice came from inside. 'Somewhere here is a self-illuminating dial. Quick!'

MKG gave a quick glance about and edged in. I followed. Peace clamped the hatch shut behind us. I felt the smooth polish of the coffin-like interior. It is one thing to be shown an escape apparatus as an interested bystander, another to stake one's life on it. I wished I had listened more carefully to Bob Peters.

'Here's the ladder to the upper hatch,' said Peace's disembodied voice. 'Wait, here's a toggle by the clock.' I heard the click of the switch and a faint light came on from the self-contained waterproof of batteries. The depth needle steadied as *Willowtrack* took up her periscope depth. The bronze glowed evilly in the poor light.

'Strip!' ordered Peace.

MKG unzipped his khaki and I tugged at buttons. Then MKG stood in his underpants, the Remington in one hand and his two plastic-wrapped packets of documents in the other. The gurgling of the forward trim tank echoed through the confined space.

Peace put his foot on the first rung of the ladder. 'Right? Remember, ballast-control will sense it as soon as I flood.' He indicated two valves at chest level. 'When the pressure equalizes, open those and step out, John.'

Peace swung himself up. A locking wheel creaked. A stream of sea-water cascaded in. However hardened a sub-mariner is, this is still the awful moment he fears above all else—when water comes rushing in. In a moment it was up to our knees.

'Pressure—watch it!' called Peace.

My eyes went to the big dial. The needle was swinging upwards. God! It seemed loaded with lead!

The water rose to my thighs. Suddenly there was a new

note. The diving officer had detected the inrush of water. He was pumping water from the for'ard trim tank.

Our discarded clothes, as if unwilling to be separated from us, clung soggily around our bodies. Peace spun the valve to its maximum. The water shot up to our armpits.

'Pressure!'

My ears roared as the air compressed in the upper area of the trunk. I began to feel dizzy. Breathing was difficult.

'Blow and go!' commanded Peace.

I nodded to MKG and inadvertently took a deep breath. It was like a hot iron shoved into my chest. I started to cry out, but I knew I had to save every breath of air for the ascent. I plunged under, tugged hard at the wheel valve. It seemed to come away in my hand—it was in perfect order.

'Don't hold your breath!' warned Peace.

I ducked under and spun the second locking valve. With quite unnecessary force I tugged at the escape door. It opened as if it had been counter-balanced. I paused. A faint sunlight glow of green came from above as I stood poised on the metal step. Then I lurched forward. An iron band clamped round my chest. The pain was acute. I let go my breath and shot upwards. Bubbles boiled from my mouth, uncontrollably. The pain vanished. It was like stepping into an ever-lightening room. Deep green changed to light, to turquoise, to blue—I was blinking in bright sunshine! I was on the surface. *Devastation*'s black hull was close and our dinghy was stroking for it.

There was a splash near me—MKG! He screwed up his eyes, grinned and swam awkwardly to me, keeping the Remington and his papers clear. Before he could speak, Peace broke surface.

He laughed. 'Blow and go! You need a tranquillizer beforehand, Commander!'

Peace cupped his hands. '*Devastation*! Boat ahoy! Here!'

In reaction, I found myself laughing out loud at the stunned surprise of the four ratings. They gazed unbelievingly as our clothes appeared one garment by one in slow motion from the depths.

The men dug their paddles in. The petty officer in charge burst out, 'Strike a bleeding light! It's Commander Peace!'

'Jesus!' exclaimed a rating.

The third poised his paddle in mid-stroke. 'The skipper—'e's become a flaming merman!'

'Slap it about!' retorted Peace good-humouredly. 'Just testing *Willowtrack*'s escape gear. Here, haul us aboard.'

The petty officer looked uncertainly at MKG. ''Im too, sir?'

Peace grinned ''Im too. Now—*Devastation*! Smartly, lads.'

The boat sped across the water. There was a burst of chatter from the men on the deck casing. Peace, naked except for his underpants, stood up.

Peters, on the flying bridge, stood thunderstruck. 'Sir!'

'This is an exercise!' yelled Peace. 'Clear the casing! Clear the bridge! Stand by to dive!'

We hustled unceremoniously through the forward hatch. The diving alarm sounded as we reached the control-room. Peace, dripping water, went to the diving-stand.

Peters's agitated voice came through the bridge speaker. 'Control—Bridge. All clear topside.'

Officers, automatically carrying out the drill, did not take their eyes off Peace. They—and the crew—would talk about this until it became a legend.

'Jettison the anchor!' snapped Peace.

'Jettison the anchor—aye aye, sir!' repeated a startled junior officer and spoke rapidly to the torpedo-room. No time to rig the ship to dive and compensate her. Peace was taking her down like a train, relying on his own skill and the diving officer's.

'Shut the induction, Bob!' he ordered.

The toggle on the BCP went over; the hatch clanged to.

'Open the vents!' said Peace. 'Take her down! Periscope depth! Left full rudder! Ahead flank! Course two-seven-zero. Smartly!'

The diving officer's hands raced across the panel. Engine-room annunciators flicked to maximum speed. I felt the propeller bite and *Devastation*, badly out of trim but diving hard, swung in a half-circle to take her westwards out of the bay.

Peace called, 'Sounding!'

'Forty feet!'

There were less than thirty under us! If a coral finger projected from this uncharted bottom . . .

'Follow the bottom down to the thirty-fathom mark. I want continuous soundings.' Peace beckoned to me. 'It's thirty fathoms for about a mile westwards of the point. After that it falls away to a couple of thousand. I'm taking her deep.'

'You don't think Tyler hasn't heard all this fuss of our getaway?' I asked sombrely. '*Willowtrack* is good—bloody good Geoffrey.'

'Tyler will come after us, you can be sure of that,' he replied tersely. 'Sonar?'

'Confused echoes bearing one-eight-zero degrees, range two thousand yards. Can't make anything of it yet, sir!'

Two thousand yards! That meant we had a flying start over *Willowtrack*. Sonar is not accurate under 2,000 yards. *Willowtrack* would be having our own listening problems, exaggerated by the racing propeller and St Brandon's broken agglomeration of coral-heads, islets and reefs. On our present course, however, we would soon be in deep water. Peace knew that the hot sun must have created a thermal layer in the water offshore anything up to 200 feet deep. Sound— even the sound of our full-ahead engines—would be distorted, reflected, deflected, by this layer. I guessed he would play the layer to the full, but he would lose it pretty soon if he headed deep and far from the land as apparently he was doing. For the moment, however, we were safe by virtue of our high-tailing start. It was a respite, no more.

Peters came across and said formally to Peace, outlined against the unreal glow of green and red from the instruments, 'Wish to report, sir, radio out of action.'

'How?' The dark shadows masked Peace's eyes and the strange light emphasized his cheek-bones, so that he looked like some avenging angel at the controls.

'While you were aboard *Willowtrack*, sir, Williams was on duty. Maybe he didn't hear her coming——'

'Her!' I gasped.

Peters became agitated: Mam'zelle Adèle, sir. She broke into the radio-room with a pistol.'

'A Colt with a hocked hammer, I'll bet,' said Peace grimly.

'Williams didn't hear, sir—maybe he was dozing from the effects of the long shifts he's worked. Before he knew where he was, she'd hit him over the head with the butt and dragged him out here—' he jerked his head towards the steel door of the radio-room—'and before we could do anything, she had locked the door. She's been there ever since.'

'My God!' exclaimed Peace. His glance went across to me, and then to the Remington case in MKG's hands. 'Better stay out of this, John.'

'No,' I shouted. 'No! You can't——'

Peters said levelly, 'I've tried to reason with her, sir. She merely says that if anyone breaks in, she'll shoot.'

Peace took the pistol case from MKG. Eyes left their instruments as he dropped a heavy 221 Fire Ball shell on to the breech platform, tilted the barrel down, and snicked the bolt shut.

I grabbed at the heavy weapon. 'Geoffrey, you can't . . .!'

His eyes were blank as he turned on me. 'There are a

hundred men whose safety depends on——' He inclined his head towards the locked door. 'You are only one. So is she. Stand by!'

Peters and MKG grabbed me by the arms.

He strode over to the radio-room and raised the Remington. 'Open!' he called. 'Open—or I fire!'

I found myself struggling and shouting as a voice answered from inside in the deadly quiet of the Control Centre.

Then the door flew open and Adèle stood there, the Colt in her hand.

'Drop it!' I yelled. 'Adèle, drop it, or he'll shoot!'

She smiled and threw the Colt at Peace's feet. 'Ah, Commander,' she said quietly.

I wrenched free and darted across. Peace swung the Remington's short barrel so that it arched over both of us.

'Stand back!'

She said matter-of-factly to Peace, 'You saw the signal about yourself—the funeral?'

'Yes.' There was no inflexion in his voice.

'As soon as I read it, I guessed Tyler would think you a fake—whatever you said,' she went on. She looked across at MKG. 'Is that the Vice-President?'

'Yes.'

'I'm glad you got him out.'

Suddenly Peace dropped the barrel of the wicked-looking weapon and with his free hand grabbed her shoulder and pulled her close. He burst out laughing. 'By all the devil-fish in Limuria!' he exclaimed. 'So it was you! *You* jammed *Willowtrack* to give me time!'

She laughed too, glancing a little uncertainly at me. 'I knew, after what you had said, that the Exec wouldn't allow me near the radio. Extreme measures were called for So I took the pistol. Williams—is he hurt?'

'No, just stunned.' He looked at her in amazement and admiration. 'And I thought . . .'

He clunked back the bolt of the Remington and spat on the tip of the shell.

She grinned. 'Epitaph for a spy!'

'Thanks to you, we've got a start on Tyler,' Peace went on quickly. 'And it'll need all our brains to outsmart him.'

Suddenly he seemed to become aware of his naked torso. He grinned at her. 'Clothes—captain's cabin! Come on, MKG, Bob, Adèle—don't just stand there, John, pick up that darned gun of hers and come!'

She smiled and hooked her arm in mine. We all went through to Peace's cabin. Peace talked from the shower cubicle as he pulled on fresh clothes, handing some to MKG also. He outlined to Peters what had happened aboard *Willowtrack*. He re-entered the cabin, with MKG, who was silent, thoughtful.

'We've got to fight this like a man with one hand tied behind his back,' Peace observed.

MKG interrupted gravely, 'Commander, there is to be no shooting.'

'Tyler is acting from the best of motives—I know that,' replied Peace. 'His first duty, as he sees it, is to protect the Vice-President. Now he's on our tail. But thanks to Adèle, he hasn't had the opportunity to get off a message.'

'It's a question of trying to out-think and out-guess him until I can get a message to the President,' began MKG. 'Tyler must be reassured from the highest level.'

'He'll take a lot of reassurance,' said Peace grimly. 'You saw that for yourself. Not even your word, MKG, was good enough for him. Our escape won't make it easier. He is convinced we are a couple of spies who have shanghaied the Vice-President.'

I found my voice at last. Adèle still kept her arm in mine. 'Tyler won't—can't—shoot for fear of injuring you.'

Peters said quietly, '*Devastation* has taken aboard an awful responsibility, sir.'

'The decision is mine, Bob,' replied MKG. 'The responsibility likewise is mine. Remember that.'

Peters glowed under the strange magnetism of the man. 'Aye aye, sir. Once Tyler's news gets around, we'll have a power of people against us.'

MKG smiled and turned and turned to Peace. 'What's in your mind—*Willowtrack*-wise, Commander?'

Peace found a chart from his desk and smoothed out the parchment. North-eastwards, St Brandon stretched for about 25 miles, shaped like a primitive bludgeon, narrow one end, thick the other. From Raphael, one of the few inhabited islands, Peace and I had explored the great barrier reef from an island pirogue; a wild jumble of coral-heads, racing seas and small passages amid bursting spray. A plume of foam, held fifty feet aloft by the trade wind, streamed perpetually across the eastern side of the reef—thundering, booming, drenching. Old André, the only fisherman Peace could induce to take us because of local superstition about the reef, had commended his soul to God at the wild sight. But we had discovered—and partially charted—an unknown inlet in the coral about five miles long and one broad. It had a seaward entrance. There was, however, nothing on ordinary charts to show it existed. When he had recovered himself, old André assured us with a grin that this knowledge of the reef passage was as good as a pension—a fish pension, he called it—for now he knew rich fishing-grounds where no other islander dared venture.

MKG read out an annotation on the side of Peace's chart. 'No vessel dare approach this seaward face of the reef.' His eyes held the question. Peters was uneasy.

Peace replied obliquely, 'Our first task is to try and shake off *Willowtrack*.'

'Easy to say,' I interjected. 'Tyler's the best——'

I could see by the set line of Peace's jaw how worried he was. He replied quietly, 'If Tyler catches either *Devastation* with the Vice-President or *Semittanté* with Little Bear, our game is up. *Semittanté*'s course is west of St Brandon—we're heading east. If Tyler . . .' He shrugged off the thought. 'Our immediate task is to lay a trail away from *Semittanté* and at the same time give Tyler the slip.'

'Go for deep water,' suggested Peters.

Peace shook his head. 'In deep sea *Willowtrack* is certain to pick us up. We must stick to St Brandon, our best bet. Already we're starting to get clear of ground echoes and the mush of sound which comes from the reef, which means that Tyler can hear us. *Willowtrack* is faster than *Devastation*. All Tyler needs to do if we head deep is to sit on our tail. He won't lose us once we're a firm contact, you can lay any money. Even if *Devastation* flees right across the Indian Ocean at maximum depth, Tyler will stick. If I try and make a break, he's got the heels of me. If I surface, he'll surface. He will stop at nothing to get the Vice-President safely back in his hands. Everything we've done has served to confirm that we've kidnapped him.'

I ran a finger-nail up the chart showing the jagged 25 miles of St Brandon's reef. 'So you're going to lose him among this lot, Geoffrey?'

'I'll try,' he replied.

MKG screwed up his eyes in that far-horizon way of his and spoke to Adèle. 'Your jamming was a fine bit of work. You see, I cannot signal the White House in my special code before a fixed time at sunset every evening. We've still about six hours to wait. Once the President knows what the situation is, he can instruct the Navy to call off Tyler.'

'Why not simply radio the President now?' I asked.

MKG shook his head. 'When I left, the President and I arranged that the sunset time only would be used.' He gestured towards the documents in his plastic bag. 'Not even the Navy knows the code. The President and I have a special preamble, just to make sure that if anyone got hold of that, it would still be recognized as bogus.'

Adèle said, ' Let me signal the White House, in plain language, now.'

' Look at it from the other point of view—from Tyler's. A signal reaches New London submarine HQ from Tyler saying the Vice-President has been snatched by—' he grinned at us—' by a couple of Red agents. Meantime, should a plain signal, without my special code, also come in, that would smell to high heaven! If I were the President in such circumstances, that, plus Tyler's statements, would certainly add up to a kidnapping.'

As we spoke, Peace was becoming more restive. He said sharply, ' MKG, I don't think the others know just how much Little Bear and the SNAP project mean to us. You're still going along with it, aren't you?'

MKG nodded. ' Provided all is above-board with the White House. I'm willing to keep the secret tight before Tyler shoots off his mouth and ruins everything.'

' Good!' exclaimed Peace. ' But there'll be no signalling while I dodge Tyler. One radio emission will give Tyler a fix which will enable him to pinpoint us within a couple of miles. Today is February 6th; on February 16th we will launch Little Bear, as scheduled.'

MKG seemed taken aback at Peace's tone. ' There is one exception to what you're saying, Commander. My signal to the White House goes out each day at sunset, irrespective.'

I now recalled Peace's attitude when the DNI had insisted on the one reservation in the mission as far as MKG was concerned, namely, that he had the right at any time to call it off if he felt it was prejudicing his high office or the nation. We seemed to be stumbling over the same obstacle again.

' We'll get it off somehow,' he replied, so perfunctorily that all my doubts remained. Would he dare? Not even Peace, I told myself, for all his faith and devotion to Little Bear and its enormous implications for the future of two great navies, would dare run counter to MKG's express wishes.

' Bob, John,' went on Peace, changing the subject abruptly, ' look at this chart——'

Peters broke in, ' If you're trying to evade *Willowtrack* why are you going full ahead now and kicking up such a racket that she's bound to hear it, if she hasn't done so already?'

The old thrill of the chase was upon me. Peters was vibrating with interest. MKG became excited, controlled as

Peace outlined his escape plan. It was, I believe, the point at which he failed to appreciate Peace's deadly single-mindedness about Little Bear and SNAP.

'At the moment I'm manufacturing a "knuckle" of sound,' he said. 'I'll lead *Willowtrack* on.'

I too was carried away. 'I've sailed with this foxy bastard.' I grinned across at Peace. 'He's laying a false trail right now. I'd say that *Willowtrack* at this moment is picking up on her sonar a confused but distinguishable echo—on a steady line, heading deep. That echo, however, won't be clear enough—' Peace nodded confirmation of my outline of his tactics—'for her to be sure that it's *Devastation*, but it's strong enough to give Tyler a pretty fair hunch. Then, suddenly, *Devastation* will go full astern——'

'Hard astern after full ahead makes a sort of "solid sound". *Willowtrack* will come right up against a wall of sound while we go ultra-quiet—every blasted thing off which makes a noise, the men without their shoes, even—and we sneak away up the coastline. We stay close to the barrier reef so that the seas breaking against it mask our getaway.'

'Are breaking seas enough?' asked MKG.

'These waves on St Brandon reef will sound like all hell on sonar,' Peace added. 'Heavy as a Force Six sea.'

'What's the weather up to?' I asked.

Peters smiled at Adèle. 'When I last had access to the radio-room, met. at Chagos reported a big cyclone build-up beginning.'

MKG's eyes again screwed up. 'Little Bear is an act of faith with me,' he said tersely. The rest of us stared, under the spell of the man. 'I have to take that space-ride. It's not only the weapon; science is the faith which put me where I am today, and Little Bear is its supreme justification.'

My eyes were on Peace. The hard mouth softened a little and his eyes glowed. Peace would stop at nothing to launch Little Bear.

'If you give Revs the slip, Commander, what then?' asked MKG.

'*Semittanté*!' exclaimed Peace. 'I must have *Semittanté*!'

MKG held up his hand. 'The moment Tyler misses you, don't you think he won't go for exactly the same target—*Semittanté*? She's as important as I am in this hunt, perhaps even more so, for if he can locate *Semittanté*, he can put paid to the mission without crossing swords with me. Tyler will sanitize the ocean between here and Love-Apple Crossing. Don't underestimate Tyler.'

'Tyler—you heard him say it himself—hasn't any forward

briefing on the mission beyond the St Brandon rendezvous,'
Peace replied. 'That was his main cause for suspicion. He
is unaware of two vital points of information: where
*Semittanté* is, or where the launch is to take place. He's got a
hell of a lot of ocean to sift, either way.'

'At thirty knots, plus all her search equipment, *Willowtrack* will pick up *Semittanté* before we do.' MKG said. 'Revs
knows—you told him—that *Semittanté* had cleared Mauritius
a few days ago.'

'Let me send *Semittanté* a bogus radio message in French
and arrange a rendezvous between ourselves and her,' Adèle
suggested.

'No,' replied Peace. 'One radio emission—' he drew his
hand across his throat—' and we've had it. Another thing I
know that Tyler doesn't: since the days of my piratical
ancestor Sir John Peace, and the corsair Surcouf, the seas
round St Brandon have had a bad name, especially the
eastern coastline where we're now headed. I'm certain that
*Semittanté* will avoid the east and take the western side of
St Brandon. It's more likely still, seeing the weather is
deteriorating.' Peace rounded on Peters. 'Bob, once we've
shaken off *Willowtrack*, *Devastation* will become a liability
to the launch. From then on, you take over command from
me.'

Peters looked disappointed, puzzled. 'Aye aye, sir. But
what about you?' he asked MKG. 'I'd like to be there to see
you safely launched, sir.'

'We—myself, MKG, John, Adèle—will trans-ship from
*Devastation* to my yacht *Bellatrix*. I gave Trevor-Davis his
orders and I know exactly where to intercept her.'

I pored over the chart, Adèle with me. 'As I see it,' I
said, ' we are at the moment about three hundred miles from
the original rendezvous-point with *Semittanté*.'

'Correct,' said Peace. 'That rendezvous was a hundred
miles south of Love-Apple Crossing.'

Peace pulled out another, smaller-scale chart and I did a
quick calculation. I stabbed at a point north of Love-Apple
Crossing. '*Bellatrix*'s route lies between Love-Apple Crossing
and Agalega; the two islands are about fifty miles apart.
*Bellatrix*'s course is a constant factor in our plans.'

The intercom broke in imperatively. Peace listened, slapped it down. '*Willowtrack*'s closing. We've work to do.'

Peace, MKG and Peters hurried out. I waited behind for a
moment. I smoothed Adèle's sun-bleached hair. She raised
her face to mine. 'Peace can't win,' she said softly. 'I don't
believe MKG will go through with it. Remember what the

112

DNI said—if MKG's secret were known, Tyler would call in the whole of the Seventh Fleet.'

I half-opened my mouth to tell her my fears about Peace, but stopped. 'I've sailed with him before,' I replied slowly, 'and when I thought he was dead, I still said to the petty officer in the DNI's garden, Peace is a brave, dangerous, ruthless bastard who has killed more men than he can remember.'


## 9 CORAL POLYNYA

Peace was at the diving-stand when we went through to the Control Centre, the eerie light enhancing his black clothes. Adèle pressed my hand and went to make her peace with Williams, the radio operator. The ballast-control petty officer had his hands out like a pianist waiting for the conductor's baton as he watched Peace. One planesman was in charge, which meant that Peace intended to change depth and course rapidly and suddenly—it is easier to manœuvre fast with one man instead of two. He glanced nervously at the gyro compass repeater and rudder-angle indicator above his head and ran his tongue round his lips. The diving officer, instead of sitting in his normal languid position behind the diving-stand, was swinging on his toes, feeling the ship.

Peace was balancing *Devastation*—taking advantage of the layer of denser water which had masked our getaway—by 'sitting' on it. As she hung, he ordered a slight intake into the auxiliary tanks. It told me we had entered a layer of cold water: Peace would 'play' that to the utmost. I glanced at the 'bug' of light under the glass-topped chart table. We were about a mile off the southern extremity of St Brandon.

As I came close, Peace turned to the dead-reckoning tracer—the instrument which shows a 'goblin's' movements —and increased the volume of the sonar sound-reproducer.

He nodded at me, tight-lipped. It was not for nothing that the DNI had filched *Willowtrack*'s sound signature from the U.S. Navy's Anti-Submarine Warfare Library.

A cloudy clutter of sound came through, then: 'Jum-jum-jum-squeak!'

'Circ pump, *Willowtrack*,' I said.

The sonar-man intoned, 'Possible contact bears zero-seven-five degrees.'

Could she hear us? At our speed the propeller could only be pinwheeling.

Peace's finger whitened on the activating button of the control microphone.

'Rig for silent running!'

A paralysing quiet fell on the Control Centre. We awaited Peace's next move. Would he try to fox the crafty Tyler with a 'sound knuckle' or try to slip away?

'Depth? Speed?'

'One-eighty feet, sir. Four knots.'

We crept along into rapidly-deepening water as the volcanic shelf on which St Brandon lies fell away into the ocean depths.

Peace rapped out, 'All stop! Left full rudder!'

*Devastation* eased round the extremity of St Brandon, the way off her.

'Back full! Rudder amidships!'

A shudder pulsed through *Devastation* as Peace dived backwards into his own echo. A long minute passed. We were racing stern-on towards *Willowtrack*.

'Ahead one-third! Take her down smartly! Three hundred feet! Course one-eighty degrees true!'

Up went the planesman's hand to the engine annunciator pointer. He said, without inflexion, 'Answers, ahead one-third, sir.'

MKG stood like a statue among the confusing agglomeration of dials, pipes, cables and eerily-lit instrument consoles.

*Devastation* crept away.

For half an hour, it seemed, no one in the control-room drew breath. Peace altered course until I saw the sonar-man's face whiten at the thunder of the seas against the barrier reef. Peace went deep—600 feet—and inched up and as close to the menacing sea-facing coastline of St Brandon as he dared.

An hour passed. Tension eased. The combination of our 'sound knuckle' and the echo effects of the reef must have baffled Tyler.

Then the sonar-man, keyed-up, exclaimed: 'Possible goblin contact, sir'

Peace looked thunderstruck. 'She's—she's parallel with us!' He grabbed his microphone. 'Rig for ultra-quiet! All stop! Hold her steady with the pumps, Bob! Nothing that is not necessary . . ."

*Devastation* coasted to a standstill. All turbines, generators and pumps not needed for the essential running of the ship were silent. Men kicked off their shoes. No one spoke.

Peace turned on the sound reproducer. Through the woolly beat of surf—there it was!—jum-jum-jum-squeak!

The sonar operator intoned softly, 'Contact evaluated as submarine, sir.'

'Range? Course? Speed?'

'Range four thousand five hundred yards. Approximate course zero-three-five degrees true. Approximate speed—' he paused, tensely. 'Slowing, sir—slowing now!'

Slowing! She had a bead on *Devastation*, all right! *Willowtrack* slowed as we slowed.

'Flood her down, Bob! Seven hundred feet, smartly!'

As the way dropped off her, *Devastation* started to sink, slowly at first, then more rapidly. Then, in a moment it seemed, she was starting to race for the bottom.

'Christ!' snapped Peace. 'That bloody salinity layer! Pump auxiliaries to the sea!'

The noise of the pumps seemed to fill the whole ship. And *Willowtrack* lay less than two miles away, ears glued to us!

A chant came from the rating at the rate-of-flow meter— it shows the gallonage going overboard: 'Six thousand out —seven thousand out—ten thousand out—sixteen thousand out——'

I glanced at the fathometer: 650 feet. Peace would never hold her! In trying to outsmart Tyler, he had been caught by the density of the water which a short while before had been *Devastation*'s friend.

There was only one thing to do, Tyler or no Tyler.

'Blow the tanks!' ordered Peace.

As it thundered into the main ballast tanks the high-pressure air seemed to shout our position to *Willowtrack*. It ceased; *Devastation* hung uncertainly. The sonar was silent. *Willowtrack* had the edge. The warm smell of polythene caught at my throat.

Then the sonar-man said, 'Goblin contact—' a look of astonishment came over his face—'she's making off, sir! Ten knots!'

Peace swung on me. 'What the devil is Tyler playing at! Here he had us nailed, then he simply pushes off.'

'Maybe he didn't hear us at all—something to do with the underwater topography,' I suggested. 'The sound could be distorting.'

Peace shook his head. There it was, however, on the sonar-scope: the retreating sound of *Willowtrack*.

Peace was uneasy. 'It's a double bluff,' he muttered. 'Wants me to run for deep water—does Tyler know the cyclone forecast?'

MKG kept his voice low. 'If you run, *Semittanté* is wide open.'

'The alternative is the simplest—*Willowtrack* didn't hear us,' I said. 'After all, there's a hell of a racket, the sea on the reef . . .'

'True,' Peace reflected.

'Contact goblin—she's speeding up, sir!'

'What the hell!' snapped Peace. 'Ahead one-third!'

We started to shadow our pursuer.

The sonar-man chanted, 'Contact fading, nineteen thousand yards . . .'

Peace's order for flank speed came too late. As mysteriously as she had halted, *Willowtrack* disappeared.

'Secure from ultra-quiet,' ordered Peace. There was no need now to keep the men tensed up. We had lost her—or had we?

The chart's moving needlepoint of light now placed us off the southern end of Seahorse Sound inlet—where the seahorse's tail started to curve, as Adèle fancifully pointed out. The inlet itself, stretching for five miles parallel with our present course, terminated at a seaward entrance with a coral 'headland '——St Brandon's widest sector. Stealthily *Devastation* inched on.

I glanced up at the big clock and MKG's glance followed mine. Six o'clock! The whole afternoon had passed.

Peace turned to us, jubilant. It was the sort of exercise his iron nerves rejoiced in. 'Lost her!'

'Certain?' asked MKG.

'Pretty well,' he replied. 'What's on your mind, MKG?'

'Shall we go through to your quarters?' he asked. 'John and Adèle, too.'

Peace's excitement gave way to caution. 'Of course, *Willowtrack* may be lying doggo.'

We went through to the cabin.

MKG said, without preamble, 'See here, Commander, now you've shaken *Willowtrack* off our necks, I must let the President know what's happening.'

'Let the President know?' echoed Peace incredulously. 'You want me to signal—to give our position away after all I've done to evade *Willowtrack*?'

MKG reddened slightly, but he remained adamant. 'I said once before, Commander, that my first duty is to the office of Vice-President. Anything might have happened since the White House signal to me yesterday. It's almost sunset now and the routine time my messages are scheduled to go off. Adèle can send it—I'd prefer her to your regular operator.'

Peace swung backwards and forwards on his heels. 'You

seriously propose that I should go to periscope depth, put up an antenna which is detectable by *Willowtrack*'s radar, and send off a signal which will enable Tyler to get a fix on my position? Have you also considered the time-factor involved in sending such a signal? How long do you think I'll have to stay up? It's not a matter of a few minutes, it's a signal halfway across the world. Reception may be bad. It usually is in a west-east or east-west direction in these latitudes. *Devastation* will be a sitting duck!'

In *Willowtrack* I had seen the clash of three wills, now I was witnessing that of two.

'I don't like to say this, Commander,' replied MKG, 'but unless you agree, you will surface and return me to *Willowtrack*. The Little Bear missioin will be off. Either you signal, or it's over with.'

*Devastation* scarcely made a sound crawling along. The cabin creaked.

'You'd call off a mission of such magnitude to send a signal which may kill it anyway?' demanded Peace.

'You, Commander, are devoted to this mission,' MKG said quietly, and his personality seemed to flood the cabin. 'If Tyler had been equally so, we wouldn't be in a spot now. But he saw his duty to the American nation and the office of the Vice-President as the greater. My first duty is to my office as Vice-President. If the mission runs counter to that, the mission will be sacrificed. The signal epitomizes my duty. It must go.'

'But *Willowtrack* will locate us,' argued Peace.

I broke in, 'You said aboard *Willowtrack* that the daily signal at sunset to the White House applied only during *Willowtrack*'s outward journey to St Brandon. After that, you said you would keep in touch through the DNI. We could come now to periscope depth, get off a brief message to the DNI that you are, in fact, in good hands—' he smiled slightly—'and suggest a return signal at a given time a couple of hours later.'

Peace shook his head. 'It would give *Devastation*'s position away,' he repeated.

'Let me send it—even Williams says I'm the quickest operator he knows,' urged Adèle. 'Very brief—half a dozen words. *Willowtrack* would never get a bearing on us for so short a while.'

We all faced Peace, whose face remained bleak. 'It's an old Royal Navy adage,' he said. 'When in battle, never break radio silence.'

'The DNI's only eight hundred miles away, the White House is eight thousand,' Adèle urged. 'I can raise Mahé in a couple of minutes.'

'A couple of minutes is all *Willowtrack* needs,' retorted Peace.

'Will you agree?' I asked MKG.

'I'll agree if the Commander will agree. One brief message to the DNI and a return to be fixed for the President's okay. Otherwise——' He shrugged.

Peace stood silent and then, without speaking, he went to an intercom. 'Bob, any sign of *Willowtrack*?'

'Not a thing, sir.'

'Very well. I'm coming through. We'll go to periscope depth.' He said to MKG, with half-grudging admiration, 'I don't like this, MKG, but if you keep it brief maybe we can get away with it.'

'Adèle and I will draft it,' replied MKG.

Peace and I returned to the Control Centre. Our instruments still showed no sign of *Willowtrack*.

'Periscope depth,' ordered Peace. 'Ease her up.'

MKG and Adèle joined us within minutes and Peace sent them through to the radio-room. Williams, grinning ruefully, came out and closed the door behind him.

Peace brought *Devastation* up to 50 feet. With a series of orders, he raised the radio antenna. I watched the clock.

One minute.

Two minutes.

Three minutes.

Then MKG came out, gave the thumbs-up sign. Peace shot off orders in rapid fire.

'Take her down—two hundred feet, handsomely! Full ahead!'

The big sub picked up speed. We came opposite the entrance to Seahorse Sound. The surf drummed on the sonar. Peace's continuing unease communicated itself to the group poring over the chart table. A new ripple of sound——

'What is it?' Peace jerked out.

'Big school of fish,' replied the sonar-man evenly.

'Could be, opposite the inlet entrance,' muttered Peace, staring at the chart. 'I hope to God that signal——'

The sonar-man's voice cracked through the silent, weirdly-lit control-room.

'Contact bearing zero-four-zero degrees! Range three thousand yards! Course zero! Speed zero!'

'My God' exclaimed Peace, jumping for the control stand. '*Willowtrack!* Stopped right across our bows! And we send off a bloody signal into the bargain to tell her exactly where we are!'

He swung on MKG, who stood there—pale. For a moment I thought he would reproach him ; then he turned back to his instruments.

'Tyler—the foxy bastard! He made an offset to ambush us, and then we go and tell him we're on our way into his ambush! Jesus! That bloody signal!' He snatched up his microphone and stabbed the button.

'Rig for steep angles Right full rudder, ahead flank, five hundred feet, smartly!'

The planesmen snapped on their safety-belts for the hydrobatics. MKG, Adèle and I grabbed the overhead trolley-straps. Tyler had been very shrewd: he had read his opponent's mind in a way which the Navy's training schools at Nuky Poo and Dam Neck never taught. Peace too, had been right about MKG's signal and his uneasiness had been on the same instinctive, non-rational basis as Tyler's—the supra-conscious decisions of the hunter and the hunted. Tyler had first shown a masterly intuitive reading of the signs and then we had handed him the rest on a plate by virtue of MKG's signal. Had this been war, I told myself grimly, the first we would have heard of *Willowtrack* would have been the swift rush of her torpedoes. It remained now to see how Tyler would push home his advantage.

I clung to my trolley-strap as the deck went down thirty degrees and the reduction gears of the giant nuclear turbines took on their full-throated whine.

'Call out the depths!' ordered Peace.

'Three hundred—three-fifty—four hundred——'

Peace raised his right hand with two fingers curved in a tight circle to the diving officer. The man nodded and gave a volley of orders, but the depth-indicator had hit 550 feet before he caught her.

'Left full rudder, three hundred feet, smartly!' commanded Peace.

My stomach gave a sickening lurch as *Devastation* turned on a sixpence and spiralled upwards. Peace held her to the first half of a tight S, rolled her off the top and went deep, twisting likes a harpooned whale.

Sonar said, 'Contact bears two-six-zero degrees, five thousand yards, speed approximately thirty-five knots.'

Tyler was clinging like a leech—he had lost less than a mile as we shot off into a series of tail-chasing gyrations. Peace reached the glass table-top, hanging on as *Devastation* peeled off in the equivalent of a steep aeroplane bank. She headed towards the entrance to Seahorse Sound, tearing towards its jagged jaws at 30 knots. He grabbed my strap to steady himself. There were rings of sweat below his eyes.

'John,' he asked, 'you didn't get any soundings in that entrance, did you?'

The fear and the thrill of what he was about to do hit me. 'No.'

Adèle said, 'At St Brandon there are stories of a deep, mysterious passage somewhere into the reef . . .'

MKG broke in, 'Commander, rather . . .'

Peace shook his head. 'No! Periscope depth!'

*Devastation* was under full power.

'Up attack periscope!'

The long tube, much thinner than the main periscope so as to leave no feather of spray on the surface, slid up at the periscope jockey's touch of a lever. Peace clipped down the handles and threw his left arm over one in the almost affectionate way I had seen so many times. He took a quick sweep round. He beckoned me over. I glanced into the eyepiece. I gasped. We were rushing straight at two big coral cliffs. Through a gauzy curtain of spray the red sun sank balefully, masking the streaming cliffs and dagger-like coral-heads. In the strange light, the coral's soft pinks, reds and yellows were blurred to leprous monochromes on which stood out in startling juxtaposition jagged, striated black barnacles, sea creatures, and weed. They seemed right on top of us, but in fact the entrance was nearly half a mile wide. I flicked the single-lens 'scope astern—no *Willowtrack*, only a wild following sea exploding against the cliffs.

We were in the entrance.

'Speed one-third!' Peace ordered.

Adèle saw my face. 'What is it?' she whispered.

I whispered back, 'If she strikes—I love you . . .'

Peace at the 'scope gave a quick glance round—and astern.

'All stop!' The engine annunciators swung. 'Rig for ultra-quiet!'

'Speed zero,' called the plotter softly.

'All stop. Sonar?'

Would *Willowtrack* come crashing into us at full speed just as we had stormed the wild passage, unable to detect us in her path because of the breaking surf? Would Tyler take the risk?

'Goblin contact slowing.'

Of course. Tyler had no way of knowing there was a gap in the barrier reef.

'Ease her down, to one hundred feet.'

The auxiliary pump clattered softly and sea-water crunched into the trimming tanks. Would *Willowtrack* hear—and come on?

'Goblin contact—speed zero.'

Tyler had funked it! But *Devastation* was in mortal danger —the swift race of the current had swung her stern towards the coral cliffs.

Peace was on the ball. 'Periscope depth! Pump from auxiliaries to the sea!'

The diving officer's handling was masterly. A 5,000-ton submarine is not meant to ride up and down like a lift, especially when a current is snatching and spinning her towards destruction.

Every eye was on Peace. Slowly, deliberately, he made a 360-degree sweep with the main periscope.

'Down periscope! Ahead one-third! Course two-two-zero.'

Straight into the inlet!

'Goblin contact lost,' chanted the soner-operator.

'Can't *Willowtrack* hear us any more?' Adèle asked me anxiously.

'No,' I replied. 'Tyler's outside the barrier reef. He could try and follow us in, if he heard us enter . . .'

MKG said tersely, 'He's outside; maybe he guesses we're inside . . .'

Peace altered course and headed down the inlet, parallel to the way we had come up the coastline, but inside the shelter of the reef now.

He joined us. His face was set. 'There are half a dozen tiny coral atolls in the inlet,' he said. 'I'm making for them. They're about the size of *Devastation*.'

MKG said quietly, 'Tyler's sure got you, Commander.'

But Peace spoke to Adèle. 'You spoke about an umbrella-shaped piece of coral in the Grand Carreaux when we were headed round St Brandon—what was it like?'

'Like—why, an umbrella, or a mushroom. There was a stem of coral in the middle and——'

'Was there an overhang?' He cupped his hands. 'A sort of roof?'

'Not a roof,' she replied. 'The coral wasn't strong enough for that.'

He leaned forward eagerly. 'Not strong enough?'

'Not at the rim of the overhang, anyway. It was a favourite with the fishermen, as the fish concentrate under the shelf . . .'

'Shelf?' he queried.

'Yes—it's so thin near the edge that if you're spear-fishing you have to be careful not to fall through.'

MKG said. 'Commander, there's no way out of this—and *Willowtrack*'s waiting outside.'

Peace swung on his toes. 'There *is* a way out—through the coral.' We looked at him in astonishment.

He gestured upwards. 'Up—through. I'll take *Devastation* up—like they do through the ice. American nuclear subs pioneered the technique of breaking through polar ice—they smashed up from below. It's standard practice now. All these subs are equipped with polynya delineators—a special type of sonar which traces the outline of a hole in the ice. The polynya, or gap in the ice, is often covered with a thinner layer of ice a couple of feet thick— a skylight, they call 'em. If a sub can penetrate thin ice like that, it can smash through a coral skylight just as easily. That's why Adèle's information is invaluable to me at the moment. I intend smashing through the coral umbrella of one of these little atolls and making *Devastation* seem to be part of the atoll itself—undetectable by *Willowtrack*'s radar.'

He turned and went back to the diving-stand. Adèle's hand was clenched on my arm at what he was about to attempt.

*Devastation* approached the first jagged coral atoll.

'Depth?' asked Peace.

'Fifty-five feet.'

*Devastation* edged closer, barely under way.

'Flood her down, Bob!'

Vents opened, water poured in.

'Three hundred feet!'

Down she went.

'Secure flooding!'

*Devastation* coasted to a standstill.

'Switch on the ice-detector!'

Eyes turned in amazement to the black figure merged against the shadows of the periscope stand. A switch was thrown and a new instrument face came to life in the Control Centre—an upward beam fathometer to detect the thin patch of 'skylight'—if it existed. A metal stylus began to oscillate against a paper-covered cylinder. A pattern appeared.

Smash-through technique worked in ice—would it do so in coral?

'Speed?'

'Zero.'

'All stop!'

'Clear water overhead!'

We had found a polynya in the coral!

The polynya delineator traced the outline of its edges. I stood by the instrument. My hands were wet with sweat.

'Ice—coral—solid—overhead!'

*Devastation* had drifted clear of the skylight! I recalled the current sweeping into the inlet.

Peace raised the periscope and beckoned to me. At first I saw nothing. I directed the prism upwards. I saw then a blurred green-blue: a school of dark turquoise surgeon-fish blended against the jagged splendour of coral on one side. A pale shell-pink fish drifted into view above and then coasted down curiously towards the 'scope. I could see his pink sides and silvery-blue back, he was so close. I swung the periscope round against the pressure of the sea—its tip was still nearly 140 feet below the surface—and winced. Within touching distance, it seemed, a coral mass towered from the deeps. It flowered, cantilever-like, surfacewards. This was what Peace intended to break through!

'Ease her up to one hundred feet,' he ordered.

I stood with him, not trusting my knees to take me across to the ice-detector.

'Call out the depths as she comes up!'

'One-eighty.'

'One-sixty.'

'One-twenty.'

'One hundred.'

The growing light showed up Peace's face in the periscope eyepiece. Its top was now only 40 feet from the coral.

'Thin ice—coral—overhead. Offset skylight,' intoned the man at the ice-detector. I saw the muscles tauten round Peace's parted lips. He held a hundred lives in his hand.

'Down periscope! Stand by to hit the coral! Bring her up!'

'Aye aye, sir!'

The only sound was the thrum of the pumps.

*Devastation* rose.

There was a sickening shock. I grabbed the stand. The sub caromed off the coral, hurtled downwards. I saw Peace check his order to blow all the main ballast—if he had done that to hold her mad career, she would have raced headlong up into the coral above without nicety of control . . .

'Pumps.'

The diving officer caught her. We hung at 120 feet.

'Again!' ordered Peace. 'Harder this time, Bob!'

I felt the strong bite of the pumps and the upward rise of

the ship. Then, from overhead, came a violent rending and crunching. Eyes went automatically upwards for the tell-tale inrush of water from *Devastation*'s crushed sail. It did not come. Fore and aft were a series of heavy thumps. Sweat ran down Peace's throat. Then—quiet.

'We're through!' MKG exclaimed in disbelief.

The long barrel of the periscope slid up with its customary hiss. Peace put his eyes to the instrument's rubber cushions —then drew back. They were wet—with his own sweat of fear. He ran his sleeve across the eyepiece. The tension was unbearable. He turned the 'scope a full circle, slowly. He drew back, his voice slack with reaction.

'Blow the main ballast!'

I swallowed hard as the high-pressure air volted into the tanks, upsetting the pressure in the Control Centre. We had broken through—now Peace was securing his handhold on the coral. He was bringing the entire buoyancy of the 5,000-ton craft to bear on the underside of the coral to clamp the sub there—part and parcel of the atoll itself. *Devastation* creaked and groaned. A film of apprehension spread momentarily over Peace's eyes as a high-pitched squeal of tortured metal, followed by a heavy crunch, came from somewhere up for'ard.

'Stand by to surface!'

The crew were dazed automatons: intricate routine checks, reports, flowed in. Peace remained motionless at the periscope stand.

'Ready to surface!'

With infinite caution, Peace blew the remaining tanks. The coral held. We were fast—part of the atoll, safe from underwater detection, safe from eyes afloat.

'Open the hatch!'

The petty officer spun the locking dogs. Peace, foot on the ladder, did not notice the dollop of water as he threw it open. He went up alone into the darkening night, into the wild plumage of spray blowing in from where the cyclones are born.

'Nine days to go!'

MKG spoke our thoughts as he and I sat in Peace's cabin, waiting for him to return from his lonely vigil on the bridge. He had been away for nearly an hour. Adèle had left us to go to the radio-room where, apparently, she was on the best of terms with Williams the operator. I felt weary, frustrated ; every drop of emotion had drained out of me. The strain of the past hours was plain in MKG's face. We were caught in a trap—and we knew it.

'The prospect of my being launched only nine days from now is dim,' MKG went on.

Adèle opened the door. She did not seem to share our depression. She was almost gay. Her first glance was for me ; she overheard MKG's remark.

'Here in the islands we say—' the Creole spun softly off her tongue—' God will plant new coconuts after the cyclone.'

MKG's warm smile for her chased away his abstraction. 'I'll have no second chance with Little Bear,' he said. 'Now that the secret is about to come out from Tyler, and *Devastation* is trapped, it looks as if Little Bear is finished, washed up. Imagine the hoop-dee-dah there'll be!'

Adèle said, 'Tyler hasn't started transmitting yet.'

'You seem to have become Williams's No. 1,' I commented.

She smiled. 'He's Welsh—emotional. Celtic temperament. No hard feelings about my hammering him on the head. I'll want that Navy code-book for *Willowtrack*'s messages.'

'Better decode anything in here,' replied MKG. 'Williams can take 'em down and you can do the rest here.' He indicated the desk.

'All the crew knows we have the Vice-President on board,' she said.

'How do they feel about it?' MKG asked.

'Williams says they're all on their toes to get you safely away.'

His eyes clouded. 'Then they also know about Little Bear?'

'No, certainly not,' she replied. 'They know you're trying to escape from Tyler—a lot of speculation in addition, but no facts. They're on your side—bit of a lark, says Williams, if *Devastation* can wipe *Willowtrack*'s eye.'

'There's very little prospect of that now,' MKG rejoined.

Peace came in, light shining on the spray on his shoulders and hair.

'Has Tyler sent anything yet?' he asked Adèle.

'No,' she replied. 'I've been with Williams. When he's not admiring my radio skill, he's muttering affectionate nothings in Welsh.'

I thought from the look on Peace's face that he was about to say something about discipline aboard his ship, but instead he shrugged and laughed shortly. 'We owe our getaway to you in the first place—help yourself to the radioroom.'

She nodded at the Navy code-book on the desk. 'MKG thinks I'd better decode in here—okay?'

'Yes, fine.'

She glanced at her watch. 'The DNI's reply should be here within an hour.'

Peace looked uneasy, but MKG said, 'Until I hear from the President that things are fine at home, I can't move.'

'And if you get the say-so from him, then you're still prepared to go ahead?' Peace insisted.

'Sure,' replied MKG. 'But I think the question is only academic at this moment. Commander, you're cornholed here and you know it. You can't get out and you can't get in farther.'

Peace shook the spray off like a dog. 'But I can get across!'

'What!'

Peace went on quickly, speaking first to Adèle. 'My plans need your help with the islanders. You'll be the kingpin, too, on the radio to keep track of what Tyler is up to. We'll take a portable—there's a powerful all-wave they use in the mess——'

'Take?' echoed MKG. 'Take where?'

'This Seahorse Sound of ours is only about seven miles across the reef from Raphael, which has the only permanent population among all the St Brandon islands——'

'You can't take a submarine through the worst coral reef in the world,' I objected.

'Who said I intended to?' he replied. 'We'll use one of the sub's rubber dinghies. We four will make our way to Raphael in one. John and I have negotiated this reef before in a pirogue when we scouted the place on our way from Mauritius to the Seychelles. It can be done. It's mighty tricky, though.'

'You deserve to luck out, Commander,' said MKG slowly.

'At Raphael we can pick up a boat, a cutter, a pirogue—anything that will sail,' Peace went on rapidly. 'Trevor-Davis and Mac in *Bellatrix* won't be more than a hundred miles to the north. We know their exact course. Interception is a cinch.'

'*Bellatrix*!' murmured MKG. 'I'd forgotten about *Bellatrix*!'

'I can't understand Tyler's silence,' I said.

'I can,' replied Peace. 'First, he didn't have time during our breakaway and second he's too wise—' he glanced sideways at MKG—'to send a signal during a hunt. Now I'll bet he's blowing a gasket, thinking, what the hell! You're assuming that he *knows Devastation* is inside the reef. How does he? The chart simply shows a barrier—no Seahorse Sound. He's thinking and re-thinking, that's what he's doing. And above all, there's the brutal fact he's lost the Vice-President who was entrusted to his care. He didn't hear any breaking-up noises over his instruments, as he would have done had we struck the reef. He can't locate us by radar or sonar since *Devastation* became almost joined to a chunk of coral about the size of the White House itself. I've cancelled all our own radio, radar and sonar transmissions. Tyler's not going to make a first-class ass of himself by signalling before he is sure of something. Into the bargain, the weather's building up. Maybe tomorrow—or the next day—he'll take the risk of trying to probe into Seahorse Sound in *Willowtrack*. By that time the birds—' he gestured to the four of us—'will have flown.'

'What is Tyler's reaction going to be when he finds *Devastation* and discovers that she is indeed a British sub and not one belonging to some hostile power?'

'Tyler's got the bit right between his teeth,' replied MKG. 'He's a tough hombre, that guy, and a nit-picking point like whether or not the sub is British won't stop him until he's got me safely in his hands again. But you've forgotten a big factor, Commander.'

'What is that?'

'Your Exec, Bob Peters. Your crew. Adèle tells me that already every mother's son of them is gossiping about having the Vice-President on board.'

'I'll order Peters to stay put here in Seahorse Sound,' said Peace. 'Let *Willowtrack* waste time trying to find her while we make a high-tailing start.'

'It's not good enough,' MKG objected. 'You're throwing the entire responsibility on to Peters.'

'Tell him the whole truth,' I suggested. 'He's one hundred per cent sound, is Bob Peters. Then he'll know how to handle the situation when Tyler locates *Devastation*.'

'The truth—yes,' Peace replied slowly. 'But truth without times, schedules, the position of the launching-site, or anything about *Semittanté*'s course.'

Peace picked up an intercom and asked Peters to join us. He glanced curiously round the group on arrival. Without preliminary, Peace said, 'Bob, you must be wondering what in hell is going on?'

Peters grinned, looking at MKG. 'They've started a book on you at the acey-deucey table, sir. I've taken a bet myself. All I know—officially, that is—is that there is to be a secret test-fire of a new weapon.'

'How many believe that?' asked MKG.

'They wouldn't be betting unless there were doubt—a lot of doubt—about it,' replied Peters evenly.

'Bob,' said Peace incisively, 'the Vice-President here is not—never was—supervising such a test fire. He was to test it out himself—by taking a space-ride to the Santa Fe station.'

'Not even the boys with the bets thought of that one,' Peters said.

'You know *Devastation* is in a trap here,' went on Peace. 'Tomorrow I'm taking one of the sub's dinghies and the four of us are cutting through the reef to Raphael.'

'Why?' asked Peters, still staggered by what he had just heard.

MKG explained the situation and the reasons for Tyler's pursuit. When he had finished, Peters said, 'Tyler's got my sympathy. Think of his agony of mind—whether to signal that his own Vice-President intends to fly into space and hold himself up to ridicule in front of the Navy and top brass, or whether to keep his mouth shut in the hope of locating the kidnappers before more harm is done. I wouldn't have signalled either. It's a decision I wouldn't like to have thrust upon me.'

Peace went on, 'Bob, you are to stay here with *Devastation*. Just keep quiet, no transmissions of any kind. String Tyler along for a couple of days in order to give us a start.'

'Stay, sir?' Peters looked disappointed. He turned to MKG. 'We'd all like to help you, sir . . .'

'Into orbit?' supplied MKG. ''Fraid not, Bob.'

'After Tyler has located me, I could double back and pick you up at sea,' suggested Peters eagerly. 'We could arrange a rendezvous west of St Brandon. I could get you to the launch point in *Devastation* . . .'

128

'No, Bob,' said Peace. 'I don't want to bring the whole United States Seventh Fleet on to your neck. No, we've got a plan.'

Peters looked appealingly again at MKG, but Peace remained adamant. 'I'll want one of the rubber dinghies ready by morning, complete with food, water, charts, compass, navigational instruments.'

Peters turned to go, then he stopped and said to MKG, 'Good luck, sir.' For a moment his habitual command reserve faltered. 'I and a lot of other people—your own people —will want you to make it, sir.'

He saluted formally and went.

MKG stared after him. 'I wonder . . .'

Peace shook his head. 'No. A nuclear sub is a big craft. It'll be difficult to hunt the small ship we'll have and it won't be in a pocket-handkerchief inlet but in an ocean one thousand miles one way and six hundred the other. See if I can't hide a ship in that.'

'*Bellatrix* is small and fast,' admitted MKG.

'I wasn't talking of *Bellatrix*,' replied Peace. 'I mean *Semittanté*! I'll intercept *Bellatrix* and then I shall go after *Semittanté* in her. I intend to cut her out. I want Little Bear. Even if I have to shoot the whole crew—' he inclined his head towards the Remington—'I mean to have Little Bear.'

'Cut her out!' MKG echoed.

'It'll be easy—we've help aboard in the shape of Dr Boz Blair and the team who are assisting at the launch.'

'I wonder what they'll think when we swing alongside flying the Jolly Roger!' I exclaimed.

Peace did not respond. 'Listen,' he said sharply. 'After Tyler has located *Devastation*—and find her he will—don't you think his first objective will be the one thing that matters since he hasn't got the person of MKG? *Semittanté*—and Little Bear. Peters will play dumb, and he may find himself being court-martialled for his part in all this, don't forget. When Tyler therefore can't extract anything from Peters, he'll go right after *Semittanté*.'

'We have only nine days,' MKG reflected. 'How long will all this take, Commander?'

'A day, maybe two, to reach *Bellatrix*, depending on what sort of boat we raise at Raphael. I'll steal one if necessary,' he went on roughly. 'Give me the same time again to find *Semittanté*. That should be easy enough. We know her course and—' his eyes warmed and he spoke to Adèle—'this man John is a magician when it comes to navigation. Another couple of days after that to Love-Apple Crossing.'

'That should leave us four-five days once we're there,' considered MKG.

'I don't like schedules,' replied Peace. 'There are too many imponderables when you're dealing with the sea.'

'The launch deadline is immovable,' began MKG, when there was a rap at the door. It was Williams, the radio operator. He held out some signals.

'Code, sir, all three of 'em. One of 'em's ours, and they could be important, that's why I brought them myself. Can't make out the other two. But—' his dark eyes were on Adèle —'maybe the lady can.'

Peace broke the formality. 'I'm damn' sure she can, Williams. This is *Willowtrack*, then?'

Williams relaxed. 'It's that Yankee sub, true enough, sir. Close—loud and clear. The other's from our people in the Seychelles.'

'Want any feminine assistance, Williams?' Peace asked, grinning.

'Argh, man,' he replied. 'And here's Ted Williams thinking he's the finest operator in the Royal Navy and there comes a slip of a girl—any time you can spare her, sir, she's welcome. Now I'll be getting back and watching that Yankee bastard—begging your pardon, Mister Vice-President.'

He grinned and went.

Adèle glanced at the three signals. 'The one from the Seychelles is very short. Shall I do it first?'

'Aye,' said Peace. MKG was very still. Adèle sat down at Peace's desk and worked on the letter groupings.

'It's one word only,' she said, handing it to Peace. 'Washington.'

'Ah,' exclaimed MKG, and the tension seemed to ebb out of him. 'Fine, fine!'

Peace raised his eyebrows.

'That's the President's code word that everything is okay,' he said expansively. 'Lincoln means the mission is off, I must return at once.'

'Why Lincoln?' I asked.

He smiled. 'I suppose I shouldn't be letting you into this secret code, but the President and I thought that by using the names of former Presidents, it would be very nearly unbreakable. Washington set everything to rights in the States, so the situation's fine. Lincoln was assassinated—things are bad. Simple as that.'

Peace had a curious look on his face. 'Washington—Lincoln: that all?'

'That's all,' replied MKG. 'No in-betweens. Either the Little Bear mission is on, or it's off. I rely solely on the President's reading of the signs at home. What he says, goes.'

Peace said nothing but turned to Adèle. 'I want to know what *Willowtrack* is saying.'

Adèle took the U.S. Navy code and worked on the groups of complicated letters. It took her much longer than the DNI's return call to the Vice-President. There was no sound in the tiny cabin except the creak of the casing against the coral.

Then Adèle read out:

'*Willowtrack x op-immed x Chief of Naval Operations x inform White House x Marvin K. Green kidnapped from aboard USN Willowtrack x taken abroad submarine stated to be British Devastation x shadowed Devastation to position Long. 16° 30' S., Lat. 59° 42' E., in St Brandon group x lost contact with Devastation same position approx 1640 GMT x Devastation's last heading 220 degrees, taking her directly on to St Brandon outer barrier reef x heavy surf x no break-up noises x no further radar or sonar contact x am lying in above position surfaced x heavy broken water and reefs x will recommence visual search daylight x*'

'No break-up noises, no contacts!' exclaimed Peace jubilantly.

'Tyler's starting his search at daylight,' MKG pointed out.

'Visual search means nothing under the blanket of spray,' Peace said. 'We can be clear away at first light.'

Adèle straightened up at the desk. 'Here's the other signal. It's also from *Willowtrack*:

'*Request immediate air-sea search for French freighter Semittanté, position not known x she carries American classified test missile Little Bear x*'

Adèle pointed to the superscription to the signal—*ComSubInd.*

'Limuria Command!' exclaimed Peace. 'Tyler's called in the Seventh Fleet. I knew he'd go after *Semittanté*?'

MKG said anxiously, 'He's asking to vector the whole Seventh Fleet to search for us.'

'No,' replied Peace, who seemed eager to placate MKG. 'You're reading the two signals together, but in fact they're in watertight compartments. The Seventh Fleet wouldn't have access to his secret signal to the Chief of Naval Operations, would it?'

'No,' conceded MKG reluctantly, 'I suppose not.'

'Tyler hasn't said a word about you to ComSubInd,' Peace went on quickly. 'He's merely asked for assistance in trying to locate a ship carrying a classified missile.'

'He asks the Chief of Naval Operations to inform the White House,' MKG said sombrely. 'Frankly, I don't like it, Commander, I don't like it at all.'

'But,' Peace argued, 'you've already informed the President that everything is in order, and you've got his okay back again. He'll naturally discount the Tyler story in the light of your prior message.'

We waited as MKG remained silent, thoughtful. At last he said, 'I suppose I can be grateful that Tyler hasn't put it on the air that I'm going for a space-ride. If ever that got out——' He shrugged. 'The papers certainly wouldn't put *that* story on the back burner!'

'These messages are all top-secret and only for the persons they are directed to,' Peace went on persuasively. 'Their contents are not likely to become public property.'

'I hope to God not,' replied MKG. 'The space-ride story, out of its true context, especially since the project has been officially axed, could do me irretrievable harm politically.' He smiled grimly. 'There are a lot of people who would like to make capital out of it against me back home.'

'Not only back home,' I added. 'What about the Kremlin?'

Peace was anxious to guide the conversation away from this channel.

'This is all speculation about things which are not likely to come to pass,' he said. 'Look at the facts: you've reassured the President only a couple of hours ago, MKG. He can read the times on Tyler's signal and make the correct conclusion, that you're safe aboard *Devastation* and all is well. The kidnapping he will discount in advance, therefore. Tyler's acting unilaterally, without knowing what lies behind the whole Little Bear saga. The President will call off the dogs and silence Tyler. It is our duty to the mission to go ahead.'

MKG looked keenly at Peace. 'You're pretty set on it, aren't you, Commander?'

'Yes,' replied Peace, 'I am. We can still carry it through in secrecy if we follow my plan and escape through the reef.'

MKG seemed to hesitate between Peace's reassurances and his own inward doubts. He said, 'Commander, is it not possible for me to signal the White House via the DNI again ——'

132

'And give our position away after all we've been through to dodge *Willowtrack*?'

MKG looked thoughtful. 'I'm not happy about it, Commander, but I see your point. Will you give me a categorical assurance that, whatever the circumstances, you will signal the White House as soon as we intercept *Bellatrix*?'

I saw the relief flood into Peace's face. 'Yes. But by that time, in any event, I think all this—' he waved the signals— 'will have been called off and we'll be on our way unhampered to Love-Apple Crossing.'

'Maybe Tyler is taking a lot upon himself without explaining much,' MKG said. 'We're on the inside, which makes it easy to understand.'

'I wonder what Admiral Thornton's reaction will be when he receives a message like that out of the blue?' I said. 'He doesn't even know that *Willowtrack* is in waters under his command.'

Peace seemed unwilling, now that he had gained his point, to go on discussing it. 'I'll check over the dinghy myself for our trip in the morning. I'll put in life-jackets, too.'

I felt weary after the long strain of the chase and the mounting tension which the signals brought with them. I said to Peace, 'Mind if I go up on to the bridge for a breather?'

I looked over at Adèle, who smiled.

Peace was abstracted. 'Don't go up on to the flying bridge or move around topsides. I don't want *Willowtrack*'s radar picking up a moving object to make her suspicious. Take oilskins. The bridge shield isn't enough to keep off the spray.'

Adèle and I made our way through the silent Control Centre. It had the air of a stage after the players have gone. The watch was on duty, but there was nothing of the previous bustle. I undogged the hatch and we stepped out into another world, the world of St Brandon, the world of the two of us. The spray was salt on her lips as I kissed her. It looped high into the air above our heads—like standing under a shower. The tall black sail projected through the hole it had made in the coral, but the hull itself was out of sight. Landwards—or rather, towards the west where the coral thickened into innumerable swashways in the reef—I could see the glint of breaking seas sparkling against coral in the starlight. Through the gauzy curtain seawards I spotted Orion's Belt. The wind blew hard into the inlet from the north-east —the direction of the entrance—but inside it was strangely calm. Seahorse Sound seemed to have the spurious reality of a film set—water cascading, spray blowing, yet there was no bite to it.

Adèle swept back the yellow oilskin hood. The spray turned to stars in her hair. She drew in a deep breath. 'St Brandon—oh, the smell of it! I smell the Grands Carreaux! You can't imagine what it is like on a London winter's night to yearn for this island-smell . . .'

I kissed her again. 'Let's come back when this is all over.'

She drew back only far enough for me to see her eyes, sea-bright. 'We can't, you know—St Brandon is a man's world. The *jouissance* stipulates, no women. They're hellcats, trouble-makers——'

I kissed her silent, but she drew away and was grave. 'This—this thing of MKG's—it seems to be unleashing forces that he, or we, never dreamed of. It makes me frightened.'

'He's in advance of his times,' I replied, pushing back her hair. 'It's not only the justification of a weapon which this mission stands for, it's the justification of everything he himself stands for, the age of science. There is no one else in the world in the same position as he is. Top scientist, top leader, top nation.'

'I see it, yet I fear,' she said. 'The Seventh Fleet, the most powerful naval task force on the high seas, and it's coming against four people in a rubber dinghy——' Suddenly she shrank back under the perspex spray-shield. She pointed landwards: 'A light! Someone is coming!'

I raised my head cautiously above the streaming shield. A vast arc of heaven met a vast arc of sea somewhere over Africa. I could distinguish a yellow star or two—nothing else.

Her voice was low, imperative. 'White—it's a white light! In the direction of the main reef—there!'

'Then it's not *Willowtrack*.'

'Who else but *Willowtrack* knows we're here?' She gripped my arm so hard that I winced. A pinpoint of white light rose and dunked itself.

'A boat!' I exclaimed. 'Heavens, how it slews!'

She watched for a moment. 'There! Again! He's coming through the reef proper!'

I picked up the intercom and pressed the energizing button. 'Control—Bridge—Garland here. I want Commander Peace.'

'Bridge—Control,' replied an unfamiliar voice. 'Hold it.'

There was a pause and then Peace's voice came through, sharp. 'John, what are you playing at? Do you want *Willowtrack*——?'

'There's a light—a boat, I think—coming towards us.'

134

There was an electric silence.

'I'll be right up.'

I heard the quick clump of his boots inside the sail as he raced up the steel ladder. In a moment, he and MKG were beside us.

'Where away?'

'North-west,' I replied. 'A shade north.'

We peered into the blackness. There was nothing but the steady drumming of the sea and a speckle of spray.

'There!' exclaimed Adèle. Peace was at her side, following her pointing finger.

The light zig-zagged, shone, disappeared, shone again and stood out steadily.

'He's at the nose of the seahorse!' said Peace. 'Where it faces deepest into the reef. See—he's steady—he's out of the millrace of the reef.'

'I'm trying to jell my ideas on this,' MKG said slowly. 'Surely it can't be Tyler; he wouldn't show a light!'

'He's coming this way!' Adèle said.

Peace snapped, 'Get me the Remington, John!'

I dived below and decided that rather than take a naked weapon through the Control Centre, I would carry it in its case. I hurried through, all eyes upon me. Peace flipped open the top of the box. He slid back the Remington's bolt. It didn't have a deep clunk like a rifle but a light click—like a terrier's bark alongside a bloodhound's. Peace loaded. The light was coming closer.

'Quiet!' Peace ordered.

The light, startlingly bright by contrast with the general wateriness, drifted slowly towards the dark shape of the submarine merged against the coral. There was a sudden crack. Peace crouched forward with the gun. Adèle put out her hand to him. 'It's the flap of a sail,' she whispered. She looked hard into the night and murmured something in the soft Creole to herself. She turned, and her eyes were alight.

'It's a St Brandon man. Look, that's a cutter's sails—you can tell old André's style of sailmaking anywhere—that odd snip in the luff . . .'

'André!' exclaimed Peace. 'By God, John, MKG, this is our big break! André!'

'André was the fisherman who brought us through the reef when we charted it,' I explained to MKG.

'Quiet!' warned Peace. 'He's coming on.'

'He still doesn't see us!' exclaimed Adèle.

Peace reminded her that we were part of the coral. There was another slap of the sail and we saw the boat's stern under the white light. It was the same sort of contrivance fishermen use throughout the Mediterranean—bright acetylene, mounted aft, to attract the fish. The cutter drifted closer, unaware of *Devastation*. André slipped a pair of oars into the row-locks. Across the water, half-obliterated by the noise of wind and spray, came the sound of singing.

Adèle's eyes were as bright as the acetylene. 'It's a sort of song-prayer—he sings to the devil-fish of the inlet to leave him in peace, because he's only catching small fish, fish too small for the devil-fish to enjoy.' She cocked an ear. 'It's snappers and *varra-varra* and *rouget* he's after tonight.'

André unshipped his oars and started to cast his net.

'Hail him, Adèle!' said Peace.

Adèle cupped her hands and called in Creole. The old man faced away from us. His back jerked at her words and he swung round, his squat, powerful frame silhouetted against the white light. He called to us in reply.

Adèle gave a ripple of laughter.

'What does he say?' I demanded.

'He says good-evening, nixie, I know I am a wicked old man, but it is dominoes and not women which are my downfall. He thinks I am a sea-spirit—dominoes are the great gambling game at Raphael.' Adèle was like a girl. She called again, bubbling with laughter.

'He says, nixie, you see I am an old man—I cannot make love to you like the young ones at St Brandon. Let me go. Besides, as you know, the *jouissance* forbids women at St Brandon, and a man gets out of practice. Let me go back to Raphael and to-morrow night I will bring you a young man.'

'He doesn't sound scared,' observed MKG.

'Oh, no, he isn't,' Adèle replied. 'They believe in nixies and devil-fish at St Brandon. It's a question of talking smart so that the nixie will let him go. He'll never come near Seahorse Sound again, though.'

André peered, trying to locate Adèle's voice.

Peace called. 'André! André! You old sonofabitch!'

In slow motion the old man sank down on the thwart, his hands clasped as if in prayer. Adèle shouted something, but his reply was half-lost.

'He says shame on you, nixie, for changing yourself into my man of the sea who was my friend and a very brave man. I know now that I am dead, for he and I and the other were the only men ever to come into Seahorse Sound.'

'André. It's me—John Garland.'

The bowed head did not rise. Adèle called again and again. At length he rose. She translated.

'He knows he is dead,' she smiled. 'He has heard the voices of the two men he guided to Seahorse Sound.'

MKG broke in, 'André you say, knows all the passages through the reef—we won't need the sub's dinghy now.'

Peace banged his fist excitedly on the bridge shield. 'This is our moment! We go—now—just as we are—with André. The gear in the sub's dinghy can be shifted into André's boat. Don't forget the transistor radio and the Navy code.'

MKG and I stumbled down the steep ladder into the sub's interior. It was a moment's work to explain the situation to Peters. The dinghy's gear—sextant, charts, compass, oilskins, food, water—had been neatly laid out in the mess. Two ratings helped us carry it to the bridge. As we went up, we felt the thump of André's boat alongside. Peters dismissed the two helpers from the bridge. André stood in his boat gazing in wonderment at the black sail rising out of the coral.

'Toss a line,' ordered Peace. 'Here, André.'

Like a man in a dream, but not lacking in seamanship, André spun a rope and cast it high. Peace knotted it securely to the base of the radar antenna and swung a leg over.

'She's all yours, Bob,' he told Peters.

Peters gripped him firmly by the hand. 'Are you sure I——? Wish it was me, sir.'

Peace said quietly, 'I'm afraid for you it's a case of they also serve, Bob. Hang on as long as you can to give us the best chance. John, help Adèle.'

'Help!' She smiled. 'I've climbed ropes since I was five.'

MKG gave a brief glance round the minute bridge—a strange look of farewell.

'Good luck, sir,' said Peters. His hand went instinctively to his forehead to salute, but he drew it back when he realized he stood capless in the blowing spray.

MKG simply leaned out and touched him on the shoulder. I think Peters would have gone to the ends of the earth for him, then. MKG went down hand-over-hand into André's boat. I dropped down next to the old fisherman and Peace. Tears streamed unashamedly down the old man's face and he hugged us.

Adèle translated, 'He says he does not know what strange ghost of a ship it is which stands part of the coral—he has never seen one like it before. Yet he is glad for to how many is it given to meet a nixie and live?'

Peace clapped him on the shoulder. 'Ask, will he take us to Raphael—tonight?'

Adèle translated. 'Not to Raphael—he is willing only to take you near Raphael.'

Peace hardened. 'What's all this about?'

The gay, rippling note was back in Adèle's voice. 'If he returns to Raphael by morning and says, I have a nixie and men who appeared out of the high spray as if from nowhere aboard my boat, the other fishermen will say, there is a new wreck on the reef and André has found her. For look, he is drunk with *bacca* stronger than the red wine of Mauritius. It is—is— 'she laughed—' he calls it, the wine that looks like stirred-up sand in a coral pass and is as dangerous—whisky! No! From Poulailler to Puits-à-Eau the fishermen will watch him and follow. His life will not be worth living. They will find Seahorse Sound. He will then lose his " pension " of fish which is unknown to anyone else. No, he will not take you to Raphael.'

I saw the stern clamp of Peace's jaw and I said quickly, 'Will he take us beyond Raphael?'

André made an expressive gesture which embraced the whole arc of the sea. 'Anywhere—but not Raphael.'

I glanced at Peace and he nodded. *Bellatrix*!

'Say, our yacht—the one he admired so—is at sea maybe a hundred miles north of Raphael. That is where we wish to go.'

André in reply snatched up a bright red fish from the bottom-boards—one of the *veielles* which haunt the sheltered lagoons and coral overhangs—and snapped it with a curious deft movement across his knee, handing one half to Peace and retaining the other.

'It's a deal,' translated Adèle.

André shoved the hardy little cutter clear. She was about 25 feet long with a broad beam and flared bow—the sort of boat which claims kinship with the New Bedford whalers, the longboats of Tristan and the flatbooms of the Skeleton Coast. All are built to ride and fight wicked seas. She was half-decked, with a peculiar lateen sail—heritage of some dead-and-gone dhow plying from Zanzibar to Calicut and blown far off course to Limuria. The first chop of the short seas hit us as André hoisted it. I made for the tiller, but MKG said, ' This isn't going to be such a cinch—I know boats.'

We headed for the reef.

André gestured to Peace and me to conn the boat. The driving spray seemed thicker. The stern light was out and I could not see a handbreadth ahead, but André tacked to windward, turning now and again with a peculiar gesture of his left hand—his thumb like the tiller-head and the palm and fingers the tiller itself—to guide MKG. The Vice-President sat bareheaded, eyes screwed up in that peculiar mannerism of his.

André let the sail go with a clatter. He gestured—hard aport. The cutter swung wildly on a stern roller for a moment before MKG caught her. André whipped up the sail again and the boat rushed into white water. The stern corkscrewed violently, the tiller kicking loose momentarily from MKG's hands until he snatched at it again. This was the place where the Indian Ocean roiled its guts on the first land for 2,000 miles. The seas boiled, foamed, thundered, caromed, dragged, volted. A mass of coral loomed. I yelled in fear to André. He gave her half a reef and we snaked by a plume of foam within a hand's touch. We broke into the main pass in a series of rapid turns, André using the sail to keep us ahead of the thrust and rush of the sea. There were kaleidoscopic close-up glimpses of yellow, red, pink and blue coral; barnacle-black rocks and white, savage water.

Time and again Peace and I crashed the heavy wooden oars against the coral to fend us off. Our oilskins were waterlogged. My first guess that we were well inside the barrier was due not to the lessening of the spray but to a peculiar silveriness which came over the boat and reef. We swept, apparently out of control, round a 12-foot-high buttress of yellow coral and for the first time the lash of the spray was out of my face. I turned. The stars were hard, defined, white in the west towards Raphael. The sail was silver-blue. The wild magic of the barrier reef was upon the boat. It deepened the grave abstraction of MKG's eyes; it laid beauty on beauty in Adèle's face. It blurred the cruel line of Peace's mouth and overlaid André's mahogany with a patina of St Brandon's glory.

André dropped the sail. 'Oars!' passed on Adèle. There was an engine, Peace had found, in good working order, but there was no petrol.

Peace and I clunked the oars home into home-made rowlocks. After a few dozen strokes we stripped off our oilskins, which began to steam from our sweat. On the horizon behind MKG appeared a long thin line of pearl.

I cried out, it was so exquisite. Adèle, crouched on a thwart, looked towards me and said something softly in Creole.

The spray was gone now and the sea, at our backs, grumbled. On every hand lay wet coral—yellow, red, pink, blue— stretching as far as our limited horizon would allow, and between were sea-threads of aquamarine, turquoise and blue. To starboard, a dark, ill-defined green mass rose out of the sea—Raphael! We were safe.

MKG stretched himself stiffly. 'Eight days to go.'

Red-eyed from the spray, Peace spoke to André through Adèle. 'The weather—they say there's a cyclone coming?'

The old fisherman shook his head and pointed at the red coral. 'Not yet, not yet. When it is near, that turns dull.'

Peace unrolled the damp chart. He pointed to a spot north-north-west of St Brandon. 'André, my yacht is somewhere here. . . .'

The old man stared in blank incomprehension and rattled off a volley at Adèle. He says he doesn't know what you are talking about, or what that thing is.' She indicated the chart.

I found the compass I had brought from the sub—I didn't like the look of the cutter's old compass, any more than MKG did. 'It hasn't been boxed since Old King Cole ordered the bowl,' he remarked.

Adèle leaned over the chart. 'May I see? The islanders have their own names for places . . .'

Peace pointed. '*Bellatrix* will be a hundred miles north-north-west of Raphael.'

Adèle stared at the map and clapped her hands. There was a rapid-fire of Creole and André shrugged and laughed too.

'What does he say?'

'" Thank you, sweet Jesus, that I am unable to read and write, when all they mean is Purse-Fish Bank."'

'What is a purse-fish?' asked MKG.

She shot the question at André, who grinned and sketched a caricature with his expressive hands—a grotesque thing with mean eyes and a Roman nose and—André took in the whole compass of yellow coral—as garish as that.

'Tell him to strike south of Raphael to start with,' said Peace. 'Now we've got a boat, I don't want the islanders to see us any more than André himself wants to be spotted.'

The reef lost its violence. We rode easily through the channels, Peace and I in the bows. Our course remained south of Raphael till the white guano fang of Siren Island lifted out of the waves. Then we swung north-north-west to intercept *Bellatrix*—I had drawn a straight line on the chart showing her course after I had left her to Trevor-Davis's charge. Under the steady bite of the trades on our beam, we snored along while MKG and I shared yachtsmen's appreciation of the cutter's sailing qualities.

Despite the balminess of the morning, our enjoyment was

underlaid with unease. Had Tyler broken the news of the space-shot? Was the news of MKG's disappearance public?

MKG fiddled with the radio to get a Voice of America newscast, while Peace waited a little impatiently for Adèle to see what Tyler and the Seventh Fleet were up to. The newscast blared through. Nothing, beyond day-to-day events. MKG breathed a sigh of relief. But his anxiety was not allayed, for when Adèle switched to the Navy wavelength and the quick groupings started to come in, he muttered, 'Now for the kicker.'

It wasn't long in coming. Peace read out the decoded signal Adèle passed to him.

*'Willowtrack to Command Intelligence Center, carrier Rio Grande x top secret x op-immed x repeat my request immediate assistance search Vice-President x'*

Admiral Thornton's reply was terse:

*CIC to Willowtrack repeat to Chief Naval Operations x top secret x op-immed x entire Seventh Fleet on its way x deployed under my personal command as hunter-killer group x proceeding all speed St Brandon area x*

*Willowtrack to CIC x last contact with Vice-President aboard British submarine Devastation x no further contacts x*
*CIC to Willowtrack x Keep station x*

'Hunter-killer group!' exclaimed Peace.

MKG was withdrawn, thoughtful. 'I can't make it out,' he said at length. 'The President had my signal last night. Why has he allowed this operation to be mounted?'

Because, I told myself secretly, he believes Tyler; he is under the impression that MKG has been kidnapped. Tyler's dramatic news came *after* MKG's signal, and the President himself had given the okay *before* learning it.

But Peace pointed to the superscription to the signal. 'These are inter-Navy signals and I expect, from my knowledge of official channels, that the White House hadn't had time to step in before Thornton acted on his own initiative, in the light of the seriousness of *Willowtrack*'s appeal. After all, it is less than twelve hours since you let the President know you were safe.'

MKG didn't seem convinced. I, too, wondered whether

Peace wasn't trying over-hard to rationalize every adverse fact in order to keep the mission going. Perhaps MKG felt so also, because he gave Peace a long, appraising look before he said, 'There would be a red-hot line from Naval Operations to the White House on news like this. The operation could have been called off within an hour. This is top priority, by any standards.'

There was a long silence, broken only by the crunch of the seas under the cutter's planks.

Then MKG said, 'You're sure the President got my signal via the DNI, Commander?'

Peace met his gaze squarely. 'I give you my word of honour. Until you yourself revealed what Washington meant in your secret code, none of us had the slightest idea. It could have been the recall, for all we knew.'

'Yes,' admitted the Vice-President, 'that is correct. But you can't have the whole of the Seventh Fleet racing out of base on an unexplained mission and expecting no one to ask why. And once they ask why, the story of the kidnapping and the space-shot must come out.'

Peace broke in, as if to steer his thought away from these graver implications, 'There was no mention of the space-shot. No mention of *Semittanté*.'

'Tyler is not going to put that on the air before he's seen Thornton personally,' replied MKG. 'It's too big, coming hard on the heels of his other news.' There was another pause, broken only by a sputter of static from the radio. 'Commander,' said MKG, 'your heart is in this mission and so is mine, or else I wouldn't be sitting in an open boat in the middle of the ocean. But the mere fact of the Seventh Fleet being brought into this may be enough for me to decide that the time has come to call off Little Bear. The decision was to rest at all times with the President and myself. This whole thing may well be construed as endangering my office and my responsibility to the Presidency. I cannot decide this alone. I must signal the President for full assurance. I must have his approval.'

Peace motioned towards the radio set. 'We haven't a transmitter, only that.'

MKG nodded. 'I want your word that as soon as we pick up *Bellatrix*, you will send a signal.'

Peace's jaw tightened. 'And give our position away again?'

'You may choose your own time,' said MKG, 'but it must be soon after we reach *Bellatrix*.'

'And meanwhile?'

The Vice-President gave a wry smile. 'I'll be a very

interested spectator of the Commander dodging a hunter-killer force in a small boat—if he can.' He glanced into the lightening sky as the cutter hurried through the long seas. 'Tyler has sure goosed them into action and this—his eyes were sombre now—'has become an aseptic area as far as the United States Navy is concerned.'

His reserve brought a restrained air to breakfast. André fried some fish on a paraffin stove under the forward decking. He also produced a gunny-sack of salted sea-birds—he gave them a Creole name, but Adèle told us they were glossy ibis. Adèle herself sat with a headphone over one ear, listening in case either Thornton or Tyler should break silence. We munched the salted ibis and drank hot, steaming coffee.

Peace threw the dregs of his cup overside. 'I *must* know what the hunter-killer force is up to.'

'Not a chirp,' replied Adèle.

'What will they throw at us?' I asked.

'The standard HUK force in the U.S. Navy consists of carriers, destroyers and a couple of nuclear subs,' explained MKG, as if glad to talk. 'The carriers operate dunking helos and search aircraft. Blimps, too—but in this sort of weather they're not a proposition. Subs are really best for tracking subs, but only in co-operation with cowboys and helos.'

Adèle looked up from her radio dials. 'It's like the sound-track of a Western!'

MKG laughed for the first time that morning. 'That's what they call them—destroyers are cowboys, subs are goblins, a dunking helo is a helicopter which hovers and lowers a sonar ball into the water.' He stretched himself. 'With a day and a boat like this, it's a shame that the world's trying to get on my back.' His easy charm relieved the earlier tension and brought almost a holiday excursion air to the boat.

Peace's thoughts, however, were obviously on the massive build-up over the horizon. 'They'll use a grid pattern search.'

'They must have a datum point for a grid search,' replied MKG.

'Seahorse Sound,' I said.

Despite his reservations, I think MKG was infected with the thrill of the chase. 'Only after the HUK force has located *Devastation*.'

'That won't take the Seventh Fleet long.'

Peace said, half to himself, 'Eight days from now—almost to the hour—the Little Bear launch is scheduled.'

MKG touched Peace on the shoulder. 'I wish this thing hadn't gotten snarled up, Commander. All I need is the President to say it's okay.'

143

Peace said, 'I wish the eight days were past.' He glanced at the horizon, as if he half expected to see his victim: '*Semittanté*! I must have *Semittanté*!'

MKG smiled. 'The Navy has a word for a ship like her, an enemy surface ship—we call it a skunk.'

'Our skunk will be in everybody's mind after Tyler's call,' I said.

'Thornton doesn't know her significance in relation to the Vice-President—yet,' replied Peace. 'Tyler isn't going to foul his own doorstep by sending off what would appear to be a fantastic message. My bet is that he'll wait to meet Thornton to tell him.'

'I rather agree with you, Commander, and that gives me hope still for the mission. Tyler's a regular guy, a tough guy, but he knows the form.' Some of his earlier mood returned. 'Guessing's fine, Commander, but wait until the squeal comes in when Thornton and Tyler meet. Tyler won't play this so cosy once he knows Thornton believes him.'

Peace glanced again at the sky. 'Nor will the Seventh Fleet.'

A dollop of sea made Peace grab at a stay to keep his feet. He nodded overside. 'But we're getting a big ally—soon.'

'The sea?'

'Chagos has issued a gale warning, possible cyclone,' replied Peace. 'We can find *Bellatrix* under cover of it without the Seventh Fleet being able to spot us.'

'Chagos is eight hundred miles away,' I said.

Peace turned to MKG. 'John knows the cyclone pattern as well as I do. This one could be perfect cover for us. Cyclones originate round Chagos and then shoot across the ocean in a south-westerly direction until they hit the St Brandon area. They either blow themselves out there or race for Madagascar and the Mozambique Channel.'

'Assuming that it does just that,' asked MKG. 'How long will a cyclone take to reach us?'

'Three-four days,' answered Peace. 'I'd say that already the Seventh Fleet Navy aviators are casting anxious glances eastwards.'

The morning remained brilliantly clear, but on the eastern horizon there was a curious opaqueness.

Peace said to Adèle, who sat hugging her knees on the thwart next to me. 'Ask André what he thinks of it.'

André had been fussing with the lateen-like sail. trimming it to the wind, which had now changed its steady thrust to intermittent, heavier gusts.

144

'He says, the great cyclone of 1947, when St. Brandon was completely submerged, began on a clear day like this.'

'What was the wind-velocity?'

Adèle smiled. 'He wouldn't know what *you* meant, put like that.' She spoke rapidly, circumlocuting. 'The radio station on Agalega reported one-twenty knots.'

MKG gave a low whistle.

André went on, indicating MKG, 'He says it is better to be out in a small boat like this in a cyclone than a big ship,' translated Adèle. 'The waves can break a long ship's back, but this one—never.'

André took the radio and Adèle said, 'André says there are radio warning stations on St Brandon and Agalega. Agalega is operated by Chepé, who is a master shipbuilder and a sailor. He uses his brains to see whether there is really a cyclone coming. He does not merely pass on what some—some—' she paused—'sonofabitch in Chagos thinks.'

The old fisherman shook the radio. 'Chepé! Chepé!'

Adèle's eyes were on mine. 'He's calling Chepé. He thinks because Chepé can hear Chagos, there is no reason why he cannot hear André, who is much closer anyway.'

The old man fiddled angrily with the dials, but with Adèle's help we were rewarded by a sing-song voice. André pointed in triumph and grinned. 'Chepé!'

Adèle was puzzled. 'Even I do not know what Chepé is saying: he repeats, the frigate birds are coming in from Love-Apple Crossing and the Agalega lagoon is full of noddies.'

André looked grave. Adèle spoke for him. 'Big cyclone. Chepé is telling the fishermen in the sort of terms they understand.'

A stylized voice came through after a flood of Creole. It was still Chepé, but he was repeating by rota. 'Agalega—Agalega met. calling. General gale warning from the northeast. Chagos met. station reports Force Five wind and sea building up.' There was another volley of Creole. André shook his head at the eastern horizon.

Adèle translated. 'This morning I saw a giant ray a mile south of Taillevent Head.' André pursed his mouth. 'It is bad—very bad. A ray going south-west from Taillevent means he is running from the coming cyclone.'

'This could wreck the launch schedule, apart from any other considerations,' said MKG.

'No,' replied Peace. 'A cyclone generally lasts no more than four-five days. We still have eight. Thornton's men will never find us in a full-scale blow.'

MKG smiled wryly. 'I grant it's good cover, but what about the rest—open sea, tiny boat?'

'I'll pick up *Bellatrix* either tonight or tomorrow before the full force of it hits us,' asserted Peace. 'And once I have *Bellatrix, Semittanté* is ours.'

'In short, you choose a cyclone rather than the Seventh Fleet?' There was an undertone of admiration in MKG's voice.

'Any day,' replied Peace. 'The sea is on my side.'

'It always has been,' I added.

He looked at me for a long moment. 'Yes—but, like now, I am never sure.'

Adèle said, 'Before we find *Semittanté*, won't the Seventh Fleet fliers come looking for this cutter?'

'So what?' asked Peace. 'Spread over the Sea of Limuria are hundreds of island cutters, pirogues and fishing craft. Even if a Navy plane comes—you can't distinguish us from the others.'

'Yes, you can,' replied Adèle. 'In this, I look like no other Limuria woman. I . . . I . . .' She smiled delightedly and spoke to André who, wonderingly, handed over his knife. Adèle seized the material of her pants and hacked round the leg, reducing them to shorts.

'And fishermen wear hats.' She spoke again to André, who pointed to the forward decking. Adèle came back with four enormous latanier-leaf hats, which she crammed down amid laughter on our heads.

'No fisherman wears a jersey like yours,' she told Peace. 'It must come off. Yours too, John. And—' she went on shyly—'yours also, Mister Vice-President.'

'MKG,' he corrected. 'My by-line on this edition is MKG.'

When we had pulled off our sweaters and concealed our faces under the ragged-edged hats, André grinned. 'Chepé would laugh at this,' Adèle translated. 'He is my cousin and a man to laugh. Maybe you will drive the cyclone away, looking like that.'

MKG checked his watch and asked Adèle to switch on the radio. Limuria is nine hours ahead of Washington. Although static masked the Voice of America and other American stations, there was no mention of the Seventh Fleet's mission.

Peace impatiently asked Adèle to tune it to the Navy waveband. The seas seemed to have assumed a sinister glaze and I didn't care for the look of the eastern horizon any more than André did.

Here it came—a pattern of quick-fire Morse. Adèle jotted

down the close letter-groupings and deciphered them with the aid of the Navy code-book.

*CIC to Willowtrack x am sending for you for personal report when in range x return with helo to Rio Grande x*

*Willowtrack to CIC x helo pick-up of myself impossible x weather deteriorating rapidly x*

I could visualize the big seas smashing against St Brandon's reef. Here, scores of miles away, apart from their strange sheen, they had taken on a long surge. The gay blue of Limuria had turned to grey, presaging trouble.

Thornton's reply showed the sandpaper temperament for which he was famous:

*CIC to Willowtrack x stand by x helo will pick you up as ordered x*

We drove north.

By afternoon the lateen sail was snugged down to two reefs. It was blowing hard from the north-east and the seas had a nasty lop to them. Adèle kept radio watch on the Navy wavelength; only once Peace reluctantly agreed to listen to a newscast, but there was nothing.

With the lowering seas came cloud from the east. We thankfully pulled on our jerseys. There was little point in camouflaging ourselves as fishermen in the deteriorating visibility. Peace began to grow anxious lest we should miss *Bellatrix*. The sun was hidden by overcast and, according to my dead reckoning, we were on a collision course with the yacht. It would, however, be possible not to spot her at a couple of miles in the threatening seas.

After hours of silence, a clatter of Morse came through. Adèle, sheltering a scrap of paper from the spray, noted down the groups. It was Tyler:

*Willowtrack to CIC x helo lost on pick-up attempt x rescued survivors x*

*CIC to Willowtrack x have dispatched second helo x stand by for pick-up 1600 GMT x*

*Willowtrack to CIC x submit weather conditions impossible x*

*CIC to Willowtrack x repeat stand by helo pick-up 1600 GMT x*

I pictured Tyler's predicament in trying to save the second helo from the fate of the first. At four o'clock GMT—eight p.m. by Limuria time— St Brandon's reef would be a wild hell of dark water. It showed the significance Thornton attached to the news of the disappearance of the Vice-President. Tyler's seamanship must have been magnificent to have

147

rescued the first helicopter's crew. MKG's face was grim.
Another two men were risking their lives for him.

The cutter drove on.

Adèle took the radio and wrapped herself in an old blanket
under the for'ard decking out of the spray. The cutter was
making a good nine knots—better than Peace had counted
on. Somewhere ahead in the waste of waters was *Bellatrix,*
merged with the grey gloom. Peace took the sail from André
and sent him into the bows to try and spot the yacht. MKG
and I took turns at the tiller, but I decided to join André.
Water burst along the planking, blinding me. In contrast to
the grey east, the horizon in the west was still unnaturally
bright.

Then I saw it.

The sea seemed to be fashioned from a solid, not fluid,
medium. The wall of it rose up square, about half a mile to
windward. Unlike an ordinary wave, its top was not spume-
white and boiling: this was calm, squared-off, confident of
its mighty power. Icy fear gripped me, I recognized it, although I had never seen one. I tried to find the three words,
but fear strangled my voice.

' *Raz de Marées* !'

Only André, a foot away, heard my terror-deadened cry.
All I knew was that I was pointing frantically at the awesome thing rushing down on the cutter.

' *Raz de Marées* !' yelled André.

Peace turned in disbelief. But MKG saw and the tiller
went hard over so that the bow—our only slight chance—
pointed at the advancing wall of sea. Peace cleated home the
sheet and whipped a bight of it round the mast and his chest.
I stood staring stupidly at the living grey death bearing down
until André's hard hand jerked me under the bow decking.
Adèle emerged and stared, wide-eyed.

' *Raz de Marées* ! I croaked. ' Brace your feet—hang on—
for God's sake, anything—it's almost here !'

It seemed as if our backs rose vertically. The cutter's bow
went up and up. I heard the low moan of the giant wave
before I felt the hammer-blow of the water against the hull.
If the boat's head fell off now——! But MKG had her, holding the tiller amidships with both hands.

Up! Up!

She yawed, faltered. MKG's hands worked the rough tiller.
She came back—reluctantly, with awful lethargy. She was
making out!

Then Peace shouted, pointing.

Away to port were the lights of a ship.

*Bellatrix*!

The DNI had chosen his man well. Trevor-Davis had put on all the yacht's lights, including the masthead ones, before it was fully dark, in anticipation of being intercepted—as Peace had told him—before *Bellatrix* reached St Brandon.

We watched, awestruck. The graceful yacht canted steeply under the huge wave, shuddered, rose, broke free.

Peace lit the cutter's acetylene light and fired a flare. My admiration for the quiet Trevor-Davis increased still more as *Bellatrix* swung round towards us—alone in the wheelhouse, he was keeping an eagle's-eye watch all round the compass.

Within half an hour we were drinking Glenfiddich in *Bellatrix*'s sycamore-panelled lounge, the cutter towing safely behind the yacht. Mac had come through on Peace's invitation and met MKG. He seemed much better pleased to see Peace than the American leader. I was reminded again of his gutter-gang loyalties, his unquestioning devotion to the submarine ace.

Peace took over from the exhausted Trevor-Davis—except for a few cat-naps while steering on the Sperry auto, he had been almost continuously in the wheelhouse, he told us. The only sign of the long shifts on Mac was his moroseness as he downed a half-tumbler of straight Scotch.

*Bellatrix* drove north into the wild night—for *Semittanté,* for Love-Apple Crossing.

# 11 THE CUTTING-OUT OF LITTLE BEAR

A hard hand was on my shoulder. I was awake and sitting up, my reflexes ahead of my senses. For a moment I saw only a man in paint-streaked overalls. It was Mac.

'Skipper's orders,' he said briefly, in his harsh Glasgow accent. 'It's after midnight. He wants you in the wheelhouse.'

I rubbed the sleep out of my eyes. The tough Scots engineer seemed as tireless as Peace—or was it his devotion to him that would not allow him to let up while the submarine ace still remained on his feet? The only outward sign was his moroseness and hangover-like shadows under his eyes.

'What the hell are you doing painting at this time of night?' I asked.

'Air-sea search—hunter-killer group—I've heard it a' till I'm sick. So the skipper decided to camouflage *Bellatrix*—'

he spat uninhibitedly on the carpet. 'Paint the bluidy ship in a flippin' cyclone! Aye, so I painted her.'

My watch said a couple of minutes after midnight. A new day had been born.

February 9th—seven days to go.

'They'd spot the old white for miles,' Mac went on. 'So now she's grey—mixed with sea-water.' He gave a grunt and went.

Adèle, MKG, Trevor-Davis and I had all gone to bed immediately after a lash-up dinner, but Peace, tireless, took command. MKG had insisted on drawing up a message to be signalled to the President via the DNI. Peace had objected to its length—it was only a few sentences—and I felt the undercurrents as MKG was obliged to cut it down. MKG had wanted Adèle to send it off right away, but again Peace had intervened. He had reminded MKG that although he had agreed to send a message, the time was his to choose. Silently MKG had agreed, but it was clear that Peace was hanging on to the mission, whatever it might cost.

I had taken a liking to Trevor-Davis, and Peace, putting him in the picture about MKG, had congratulated him on his insight, for without *Bellatrix* our plan would have been hamstrung. How exhausted Trevor-Davis had been was apparent over drinks—once or twice his head had fallen forward on his chest and it was only his will-power which had jerked him awake again. MKG, reserved because of Peace's attitude, went off to the luxurious guest suite in the stern which Peace had allocated him. I was next door and Adèle in the adjoining big cabin.

I pulled on fresh clothes from among those I had left behind when—it seemed years ago—*Devastation* had intercepted the yacht. The deck vibrated under my feet as the waves jounced her. Peace was pushing her very hard. I was thrown against the lintel as I opened my door. Holding a grab-rail, I started along the passageway. Adèle's door was swinging with the yacht's motion. I reached for it, jamming myself in the opening in order to secure it.

Her cabin, like mine, was panelled in sycamore, but the colour scheme was pale green and gold. A bed was near the door. Over its foot the blankets had been thrust back so that only the sheet remained. A pair of red silk pyjamas lay carelessly on the pile. Adèle slept on the white pillow, the sun-bleach of her hair making an undefined shadow in the darkened room. Her eyes were closed. She was completely naked. The lift of the ship moved her breasts gently. Her knees were drawn up and her hands, palm to palm, were clasped between them. I shut the door and went to her, darkness blurring the sleeping form. I bent over her. The warmth of sleep and fragrance of her perfume brought the blood drumming in my ears. I kissed one eyelid, and then the other. She stirred a little and said something in Creole. For a long moment I stood looking at the lovely, naked body. Then I secured the door behind me and ran quickly for'ard to the wheelhouse.

Peace was steering. The yacht's motion seemed wilder and all three revolving viewers were on to try and keep the screen clear. The wheelhouse was dark, except for the concealed compass light. The gyro compass, radar and radio were off. Peace wore his favourite black turtle-necked sweater and black Dacron pants; stubble emphasized the hard line of his lips.

He said, without preliminary, 'They've got *Devastation*.' He jerked his head at some signals clipped together. 'That's U.S. Navy stuff. Take the wheel, will you—mind, she's a bit dicey.'

I took the spokes, kicking and bucking under the cross-sea from the north-east.

'Steer three-four-five degrees magnetic,' said Peace.

'What about the gyro?'

'I've got all unnecessary electrics off. I daren't risk any transmissions being picked up. Same goes for radar.'

'So you haven't sent MKG's message, then?'

'I decide when,' he snapped. 'The opportune moment hasn't arrived yet. I don't intend to give away *Bellatrix*'s position as I did *Devastation*'s. You can bet that every direction-finding aerial in the Seventh Fleet is working overtime.'

'You're riding him pretty hard,' I went on. 'MKG can call off his mission any time, remember.'

His eyes blazed in the dark wheelhouse. 'It's my mission as much as his! Remember that, too!'

I shrugged and checked the log. 'Thirteen knots—not bad in this sea, if she'll hold together.'

'I'll drive the bitch right under,' he retorted.

'How did Tyler locate *Devastation*—radar, sonar?'

'Neither. Peters simply broadcast here I am—loud and clear, right into Tyler's ear, who was waiting outside the reef. He made the excuse that *Devastation*'s radio had been damaged during my—er—little escapade in breaking through the coral.'

'Peters might have given us more time.'

'No,' he replied. 'Bob played it right—kept his yardarm clear. He gave us the maximum opportunity to get away. He knew that once the helos and search aircraft were overhead, he didn't stand a chance. By breaking silence this way, he stopped anyone putting the screw on him.'

'What did Peters tell Tyler about MKG?'

'Bob's playing dumb, being very formal and proper. Yes, he said, there was aboard *Devastation* a man who corresponded to the description of Marvin K. Green, but since he'd never seen the Vice-President, he could not say.'

'Did Peters radio all this?'

'He had to, in order to communicate with Tyler—they haven't been in physical touch. Think of what St Brandon reef is like with this sea and wind! Peters, by having announced himself, also puts the DNI in the clear and the British part in the mission—Peters maintains that he acted under orders to pick up an American VIP, name unknown, for secret, missile tests in the Seychelles. He knows nothing else, he states. Then, at the first opportunity when his radio has been fixed, he reveals his position and comes clean. No, Bob's been very clever.'

'How did he account for our disappearance?'

Peace laughed. 'This is how Bob put it: the American VIP, purporting to be an expert on inertial navigation, came aboard *Devastation* in " unusual circumstances ". This man, together with a naval officer who went by the name Peace, disappeared with another man called Garland and a woman named Adèle, whose surname he does not know. That, asserts Bob flatly, is all he knows about the whole thing. He's playing awful dumb. He's even offered *Devastation* to assist the Seventh Fleet!'

'Is Tyler still aboard *Willowtrack*?'

'Yes. It's impossible to get him off in this weather for all Thornton's wishes—the second helo Thornton sent also crashed, but Tyler picked up the crew. One of them is badly smashed up. After that, even Thornton decided to play it more gently. But he'll be up with *Willowtrack* by morning.'

'That's a respite.'

'It's not. Thornton wouldn't waste a whole night.'

'What do you mean?'

'He's taken *Devastation* as his datum point. Fanning out from her, he's launched a carrier task-force grid search.'

'My God! But how do you know all this—the signals are in code——?'

He smiled grimly. 'I dragged Adèle out of bed. She's been decoding for hours. I sent her back when she couldn't keep her eyes open any more.' He slapped the clip signals. 'It's all there: Thornton has split the Seventh Fleet into three hunter-killer groups, each with one carrier, three nuclear subs and six destroyers. And you ask me why I haven't sent off MKG's signal! Thank God for that U.S. Navy codebook, and thank God for Adèle. At least I can keep track of the opposition's moves.'

'Geoffrey,' I said slowly, 'do you really think it's worthwhile trying to play this kind of hide-and-seek? This massive force will catch up with us as soon as it's light enough to see.'

He came across and stood by me. 'While I have one card left, I go on playing the game—to the finish. You should know that, John. It's because the odds started to mount up early that I called in your help in the first place.'

At that moment, I remembered the still face in the coffin and the host of thoughts it had aroused in me. Not least among them had been Peace's unswerving loyalty—to the DNI, to the sea. He was invoking that now; he had always been at his best when the odds were stacked against him.

He was terse, edgy. 'I wonder if Mac can get more out of these engines . . .'

He knew the answer as well as I did. 'It's not the engines, it's the hull.'

'There's a general cyclone warning. The centre is moving rapidly from Chagos towards us.'

'We have a week still to the launch.'

'I'd rather it was less. Give the cyclone three-four days to blow itself out. No cover after that.'

'Don't forget, Geoffrey, the two big unknowns in Tyler's search are, first, where is the launch from? Second, where is *Semittanté*?'

'The signals indicate that Thornton has called his three HUK forces Red Force, Blue Force and Green Force,' Peace went on. 'They fan out from Seahorse Sound. Green will cover the southern quadrant Mauritius-Rodriguez-Réunion and along a line to the eastern coast of Madagascar. Green's no worry—he's way outside our area. Blue has been assigned everything between St Brandon and Chagos, east of the 60th parallel. That mean Saya de Malha and a lot of *Devastation*'s first route to St Brandon. There's an outside chance that one of Blue's search aircraft might pick us up. But Blue Force is steaming and flying right into the heart of the cyclone . . .'

I gestured beyond the spinning screens. 'No one can fly in this.'

'Thornton's men do,' he rejoined. 'Christ! Imagine a carrier take-off on a night like this! They're in the air tonight, all right. Two aircraft have been lost already, but they rescued the crews. Thornton's flying them off, regardless.'

153

'God pity them!' I exclaimed involuntarily. 'The best place would be a sub.'

'A sub's sonar would be ineffective in these seas—they'd damp out the sound of a ship's engines. Besides, a sub is not the most useful HUK weapon, alone. But teamed with helos or aircraft, it's deadly.'

*Bellatrix* yawed heavily and I found myself sweating at the effort to bring her back on course.

Peace went on, 'I hadn't the heart to cut old André's cutter loose. It's his everything. Besides—' he turned away so that I would not see his feelings—' I like that bloody old boat.'

'The third HUK force?' I prompted.

'Red,' he replied slowly. 'Red force is our danger. They've been assigned the biggest bloc, but it includes us—St Brandon westwards to Madagascar and north to the Seychelles.'

'Love-Apple Crossing!' I exclaimed. '*Semittanté*!'

He nodded. 'Thornton has put Tyler in command of Red Force, operating from *Willowtrack*.'

'Tyler thinks like you do, Geoffrey.'

'He damn' near cornered me in Seahorse Sound.'

'If Tyler's Red Force picks us up, the game is over. In some ways *Bellatrix* is a liability.'

He looked at me sharply and then said slowly, 'A liability, yes, she's made of steel, which makes her easy to pick up by radar.'

'So is *Semittanté*.'

He remained thoughtful.

'When do you expect to sight *Semittanté*?' I asked.

'Mid-afternoon today. I'll have to risk using our radar a little then. It's almost certain she won't hold her course in this weather.' He broke off suddenly. 'I'm going aft to make sure the tow to the cutter is secure. Maybe I'll double-lash it, even.'

When he returned, he seemed pleased about something. Then he glanced at his watch. 'Adèle's slept long enough. Something important may be going on.' He jerked his head at the radio. 'I think it's your privilege to call her, John.'

'Let her sleep,' I answered. 'She's dead-beat.'

'No,' he rejoined. 'The DNI sent her to do a job and this is the time for her to do it. At this stage of things, she's worth any two of us put together.'

I went. I paused at her door, wondering whether I should knock until she awoke. Then—I pushed it open and went in.

She lay almost exactly as I had left her. I stood in the darkness, looking down on the slim person who had come, in such a short time, to mean so much in my life. The quiet

154

serenity above the high cheek-bones was as calm as the rest of her was disturbing. 'Worth any two of us put together'— Peace's words held a new context for me: she was worth any two other women I had ever known. In that certainty, I pulled the blanket up to her shoulders and clicked on the bedside light.

She must have been sleeping on a hair trigger, for she woke instantly, alarm in her eyes. 'John!' She glanced at her pyjamas and laughed. 'How long have you been here?'

I sat down on the bed next to her and put off the light. For a short moment, it seemed—then the telephone bell shrilled. It was Peace. 'Adèle—come quickly! Thornton's on the air!'

She threw on some clothes and together we raced up to the wheelhouse. Peace had the radio on. Adèle pushed the hair out of her eyes and under a shaded light decoded the complicated groups.

*CIC Seventh Fleet to all ships and aircraft x return to base x stand by for further orders daylight x*

'Thornton's called off the search for tonight,' Peace exclaimed with satisfaction.

It was a bonus of six hours. I made a quick calculation. 'Long enough for us to cover almost a third of the way to *Semittanté*.'

Peace remained without speaking, so that both Adèle and I looked at him in surprise.

'MKG's message,' he said slowly. 'Now would be the time —the air will be full of routine signals and the boys will be relaxing with the prospect of some sleep.' He pulled it from his pocket and read aloud:

'*Request your personal and categorical affirmation that it is in order for me to continue with Little Bear mission in light of developments—MKG.*'

'Group it up in Royal Navy code,' he told Adèle. 'And then send it to the DNI—quick as hell. Try and send it at a moment when Thornton's fliers are making their landing approaches—the carriers will be using their DF equipment on them then.'

Adèle took the paper and hesitated. 'There's no mention here of a return signal, or a fixed time for it.'

Peace's reaction astonished me. 'Send it!' he snarled. 'You're here to take orders—from me!'

Adèle recoiled at his vehemence, glanced at me, and then sat down without speaking at the angled light. She coded the message and then listened on the U.S. Navy waveband. If Williams had been there, he would have admired Adèle's transmitting even more than he had done before. The Morse chattered off her deft fingers like machine-gun fire.

She stopped, looked up at Peace, who seemed to watch her every movement, and then wrote down an incoming signal. ' The Seventh Fleet has picked up a series of radar contacts round Raphael.'

' The fishing fleet,' answered Peace.

' One very firm one among them,' she added in an impersonal voice. ' Metal, a couple of hundred tons, off Siren Island. Tyler thinks it may be important.'

' Island steamer,' replied Peace.

The thought struck me. ' Does Tyler know about *Bellatrix*?'

' No,' replied Peace. ' How could he? But when he and Thornton meet and the name John Garland is mentioned as having sailed the yacht of the late Commander Peace from the Seychelles, they'll put two and two together—and *Bellatrix* will be their target.'

' How far has the search ranged so far?' I asked.

' Red Force—and we're principally concerned with Red—doesn't seem to have got beyond a limited number of sorties over St Brandon itself,' answered Peace. ' In this weather it must be hell trying to identify anything.'

' Impossible visually, I should say.'

Adèle did not join in the conversation, but she yawned and tried to keep her heavy eyes from closing.

With an odd warmth after his earlier attitude, Peace said to her, ' You go and get some more sleep, Adèle. It looks as though things will be pretty quiet now until morning, seeing the search is off.'

She smiled her thanks as she went ; to me her eyes said everything.

Peace switched off her angle-light, leaving the wheelhouse blacked out once more. He came and stood by me at the wheel, his face shadowed by the compass-light. I was about to take him to task about Adèle when he said : ' Tyler's force will have to waste time during daylight by first following up the radar contacts they made tonight—maybe half a day. By that time we'll almost be up with *Semittanté*. And almost out of range of carrier-based aircraft, assuming that the carrier itself stays in the vicinity of St Brandon.'

The thought hit me with the force of one of the seas against *Bellatrix*'s hull. ' Geoffrey—*Semittanté*! What if the signal has to report her position?'

He was uneasy, almost as uneasy as he had been over MKG's signal. ' Adèle picked up a signal about just that while you were asleep—it's amongst that lot there. Safer not to put

156

the light on. I'll tell you: Thornton and the Chief of Naval Operations have had an exchange over the point. Thornton says that to signal her will scare her away. He believes that she is part of the kidnapping plot, that her skipper is one of the gang who kidnapped MKG. Thornton doesn't know yet that she's important beyond carrying an American classified weapon. Of course he doesn't know about the space-shot yet. So for the moment Thornton's view has prevailed and they're not signalling *Semittanté*. For the moment, that is.'

'I wonder how long that moment will last?'

'Aye,' he reflected. 'Maybe only until Thornton talks personally to Tyler.'

But behind it all lay the one unanswerable question—why had the President not informed the Seventh Fleet? *He* knew *Semittanté*'s part in the Little Bear mission.

'Hasn't *Semittanté* sent out any routine signals?' I asked.

'No—why should she? An old tramp like that is lazy—probably listens to the weather reports every so often, that's all. From our area I've had cyclone warnings from the met. stations all round—St Brandon, Tromelin, Agalega—old Chepé again—and Madagascar.'

'I thought Adèle was the radio operator,' I said.

'These were *en clair*, anyway,' he replied. 'But I can manage the odd bit of Morse myself, you know. Not the high-powered American stuff, of course, but Royal Navy, yes.'

I gestured beyond the screen. 'It's getting worse.'

'It *is* getting worse,' he answered with satisfaction. 'The worse the better, so far as we are concerned. They've pulled the South-Africa-Australia jets into Mauritius on the strength of a POMAR report.'

Peace went on, 'If it were only a question of dodging short-range carrier-based aircraft, I'd rate our chances pretty high, since they'll be out of the picture once the cyclone reaches full strength. But you haven't heard this—the signal came through while you were asleep—the Americans are flying out a squadron of big VP-5's from Greenland to the Seychelles to assist in the search for MKG. They're the planes for the long-range Atlantic patrols. At a guess, I'd say a VP-5 can stay in the air the best part of twenty hours and cover thousands of miles. And instruments—they have everything that opens and shuts.'

I concentrated on holding *Bellatrix* on course so that Peace should not sense the tumult of my thoughts. What he had just said confirmed my fears—the President himself believed that MKG had been kidnapped! Why, I questioned, had he allowed the massive air-sea search to proceed if he were

157

satisfied in his own mind that MKG was safe? Why fly out the deadliest patrol bombers half-way across the world to look for someone he knew was proceeding according to a secret plan? Or had—I had almost rejected the thought as unworthy when I remembered Peace's bulldozing attitude towards the mission: that at all costs he would put SNAP into space and prove Little Bear.

*Had Peace faked the messages to the President?*

My mind went over each point in turn. No, they could not have been faked, I argued, because Adèle herself had decoded the President's okay, the single-letter word 'Washington'. But—Williams had brought it through to the cabin. Could Williams be part of an elaborate hoax? I rejected the thought. I myself had seen Adèle send off the Vice-President's own signal; we were now awaiting a reply which could come through at any time. Strange—Peace had sent Adèle off to bed . . .

I deliberately broke the silence to still my doubts. 'Not even VP-5s could operate in a cyclone.'

The radio crackled and Peace cocked an ear. 'Our call sign!' he exclaimed.

'I'll fetch Adèle,' I said.

He listened. 'No, it's Royal Navy stuff. I'll manage.'

He sat down at the table behind me and switched on the small light. In a minute or two the Morse stopped. I glanced back at Peace over my shoulder. He was sitting, staring silently at the code groups in front of him. For the next ten minutes my whole attention was occupied with keeping *Bellatrix* on course. It seemed as if we were running into the outer fringes of the cyclone, judging by the violence of some of the gusts and the mounting sea. In a calmer patch I turned to speak to Peace, but the words died. He sat staring still at the signal, which he seemed to have decoded, his expression so withdrawn and hard that I knew what his anger would be at disturbing him. Another ten minutes went by. I risked another look. Now he was writing something on a signal pad, laboriously consulting his code-books.

Half an hour must have passed before he spoke. 'This should satisfy MKG.' He waved the signal.

'What does it say?'

'*Washington x you have my personal authorization to continue with Little Bear mission as planned x*'

His voice was without inflexion. I glanced keenly at him. 'You don't seem very thrilled about it.'

He shrugged. 'I don't like being strung on to the end of a radio line for every little action I wish to take.'

'This is not a little action,' I pointed out. 'MKG's whole future depends on it.'

He grunted, staring at the racing seas.

'Shall I take it through and wake MKG?'

'What the hell for? It'll keep till morning. It doesn't alter anything, anything at all.' He went to the table and gathered up the signals.

'Better let Adèle check them over,' I said.

For a moment before he clicked out the light his eyes were full upon me. They were not pale like the DNI's, but the cold deadliness was the same.

'I told you, I am quite capable of handling Royal Navy signals,' he said levelly. He brushed past me and stood staring out into the wild night.

'It's *Semittanté* I'm worried about,' he muttered—and by breakfast it was all *Semittanté* as the vast drama of the Vice-President cracked open after Thornton had interviewed Tyler.

MKG, shaved and dressed in some of my clothes, looked grave as he stood with Peace, Trevor-Davis, Adèle and myself in the wheelhouse. Trevor-Davis, rested, pursed his lips at the sea, which had worked up during the night into long swells on the heels of the fresh north-easterly gale. The driving overcast ceiling seemed no more than a couple of hundred feet as *Bellatrix* shouldered her way through the greyness. Adèle brought us coffee in the dim light which passed for daybreak. Her eyes were on me, sharing our secret of the night. André would not be refused the privilege of steering *Bellatrix*. It did not need Adèle to translate that he was in his seventh heaven.

MKG read the President's message with satisfaction when Peace first handed it to him, but when Thornton came on the air within half an hour, he was silent.

Thornton signalled the Chief of Naval Operations:

*Tyler interrogated by me personally x endorse his view Marvin K. Green kidnapped x one of the kidnappers using name Geoffrey Peace bracket presume fake since Peace is dead unbracket French freighter Semittanté carrying deck cargo purporting to be coconut oil processing plant x it is in fact United States classified experimental missile Little Bear x Semittanté cleared Mauritius February 3 present whereabouts unknown x Tyler also asserts that Vice-President intends to be launched to Santa Fe Moon Station One in Little Bear from unspecified point Sea of Limuria on unspecified date but presumed within next few days x repeat Vice-President intends to be launched to Santa Fe Moon Station One in Little Bear*

*missile x Commander British submarine Devastation says
he unaware all this x have deployed Seventh Fleet into
three HUK groups for grid search entire Sea of Limuria x
search impeded general cyclone warning x number radar
contacts St Brandon reef and neighbouring islets under
investigation eyeball check x*

MKG said, 'After that, I feel I need a hooker of rye. If it
had not been for this message of the President's to me, I'd
call it a day so far as Little Bear is concerned. In the light of
it, we must go on, but it sure looks as though we're up the
creek.'

Peace's face was bleak. 'Up the creek, certainly, but with
two paddles—*Semittanté* and *Bellatrix*.' He nodded beyond
the streaming windows. 'I have a cyclone, I have a wide,
wide sea. The sea has always been my friend.'

'Up to now we've gotten along just jim-dandy,' MKG
mused, 'but now I wonder . . .'

Peace said briskly, 'Perhaps the recall signal has already
gone out to the Seventh Fleet from the President.'

MKG shrugged. 'Then where is it?'

Peace said, 'Adèle was dead on her feet last night. There
was no regular radio watch.'

He looked keenly at Peace. 'Then what about the President's signal to me?'

'I took it,' Peace replied. 'It was Royal Navy code. I
recognized *Bellatrix*'s call-sign.'

'Perhaps in view of its importance, Adèle could check . . .'

'I checked it myself,' he retorted. 'There's no need.'

In the middle of this, Adèle handed Peace a decoded
signal:

*CIC Seventh Fleet to C-in-C British Limuria Command
x top secret x where is yacht Bellatrix? x is Peace alive
or dead? x where is Garland?*

Before he had finished reading it out to us, the reply had
come in:

*C-in-C British Limuria Command to CIC Seventh Fleet
x top secret x Bellatrix sailed February 1 ex Mahé Garland in command x believed destination South Africa via
Madagascar x Peace is dead x you were there x*

Peace read it out triumphantly to MKG. 'You see, Little
Bear is still very much on in the DNI's view, and that means
he must also have been in touch with the President,' he said.
'Otherwise he wouldn't have replied in these terms.'

'The DNI's certainly playing it cool,' was MKG's rejoinder.
*Bellatrix* drove on.

By early afternoon there was more encouragement for us.

Thornton, commanding Blue Force, called in his terriers in the face of impossible weather between St Brandon and Chagos. Looking at our driving overcast—we were 600 miles from Blue Force—I marvelled at the intrepidity of the American fliers in staying in the air for as long as they had. Tyler began recalling his dogs, too, as the cyclone marched inexorably towards him. They did not stand a chance of getting within real striking distance of *Bellatrix*. Green Force, far away to the south, reported ship contacts south and south-west of Mauritius, but one after another they were getting clearance.

What worried MKG, however, was that news of the massive American search was starting to become public. Mauritius Radio, usually at the fag-end of world news, did not realize yet that it would soon be the focal point of world attention. The midday bulletin, put across with amateur fervour, said:

'Powerful forces of American carrier-based aircraft swept across the harbour of Port Louis at intervals this morning in a south and south-westerly direction. Vessels entering the harbour report that they have been investigated and interrogated by the aircraft. The United States Consul in Mauritius denies all knowlege of the operation. It is, however, presumed that these squadrons are part of the American Seventh Fleet which is nomally based on the Seychelles, and listeners may well ask themselves, for what purpose is this task force so far from its base . . .'

The radio cut as *Bellatrix* leaned heavily to leeward. She came back quickly and rolled her starboard side under. For a moment the screen wipers churned green sea. Above the growl of the wave-punch came the sound of tearing, splintering. Peace and I reached the wheelhouse door together. The luxury wooden gangplank, lashed to the side, cartwheeled and vanished overboard. The starboard boat, torn from its davits, bumped along the deck until it hit the rail aft, poised for a moment, and then disappeared too. Metal stanchions were left twisted and snapped in its wake.

'And the cyclone hasn't hit us yet,' remarked Peace. He glanced at the clock. 'Two hours still before we can really start looking for *Semittanté*.'

Two hours—it seemed like two years. Peace, Trevor-Davis and I rigged relieving tackles on the streamlined mast and repaired the radio aerial. The lack of operational messages seemed to create a silence in which all listened for *Semittanté* —waiting, waiting. The hull seemed to develop a whip-lash tendency as Peace drove the yacht, often bows under with André fighting the wheel, into the increasing sea. He would not slow down. 'Clyde-built,' was all he said. 'She'll take it—till she dives under.'

The wheelhouse gratings were awash; we hung on to anything we could find. Adèle jammed herself on a tiny stool by the diminutive chart-table to operate the radio.

Shortly after 3 o'clock Adèle held up her hand and turned up the volume on the merchant shipping band. It was the message which we had dreaded. It said, in plain language:

'This is the commander of the United States Seventh Fleet in the St Brandon area. I am calling the French freighter *Semittanté* . . . *Semittanté* . . . *Semittanté* . . . report your position immediately please on this wavelength.'

We crowded round the set, gripping one another's shoulders like a Rugby scrum to keep steady in the heavy pitching.

'Any ship or aircraft knowing the whereabouts of the French freighter *Semittanté* must report immediately.'

'We could pass *Semittanté* at a couple of miles and not see her in this weather,' said Peace, grim-faced. He turned to Adèle. 'Tell André—there's an old ship hereabouts. We must find her—soon.'

She spoke rapidly in Creole and translated his reply. 'She'll be that way . . .' She pointed to leeward.

I said, 'I've been making a rough offset allowance, taking wind force and run of the sea into consideration, but my calculations are purely hit and miss.'

Peace switched on the yacht's radar. The cathode screen glowed. He worked slowly round the compass. 'Nothing.'

'What's the radar's range?' asked MKG.

'Ten, maybe twelve. Could be anything in this sea, the way we're lifting.'

The radio blared: '*Semittanté* . . . calling the French freighter *Semittanté* . . . report your position immediately . . .'

The rain drilled against the wheelhouse. Peace said irritably, 'John, make a sweep round, will you—round and bloody round.'

The green light circled. The screen remained blank. I looked up as the wheelhouse grew momentarily brighter. The rain eased; there was a break in the driving wrack.

André called and pointed excitedly. Adèle, wide-eyed, crouched at the radio, repeated, 'A ship!—a ship!—to port—to leeward!'

Peace was at the old fisherman's side in a flash. I fixed the radar on the quadrant he had indicated. It was empty. The greyness stretched away into a gauze-murk horizon of a mile or less.

André gestured at the controls. 'He says you're going too fast—you're passing her,' supplied Adèle.

Peace yanked back the engine-room telegraph. MKG's eyes went from the radar screen to the old fisherman. 'If I were a horse-player, my money would be on the radar.'

André spoke quickly to Adèle. 'There's a ship out there—he feels it—he caught a glimpse of her in that clear patch.'

'Tell him the radar shows nothing,' said Peace.

She translated and grinned. 'He says that thing has no soul. Fishermen and ships share the sea between them . . . there!'

For a moment something that wasn't the grey heave of the sea showed broad on the beam, a line of deeper grey and breaking water.

'By God!' I exclaimed. 'I saw her!'

André gave the helm a spoke or two. *Bellatrix* high-kicked.

'It was only a whitecap—you can kid yourself so easily,' said Peace. He fiddled with the radar. 'Wait, though, something here—not at all firm . . .'

André and I shouted together. Westwards, in a stray patch of sunlight, was a ship, rolling and pitching in the heavy swell, whiteness under her single screw.

'Put that thing off!' I called to Peace. 'We've got her! No need to endanger our position.'

Adèle's radio said, '*Semittanté* . . . calling French freighter *Semittanté* . . . report your position on this wavelength . . .'

'If she does so now, it's the giveaway for both *Semittanté* and *Bellatrix*,' commented MKG. 'One fix and Thornton will dispatch half a dozen subs. Weather doesn't worry them, five hundred feet down.'

'No response from her yet?' Peace demanded anxiously of Adèle.

'Not yet.'

'John!' he said harshly. 'Go and get me the Remington. Take the .38 Special for Mac. Find yourself an axe.' He turned on Trevor-Davis. 'You conn the yacht—André's a magnificent helsman but you'll have to say it with signs.' He quickly outlined the hand-signs which had brought us through the reef. He turned back to me. 'I'll take the bridge, Mac the engine-room. Yours is target No. 1, John—smash the radio before she can get off a message.' As he spoke, the colour drained from Adèle's face.

'John——' she began.

I stopped her. 'It's got to be done.'

Peace said, 'Boz Blair and his team can be a big help, if we can get it over to them what this is all about.'

163

'I'll call 'em up on the loud-hailer,' MKG suggested. 'Tell them it's me—there's time before we go aboard.'

Peace stopped him. 'You're staying right here, MKG.'

'I'm fit—fitter than any of you,' he protested.

Peace said, 'It isn't funny, jumping in a sea like this at the end of a rope from one ship to another. We can't afford to let you smash a rib or a leg.'

Trevor-Davis offered, 'I'll lay alongside in the lee. The going will be easier for you there.'

Peace nodded.

'What . . . what will you do to the crew?' Adèle asked in an anguished voice.

Peace laughed. 'We're not pirates—yet. Odds are that they'll be so surprised they won't offer any resistance. Particularly if we can get word to Boz Blair.'

'There's Boz and four others,' MKG reminded us.

Adèle said, 'I'll try and jam anything *Semittanté* tries to send.'

Peace looked at her appreciatively. 'Good girl. If you're as successful as you were with *Willowtrack*, we should be okay. John, get the guns will you?'

In Peace's cabin I took the sinister Remington from its case. It sat easily on my hand and the big stock, which looked cumbersome, was in fact beautifully balanced. I shoved a box of shells into my pocket and grabbed the Colt I had taken from the unknown intruder.

Mac's engine-room was cleaner even than a nuclear sub's, which itself looks like an operating theatre. The crash of seas seemed louder below.

Mac eyed my pistols. 'Thinking of murder?'

I explained quickly and a sinister grin spread over Mac's face. He took the Colt and spat into the muzzle.

'Aye,' he said. 'It's like I said when we thought he was lying deid in t'coffin—we'd be a power poorer without our bluidy bastard skipper.'

He grinned again and slipped a monkey-wrench into the back of his overalls. Together we went back to the wheelhouse. We found Peace bending over the compass housing. He had unscrewed the glass with his flick-knife.

'What on earth . . .?'

His face was flushed with excitement at the prospect of the coming action. 'Listen—in this weather, we can't very well turn the French crew adrift in their boats unless we really want to murder them. We'll give them *Bellatrix*.'

I couldn't believe my ears. 'But they'll simply radio Thornton—shadow us in *Semittanté*!'

'Just that,' he grinned. 'Once we've cleaned up the crew, we'll come back aboard here and smash up *Bellatrix*'s radio, radar and the gyros. We'll have to come back anyway for my diving suit, radio, code-book. The French will have to rely on the magnetic compass—this one. We'll set our course into the heart of the storm. Skipper du Plessis, righteously mad, will follow us—while he can see. As soon as it's dark, he'll shadow our daylight course by compass. What he won't know is that there's a knife-blade in here which will throw him ten degrees out. Sooner or later either Red Force or Blue Force will pick him up—he'll run right into their arms.'

Trevor-Davis shook his head sadly. 'To regard a lovely craft like this as expendable . . .'

'You gave me the idea, John,' said Peace. 'You said *Bellatrix* was a liability. Now, with the Frenchman, she's become an asset to us—the perfect decoy.'

André said something and we followed his pointing hand.

'He says *Semittanté* is turning away.'

'Anything on the radio, Adèle?'

'Nothing from her. Plenty of " report your position " from Thornton.'

'Perhaps she's spotted us,' suggested MKG.

'She doesn't know about *Bellatrix*,' rejoined Peace. 'I'd say she was merely easing off the wind.'

The old-fashioned stern of the tramp, which must have been built about the time Red Raborn confounded the critics with the first Polaris, rose and fell in the trough.

'Look!' I exclaimed.

'Little Bear!' MKG gasped.

There it was, lashed on the deck askew from the starboard railing towards the stern on the other side: a long wooden crate about eight feet square and sixty long, looking like a number of automobile shipment crates fixed together.

'I'll call her first on the loud-hailer,' said Peace. 'If she'll let the pirates aboard peaceably, so much the better.'

André under Trevor-Davis's guidance closed in. A heavy sea broke over the tramp's rusty bows and creamed over winches and hatches. An oilskinned figure appeared on the bridge wing.

'*Semittanté* . . . *report your position* . . .'

The voice was obliterated by a clatter of Morse. Adèle whispered, 'United States Seventh Fleet, this is *Semittanté* . . .'

'Jam him, for Christ's sake,' snarled Peace. He grabbed André by the shoulder. 'Alongside! Quick!'

André understood. He read the meaning of the guns in

our hands. He spun the wheel and opened the throttle—
*Bellatrix* was back on the auto gear.

MKG switched on the loud-hailer. He deliberately made his
vowels longer. 'Boz!' he called imperatively. 'Boz—it's
Marvin Green here—MKG! Do you hear! A couple of
Limeys are coming aboard with hand-guns—help 'em, willya
. . .'

All I saw was the rusty, red-leaded side of the plunging
old tramp looming like a skyscraper. André shaved round the
stern and banging screw into the quieter water in her lee.

Trevor-Davis looked enquiringly at us, waiting for the
right moment.

Peace jacked a shell into the Remington, snapped home the
bolt. 'Come on!'

Mac and I raced with him to the twisted starboard decking.
*Semittanté* lurched towards us, the red-painted patches grinning like bloodied lips as the high side sought to crush the
slender yacht. Then the sea spurted and the hulls drew apart,
like an outward-facing V. Peace shouted an oath at Trevor-
Davis and André, but his voice was lost in the cavern of
boiling seas. Down went *Bellatrix* until we looked into the
foul bilge vents of the old tramp, and then sky-rocketed on
the next wave. Peace swung a Jacob's ladder of thin nylon
rope in his hand. A shot crashed out: a man with a gun, in
yellow oilskins, stood at the head of the bridge ladder. The
strike of the bullet was lost in the noise. Even under the
whip of excitement I admired Trevor-Davis's handling of the
yacht: she rose past a scum-shrouded porthole to deck level
and he held her there.

'Jump!' yelled Peace.

We leaped as one man. Peace landed agilely on the ship's
rail and dropped to her deck. But the wet wood slipped from
under my feet and I crashed down. *Bellatrix* fell away like
a lift. I saw the death-engulfing water. I toppled overside
and snatched with the axe-head at the rail. It bit. In a flash
Peace hauled me clear, gasping, on to the deck. I didn't hear
the second report but only saw the splinter of the bullet a
foot from my head. I looked upwards and saw the ugly
muzzle pointing straight at me. The man on the bridge
steadied for the shot. I cringed away. Peace started at a
crouching run for him, but I knew he would never make it.
Then a figure raised an arm over the man's head and struck
him down with a length of piping. He sagged and fell ten
feet to the deck below.

Peace almost ran down my rescuer. 'Thanks—Boz! It is
Boz?'

'Sure, sure,' exclaimed the stocky scientist. 'I heard MKG's voice—was him, wasn't it?'

'Yes,' replied Peace. 'No time now to explain—the bridge. Come on, Boz!'

They tore up the ladder and I paused only for a second to trace the course of the radio aerial from the masthead down to a peeling deckhouse. At the door a heavy sea threw me full-length.

'*Semittanté* calling . . .' chattered the Morse. I prayed for Adèle's jamming skill.

I kicked up the door. The operator, an acned youth in a sweaty towel shirt, gave a terrified glance as it burst open. I cannoned into him as he jumped to his feet. I smashed the axe down, once twice, across the Morse key and the aerial wire. There was a small puff of blue smoke and a smell of burning rubber.

The youth gave a high scream. I lifted the axe. 'Shut up!' The inhuman sound ended in a gurgle. I jerked my head. 'Out! Get out!'

He edged past me, terror in his eyes. I found the key and locked the shack. I gestured for'ard and saw him down the main deck companionway. I swung the axe as a heavy figure sprinted along the deck at me.

'Hold it, buddy!' The Texan voice was unmistakable. 'I'll look after him!'

'Thanks.' I made for the bridge.

The quartermaster lay on the gratings with a weal across his forehead. Peace was trying to quiet the kicking wheel. Boz Blair had exchanged the length of piping for the Remington and was standing at a half-crouch trying to cover two men in a corner.

Peace said, before he saw me, 'Just mash the tit if they move, Buz! Don't let 'em come at us.' Then he saw me and grinned. 'Okay?'

'Okay—he was still transmitting, though.'

'I wonder if he got past Adèle's jamming.'

'These bums look like wanting to jam us all any moment,' said Boz. 'Here, you're better with this than me.' I swapped my axe for his Remington.

Peace said, 'Good work John! Now give your French an airing. That bastard—' he indicated the unconscious man —'came at me with a fire-extinguisher.'

'The engine-room?' Boz asked quickly. We told him. He whistled. 'One man!—I'll round up a couple of my boys and help Mac.' He darted off. Peace picked up the engine-room voicepipe. His eyes clouded when there was no reply.

'Which of you is Captain du Plessis?' I asked.

The flow of invective from the smaller of the two was impressive. Peace and I let him finish before grinning at each other. 'That's him.'

'Tell him we're taking his ship I'll give him and his crew five minutes. They're going aboard *Bellatrix*. I hope Mac's all right . . .'

'Pirate! Murderer! Thief! Abductor!' screamed the little man .

'He knows all the words,' I said.

The skipper came forward shaking his fist. The other officer looked ready to jump me. I raised the Remington. He stopped.

'He says piracy on the high seas is a hanging offence. He will see you hanged, if it takes him all his life.'

'Tell him an exchange of vessels isn't piracy. In fact, he should be pleased. He's getting a luxury yacht in exchange for a clapping-out lump of floating ironmongery.'

I couldn't give full value to the French, but none the less the little skipper turned purple.

Peace went on, 'Tell him to line the crew up on deck. Anyone who stays behind is liable to get hurt.'

The voicepipe gave a whistle. Peace picked it up and there was a rattle of unmistakable Glasgow gutter oaths. He gave me the thumbs-up sign.

'Pirate! . . . Thief! . . .'

The big Texan whom I had met came clattering up the bridge ladder with what looked like a stoker's iron in his hand.

'Aw, put a sock in it!' he told the Frenchman. 'Come on —join the other suckers!' Bewildered men in a disreputable array of dirty garments began to emerge on deck, guarded by three Americans, two of them with guns. The crew looked more resentful about being lined up in the rain than about losing their ship. The Texan shoved the French skipper and the other officer down the ladder. I gave him the Remington. He stopped for a moment at the head of the steps. 'MKG okay? The air's been full——'

'Okay,' replied Peace. 'Little Bear's still on.'

'Fine.' The long vowel made it sound the most wonderful adventure in the world. He stomped down the ladder.

Peace took an electric loud-hailer megaphone. '*Bellatrix*!' MKG's voice came back, metallic, anxious. 'Are you okay —we heard shots?'

'Okay,' replied Peace. 'Ship's ours. I'm heaving her to. I'll stream oil to give you a smooth patch. Trevor-Davis, tell

168

André I want his cutter hoisted aboard Semittanté. We'll cut one of the lifeboats adrift and haul his boat up in the davits in its place.'

The Americans guarding the crew all grinned as I passed. I hacked at a lifeboat's falls with my axe until it fell with a splash. *Bellatrix* held off until, at Peace's orders, Mac had blown hundreds of gallons of oil overboard from the old tramp's tanks and made a tolerably fine smooth patch under the stern. Then, with a display of fine seamanship, André laid her alongside. I dropped on to *Bellatrix's* deck at the end of a rope.

'We've got to move fast—that message of *Semittanté's*,' I told MKG and Adèle.

'I don't know how successful my jamming was,' she replied.

I switched off the current in the wheelhouse and raised my axe. Trevor-Davis's eyes held a mute appeal, but he said nothing as the blade splintered the radar screen; another blow was enough for the radio. For the gyros, I reversed the blade and the sensitive instruments were soon a tangle of metal. I unlocked the automatic pilot and smashed its controls. We gathered up Peace's diving suit, the code-book and portable radio.

Boz Blair came to the rail and looked down into MKG's face. Then the Vice-President swung up the rope to be grabbed by eager, welcoming hands from the American team.

Through Adèle I explained to André about the cutter. He looked up at Peace on *Semittanté's* bridge and said gently, 'He truly understands how a man can love his boat.'

Was it simply that?

I knew the answer after we had hoisted the cutter inboard and Boz's men had hustled the spitting skipper and his motley crew aboard *Bellatrix*, which now lay wallowing half a mile astern of us.

'We'll use the cutter,' Peace told the group of us gathered on the tramp's bridge. 'I am going to scuttle *Semittanté* at Love-Apple Crossing.'

'Scuttle!' burst out MKG. 'Scuttle our only chance—Little Bear!'

There was a murmur from Boz Blair's team and the genial face of the stocky scientist became grave. MKG had given them an outline of the hunt; like *Devastation*'s crew, they took it in a holiday spirit. The tall Texan's name I learned was Pete Allingham, and the other three missile experts—looking curiously disreputable in a variety of sailors' rigs—were John Palmer, Nat Reece and Lofty Reilly. Trevor-Davis, our expert, seemed completely at home in his silent way with his American opposite numbers.

'Every moment now is important,' replied Peace obliquely. He picked up the engine-room voicepipe. 'Mac—give her everything she's got.' His eyes fell on Adèle who stood next to me. 'I had better not repeat what Mac thinks of the engine-room!'

'From the sound of it, he at least will be pleased to see this crate scuttled,' said Boz Blair.

The screw began to thump. Peace brought her head round towards the storm and then handed over the wheel to André. We waited.

'*Bellatrix* was a liability, now she's an asset,' Peace explained, looking round the silent launch team. 'You must see it like this: *Semittanté* is a bigger liability still. We simply have to get rid of her. We're being squeezed between weather, position, and the launch deadline.'

MKG explained, 'But to scuttle Little Bear after all we've been through to get here, and God knows, there have been times in the past couple of days when I have doubted if my decision——'

'Little Bear goes down with *Semittanté*,' Peace cut in.

Boz Blair gave a gasp and stepped forward, but Peace went on quickly before he could protest. 'In a few hours' time it will be six days to the launch, not so?' Boz merely nodded —the suggestion that his missile should be sent to the bottom of the sea had left him speechless.

MKG started to speak, but Peace silenced him with a gesture. 'I'm not sanguine enough to think I can evade Tyler for six days. You know and I know that Tyler and Red Force will track down anything that floats. They may already have a fix on *Semittanté*'s position; Adèle's not sure. Once the VP-5's are in the air ...'

Allingham whistled. 'They got VP-5's out on our tail too?'

Peace nodded. 'With them around, I don't rate our chances very high.'

He explained that they would use the new MAD gear—an abbreviation for Magnetic Anomaly Detection. It was an electronic marvel used by the VP-5's. It picked up variations in the earth's magnetic field and showed up objects like wrecks, or other undersea metal objects. They had, he stressed, to be metal. Boz's team warmed towards Peace. He was talking the sort of technical language they appreciated.

'Even *Semittanté* sunk at Love-Apple Crossing won't be safe from the VP-5's,' he added.

'Then what's in your mind, Commander?' asked Boz. 'This sure is some wind, too.'

'Cyclone,' corrected Peace. 'It's our big hope. It could last between four and five days. But it's good only to stop Tyler's search aircraft—it won't worry the nuclear subs. We'll take a leaf out of their book by sinking *Semittanté*. Tyler in *Willowtrack* could pass by Love-Apple crossing with the heat full on and—inside the coral barrier—he couldn't detect *Semittanté*, sunk. He's looking for a ship afloat—so are the VP-5's.'

'Fine and dandy, if all you're about is escaping Tyler,' remarked the tall Texan dryly. 'But not us. What about Little Bear?'

'We'll lash Little Bear securely to *Semittanté*'s deck. That'll be your job, Boz. The water in Love-Apple Crossing lagoon isn't deep—fifty, maybe even forty feet. Little Bear's operational depth is six hundred feet, so it won't harm her. The day before the launch I'll go down in my skin-diving suit and cut the missile free. It's buoyant, it'll float up. Then it's over to Boz and you fellows to see she's all set for the launch. Then we'll tow her out to the launch-point.'

I heard Boz's indrawn breath of admiration, but MKG's eyes were on Peace. 'You're not snowing me, Commander?' He screwed up his eyes in his characteristic way.

'It's the only way left.'

The Vice-President's face was expressionless. Then he said, 'The DNI said you were quite a guy, Commander. I believe it.'

'Me too,' grinned Boz. 'Why, it's a cinch—we can get out the DATICO gear and space-suit beforehand——'

'What's DATICO?' I asked.

'Digital automatic tape indicated check-out,' enthused Boz. 'It's like a small tape-recorder for the final moments of the

171

countdown. When MKG mashes the firing-button for Little Bear six hundred feet down, DATICO goes into action. One minute later Little Bear emerges—she don't even wet her ass, as we say in the Navy.'

The other scientists started to grin at Boz's enthusiasm. 'All the instrumentation is packed with Little Bear,' he went on. 'Did it myself. Know where every damn' thing is, exactly —from the VLF set to the space-suit . . .'

I was already lost among Boz's technicalities, but he rushed to fill the gaps in my missile ignorance. 'Very Low Frequency radio,' he explained, grinning. 'We—the Navy—found years ago that you can send very low frequency signals—between five and fifteen kilocycles—almost anywhere in the world over an ocean surface. So we built the biggest VLF station in the world at Cutler, Maine . . .'

'Aw, Boz, don't give the guy a lecture,' said the Texan good-naturedly. 'All he wants to know is, will the goddam' thing work?'

Boz cut short his technicalities. 'Sure, sure. I'll operate the VLF transmitter to MKG's marker buoy—Little Bear's marker—and at T minus sixty a red light comes on on his instrument panel——'

'But a crated Little Bear is not exactly a Little Bear ready to blast off,' I ventured.

Boz interrupted. 'The top, which is in fact the capsule, is covered by a plastic membrane which will withstand water pressure up to seven hundred feet, but it ruptures at the thrust of compressed air from the firing-flask—just like the ordinary Polaris. The inertial navigation—SINS—holds the missile continuously vectored on a point in space, in this instance, the Santa Fe staging station . . . which reminds me; I must check the calibration of the space-docking computer . . .'

'Aw, gee, Boz, quit it, willya!' exclaimed the Texan. 'The guy's drunk with words, can't you see! How in hell you're going to live without this damn missile once she's on her way, I dunno.'

MKG said, 'Commander, it's easy to say, tow Little Bear to the launch-point, but what with?'

'The cutter,' replied Peace. 'That's why I wanted her safe. I've had a look at the auxiliary engine. It works, although André won't use it if he can help it.'

'You can't tow a twenty-ton missile out to sea with a cutter's engine,' I objected.

'You can,' said Peace. 'Ask Boz here: Little Bear is the finest hydrodynamic and aerodynamic machine man has yet evolved—eh, Boz?'

'Sure,' replied Boz. 'You have some damn' original ideas about missiles, Commander.'

Peace grinned back at him. 'Little Bear is designed to travel—through water, air and space. She offers the minimum resistance to water. Only a few horsepower is enough to pull that pencil-slim shape through the sea. In fact, I think the cutter could do it with all of you at the oars, but I'll spare you that. Blast-off point is not more than a couple of miles offshore.'

He looked enquiringly round the team. Trevor-Davis said, 'I would have liked a couple of days, not just one, to check her over.'

'We pre-set the inertial navigation back home—she's continuously vectored on Santa Fe,' replied Boz.

'The accelerometers, though—it's been a long voyage——' began Trevor-Davis.

'We set 'em also—the gyros and the accelerometers of the stable table,' said Boz.

'I'm anxious about the correct toss-off point.' Trevor-Davis seemed to find his voice in talking about the abstruse technicalities of the missile.

'New jetavators with a simple thrust-reversal system—blow-out points explode along the leading edge of the second stage and then thrust backwards, but the capsule flies on . . .'

Trevor-Davis let out a sigh of relief. 'That takes a load off my mind. I wasn't too happy about the old ones.'

Peace said, 'It's my turn to break up this fascinating conversation, boys. We've got a lot of work to do. John, go and fix the radio aerial you chopped—I must know if Tyler heard *Semittanté*'s call. And Adèle, ask André before you go if he'd like the job of being permanent helmsman of *Semittanté*.'

She translated and he nodded, pleased. Adèle kept close to me. She was pale and quiet. I put it down to the strain of the cutting-out operation.

'Tell him to steer zero-seven-zero degrees,' ordered Peace.

'Zero-seven-zero!' I exclaimed. 'You're steering right into the arms of Thornton's Blue Force!'

MKG, Boz and the team looked startled.

Peace's answer was again evasive. 'See if *Bellatrix* is following us.'

I stepped out on to the bridge wing. The wind ripped at my clothing. A mile or so behind, *Bellatrix* was in our wake. I went back, thoughtful. '*Bellatrix* can sail rings round this old basket,' I told the waiting group. 'She has only to stay where she is.'

'Precisely,' replied Peace. 'At this moment her doctored compass reads zero-eight-zero—ten degrees out. When Blue or Red Force catches up with her, she'll report that when last seen *Semittanté* was steering that course—clean away from Love-Apple Crossing. Tonight, when it's dark, we'll give the yacht the slip.'

The admiration in MKG's face was overlaid with doubt. 'But Tyler, Commander——'

'Tyler is smart, bloody smart. I'm doing with *Semittanté* what would be a classic manœuvre for a sub: I'm breaking away upwind into a heavy sea which will mask the sound of my engines. Once Tyler or Thornton pick up *Bellatrix,* which is only a matter of time on the course she's steering, they'll bring every Red and Blue sub, destroyer and search plane into that area, which is on the edge of the Saya de Malha. I want Tyler to think I've run for the shoals and banks to use the shallow seas and breaking water to damp the sound of this old tramp's engines. I want them to concentrate the search there. But in fact I'll be hundreds of miles away in the opposite direction, at Love-Apple Crossing.'

'Aren't you playing this game a little too cosy, Commander?' asked MKG. 'Sure, sure, guessing's fine; Tyler will do this, Tyler will do that. But what if he doesn't? What if Tyler out-thinks you, smells the double-cross?'

'We sit at Love-Apple Crossing, waiting.'

'What!'

'A bunch of fishermen with an island girl—everyday islanders, all of us. We'll have lines over the side of the cutter and big hats on our heads. Adèle or André will answer any questions in incomprehensible Creole. Under our keel will be Little Bear, also waiting.'

MKG assumed a remote faraway look which was to become more and more frequent in the coming days. He clapped Peace gently on the shoulder.

Adèle said, with a peculiar inflexion, 'John, shall we get the radio going?'

We left the group and went to the radio shack.

As we entered, I started towards the cut aerial, but Adèle closed the door sharply. I turned to face her. She was standing with her back to the door, her face dealthy white. She started to pull a scrap of paper from her blouse, but her hands trembled so violently that she could not manage it.

'It was a fake!' she choked. 'I suspected him before, but here's proof——'

A deadly fear spread over me. 'Peace?'

She nodded, and handed me the scrap of paper. It was simply a jumble of letters. I shook my head at it.

'He forgot this, among the others he faked. You see, the signals pad is carbon-backed—one copy for filing, the other for the captain. This is the copy.'

She took the slip and read out the code:

'*President of the United States to Marvin K. Green, via Seychelles x unless you reply personally to this via same channel within six hours I shall assume the kidnapping report of Willowtrack to be correct and that you are no longer a free agent x whatever the circumstances, the Little Bear project is to be called off now x*'

There was a long silence. I said, 'The version Peace passed on to MKG read something like this: "You have my personal authorization to continue with the Little Bear mission as planned."'

Adèle sat down in the operator's chair, taking a grip on herself. She nodded at the severed wire. 'Fix that first—anything may be happening.'

It was only a matter of minutes to fix the wire. Adèle checked the set. My thoughts were in turmoil.

'Do we tell MKG?' she asked, her eyes on me. Perhaps she wondered whether my own loyalty to Peace would prevail.

'The implications are too colossal to contemplate,' I said. 'No wonder Thornton and Tyler were throwing everything into the search.'

'Far from the President recalling the Seventh Fleet, he must be urging them on,' she said, fiddling with the dials. She held up her hand. 'Wait!'

It was Mauritius Radio:

'... an announcement of major importance. The President of the United States announces that an incident has taken place which is without parallel in American history. The Vice-President, Markin K. Green, has been kidnapped by foreign agents. The White House states that although the circumstances of the abduction are not clear, it appears that the Vice-President was on his way to superintend the test-firing of a secret new American missile in the Indian Ocean when the kidnapping took place. The Vice-President was seized aboard the nuclear submarine U.S.N. *Willowtrack* and conveyed aboard another submarine, which was then shadowed to a remote atoll barrier reef named St Brandon. Although this submarine has since been located, the Vice-President has disappeared. In view of grave fears being expressed for the safety of Marvin K. Green, the United States Seventh Fleet in Limuria waters has been deployed under command of Admiral Thornton and is now searching the area. The search is, however, being impeded by a cyclone.

'The White House announcement adds that the situation is aggravated by the fact that the secret missile which was to have been test-fired by the Vice-President has also disappeared. It was being transported in a French freighter named *Semittanté*. Captain Revs Tyler, the famous American submarine ace who was decorated for his epoch-making dash under the ice-cap of Antarctica, is in command of *Willowtrack* and is leading the search.'

'Peace must know he can't get away with it!' exclaimed Adèle. 'How could he have faked that signal from the President?'

'Because,' said a menacing voice from the doorway, 'nothing can justify Little Bear except MKG.'

We spun round. It was Peace. He stood swinging with the motion of the ship, spray on his turtle-necked sweater and black trousers. He held the Remington lightly by the triggerguard and in his other hand was the hocked Colt. The lightness of his movements lent him the air of a predator about to spring.

I jerked my head at the loudspeaker. 'You heard that?'

'Aye,' he said, 'I heard.' He watched us both for a moment and then closed the door behind him, still with that air of coiled power about to strike. He spoke to Adèle. 'How did you find out—did I muff the code?'

'It's of no consequence how we know,' I retorted angrily.

'It is,' he replied. 'I want to know how many people I have to deal with.'

'The signals pad had a carbon backing,' said Adèle. 'You overlooked it.' I wondered whether I could jump Peace. Adèle sensed it. 'John, don't!'

'So it's only you two, then,' said Peace. He put the weapons on the table, but he stayed close.

'Geoffrey,' I said, 'your devotion to Little Bear has gone beyond the point of sanity.'

'Sanity does not enter into this,' he answered. 'Every mile an hour the gale puts on, every foot the sea rises, puts the odds more on my side. Are—you—going—to—tell—him?'

I walked deliberately past the pistols and confronted him. 'We've sailed before on tough missions, Geoffrey, but we won through because right was on our side.'

'Who are you to set yourselves up as a judge of my

176

actions?' he blazed back. 'Right! What is right in this instance? Is it wrong to have one's heart in a weapon whose lethal efficacy is obscured by petty rivalries between Services and a bunch of politicians who don't know Polaris from a pump-handle? This thing is big—bigger than we dream of! It is power, power unlimited in the hands of the nation who owns it! Now it's to be sold down the river because some bloody fool thinks we've kidnapped the Vice-President!'

'That's not the way of it and you know it,' I snapped back. 'MKG risked himself and his standing in the first place by consenting to the test-fire. That is the measure of his faith in Little Bear. But then it was secret and he was safe-guarded. Now the whole world knows; his position is endangered; the President has called it off. You can't go on with it!'

'The Seventh Fleet plus the whole world versus us!' he said. I looked at him and marvelled inwardly. He wanted the odds as high as that.

'Are you going to tell him?' he repeated.

'If we don't, someone else will,' I said. 'There's Boz Blair, Pete Allingham——'

'No. This is the only radio aboard Semittanté. I've told Mac to keep the transistor under guard.' We did not reply and he went on, 'By tomorrow we should be at Love-Apple Crossing. I shall sink Semittanté. The space-shot will still go on.'

'MKG is undertaking it voluntarily,' said Adèle. 'You force him to take a space-ride.'

'If he doesn't know, he will go through with it,' he replied. He swung on us, his voice harsh. 'Think, if you break the news to him, you will sacrifice the West's nuclear weapon lead for the next decade at least. Can you reconcile that with your consciences? The consequences of your discreet silence are immeasurable in the field of future peace. Has either of you the right, without express permission from the DNI, to back down on the mission? *Have* you?'

'You'll be launching MKG under false pretences,' I said.

'Put that way, yes. But it does not invalidate the weapon or the need to show the world how mighty a thing Little Bear is.'

I looked deep into Adèle's eyes and saw the conflict raging in them, too.

'Give me just one day until I can scuttle this bag of bones,' Peace went on vigorously. 'Leave it to me after that. All I ask is your silence.'

'And if not?'

Peace picked up the telephone, dialled the engine-room. 'Mac—come to the radio-room. Drop whatever you are doing.'

The sea beat like drum-fire against the old hull. It seemed like hours until Mac came.

Peace picked up the Remington, handed it to Mac. He took the Colt himself. Adèle was pale.

'Mac,' he said, 'the President has blown the gaff on the Little Bear mission. MKG doesn't know. John and Adèle heard the broadcast. The others don't know, either. If MKG has an inkling, the mission is off. I faked a signal so that he would carry on. Now—' he waved at us—'it's in danger.'

Mac eyed us with his bloodshot eyes. 'I'm an old shipmate of Number One, sir, and I wouldn't like to hurt him. There are plenty of spare places in the engine-room where I could look after him. The girl's easy.'

'It means as much as that to you, Geoffrey?'

He didn't look me in the face but nodded. 'I'd rather you came along, John, but nothing will stop me—do you hear—nothing!'

'And if Tyler and Thornton catch up with you?'

'I'll see you right,' he replied. 'I'll take the whole rap. I'll say, what you did, you did under duress. Try and see it as a hunt, without the other implications, which aren't your concern anyway—they're MKG's.' He turned to Adèle. 'I need you, too. The end will justify the means.'

'What if MKG comes and listens to the radio here?' she asked. 'Soon every radio station in the world will carry the story.'

'The seas will be breaking right across the deck shortly,' said Peace. 'I'll put the radio shack out of bounds to everyone except John on the grounds of limbs or ribs being broken. I'll tell 'em we can't afford injuries to the launch team, or to MKG.'

I made up my mind. 'You deserve to luck out, Geoffrey,' I said. 'I'm not with you in the way I was before, but for old times' sake, I'm not against you. I can't speak for Adèle.'

She hesitated and then said, 'It's too big a decision for me to take alone. I would like to signal the DNI——'

'That's out of the question,' answered Peace. 'You are still under his orders, remember. As far as I am concerned, they stand. He didn't offer *you* any loopholes: if this happened, then that. He ordered you, go ahead.'

'Like John, I am not for or against,' she said unhappily. 'You have my word for my silence too.'

Peace nodded to Mac, who left, morose as ever, throwing down the pistol.

Peace opened his mouth as if to say something as he left, but changed his mind and said formally, 'Thank you both. This is the only way left. I'd rather it had been otherwise.'

When he had gone, Adèle concentrated on the radio and I rigged a lifeline from the radio shack along the upper deck. The barometer was alarmingly low and squalls burst at intervals from the north-east. Although it was barely five o'clock, the sky was dark and grey scud streamed across the heavens. I didn't care for the way the old ship was behaving, either. She was putting her bows under and the seas were sweeping right back to the winches on the foredeck. It was the beginning of a wild night. Somewhere in the north-east was the centre of the cyclone—a wild-lashed convulsion of sea which had sent better ships than *Semittanté* to the bottom.

As I put the last knots into the lifeline, I saw Boz Blair and his men struggling to secure the long crate containing Little Bear. I went aft and helped them double-lash the crate to the deck with a two-inch manila. We then ran a heavy wire through one of the deck winches and drew it tight for additional security. Shouting above the howl of the wind, I reminded Boz to cut it free when we scuttled the ship. Astern, throwing her bows high in the air and much closer now, was *Bellatrix*.

Boz indicated the end of the case. 'Lend me your axe!' he shouted. 'Gotta get the loose gear out and stow it in the cutter.'

I handed him the axe and he chopped open the crate. Under heavy plastic waterproofing we found three small cases, one marked 'SPACE-SUIT', the second 'DATICO' and the third 'VLF RADIO', in clear stencilling. Boz yanked one towards him, freeing the lashing of tarred paper and plastic. Beyond —and a thrill of awe passed through me as Boz gestured— Little Bear's nose-cone reflected the dull light.

The interior of the crate smelt like a new car—tarry, plastic, sterile. Boz and I crawled in farther. Behind the thick plastic protective membrane of the casing was the capsule, its rubber-cushioned seat and safety straps facing us from behind the perspex. There was an array of instruments and, fixed in the transparent canopy on a stay, was some sort of gyro or altimeter. A thick rubber cable, heavily water-proofed, was sealed into the side of the casing. Attached to one end was a metal ball which looked like a dunking helo's sonar buoy. That was all we would see on the surface once

179

MKG was submerged in the missile. A telescopic radio antenna was attached to the hull. The sight of the sleek metal cylinder seemed to mitigate, somehow, the burden of the secret inside me.

Hearing a sound, I spun round, my nerves sandpapered by the sight of the sinister weapon and the crisis it had caused. It was the Texan.

'The dame wants you in the radio shack,' he said. 'Seems it's off limits to all of us now—and I must admit it's goddam' rough going up there.' He explained Peace's ban to Boz. 'Commander doesn't want any broken limbs amongst us.' Like Boz, though, his interest seemed entirely focused on Little Bear.

At the radio shack, Adèle said, 'Geoffrey wants you to black out this place. He doesn't want a light showing anywhere tonight.' She smiled gravely at me. 'Every radio station in the world is interrupting its programmes with monotonous regularity to give the latest on the MKG crisis. I thought the Voice of America announcer would have kittens the first time he came on the air with the news.'

I stayed and listened with her. Stunned reaction, incredulity, disbelief—the ether could not hold them all. Space experts discounted the attempt, but the National Space Administration seemed to give credence to it by saying the earth would be in the most favourable position for a space-shot a week hence. Experts, within the bounds of security and supposition, tried to assess Little Bear's chances of reaching Santa Fe. The President remained silent. The one thing the listening world did not seem to take into account, however, was the cyclone. Arm-chair strategists and geographical experts all had their say about how easy it would be to locate any ship, anywhere, any time, in the Sea of Limuria.

Tyler and Thornton were ominously silent. I thought of those deep-diving subs 500 feet down closing relentlessly towards us, patiently searching, searching.

I had finished the improvized black-out when Adèle raised her hand.

Here it came!—the close Morse grouping, the expert, rapid sending of the Seventh Fleet. Adèle's hand danced over the paper.

>*Blue Force to Red Force x Semittanté transmission too short for reliable fix x on basis of fixes from Blue and Red Forces evaluate her position as north-west St Brandon and west of Saya de Malha x subs on their way x weather deteriorating x how is it with you?*

Tyler was brief:

*Damage and casualties all surface ships x cowboys hove
to x search birds roosting x Willowtrack making all
available speed with two other subs to general area indicated by Semittanté fix x*

I took it to Peace on the bridge. 'They'll be here by morning,' he said.

MKG stood silent by the wheel, his thoughts beyond the
streaming windows, across the storm-swept sea.

*Semittanté* plunged into the night.

Two hours later, after Mac had reported that *Semittanté*
was taking in water through cracked bow plates, Peace altered
course in complete darkness towards Love-Apple Crossing.
As she swung round to take the sea astern, *Semittanté* gave us
a breath-stopping moment. A heavy sea broke aboard, carrying away the starboard boats and tearing the for'ard hatchway from its coaming. Tons of water poured in. *Semittanté*
lay over like a heeled cur; I thought she would never come
up. Mac's voice in the voicepipe was fluent with profanity.
He wasn't sure if the pumps could cope, he said. Boz's men
and I tried to lash a tarpaulin over the shattered coamings, but
it was torn from our hands and whirled away into the night.
Bruised, with fingernails bleeding, we fought our way back
to the bridge.

Chagos, Mauritius, St Brandon, Tromelin, and Chepé on
Agalega broadcast continuous cyclone warnings. It seemed
that the eye of the storm still lay well to the east. Adèle at
my insistence tried to snatch some sleep on a rough couch I
arranged in the radio shack. Peace, MKG, André and I kept
the old ship alive while the launch team dozed fitfully in the
chart-room. With the run of the sea and the wind astern, she
made for her last resting-place.

When it was light enough to see at about eight o'clock the
next morning, Boz brought us all hot cocoa and bully-beef
sandwiches. We ate the rough fare hungrily. There was no
sun, only a transparency in the grey, but the sea seemed somewhat easier. There was no sign of *Bellatrix*.

I took Adèle's 'breakfast' to her and she reported silence
from the searchers, but the news bulletins were anything but
silent: Moscow offered Soviet planes and tracking stations
'in the interests of world peace'. The BBC said that 'if the
kidnappers were British, they were unscrupulous adventurers
who had assumed the name of one of Britain's most illustri-
ous naval officers who had been buried recently with full honours
in the Sea of Limuria.' When Peace joined us, he saw in this
an official disavowal of himself, but shrugged his shoulders
and said it had happened to him before. Behind-the-scenes

pressure must have been intense, for this disavowal was reinforced by an offer of the British missile-tracking cruisers *Loch Vennachar* and *Loch Rannoch*. But, it was added—and Peace saw in this the DNI's hand as a means of keeping the mission alive—these ships were at present storm-bound in the Seychelles. Speculation ran riot about the massive operation which the Seventh Fleet had mounted; Thornton's silence was attributed to security, not to the cyclone.

I felt uneasy in MKG's presence when we returned to the bridge and I was glad when Peace called me to the chartroom.

'What do you make of it, John?'

I studied our line of dead-reckoning pencillings on the chart which we had made during the night. 'We could be thirty miles any way.'

'If you are remotely right, we should sight Love-Apple Crossing about four or five hours from now.'

'Sight!' I laughed ironically. 'Love-Apple Crossing is maybe half a mile long and a quarter broad. It's ten feet above sea level, with the exception of the northern end near Vingt-Cinq Coups. On a calm day you wouldn't sight it at ten miles; today, not at ten cables.'

'True,' he reflected. 'Nothing but a sandbank with some piddling little palms. But if we miss Love-Apple Crossing today, we could beat about for days looking for it. We have six days left to blast-off.'

'Providing this old crate holds together.'

'And she's leaking like a sieve,' he said. 'Mac's worried. And if Mac's worried, the situation is critical.'

He turned back to the chart. 'So you think this is a lot of bull, John?'

'Frankly, yes.'

'You really haven't a clue where we are?'

'I said so.'

'What is the alternative?'

'André. He has some peculiar built-in sea-sense which tells him things which even Tyler's radio sextants and inertial navigation wonders don't.'

'The triumph of spirit over science,' Peace said quietly.

'Could be. Ask him, anyway.'

We stumbled on to the bridge as *Semittanté* staggered over another wave. I fetched Adèle from the radio shack. The news bulletins were ceaseless on the Vice-Presidential crisis. It seemed unreal that the man at the centre of the storm should be standing, unaware of the quick-fire of news, within yards of it. Peace, I noted, had been careful always to be with me when I spoke to MKG.

When Adèle, who was constrained with Peace, passed on our message to André the old fisherman, grey with fatigue from his long trick shared with MKG at the wheel, gestured for me to take the spokes. He went to the starboard bridge window.

'He says, Love-Apple Crossing is out there. He thought you were bound for Agalega previously.'

'Could he find it?'

For the first time I saw André rattled. 'Of course, he knows exactly where the ship is. This is yellow tunny sea. The Japs fish them off the Saya de Malha, but this is their main route.'

'Cut the fishing stuff,' retorted Peace. The strain of the night had told more on him than he showed outwardly. 'Tell him, we're lost. Will he take *Semittanté* to Love-Apple Crossing? If so, he's in command.'

Adèle translated. Surprise and delight passed across the old man's face and he went forward and kissed Adèle's hand with a gesture which I think must have been a survival of eighteenth-century French manners in Mauritius. He bowed to Peace and put his hand on MKG's shoulder. He spoke long and eloquently to Adèle. She smiled and it lighted up her strange, lovely face.

'At Agalega, he says, the children from La Fourche play on the beach with the rose and blue and carmine shells—shells which are found nowhere else in all Limuria. Chepé's wife is from the Amirante Isles and everyone knows that Amirante women are . . . are . . . how do you say, they see things . . .'

'Fey,' I supplied.

She smiled her thanks. 'Chepé's wife is fey. She reads fortunes in the shells. She told André that one day he would be the captain of a great ship, greater than any he had known. Now he thanks you because you have made it come true.'

'Great ship!' sniffed Peace, but he smiled affectionately at the old fisherman.

'There is more,' went on Adèle. 'He would never forgive me if I cut it short. This is a woman's fortune, he says, which may or may not be true. But—' she hesitated—'he feels that the real captain of our spirits here is——' She nodded at MKG.

The strain of the long night showed on MKG's face, too. There was a rim of salt and dried sweat on his hair-line and his eyes were bloodshot.

MKG said, 'Tell him, Adèle, tell him my mission.'

Peace said, 'Wait . . .'

MKG said, shaking his head, 'I want him to know.'

Adèle explained, stumbling over the words. 'You see, there is no word for rocket or missile in Creole. I must try and explain it simply, in other terms.'

André still had his hand on MKG's sleeve.

'Does he know we are being hunted?' asked MKG.

Adèle replied, 'Yes, we are running like a school of frightened tunny with devil-fish after them.'

The old man bowed ceremoniously again to Peace and me and took the wheel. He swung *Semittanté*'s head about five degrees to starboard.

'How soon does he think he will be at Love-Apple Crossing?' asked Peace.

'Early afternoon.'

'We're back in the ranks, John,' Peace said with a faint glimmer of humour. 'Let's see what's on the air, Adèle.'

'Let me know if there's anything——' began MKG, but Boz Blair broke in with some technicalities about Little Bear and I was glad to escape from the bridge.

In the radio shack, Adèle searched the air for signals from the Seventh Fleet. Again nothing but menacing stillness. Peace listened expressionless to the newscasts about the crisis. Adèle tried the Navy wavelength again. She stiffened at the call-sign.

'It's Tyler!'

Peace and I read over her shoulder as she decoded.

> *Willowtrack to CIC x intercepted yacht Bellatrix position long. 60° E., lat. 10° 30′ S.*

The radio spluttered its reply and Adèle went through the agonizing slow business of decoding.

> *CIC Blue Force to Willowtrack x is Vice-President in yacht? x*
>
> *Willowtrack to CIC x no radio contact with Bellatrix x seas make boat contact impossible x yacht seems full of men x*
>
> *CIC to Willowtrack x stick by that yacht fellah x*
>
> *Willowtrack to CIC x you bet x closer than his shirt x no answer to my light signals x*
>
> *CIC to Willowtrack x concentrate all forces Bellatrix area x where is Semittanté x*
>
> *Willowtrack to CIC x Bellatrix flag signal flies word Semittanté x*
>
> *CIC to Willowtrack x what hell's he playing at x*
>
> *Willowtrack to CIC x closed yacht in heavy seas x trying*

184

> *to get a man across x at least 20 men aboard Bellatrix x*
> *no sign Vice-President x*

I could picture the scene: Tyler, frantic for information, jockeying the big sub, awash to her casings to give her maximum stability in the swells, as close as he dared to the strangely silent yacht. Despite everything, the thrill of the chase raced through my veins. I was half-glad, half-ashamed, that I had given my undertaking to Peace about MKG.

Here it was:

> *Willowtrack to CIC x fired line from Willowtrack bridge*
> *x chief quartermaster volunteered to go across x difficult*
> *evolution but achieved it x with loudhailer says no sign*
> *of Vice-President x men all foreigners x unable to under-*
> *stand what they say except they repeat Semittanté point-*
> *ing to themselves x*
> *CIC to Willowtrack x what language x*
> *Willowtrack to CIC x leader repeats du Plessis x*
> *CIC to Willowtrack x du Plessis captain Semittanté x*
> *try French x I want that man x detach Shenandoah ex*
> *Red Force and bring him to me x*

Peace whistled, but he became less tense. 'One less sub to hunt us.'

'It's going to take the best part of today for *Shenandoah* to reach Blue Force and get du Plessis aboard Thornton's flagship,' I observed.

He glanced keenly at me, still talking about the hunt in positive terms.

Adèle said, 'Are you intending to show those messages to MKG?'

Peace gathered them up. 'Of course. These are operational. There's nothing in them about—the other side of the picture.'

'All operational messages?' she insisted.

The smile didn't reach his eyes. 'Subject to my approval.'

'I feel pretty cheap standing next to the man with the knowledge I have——' I began.

Peace's tone hardened immediately. 'There's no point in discussing it further.'

'Doesn't he want to signal the President again?' asked Adèle. 'After all, it's days still until the launch.'

'He mentioned it, but he realizes as well as we do what the consequences would be of a signal while they're hunting us.'

Hunt! Peace and I had risked death together in the past, both as the hunter and the hunted; despite myself, the thought surged up in my mind, what if Peace after all was right and the outcome of a successful mission would be worth the immediate risks involved to the Vice-President? Peace had been right before when the whole world believed him wrong——

'I'll take these to the bridge,' he said, picking up the signals.

Adèle listened gravely to me after he had gone when I told her of our past missions, of my mixture of feelings about Little Bear and MKG. Before she could reply, a stream of signals started to go out to Red Force allocating them new dispositions. *Shenandoah* grumbled at being taken from the hunt to taxi Captain du Plessis. Thornton and Blue Force abandoned their previous search area and turned on a heading towards *Bellatrix*. Tyler ordered all his ships into the same area.

Peace had bought another day with his ruse.

By early afternoon the squalls started to increase in violence and frequency from the north-east. *Semittanté* took a fearful beating. The gusts, catching the old ship under the bow, laid her under with a peculiar, sickening corkscrew motion. It was impossible to stand on the bridge without holding on; the hazard of the lifelines to the radio shack was more than real. Boz and his men risked their lives to check Little Bear's lashings. *Semittanté*'s deck was continuously awash in the violent cross-sea, which jounced and jerked, pummelled and hammered her. Three of the lifeboats hung smashed, but the cutter with its precious load was secure. I had demanded some jerrycans of petrol for its auxiliary engine from Mac—the tank, I found, was empty. Tyler and Thornton were on the air without a break. Both HUK forces were taking a tremendous hammering, they reported.

André and MKG were fighting the wheel when I felt the tempo of *Semittanté*'s motion change—from the long, swooping dives with water pouring off the rusty bows to a quick, shuddering action. The bottom seemed to be dropping out of the barometer, which stood at 28.80 of mercury. We had run into a fearful cross-sea. On Peace's orders I brought Adèle to the bridge—we were afraid that the radio shack might be swept overboard.

André shouted above the din, 'Love-Apple Crossing!'

Beyond the bridge visibility was down to about fify yards. The sea was shrouded in spray; the summits of the waves were carried aloft bodily in a white shower of salt as high as a carrier's deck. It was a formidable, awe-inspiring sight.

Adèle translated. 'We are coming in from the east, straight towards the lagoon.'

'Where is it?' demanded Peace.

André pointed, but we could see nothing. Then, slightly to port, I caught a glimpse of a coconut tree bent like a whip on a low point of land.

'There!' I yelled. 'That's it—look!'

Adèle said, 'Vingt-Cinq Coups.'

'The flogging,' said MKG quietly, 'is coming to old *Semittanté*.'

Trevor-Davis gave a thumbs-down sign to Pete the Texan.

Peace swallowed hard. 'Can André take her through the reef into the lagoon—in this?'

André's reply was grave. 'It is a very big ship and the pass is narrow.'

Peace slowed the engines. 'It doesn't matter if she strikes, so long as we get her *inside*.'

Without warning, the wind cut.

*Semittanté* lay in a vacuum of silence.

Adèle grabbed me. 'John darling, what——?'

'Cyclone centre,' replied Peace. 'We're dead in the heart of it. We're in the middle of the whirlpool: everything spins around creating a small patch in the very centre which is absolutely without movement. I've never seen it myself, though, until now.'

Our voices were loud, unnatural.

We waited—hours, it seemed, though it could not have been more than five minutes.

Then Adèle said, 'André thinks he can take her in now.'

The narrow spit of land was a dirty grey compared to the fanged whiteness of the water. The reef was a horseshoe of wild surf. At Vingt-Cinq Coups was a small roofless hut and a strange square trellis of iron.

Peace said, 'That axe, John; we may have to cut the cutter clear if we strike. Boz, slack off that wire cable round Little Bear. I'll be here at the wheel with André. As soon as we get inside the lagoon, get up for'ard with Pete Allingham and knock the shackle out of the anchor cable. I want everyone else in the cutter, ready. Then get below and open the sea-cocks with Mac. Adèle, I want you with me.'

She hesitated and looked deep into my eyes. Hers told me all I wanted to know.

I went for'ard with the big Texan. The unnatural quiet persisted. Twice I was thrown to the deck as the cross-sea dealt the old tramp a quick left-right to the jaw and water swept across the deck.

The bows swung high. I looked down into the entrance race.

I saw the coral-head too late.

André's course was slightly off centre in the reef passage. I yelled frantically, gesturing. The bow paused—plunged down—on to the dagger of coral.

The crash and scream of metal threw me hard against the deck. Up she came to impale herself again, but the bow swung away and the second strike was only glancing. She limped clear, tired to death, her head starting to droop. Then the sea quietened—we were through!

Pete and I clouted the inch-thick anchor shackle. Once—twice. It gave and the anchor fell in a shower of sparks.

I ran for the engine-room while Pete made for the cutter. 'Mac!'

It was as quiet as a cathedral, except for the ominous sound of water flooding in.

'Mac!'

'Here!'

I dropped into the shaft, up to my knees in sea-water. Mac fought to open the rusty sea-cock. We threw our combined weight on the heavy wrench and it gave, water spurting over us. We raced on deck, making for the boat. André was speaking rapidly, pointing seawards. *Semittanté* was settling at an awkward angle, making the launching of the cutter difficult. She could not be cut clear now—she would simply smash herself against the steel side.

I jumped into the boat. An icy spear of fear went through me. Adèle was missing!

I clutched the fall and swung myself back on deck.

'For Christ's sake!' yelled Peace. 'She's going down like a stone——'

*Semittanté* gave a lurch.

'Adèle!' I screamed above the din. I sprinted up the sloping planks, hauled myself bodily up a steel ladder, and propelled myself to the radio shack by hauling myself along the ropes of the lifeline I had rigged. I kicked once, twice, at the shack's door, which had jammed from the angle of the sinking ship.

'Adèle!'

She sat at the radio, headphones on, and stared unseeingly. For a moment, I thought she was dead.

'The ship's sinking—any moment—come, for God's sake!'

She seemed to come back from a great distance. Silently she pushed across the transcript of a newscast. It was headed Voice of America.

It read: *Flash. The White House announces that the President has suffered a severe stroke. His condition gives rise to the gravest anxiety.*

# 13 GRID E-13

A violent lurch, accompanied by an ominous rumble from below, jerked me out of my stunned reaction.

I crammed the transcript into my pocket, tore the headphones off Adèle's head, picked her up and staggered out. The wild motion of the dying ship ripped the flesh from my hand as I hung on to the lifeline rope. Then, as she steadied, I made a half-sprint down the ladder and deck to the boat. Peace had already eased it down about ten feet, but shouted to the others to stop when he saw me.

*Semittanté* lurched again.

Keeping Adèle over my shoulder, I grabbed a loose fall with one hand and wound my knees and ankles round it. Faces in the boat, so small below, were turned towards me. Underneath lay a maelstrom of death.

The rope burned hot on my torn palm. Eager hands reached up and pulled us into the cutter.

*Semittanté* gave another wild lurch.

'Forward bulkhead gone!' shouted Peace. 'Pay off those falls—handsomely! We don't want to go down with her!'

André gestured seawards. I saw the cause of his alarm. Half a mile away loomed a threatening bank of grey. There was a steady roaring like an express train. Sweating and cursing, we lowered the cutter, fending her off the rusty side while the angle steepened as *Semittanté* went to her grave. We clawed and shoved. Now the boat hung a foot or two above the sea. I grabbed an oar and swung round. I felt I had been struck in the face by a grey fist. The cyclone hit us anew, throwing the cutter against the steel side. Above its scream was another noise—the frightening snap of planking. Ragged rivets ripped the oilskin at my shoulder. *Semittanté* rolled, towered above our stricken craft. I reversed my oar. It slipped helplessly and then lodged against a buckled plate. Peace knelt in the bows with another oar. I saw his muscles bulge. Simultaneously, I threw all my weight against the rough wood.

We were clear!

The wind snatched the cutter away like a feather. Water poured through her broken planking. I whipped off my sou'-wester and baled. The others did the same. André snatched Peace's oar and used it to steer—the tiller was useless, she lay so far over on her beam ends. It was impossible to breathe

189

facing the wind and speech was out of the question. We all baled frantically. Despite our efforts, the water rose.

Then suddenly the cutter slewed, stayed in mid-course, bumped, crashed—and we were thrown in a heap on to sand! Peace picked himself up and gestured, 'Get her clear of the breakers!' His mouth formed the words, but I heard nothing in the gale. Adèle raced forward and looped the bow painter over her shoulder. She, too, realized the danger of another sea hurling the boat on to the iron sand. Peace and MKG, André, Mac, Boz Blair's men, Trevor-Davis and I all threw our weight against the cutter. A long splinter ripped my torn hand, but I was unaware of the pain. MKG stumbled and fell, but he was up in a moment with Pete's help, hanging on to a rowlock.

The cutter slid forward. André shouted, pointing. Up a shallow gradient, I saw the stone structure I had spotted from the sea. Dragging, heaving, our backs breaking while the wind thundered and tore at our clothes and the sea at our feet, we inched the boat out of the breakers towards the hut. It seemed to be made of heavy squared coral blocks. We headed for a ruined doorway.

The cyclone's howl took on a new note, and I saw, outside the hut, a twisted metal grille, capped by two handcuffs like rowlocks. The lattice made the cyclone scream like the slaves who were lashed to death on it. This was the flogging-grating which gave the place its name, Vingt-Cinq Coups—Twenty-five Lashes.

We manhandled the boat through the doorway, into shelter, away from the mad wind. As we up-ended the shattered hull and crept in under it, I pressed the crumpled Voice of America paper into Peace's hand.

For four days the cyclone turned the sea to frenetic fermentation and the wind to a maniac which screamed its torment through the flogging-grating. Surf boiled like thunder against the reef. The high recurring note of the wind reminded me of the uninhibited keen which breaks into a shanty to cry the sailor's death-fear of the sea. It made speech impossible and sleep, exhausted though we all were, a nightmare. My dozing moments were punctuated by jerks into dazed wakefulness, as though I were goaded by the thought of the message I had given Peace. It seemed scarcely possible that the man who lay as if dead under the boat with us might by now be President of the greatest nation in the world.

*And he did not know!*

I salved my conscience by telling myself that it was impossible to communicate at all in the din of the cyclone and that the whole question would have to be solved when it was over. Four days! What was happening constitutionally during those four critical days in the United States, where the highest office of the nation might by now be left unfilled? The searchers, like us, would be stormbound. I simply could not face up to it. Peace had taken up a position on one side of Adèle and me, and Mac on the other. I sensed, though conversation was impossible, that we were under guard.

Our misery was made worse by the spray, salt and rain which percolated through the cutter's smashed planking over our heads. Boz carefully moved the DATICO gear, the VLF firing radio and space-suits to the driest spots. Mac buried the jerrycans of petrol in the sand to deaden the smell of fumes. Since the tank of the cutter's auxiliary had been empty when we left *Semittanté*—the reason why I had obtained the jerry-cans from Mac—there was no need for us to worry about its standing upside down. We tried unavailingly to stanch the planking on the inside with our oilskins. Our mouths were raw with blown sand.

The hut, Adèle had told me aboard *Semittanté*, had been built by an eighteenth-century freebooter who had eloped with his mistress from Mauritius and been wrecked on Love-Apple Crossing. They had waited fifteen years for a ship. It never came. She died. Her grave lay outside.

Previous cyclones had reduced the outlying parts to rubble, but the centre remained, made of substantial blocks of four-foot coral. We could not stand up against the force of the wind; we could only crawl behind the shelter of the ruined walls. Whenever I did so, either Mac or Peace accompanied me, while the other watched Adèle. We were evidently to be allowed no opportunity of telling what we knew. The rest of the island except the high-lying point where we were was completely submerged. On the second night, Adèle lay in my arms in terror as the seas started to break into the shelter. MKG, his face caked with salt and stubble and his eyes red with sand, watched as the ocean reached out, sought our deaths, but could not quite touch us. A deep gloom fell over the launch team. We had eluded our pursuers, but the cost was plain: the stove-in cutter would never float again. I con-soled myself with that thought in making bearable the secret inside me, which seemed to burn like fire whenever I looked across at the fine-drawn, tired features of the Vice-President. Radio reception was impossible with the storm and the blanketing effect of the walls and the boat. We could not have heard it, anyway.

Two days were left till the launch.

One afternoon, after I had lost count of time, something awoke me. Adèle, her thin sweater stained with dried-out sea-water and her pants shrunk above her ankles, lay against my shoulder, the softness all gone from her fine, bleached hair. André's back was instinctively to the storm. Peace, his face gaunt, stubbled and dirty, sat propped up watching, the top of his black turtle-necked sweater caked with white salt. Mac lay sleeping on our other side. MKG, encased in an oilskin to try and keep out the file of the sand, slept under the decking aft with Boz, Trevor-Davis and the other scientists.

The sand began its attrition the moment I opened my eyes on the grey, sleep-drugged, wet group—alive, but little more. We had eked out an existence on André's sack of salted sea-birds, although I wanted to gag every time I smelt one. Fire was out of the question; even the acetylene lamp would not stay alight, so we gave it up and lay in a twilight, uncaring state. Now, something touched my sailor's sense. Something, somewhere, was amiss . . .

The grating had stopped screaming.

I heard—*heard*—Adèle's breathing against my neck. I lifted my head to speak to her, but the sand locked my tongue. Unceremoniously, I spat.

'The wind's dropped.'

My voice sounded like the crash of a shot in the confined space. Peace's eyes were alight. MKG and Boz started up, Boz letting out an oath as his head hit the planking above.

'By God!' exclaimed Peace. The salt caked the muscles of his face. 'Here—Mac! MKG! André!'

The others blinked unbelievingly and Adèle pushed herself upright to a sitting position. Peace crawled across to MKG and clapped him on the shoulder. 'Let's get out of here—we've still got today and tomorrow before the launch——'

MKG grinned back uncertainly. 'Let's get this damn' thing off our backs.'

Still acting like automatons, we threw our shoulders under the cutter and tipped her over. We got shakily to our feet, staring over the low wall which had saved us.

Love-Apple Crossing had been sandpapered clean, except for a few snapped-off palm-tree trunks. Acres of white spume coated the lagoon and the shore. A sodden sea-bird lay snarled in the flogging-grating, pulped and smashed. The sun broke through as we stood in silent awe at the spectacle of devastation.

Peace said, 'If the cyclone is over at Love-Apple Crossing, it's been finished in Tyler's area since last night.'

MKG said, 'The radio——'

'The batteries are failing,' he said curtly. 'It will be used for operational messages only. There will be no time to listen to newscasts when we might miss a vital signal from either Tyler or Thornton. Only Adèle operates the radio.'

'Aw, gee,' objected Pete Allingham good-naturedly. 'I was looking forward to a little cha-cha-cha to brighten this tropical isle of beauty.'

'There'll be enough music of another kind to face,' said Peace cryptically.

Adèle, anxious to steer the conversation away from the subject of the radio, said, 'Look, all the *bois manioc* has been washed away!'

André spoke. 'André says,' she translated, 'it is like the great cyclone of 1958—the landmarks are all gone.'

'That may make it tougher for Tyler's men,' I added.

'From a thousand feet up Love-Apple Crossing now probably looks more like a reef than an island,' Peace reflected.

'Except,' remarked Adèle, indicating the grating and the hut, 'for this.'

'That coat of spume will hide Little Bear if they come over the lagoon,' said MKG, screwing up his eyes.

'Unless the boat is fixed, we can forget about the whole thing,' Boz Blair said gloomily.

MKG turned to Peace. 'Why don't we see if we can fix that cutter? You and André go take a look and the rest of us will scout for wood.'

Peace nodded reluctantly. 'I'll need John as well, and I want Mac to check the engine and Adèle to see what the hunter-killers are up to.' Once again we were to be segregated from MKG.

'If there's any news of significance . . .' began MKG, but Peace cut in quickly, 'Of course, Adèle will note it down and we'll let you know. But I'm not going to waste precious power on hearing what Russia is up to, or whether Mrs Jones from Cardiff has murdered her six children.'

MKG looked unhappy. 'We've been completely out of touch for four days now, Commander.'

'The sooner we can find some timber, the better for Little Bear's chances,' he replied. 'I said, Adèle can make a note of any significant news.'

'Come on, fellers!' Pete Allingham gave a whoop and jumped over the wall. The others followed, grinning like schoolboys. Their carefree air seemed to drive away MKG's dark thoughts. He put his hand on the coral wall to vault over it, then he, too, grinned and said, 'Think the astronaut of the day after tomorrow had better get back into training.

I'll trot round the beach a couple of times.' He followed the others at an easy lope.

Peace went back into the hut and fetched the radio. This was the small set we had used in the cutter before. The VLF set was purely for firing Little Bear and could not be used for normal reception.

As Peace put it down, I asked, 'How long are you going to continue with this lie?'

His voice was controlled, but the emotion behind it was tight-packed. 'For as long as I think necessary,' he replied. 'Don't you see how this enhances the value of the space-shot? MKG may be the first President of the United States to step into space.'

'You're perpetuating the biggest fraud in history,' Adèle protested. 'It was bad enough when the President was fully in control of the situation, but now . . .'

I looked at the hard eyes, alive with dedication to Little Bear. I knew in my heart that Peace would stop at nothing. I had noticed his kinship with the DNI before; it was ablaze in his face now.

'What you are doing is not only madness, but criminal,' I said heatedly. 'For four days now the President of the United States has been critically ill. Suppose he dies? He may be dead already. You know as well as I do that quick continuity is vital in the Presidential succession. When John F. Kennedy was shot, Lyndon Johnson was sworn in within an hour and a half.'

'I'm glad you mention President Johnson,' Peace replied. 'He was sworn in in a plane; there is no reason why MKG cannot be sworn in at Space Station One, if need be. Where the foot of the American President treads, that is American soil.'

I turned helplessly to Adèle and looked into her troubled eyes.

'Mac,' Peace said crisply, 'I want you to fetch the Remington and the Colt and get the sand out of them. Get 'em in good working order—soon as hell.' He spoke to us. 'If the President dies, the Speaker of the House can act until the new President is sworn in.'

'This is no argument——' I began, but he waved me quiet.

'I'm not interested in arguments. If Tyler and Thornton don't catch up with us, I intend MKG to be shot to Sante Fe. I also intend to have your silence—at any cost.'

Mac had reappeared with the two weapons. André was engrossed in examining the boat.

There was a long pause. 'I mean, at any cost,' Peace repeated.

'This is madness,' I said.

'Are you prepared to keep quiet?' he demanded. 'Two days—that's all I ask.'

I shrugged and turned to Adèle, who made a hopeless gesture.

'Good,' said Peace. 'Mac or I will be watching you all the time. Now get the radio going.'

Mauritius Radio came through:

'The White House announces that the Seventh Fleet in the Sea of Limuria has resumed its intensive search for the person of Marvin K. Green, Vice-President of the United States, and the missing French freighter *Semittanté*. Admiral Thornton's fleet has been strengthened by two more carriers from the United States Eastern Fleet. Long-range VP-5 maritime reconnaissance aircraft will fly southwards from the Seychelles tomorrow in co-operation with the Seventh Fleet.

'Fears for the safety of *Semittanté* have been expressed in view of the violence of the cyclone, which was the worst recorded this century at the meteorological stations at Chagos and St Brandon. The cyclone is, however, now moving eastwards out of the search area. Captain du Plessis, the shanghaied master of the *Semittanté*, is rendering all possible assistance in the search and is at present aboard Admiral Thornton's flagship.

'Meanwhile, as anxiety about the President's condition deepens, the United States is torn with the biggest constitutional crisis in its history. As listeners already know, the Speaker of the House, Mr. Donald Langley, was sworn in as *pro forma* President until some clarification has been received regarding the whereabouts of Marvin K. Green. Speaker Langley has appealed publicly to the kidnappers to hand over the popular Vice-President, with the promise of a full pardon. There has been no response to this appeal. There was a violent scene in Congress last night when a group of Southern senators sought to bring in a motion applying the disability clause to Marvin K. Green, whose popularity with the man-in-the-street now appears to be higher than it ever was. The Congress reaction is stated by observers to be a reflection of the nation's state of nerves. Commerce has reported a serious decline in trade and Wall Street has fallen to its lowest level in twenty years. Speaker Langley has appealed to the nation to remain calm in this time of crisis.'

Peace had been scribbling while the broadcast progressed.

'What are you doing?' asked Adèle.

'I'm faking a broadcast for MKG's benefit,' he said brutally.
'It'll be quite harmless. Routine sort of thing. None of this.'
We remained silent.

'Try the Seventh Fleet,' he ordered.

The waveband was crowded with traffic.

' . . . Grid position E-7 negative,' said an American voice.
'Will commence search Grid position E-8. Over.'

'One of the carrier search planes,' muttered Peace. 'I
wish I knew where Grid position E-7 was.'

'Weather clearing rapidly from east and north,' reported
another plane.

Then came a code signal, which Adèle deciphered.

> CIC to combined Red and Blue Force x carrier aircraft
> and helos to search area between Saya de Malha and
> Agalega according to predetermined grid pattern x VP-5's
> ex Seychelles will carry out similar grid search south and
> south-east from Seychelles to St Brandon x all surface
> ships to take part x report contacts immediately x

'The heat is on,' said Peace. 'They're coming at us from
the east and the north.'

As he spoke MKG, Boz and the other scientists came up the
slope towards us.

'Adèle,' Peace commanded, 'ask André what hope there is
of his fixing the cutter?'

'He says it is badly damaged,' she replied. 'Two bottom
planks must be completely replaced before she will float. He
has an axe, but, as you can see for yourself, there is no timber.
If there were but one *tatamaka* tree or one *bois mangue* to be
found, we could do something.'

'What about those coconut stumps?' Peace demanded.

'We use coconut for making oars,' replied Adèle. 'The
cutter is of best *tatamaka*, which is hard. The stumps will be
useless, he says.'

The general gloom on the faces of the scientists indicated
that their hunt for timber had been unsuccessful. Peace
handed MKG the faked newscast. He read it without interest.

'Why not simply rip off some of the cutter's decking and
patch the planks?' I asked.

When Adèle had passed it on, André went and fetched the
axe. He stood with his feet apart and went through the
gestures of chopping, shaping, fitting. He shook his head.

'The deck is *bois mangue,* not *tatamaka* like the hull,' she
explained. 'He is very proud of his boat. Even Chepé, who
is a master shipbuilder, admires it. He explains that he
shaped every piece of decking with an adze so that they all

fit—each one has its own particular place and will be useless elsewhere. Besides, the decking is much too short for the
hull, even if he reshaped it.'

'Axe,' corrected MKG. 'He shaped the planks with an
axe.'

'No,' replied Adèle. 'It is an adze, a shipbuilder's tool.
It looks like—a garden hoe. They stand on a log and chop
towards their toes. The adze is as sharp as a razor. But
André says that the axe will do for a patch—if we had some
timber.'

André gestured towards the spit of sand, now looming
whiter as the sky cleared and the wind dropped.

'He wants to walk over to the western side of the island
where there used to be a small pocket of *bois mangue*, but he
warns you, it is most likely to have disappeared in the storm.'

The radio began with Morse and Adèle decoded while the
rest of us waited around. Peace looked anxious. She handed
him the signal first, and he read it out:

> '*Interrogation Captain du Plessis of French freighter
> Semittanté now complete x helos to search grid pattern
> east and west of Semittanté's last estimated position in
> Grid E-10 x estimates place Semittanté west of this
> position following cyclone x*'

As the signal had come in, I noticed Mac move up un-
obtrusively with the Remington, pretending to clean it with
a scrap of cloth. The move was not lost on Adèle, either.

As Peace explained the earlier search messages to MKG
and the others, André, Adèle and I set off. We stumbled
through the sand piled high in drifts at the base of Vingt-
Cinq Coups; farther away the gale had stripped away the
topsoil down to the coral bedrock.

Of the pocket of timber, nothing remained but a few untidy
sockets in the earth. André gestured hopelessly and then
indicated the low northern slope of the island. Adèle and I
walked hand in hand.

Adèle said, 'I thought Geoffrey Peace was your friend.
We're virtually prisoners. And that awful engineer!' She
shuddered.

'I think Mac would do anything for Peace,' I said slowly.

'Even to shooting us?' she asked.

'Little Bear means—well, I don't have to say it,' I said.
'Peace has side-stepped what is the main issue as far as we
and the world are concerned, namely, MKG's position as Vice-
President. His single-mindedness is something frightening.'

'And deadly,' she said. 'If MKG had the slightest suspicion, he'd call the space-shot off. All we can hope is that one

of Tyler's planes finds us—quickly. I feel ashamed every time I look at MKG.'

'It may solve itself,' I said. 'We can't tow Little Bear without a boat. Even if we could, the searchers——'

Instinctively I looked seawards. Even now, Tyler and his hunters might be lying off Love-Apple Crossing.

André let out an exclamation. Adèle wheeled on him. He was pointing to the lagoon.

'There!'

In the lagoon, maybe a hundred yards away, was a long, dark object. There was a rapid-fire of Creole from André, who started towards Vingt-Cinq Coups at a shambling run. I turned to Adèle and stopped in amazement. She was stripping off her clothes! In a moment the whole loveliness of her sun-tanned body stood in sharp relief against the pure white sand.

'Come on!' she called. 'Quick! Help me!'

She raced into the surf, breasted it, paused and signalled me on with her upraised arm. I, too, pulled off my clothes in bewilderment and followed her. Beyond the breakers, Adèle hung on to something. In a few strokes, I was at her side. She clung to a dark log whose top branches only remained.

'*Bois mangue*! It's a whole tree of it! André's eyesight is uncanny.'

She squirmed on to the floating log like a seal and sat astride, laughing. For that moment the massive search, the great Presidential drama, the whole outside world, seemed to recede. Her joy and her laughter were—for me.

'Don't look so serious, my darling . . .'

Her naked loveliness caught me by the throat as she sat there, her eyes dancing. I trod water and looked up at the firm curve of her breasts and the wild loveliness of her wet hair. I said, 'When we're married, we shall come back to Love-Apple Crossing.'

She leaned down and kissed me, sweet and salt together. 'Love—Apple—Crossing,' she murmured. 'Yes, back to Vingt-Cinq Coups—our happiness will make up for all the unhappiness of those old lovers.'

'Adèle——' I began, but she kissed me again and pushed me away. She slid off the log. 'Come, we must get the log ashore before the others arrive and see me like this!'

Together we floated the log to the beach, pulling it well clear of the surf above the highwater mark. Adèle barely had time to drag on her clothes before the others, led by Peace and MKG at a run, reached us. André panted out a flood of Creole. Boz gave a whoop of joy when he saw the log and seized the big Texan. Together they did an impromptu war-dance on the sand. André grabbed MKG's hand and even Trevor-Davis was moved to clap his American counterpart on the shoulder. Only Mac had not bothered to come. André put a foot on the log like a trophy hunter and burst into Creole, while the rest of the scientists stood round grinning like kids.

Adèle and I alone did not share in the general rejoicing. She translated André: 'He says bring the axe right away and he'll have the cutter ready by midday tomorrow.'

Boz looked concerned. 'That leaves the afternoon only to check her over.'

'Sorry, Boz,' replied Peace. 'That missile is staying down until the last moment—and that means until only a few hours before the launch itself.'

Boz turned in protest to MKG. 'I gotta check——'

MKG said quietly, 'Commander's right, Boz. I know you'd like to go over every rivet, but the risk is too big.'

Boz drew his fellow-scientists in with him. 'See here, MKG, I know we checked and re-checked everything before she was stowed, but that is nearly six weeks ago now.'

'She was fine then, and there's no reason to think she isn't fine now,' replied MKG. 'You set the stable table yourself.'

'The same goes for SNAP,' added Peace. 'She also should be fine. We haven't pulled rods since she went aboard.'

Boz remained dubious. 'Sure, sure. We went over everything with a toothcomb before. Everything jim-dandy. But what if——'

'How long does it take to start the nuclear power plant?' I asked.

Boz smiled, despite his preoccupation. 'Pull rods,' he corrected. 'That's what it's called. Till she's fully activated, two hours. You've also got to spin up her gyros and stabilize the stable table.'

'You're making a lab job out of it instead of a field test,' MKG chided him gently. 'You know that's part of the count-down routine, Boz.'

'Data and compensations——' Boz started to say, but MKG waved a hand. 'You know it can be done without all the trappings, Boz. Let's stick to the essentials, especially since Tyler will be just over the horizon.'

Boz and the scientists looked unhappy. I think they would have liked to strip down the entire missile.

MKG's remark about Tyler was with me still. 'Can't the Seventh Fleet interfere with you once Little Bear's in flight?'

Boz and MKG exchanged amused glances. 'No, Little Bear

199

has no radio or radar acquisition. Once Boz presses that "fire" button, nothing can stop me.'

Peace nodded at the log. 'The sooner we get this up to Vingt-Cinq Coups, the sooner André can start.'

MKG said, 'I feel I want that next to me, even when I sleep.'

'Tonight will be a lovely night, after the cyclone,' said Adèle. 'Clear, with stars and a moon.' MKG caught the strange note in her voice, but Peace said quickly, 'Searchers' moon. I'd prefer it pitch-black.'

Half an hour later, gasping and stumbling, we brought the log to Vingt-Cinq Coups. André barely gave himself time to recover his breath before he took the axe and, barefooted, his toes gripped the rough timber, he started a long, slow, rhythmical chopping stroke.

Peace ordered Adèle to check the Navy waveband; immediately she asked for a pencil. She decoded the signal and handed it to him.

'Listen to this, MKG, John,' he said. 'Love-Apple Crossing is Grid Position E-13. Fifty miles to the immediate east is Grid 1-12, and to the west is 1-14. Northwards 1-11 and southwards E-10.'

They would first search a band only 50 miles south of us! It seemed impossible that we could escape detection, I told myself, perhaps in mitigation of my surrendering to Peace's threats.

'Hear that, Boz!' exclaimed MKG. 'When they don't find anything there, they'll turn north—here.'

'It's one hell of a risk,' said Boz.

'We're being squeezed between the risks and the deadline,' replied MKG. He turned to Peace. 'By heavens, Commander, I wish I knew the reason why the President hasn't called off the Seventh Fleet's search. Maybe it's even a giant cover on his part because the secret was outing anyway. I don't know. I've thought and thought it over. But with only two days to go, this thing has really gotten into me and it'll take a hell of a lot more than Tyler and Thornton to make me turn back now.'

I saw the elation in Peace's face as he turned to meet my eyes.

'What we need is some real liquor for a celebration tonight,' the big Texan said, laughing.

'Celebrate when I'm on the way in Little Bear,' replied MKG. 'And don't toast me only—toast the Commander here.'

The secret hammered in my mind until I wanted to shout it out to the whole of Limuria. Adèle must have felt the same

200

as I did for she went over to André's log and came back with one of the shavings.

She held it out to me. 'Smell! There's no smell like *bois mangue* in the world.'

It was pungently aromatic—perhaps it owed something to a common ancestor with camphor in the East Indies—with a hint of cinnamon which lingered.

Until it was too dark to see, André swung his axe, refusing assistance. Peace declined to switch on the radio. Mac grunted over the cutter's engine, but I noted that the Remington was close in the stern locker near his hand.

The wind dropped and the sea merely grumbled now against the reef. We lit a fire of *bois mangue* chips and grilled fish which Trevor-Davis had speared in the lagoon. The tiny fire etched the sinister black grating above us with scarlet; the moon rose; under its softness the sea resumed its long, languid Limurian lope, a sigh instead of a snarl. Limuria returned to her gentleness.

We sat with our backs to the coral wall, smoking, looking across the lagoon. MKG was in the middle—scruffy, unshaven and nondescript, but we were drawn to his personality like moths to a flame. He seemed to have put his questionings behind him and his eyes were bright. We all had too much to say for words.

MKG turned to Adèle and pointed with the glowing tip of his cigarette to a bright constellation in the south. 'Pity Love-Apple Crossing is so far south. I would have liked to show you Little Bear in his own place in the firmament.'

'Why can't we see him?' asked Adèle in a small voice. Perhaps the thought was eating her, too—what if Little Bear did not go according to expectation?

There was a lightness in the Vice-President's voice, by contrast. 'You can't spot Little Bear in the southern hemisphere,' he told her. 'Nor Polaris, which is in Little Bear's tail.'

Orion's Belt was a jewel above our heads; on the right the Southern Cross hung over the limitless ocean. The silence was immense. In my heart I knew that if ever MKG came back, he would bring with him something of the incalculable horizons which lay before our eyes to add to a personality so full and strong that I, for one, had never encountered anything like it before. *Could* the end justify the means in this fantastic space-journey? I hastily stopped my thoughts; I was beginning to think like Peace, without considering the vast consequences of the act.

I said, breaking the spell, 'How long will your flight to Santa Fe take, MKG?'

'A few hours,' he replied. 'I'll orbit a couple of times to get the automatic docking computer lined up on its target, which is the space station. We know Santa Fe's orbital position exactly at any time. It's a relatively easy thing since we developed the locking beam which Acton and Davis used so successfully.'

Boz came and squatted on his haunches in front of MKG. 'Can't we float up Little Bear as soon as the cutter is ready, MKG? That check——'

MKG flicked away the glowing end of his cigarette. 'Sorry, Boz. The longer she's out of sight the safer. It'll louse up the whole project if she's spotted at the very last moment. And it's getting that way, time-wise.'

'Tyler's fliers will be over Love-Apple Crossing tomorrow,' said Peace flatly.

'Guessing's fine——' objected Boz.

'I'm not guessing, Boz,' answered Peace. 'The helos and carrier planes will have sanitized Grid E-12 east of us by tomorrow. Then—Love-Apple Crossing, Grid E-13. That's the way it goes; one grid finished, the next grid begun.'

MKG said, 'It's as relentless as . . . as . . .'

'A countdown,' said Peace.

'I gotta have more time,' insisted Boz. 'I can't risk a failure.'

Peace said quickly, 'Can you work in the dark on Little Bear, Boz?'

'No.'

'See—there's one hell of a moon,' went on Peace. 'What if I go down at sunset, cut Little Bear free?'

Boz swung excitedly on Peace. 'You're sure an ideas man, Commander.'

'It will leave Little Bear completely vulnerable for the two hours it takes to pull rods and fully activate the SNAP motor,' said Peace. 'Maybe not completely, for it'll be dark and there'll be enough moon for Boz and his team to work by. There's André's acetylene lamp until they can draw their own power from the missile's power plant.'

'Jeez!' exclaimed the Texan. 'That'll give us a whole night to test her, Boz!'

When Peace spoke, I detected the real reason for his concession. 'You'll want to help the boys for a while, won't you, MKG? Don't get short on sleep, though—you and Boz and the others can rest up here tomorrow afternoon.'

In other words, Peace would keep the radio well out of the way until it was too late to retract.

Boz and the scientists were enthusiastic. 'See here, Commander,' said Boz. 'As soon as the power starts coming through from the reactor, we'll submerge her up to the capsule. We'll have power then to operate the ballast pumps.'

The Americans and Trevor-Davis crowded round MKG, squatting like Boz on their heels.

Boz turned to Trevor-Davis. 'Can do, fellah? That SNAP is your pigeon.'

The thought of getting back to mechanics seemed to animate the silent Englishman. 'Can do,' he replied. 'I'll want light, though, from the acetylene.'

'We'll have to risk it,' said Peace.

'It's not such a big risk,' said Adèle. 'All the fishing boats in Limuria will be out now that the storm's over—I expect everyone is as hungry as we are. Tyler's men will see hundreds of fishermen's acetylene lights at sea tonight and to-morrow.'

'Good!' breathed Peace.

Adèle jerked up and pointed south. 'Look at that light! What a meteor!'

A distant stain of red, followed by brilliant white, blotted out the Southern Cross for a moment.

'It isn't a meteor,' said Peace grimly. 'That's a flare dropped from a plane.'

Adèle gave a shiver and a silence fell upon us. Would Tyler discover Little Bear—with a flare like that tomorrow as the missile lay immobile on the surface of the lagoon?

Peace broke the silence. 'Tyler's driving his men into the ground. Anything that floats, they'll find.' His voice became hard. 'Tomorrow we—that is, Mac, André, John and Adèle and I—will play at island fishermen in the lagoon. Boz, you and your boys will need all the sleep you can get if you're going to work right through the night. We'll bury the DATICO gear, the VLF radio and the space-suit here in the sand of the hut in case we have some nosey helo overhead. The dunking helos will come first, then the VP-5's.'

'It sure looks as if we're on the hook,' remarked the big Texan.

'On the hook, but not landed,' Peace replied. 'Everyone will play absolutely dumb if a helo comes over—in the boat we don't speak, except Adèle, if she wishes. in Creole. If a helo comes over the hut, act like sleeping fishermen. André's safe anyway. None of us look too zazzy in our present rig. We'll pass for islanders.'

203

MKG laughed and assumed a Southern drawl. 'For them kind words, Commander, I thank you from the bottom of mah cotton-pick'n' heart.' His easy confidence broke the tension.

Peace went on, 'While we're playing round in the lagoon tomorrow, I'll put a marker over Little Bear so that we know exactly where to look after dark.'

'What if the fliers spot *Semittanté*?' I asked.

'The water will be as clear as glass,' added Adèle.

'They will,' said Peace. 'They will. But until a VP-5 can get here with MAD gear, they won't know whether the wreck is new or old. The Sea of Limuria hasn't only got one wreck,' he went on. 'Look at 'em all on the St Brandon reef. I think it's unlikely that they'll divert a VP-5 specially to investigate yet one more wreck. Most likely it will be logged for routine investigation when a VP-5 comes to case Grid B-13. We can only watch and pray.'

Boz, carried away with enthusiasm, asked, 'How long do you reckon it'll take to get Little Bear into her firing position, Commander?'

'Two-three hours, maybe,' he replied. 'I'll have Mac check over the engine again tomorrow. It hasn't been used in ages, but it looks okay. I'd like to start out of the lagoon before daybreak.'

I asked, 'Once Little Bear is submerged at the firing point, there's one hour to go?'

'T minus sixty—yeah,' Boz corrected me. 'Sure, you got it. The countdown routine's pretty simple—MKG gets my messages via the radio buoy. He gives us a count every few minutes—T minus fifty-nine, T minus fifty, and so on down to zero. At T minus one I start the DATICO checkout. But forget it, fellah—that's what me and Pete and Trev are all here for. You got yourself a ringside seat—no work.'

Peace added quietly, 'And as you count, every helo, every plane, every surfaced sub in Grid B-13 will hear you?'

'Sure.'

'When Little Bear is on the surface, a helo, a sub, a plane—anything with search radar or sonar—could pick her up?'

'Yeah.'

'And when her generators get going, any nuclear sub within sonar range will hear them?'

'Sure—twenty thousand yards. Nearly twelve miles.'

'So from tomorrow evening until MKG is launched, Little Bear is wide open?'

'Wide open as the prairie, Commander. If Tyler and his merry men pal around Grid E-13, then——' Boz shrugged.

The mounting tension and the burden of our secret overlaid any satisfaction there might have been when we dragged the repaired cutter to the water's edge next afternoon. MKG and the American team slept. Peace, on the grounds that the radio batteries were failing, had kept it assiduously out of the way during the morning. Mac hovered like an evil presence. I had a restless night; I fancied I heard a helicopter's rotors and I started upright. It was noise, but not of rotors. At dawn I saw: the shoreline was thick with grey noddies, black-and-white terns and little love-terns which had returned to their home after the cyclone. A squadron, not of Tyler's men but of steel-eyed frigate-birds, hung over the lagoon, dive-bombing shoals of fish.

Adèle hitched the painter over her shoulder and paddled into the wavelets.

But André stood back, muttering.

Peace said sharply. 'Slap it about, André—the sooner we see whether she's seaworthy, the better. Mac also wants to try the engine.'

'André says every ship must have a life. She cannot go into the water like this.'

An echelon of frigate-birds circled low, eyeing us.

'Say, the cutter has served us wonderfully and so has he,' answered Peace.

Adèle translated, but André gestured defiantly. 'In the islands we have strange gods. Perhaps you will not approve. But without it, the cutter cannot go into the water.'

'For God's sake! What does he want?' began Peace, but Adèle cocked her head to the radio and turned it up. A voice said:

    *'Red Force reporting to CIC x Grid E-10, E-12 negative x am commencing search Grid E-13 and E-11 x'*

The reply came back:

    *'CIC to Red Force x report likely contact and vector in VP-5's for MAD investigation x'*

Peace stiffened. 'You hear that? They'll be here any moment now. What the hell is wrong with André, Adèle? Tell him the birds will be here soon——'

The old man looked sullen. 'He says the birds *are* here. That's what he's talking about.'

The radio said:

    *'Red Force helo FX-6 reporting now entering Grid position E-13 x helos FX-5, FX-7 and FX-8 at intervals 20*

> miles north x will co-ordinate reports from FX-6
> Marilyn's Dream x'

The carrier was brief:

> 'Keep that dream going, fellah x'

André gestured at the circling birds, spoke to Adèle, and then pointed at the new planks in the hull. Peace's mouth tightened and he went to the sternsheets, where the Remington was kept.

'No! Geoffrey, no! Not André!' I burst out.

Adèle said helplessly, 'The boat must have a life. The new planking must have a life. One must die in order that the ship may live. Without it, there is no life for his boat.'

There was a volley of Creole from André. 'In my father's day, he says, the islanders used to make a human chain of rollers to the sea, and a new or a repaired boat was launched over them. It took life, for only the strong survived. Now there are not enough strong young men any more. But there must be a life.'

For a long moment Peace paused. Then he grabbed the Remington. He slid back the bolt.

'Geoffrey! For God's sake!' I rushed forward.

Before I could reach him, Peace fired. One of the circling mass of frigate-birds fell, flopping into the water at our feet. Delight and astonishment spread over old André's face. He crashed his rough fist between Peace's shoulders, grabbed the axe, and splashed after the wounded bird. In a moment he was back, holding the bucking thing clear as it struck at him. He gestured to us. 'The boat—get it on its side—the bird must not die before——'

Peace, MKG and I heaved the cutter over. André yanked the kicking bird to his new planks and shoved its neck against them. With a deft stroke he severed the bird's neck and, as the blood gushed, he made the sign of the Cross against the boards. He went to Peace and took his forearm in a curious grip.

Adèle said, 'He says, only a man of the sea would know . . .'

I recovered my wits. 'Geoffrey, in the name of all that's not holy . . .'

'It's as old as time—or the sea,' he explained. 'When he spoke of a life for a life I remembered: ancient Mediterranean shipwrights used to demand a human sacrifice at the time of launching. The custom's mutated somewhat, but it still survives among these backblocks of the sea. Come on now!'

He glanced at the sky. There was nothing. We eased the cutter into the water. The new planks held. Smiling and gesticulating. André hoisted the sail. We headed for *Semit-anté*'s grave.

'Quick!' yelled Peace. 'For God's sake—quick! Get those hats on! Here they are!'

There was no mistaking the roar of rotors. The helicopter flew towards the lagoon entrance from the open sea.

'Switch off that radio!' hissed Peace. 'Under the decking—quick!' He threw the Remington after it and pulled on a big hat.

The helo came at us wave-top level.

'No English!' breathed Peace. MKG's face was drawn under its stubble. Adèle was wide-eyed. André's astonishment was genuine—he had never seen a plane before.

The helo swung low and hovered over us with a downrush of air.

'Look up! Look up at her! Play it!' ordered Peace.

We stood up, shouting incoherently and waving. The observer looked into our faces from thirty feet up. A loud-hailer clicked on, so that we overheard his conversation with the pilot.

'Hell, Pete, this looks a pretty beat-up bunch.'

'So would you be, if you'd been out in a cyclone in that boat,' replied the other. 'Jeez, it was bad enough in the flat-top.'

'I ain't no horse-player, but I'd lay money none of these guys is Vice-President of the United States!' said the observer. The harsh metallic laughter echoed over the lagoon. The helo swung and I caught a glimpse of a pin-up girl with the legend 'Marilyn's Dream' near the horse-collar winch.

'That goddam' ole ship is at the bottom of the sea,' said the pilot. 'We're wasting our time, I say.'

'This business sure gripes ole Revs's ass,' the other said, laughing. 'Jesus!'

'This is the first land I seen,' commented the pilot.

'Nothing but sea, sea, sea,' rejoined the other. 'There ain't a thing for us here, brother. Say—' he peered down—'there's a dame in that boat.'

'Listen, fellah, if you want a dame you can get one nice and cosy back in the Seychelles without flying a thousand miles to some goddam' spit of land.'

'Sure, sure,' replied the observer. 'I just sort of like the idea of a dame out here—dancing girls, soft music, tropical lagoon . . .'

'You sound like you got a couple of sheets to the wind right now,' said the pilot. 'Call 'em up, fellah. Ask what we're supposed to ask.'

'Okay, okay,' replied the observer. 'I got it written down.'
There was a pause. Then he called, 'Bateau?'

I shuddered at his French.

'Ship—bateau? Nau—naufrage—wreck?'

André spoke to Adèle. They laughed and pointed upwards.

'Aw, cut it out—can't you see they're just a bunch of
dumb islanders? Let's get the hell outa here.'

'I guess so. First let's mosey around the lagoon. Report
back, willya?'

'Sure. *FX-6 Marilyn's Dream reporting x Love-Apple
Crossing*—sounds like a first-run movie-house title—*negative
x sighted boat with islanders x called 'em up—negative x
lagoon——*'

'*Negative*,' added the other. 'Well, 'bye from Marilyn's
Dream, folks.'

The loudhailer cut and the helo whirled upwards. Sweat
stood out under Peace's eyes. Adèle was very still. My knees
were weak.

'Put on that radio, Adèle,' ordered Peace. 'Look!'

The helo came to a hovering stop above the place where
*Semittanté* lay. The observer's voice was recognizable on the
set as Adèle held the Navy wavelength:

*Helo FX-6 to Red Force x Grid position E-13 x Love-
Apple Crossing investigated x negative x island boat in
inner lagoon x negative x wreck in lagoon x refer for
routine investigation VP-5 MAD x wreck probably old x
lies inside reef x*

I saw a ball with a cable attached fall from the helo's winch
into the sea to mark the wreck. We waited, breathless.
The observer's voice went on:

*Routine dunking check x negative no contact x*

Peace gave a great sigh of relief. In less than a minute the
helo swung the sonar ball back into position with the winch
and, following the reef, disappeared westwards.

Peace said quietly, 'At least we know exactly where
*Semittanté* lies.'

We glided across the lagoon, silent with our own thoughts.
André, with his uncanny sense of place, brought the cutter
to rest over the wreck. Her outline was clear; Little Bear's
long crate lay on deck. Without speaking we dropped the
cutter's anchor cable attached to a length of line and a chunk
of *bois mangue*.

Then we stole back across the lagoon through the lengthen-
ing shadows, waiting for the night, waiting for the morning.

Fifteen hours to launch!

At six o'clock that evening they had not found Little Bear. In the gathering dusk the cutter lay over *Semittanté*. Peace stood ready in his rubber diving-suit to go down and cut the missile adrift. The tension triggered off by the sweep of the helicopter was now enhanced by the nearness of the blast-off. It was clear in the faces of Boz Blair, Trevor-Davis and the three other Americans who waited for the missile to check it. MKG alone seemed calm, almost detached.

The stream of operational messages from Red and Blue Forces did nothing to lessen the air of tension. Although the helo search had moved westwards from Love-Apple Crossing towards Agalega, 50 miles away, the surface forces of carriers, destroyers and nuclear subs had not yet entered Grid E-13. Nor had the VP-5's, which Peace dreaded most. They might come tonight.

Since our arrival back in the cutter, the conversation had been exclusively technical centering round the launch, for which Peace was, I think, grateful, for MKG did not renew his request to listen to newscasts. Mac chain-smoked and watched us from the background of the tight launch team circle.

Peace gave the thumbs-up sign and slipped into the calm water of the lagoon, axe in hand.

We waited.

Boz gave a sharp intake of breath. There was a flurry of water and the missile broke surface close by, shedding its tail of wooden crating. The long, silver-white thing, fifty-five feet long, six round the nose, and thickening at the tail like a sailor's bell-bottomed pants, pitched easily in the slight swell. The capsule nose-cone was behind the waterproof membrane. Beyond the reef, the sea grumbled.

'Let's get alongside her,' Boz exclaimed. 'This is where we take over.' The men started to grin, easing the tension. They had a job to do which would occupy all their thoughts and effort during the night. MKG was to assist for the first few hours and then return to Vingt-Cinq Coups. For us, the long night of waiting lay ahead.

Adèle shivered. 'It looks so small.'

MKG smiled at her, saying nothing. But Boz's exuberance was starting to return at the sight of Little Bear. 'Best in a small lucky packet, they say. Why, that goddam' great Sirius rocket——'

Pete the Texan laughed. 'Aw, come off it, Boz. If this guy gets talking about Sirius, he'll blow a gasket.'

Peace surfaced and stripped off his Scuba mask. We hauled him into the boat and eased alongside Little Bear. Boz made fast to the capsule's side hatch. André gazed in speechless wonderment. Boz held a checklist.

'It's a complex business,' he said. 'Me and the boys will go over everything during the night. How long are you staying, MKG?'

'Till about ten,' replied MKG.

'We'll come out in the cutter and fetch you back,' said Peace.

Boz had the pleased air of a showman. He gestured towards a small pistol switch in the capsule's cockpit. It projected prominently in front of the heavily-padded seat, around whose back were draped safety straps.

'See that? That controls the movements of the power plant rods. Trev here's the expert on that—SNAP!'

I wondered what was going on in Peace's mind. The sight of the missile seemed to disquiet him.

Boz went on. 'Before Trev pulls rods, which starts the reactor—or, as we space boys say, it goes critical—we have to check the instrument panels, the monitoring circuits, valves and emergency alarms. They're energized by a small battery unit until the main power starts coming through from the reactor. Each of us has his own department.'

'Let's get going, Boz,' said the big Texan.

'You wouldn't think to look at this bum that he's an expert on missile valves,' Boz remarked good-humouredly.

'It looks very dark in there,' Adèle murmured.

'I know—have to know—the position of every switch, every lever, even in total darkness,' replied MKG.

'He does, too,' added Boz. 'Right, fellahs. Now, we'll want a couple of hours before the instruments start to wake up under main power. It also takes some time after she's gone critical to mount full power for the pumps and so on. You can't do anything further here for the moment, Commander.'

'Power—noise,' replied Peace. 'Electric light—pinpoint for search planes. Pumps—target for sonar.'

'Sorry, Commander, but that's the way it is. We'll try and black out the perspex canopy from inside, but we gotta have a good light to check. We can't shorten the drill. Same with the countdown. Once we start the sequencer count, whatever happens in that last hour before the blast-off, we're committed.'

'Even if Tyler should show up?' I asked.

MKG replied slowly, 'Once I'm submerged and counting, for God's sake don't let Tyler do anything rash. This little honey will smash anything on her way up. I don't want the lives of Tyler and his crew on my conscience.'

'But it's Boz on the surface who presses the firing-button,' I said.

'This is all theorizing,' said Peace shortly. 'We'll meet the situation as it arises.'

MKG eyed him speculatively for a long moment. Then Boz took a key and unlocked the side hatchway through the casing into the cockpit.

He signed to Trevor-Davis. 'Come on, fellah, she's all yours to start with.'

Trevor-Davis lowered himself on to the cushioned chair and looked at us through the perspex. He raised his right hand, forefinger and thumb circled together. Then he dropped his hand to the pistol-grip switch. We waited. Then, on his left, a dial glowed and a needle quivered.

During the next hour as Boz and his team went to work the instruments came alive one by one—the first had been the power-level reading of the reactor. Boz told us at intervals of coming and going into the cockpit that the others were pressures, velocity of steam flow, monitoring checks. Then suddenly the cockpit was flooded with the bright glow of electric light. Trevor-Davis, who had taken over again from one of the Americans, smiled up at us. Little Bear began to vibrate as the steam built up to full pressure in the reactor.

'I think we'll leave you to it,' Peace told MKG and the team. He glanced uneasily at the east and at the moon. 'We're wide, wide open.'

Mac, at Peace's order, used the engine to take us back quickly to the shore. He seemed to have it in perfect running order. The American team had to accompany us, since the cockpit could only accommodate one man at a time. Peace, Adèle, Mac and I jumped out on to the sand. MKG and Boz nodded goodbye; all their thoughts were on Little Bear.

We walked slowly up to Vingt-Cinq Coups.

Twelve hours to blast-off!

We sat against the coral wall of the hut, waiting for the news from Mauritius. Peace's eyes wandered frequently across the lagoon to the muted patch of light where Little Bear lay.

Mauritius Radio came through:

'Up to a few hours ago, neither the person of Marvin K. Green, Vice-President of the United States, nor the French freighter *Semittanté* had been located by the massive search conducted by the American Seventh Fleet. Tonight the eyes of the world are on the Sea of Limuria. The focus of the search is now in the vicinity of the neighbouring isles of Agalega and Love-Apple Crossing. American fliers report that both these places have been heavily hit by the recent cyclone.'

Peace stirred as the announcer went on:

'In the wake of the air search are deployed no fewer than five carriers, eighteen destroyers and nine nuclear submarines. American long-range VP-5 aircraft, flying from British bases, today combed a large area south of the Seychelles group, with negative results. These aircraft are using secret equipment to detect submerged wrecks.

'Meanwhile, in the United States, the National Space Administration states, that tomorrow is the most favourable day for a space-shot. In view of this, carrier-based aircraft are flying round-the-clock missions in an attempt to stay what political observers in Washington consider the most extraordinary episode in the long history of the United States Presidency.

'The bearing of the American people at this time of crisis is no less extraordinary. Since the news broke, churches have been thronged, special prayers have been said for the President's recovery and the Vice-President's safety, and normal activities in all major cities have almost ceased. Many shops are closed and only essential services are operating. People have withdrawn indoors to the sanctuary of their homes, except in Washington, where crowds have gathered outside the White House in silent vigil while the battle for the President's life goes on. A curious silence has fallen on the nation. In New York——'

Peace leaned forward and clicked off the set. For a long time there was no sound but the wash of the sea in the soft tropical night.

'You have all this to account for if things go wrong,' I said.

Peace jumped to his feet. 'They must not find Little Bear!'

Seven hours later they had not located Little Bear.

MKG had returned in the cutter within an hour; after a broken night André had fetched us as a thin line started to show pearly-grey in the east. Now we were back at the missile. Peace had stood up in the cutter as we crossed the lagoon, trying to probe the lightening skies. They were empty.

Boz and his team were weary but triumphant. 'She's fine—every damn' thing just jim-dandy,' he told MKG. 'She's hot to trot.'

By contrast with his previous mood, MKG was light-hearted, boyish almost, now that the space-shot was at hand. He glanced down into the softly vibrating cockpit. 'Let's get her to the launch-point, shall we—got it fixed, John?'

'Just one more star-sight,' I said, holding my sextant.

'He doesn't need a sextant,' Peace said. 'He could do it blindfold.'

I took my sight and was satisfied. There was nothing to keep us in the lagoon longer. MKG looked thoughtfully at the long missile. 'Just pray that at the Jesus moment she hasn't got a hot bottom.'

Boz stiffened.

'Hot bottom?' Adèle looked startled.

MKG gestured with one hand. 'She's never been flight-tested—too much heat causes the tail to fall apart. If that happens, she'll wriggle across the sky like a belly-dancer. Goodbye Mr. Vice-President.'

She shivered and he put an arm round her.

Boz said quickly, 'Doesn't often happen any more. The cermets boys have seen to that. Just an outside chance.'

André brought the cutter close to the nose-cone while I fended her off with a rough oar. Boz hitched a rope into the nose-towing wire and Mac eased open the throttle. André gestured to me and we slipped our oars into the crude row-locks. We heaved. Little Bear moved, gathered way. In the smooth water as Peace gunned the engine, Little Bear followed as easily and tamely as a well-trained dog; I could feel the pulse of her machinery along the tow-rope.

Five o'clock.

We cleared the lagoon entrance and I gave Peace a course into the eye of the soft morning.

Five-thirty.

Boz brought the silver space-suit, which he had unpacked during the night, and helped MKG into it as we moved along. He laid the silver helmet on the thwart—stark, futuristic, against the weather-stained wood. The dawn light glowed on its gold-plated visor which would guard MKG's face against the sun.

The cutter chugged on.

Six o'clock.

Three hours to launch.

'Try the radio,' Peace told Adèle.

The Navy wavelength said, ' . . . Love-Apple Crossing . . .'
Involuntarily Peace jerked the throttle. There was nothing
more. He glanced skywards and said harshly, 'Keep it going,
Adèle!'

The minutes dragged; the engine throbbed. Love-Apple
Crossing had almost submerged its low length into the sea
barely two short miles behind. We had about half a mile to
go to the launching-point.

The radio said:

> *Willowtrack to all Red and Blue HUK subs x report
> your positions to me x*

Six-thirty.

The voice went on:

> *My position Grid E-13 approximately 40 miles due
> south of Love-Apple Crossing x course zero-zero-five
> true x speed 12 knots, rigged for utra-quiet x*

'My God!' exclaimed Peace. I explained to the tense team:
Tyler was 40 miles away, making straight at us, coasting
along with all his listening apparatus and radar going. At 12
knots he would be on us in three hours. If he received an
inkling of where we were, he could reach us in an hour at
maximum speed, if he chose!

I gave Peace an alteration of course. Boz and the team
screwed up their eyes against the sun, scanning the horizon
to the south, not speaking. The light reflected off MKG's space-
suit.

Seven o'clock.

'Stop!' I ordered.

We were in position.

'I'll flood her down at once, Boz,' said MKG. 'There's no
point in staying up. In one hour I shall start the sequencer.
Shall we synchronize watches?'

The simple action had all the excitement of a war mission.
Little Bear, with its tapered stern, lay like a giant ray in the
water.

Boz picked up the helmet.

MKG stopped him for a moment and surveyed the soft
scene, the sea, the low isle in the distance. He looked from
one to another of us. My secret thundered like St Brandon
surf against my brain—I *had* to tell him! I glanced round.
Mac alone of us was sitting, cigarette in mouth, his hand half
under the stern thwart where he kept the Remington. He
looked like a snake about to strike. I felt Peace's hand grip
my elbow like steel.

MKG waved at Little Bear and the sky. 'This will bring out

214

that great untested source of power in the American people which Lincoln saw over a century ago,' he said. 'It has been given to me to be the bearer of that sacred mission.'

'Lincoln!' whispered Adèle. '*President* Lincoln . . .'

MKG did not seem to hear. The strange timbre laced his words. 'There are no goodbyes in this. Adèle, say also to André . . .'

He paused, then impulsively took the old fisherman's arm in André's own peculiar grip, and shook it. Tears ran down the mahogany cheeks and he said something brokenly to Adèle.

Adèle, her voice thick with emotion, said: 'God be with you. Come back to Limuria.'

Boz held out the helmet to MKG. MKG looked quickly in a pocket and brought out a small bible, as if to reassure himself. The scene had a curious unreal air—like a condemned cell, where all normal activity goes on around in a highly abnormal context.

Once the helmet was on, we knew MKG's voice would become a metallic counterfeit. MKG moved forward to Boz and ducked a little. Boz lifted on the helmet and gave it a half-turn. Boz and the Texan helped him, ungainly now, through the missile's hatchway. He eased himself in and dogged it closed.

MKG was utterly alone.

There was a burp of water at the stern as the ballast pumps started. The missile tilted, its nose at an angle. Then it sank upright to about two-thirds of its length. Boz and the scientists nodded approval. MKG sat in his capsule about 12 feet above us. I think it must have been the bright flash of sunlight on the perspex which brought the frigate-bird down to investigate. I heard the swift rush of wings.

Like lightning, Peace snatched an oar and struck the magnificent bird. It fell, stunned, into the water. Little Bear, on hand signals from Boz to MKG, sank lower until it was the height of a man out of the water.

With a quick glance at André, Peace grabbed the bird .

Little Bear was head-high.

MKG looked out at us—grave, a slight smile in the deep-set eyes.

Peace snatched the axe from the bottom-boards and struck off the great bird's head. Boz and his team gaped in astonishment. Peace leaned out, holding the twitching stump, steadying himself against the smooth whiteness of the missile casing.

With the bloodied neck, Peace made the sign of the Cross on it.

Adèle gave a gasp. There was a startled outburst from André. Boz gave a quick signal to MKG. I heard the rapid whirr of the ballast pumps. MKG raised a gloved hand and gave the thumbs-up sign, his eyes fixed on us all.

The capsule-shield sank to gunwale-level.

Adèle translated André automatically: 'The strange ship has a life now . . .'

Another signal. The pumps whirred. I looked down into MKG's strong face. Was he already President of the United States?

The eyes went for the last time slowly from Peace to me, to Boz, to each member of the team, to Adèle, momentarily to Mac, and finally to Adèle. Boz raised his clenched fist as a signal. MKG reached out for a switch.

The capsule vanished.

I do not know how long we all stood numbed, trying to follow the missile into the depths. Adèle wept; Peace held the headless bird. The sea was empty, except for the tiny cutter. Only at firing-depth would MKG send up the marker buoy with its radio antenna.

Boz said at last, 'Commander, we must get at least half a mile away—probably a bit farther is better.'

Seven-thirty.

'Let's wait for the buoy,' I said.

'No time,' replied Boz. 'We must get clear.'

Rather than create sound by using the engine, Peace had André raise the lateen sail and we glided across the still sea. The sole marker of Little Bear was a group of frigate-birds tearing at their dead companion.

André dropped the sail at Peace's command. The buoy—where was the buoy? Adèle explained to André, whose sea-sight was keenest.

We waited.

Suddenly André exclaimed: the bright orange marker with its radio antenna plopped out of the sea. Boz slipped on one of the double rubber-padded headphones of the VLF set and fiddled with the dials; the other scientists busied themselves with the DATICO gear.

'I'll repeat everything MKG says,' said Boz.

Peace turned to Adèle, his voice strained. 'Keep the radio going all the time. Check Tyler.'

His words were drowned. The big VP-5 swept over us at wave-top height. The thunder of its four great engines momentarily blanked out the radio. It came so low that I could see the massive search radar dome, the pilot and the co-pilot in their seats. It was still in Arctic paint, broad orange stripes against the black hull.

The voice on the radio was vibrant with excitement:

*VP-5 maritime reconnaissance Baker Charley Sugar to all HUK and ASW forces x powerful MAD contacts Grid position E-13 x sighted submarine marker buoy approximately 2½ miles east Love-Apple Crossing x men in boat using radio x marker buoy has radio antenna x*

The reply was immediate:

*Willowtrack to Baker Charley Sugar x hold that contact x am vectoring all HUK forces to Grid E-13 x home them in x am proceeding maximum speed to evaluate contact x*

I looked at my watch.

One hour and five minutes!

*Willowtrack* was 40 miles away: she could do near 40 knots when pushed—Tyler would be here before MKG blasted off!

Peace's face was like iron. He knelt next to Boz and said into his chest microphone speaker. 'MKG! For Christ's sake, there's a VP-5 overhead. They've picked up this transmission. Tyler's coming—can't you cut it short——'

Boz pushed him away as the headphone crackled. 'No dice, Commander. The countdown routine is fixed. One hour, no less. I'll start MKG in a couple of minutes.'

'Tyler——' repeated Peace. His words were drowned as the big plane thundered overhead again, banking slowly over Little Bear's marker.

*Baker Charley Sugar to Willowtrack x strong radio emissions x reports, countdown will begin in a few minutes x*

*Willowtrack* came back:

*All Red and Blue Force aircraft, helos, cowboys and subs vectored to your area x what duration is countdown?*

The fact that *Willowtrack* was replying meant she was either on the surface or running partially submerged with her radio mast up, which would make her slower than full speed deep down. The thought of that streamlined hull tearing through the water towards us forced my eyes to the south. The horizon was empty.

Boz said sharply, 'Sequencer start! I repeat, sequencer start!' The headphone crackled. 'T minus sixty and counting!' MKG had begun the countdown.

One whole hour until Boz pressed the firing button.

*Baker Charley Sugar to Willowtrack x countdown has begun x voice says T minus 60 x*

217

After what seemed hours, Boz repeated MKG in a flat voice:
' T minus fifty. All systems go.'

> *Willowtrack to Baker Charley Sugar x nearest search plane to your position is in Grid E-16 x cannot get there in time x I am proceeding at maximum speed x will echo-range starting at 20,000 yards x is contact moving?*

' T minus forty-five. All systems go.'

> *Baker Charley Sugar to Willowtrack x contact steady x countdown now T minus 45 x*

Adèle sat next to me on the rough thwart, her face white. I saw Peace's sweat drip on to the collar of his rubber diving-suit. Boz and the Americans sat like statues. Peace glanced across at me without speaking. I read his thought: 20,000 yards, nearly 12 miles! When Tyler started to echo-range, we would know exactly how close he was.

' T minus forty.'

> *Willowtrack to Baker Charley Sugar x who is in the boat?*

The big plane swung round, inspected us. The minutes were agonizing.

> *Baker Charley Sugar to Willowtrack x eyeball check shows nine men and one woman x radio apparatus and two antenna-like portables x*

' T minus thirty.'

Half an hour to go.

My palms were clammy. Adèle spoke softly in Creole, as if to herself. I think she was praying. André said something and she turned to me, her eyes tear-bright.

' André says the ship down in the sea has its life from the frigate-bird. It will fly.'

How close was *Willowtrack*? I did a rapid mental calculation. Being partially instead of fully submerged, Tyler would not be getting *Willowtrack*'s full 40 knots. Say 35 now—over 40 miles an hour! If I were correct, he would start echo-ranging in roughly another 15 minutes. *Willowtruck* would then be 12 miles from her target!

' T minus twenty-five.'

> *Willowtrack to Baker Charley Sugar x drop following message to boat by streamer x Tyler to Commander Peace x request with all ervour at my command you call off launch x please convey this to the President of the United States x*

' President!'

Boz spun on Peace, staring incredulously.

With the speed of a cobra striking, Peace leaned forward and plucked the headphones from Boz's ears. The Colt with the hocked hammer was in his hand. As he did so, he jerked his head to Mac. He was so quick with the Remington that I did not see him reach under the sternsheets for it. He stood, balancing himself with one foot on the thwart, the wicked muzzle covering the boat.

Peace held the speaker against him so that MKG could not hear.

'Yes,' he said slowly, including all the Americans with Boz in his reply. 'The President had a severe stroke shortly before we ditched *Semittanté*. He wasn't expected to live.'

'You knew and you let MKG carry on with this?' Boz looked stunned. Pete Allingham, his face livid with anger, started to get to his feet, but Mac waved him down.

'Yes,' said Peace. 'Little Bear goes.'

'Not while I'm here to stop it,' snapped Pete. Mac raised the Remington and pointed it square at the Texan's chest.

'I wouldn't try to, Allingham,' Peace said grimly. 'He's been itching for days to try it out on John and Adèle.'

'Jesus Christ!' burst out Boz. '*You* knew too!'

'They knew, but they weren't with me,' replied Peace. 'I want you to remember that, Boz, if you have to turn me in to Tyler before the blast-off.'

'Blast-off!' echoed Pete. 'You're gonna let MKG go without knowing!'

'Yes.' Peace nodded grimly. 'What sort of effect would it have on him to tell him now?'

'No!' yelled Boz wildly. 'You can't, Commander, it's too big!'

'Sit down!' snarled Peace, waving the Colt. The headphone crackled and Peace put it on, drawing to one side to give Mac a clean line of fire.

'T minus twenty.'

The VP-5 engines thundered over us. A streamer with a weight attached fell into the sea a few yards from the cutter. André fished it out and handed it to Peace.

Peace repeated MKG. 'T minus eighteen and counting. All systems go.' His eyes never left Boz and Allingham.

'The message——' began Boz.

The headphone crackled and Peace repeated with grim humour. 'Observe countdown routine. Do not interrupt sequence. T minus fifteen.'

The VP-5 swooped down again, two men craning out of the co-pilot's window for our reply. We stared back, motionless, while they gestured at Mac's gun.

'T minus twelve.'

*Willowtrack to Baker Charley Sugar x what does boat reply?*

219

*Baker Charley Sugar to Willowtrack x boat does not reply x two men with guns in her x*

*Willowtrack to Baker Charley Sugar x my sonar reports possible contact bearing 010 degrees true x am slowing to evaluate contact x*

I saw the ripple of sweat on Peace's head under the headphones. Tyler was slowing—he would have to, in order to enable the delicate listening devices in his hull to pinpoint the contact. It would be impossible for him to do so while tearing at full speed through the water.

*Willowtrack to Baker Charley Sugar x contact evaluated as submarine machinery x range 20,000 yards x depth 600 feet x speed zero x course zero x*

Tyler had burst into sonar range at under 12 miles.

' T minus ten.'

Ten minutes to blast-off.

Then—Peace gave a gasp. He repeated, 'I have recycled to T minus fifteen. Holding.' He clapped his hand over the microphone and whipped out, 'Something's gone wrong down there! He's holding the count!'

'Thank God!' whispered Boz, his face deadly pale.

Peace stared at the speaker in silent dismay. There was a chatter from the Americans. Mac looked nonplussed. Then Peace held up his hand. He smiled with grim satisfaction. 'Recycle to T minus fifteen. Monitoring checklight fault. Counting.'

My mouth was parched. Tyler had been given five minutes —five vital minutes for Peace.

*Willowtrack to Baker Charley Sugar x proceeding emergency flank speed on contact bearing x*

Tyler had picked up a firm contact and, on the correct assumption it was Little Bear, was now tearing at us full speed at something over 40 miles an hour. He would be here before Little Bear could go!

' T minus ten. All systems go.'

*Baker Charley Sugar to Willowtrack x countdown now T minus 10 x*

Peace's hand holding the Colt never wavered. Each minute seemed an hour. The big plane circled in slow banks, centring on the bright orange marker buoy. I thought I detected a cream of white water to the south—*Willowtrack*'s periscope.

' T minus five. All systems go.'

*Willowtrack to Baker Charley Sugar x contact bears 002 degrees true x course zero x speed zero x range 2,700 yards depth 600 feet x*

'My God! Tyler's here!' burst out Boz.

'T minus four. All systems go.'

The big plane dived so low over the cutter that we cowered away under the thwarts, stunned by the noise. Mac was back on his feet first, Remington in hand.

We could still hear MKG's disembodied voice over the headphone.

'T minus two. All systems go. Stand by for DATICO checkout. At T minus one I will count to zero.'

When Peace pressed the firing-button, we knew that the umbilical cable which attached MKG to the marker buoy would be blown out by an explosive bolt and we would no longer hear him.

Boz jumped up, rocking the boat. 'Stop! Stop!'

'T minus one. I count . . . fifty-nine . . .'

'John!' Adèle's face was ashen. She pointed. A white feather of foam broke the calm surface of the sea less than a mile away. Tyler!

*Willowtrack to Baker Charley Sugar x stop him x for Christ's sake stop him x*

'. . eighteen . . . seventeen . . . sixteen . . . fifteen . . . fourteen . . . thirteen . . . twelve . . . eleven . . . ten . . .'

The big plane pulled round, coming at us.

Boz threw himself at Peace, but Peace's eyes had never left him. With a savage blow he clubbed him unconscious with the Colt.

'. . . nine . . . eight . . . seven . . . six . . . five . . . four . . . three . . . two . . . one.'

'ZERO!'

Peace clapped his hand to the headphone and leapt up.

'Gone!'

All of us were on our feet, oblivious of the big plane, oblivious of the submarine.

A white column erupted out of the sea like a depth-charge. Sunlight exploded on the perspex. Streaming water, Little Bear leaned over at a crazy angle. Peace gave a wild intake of breath. Then, amongst the white foam at the base, I saw the bite of red flame as Little Bear's motor kicked in. The missile jerked upright.

I turned to speak to Adèle, but my voice was drowned in the ear-stunning thunder of the explosion. Adèle came hard against my shoulder.

The white thing with its tail of white flame tore skywards, bearing with it the President of the United States.

The blast smacked across the sea. Above Love-Apple Crossing it brought a flock of white birds into the air, like a plume raised in salute.

*Love-Apple Crossing, 17th February, 197—*
The following transcript of a Telstar relay is incorporated in
today's log:

'Up here in space the sun shines brightly on the bareheaded man about to take the highest oath of office in the
United States, Marvin K. Green. His silver helmet and gold-
plated visor are at his side. On the left shoulder of his space-
suit is emblazoned the Stars and Stripes. The rest of the small
group who watch the ceremony stand back in the shadow of
the canopy.

'The sharp light throws into bold relief the faces of the
President and of Dr Felix Coulter, Director of Space Station
One. Martin K. Green's shows the strain of his fantastic
one-man voyage. Dr Coulter holds the small bible which the
President carried in the cockpit of Little Bear.

'Dr Coulter asks the President to raise his right hand,
which he does. He repeats after Dr Coulter: "I do solemnly
swear that I will faithfully execute the office of President of
the United States, and I will, to the best of my ability, preserve, protect and defend the Constitution of the United
States."

'The President looks down for a moment to the brilliant
blue-and-white curve far below which is the earth.

'With deep feeling, he says, "So help me God."'

# Geoffrey Jenkins

Geoffrey Jenkins writes of adventure on land and at sea in some of the most exciting thrillers ever written. 'Geoffrey Jenkins has the touch that creates villains and heroes — and even icy heroines — with a few vivid words.' *Liverpool Post*. 'A style which combines the best of Nevil Shute and Ian Fleming.' *Books and Bookmen*.

SOUTHTRAP £1.35
A BRIDGE OF MAGPIES £1.25
A CLEFT OF STARS £1.25
THE RIVER OF DIAMONDS £1.15
THE WATERING PLACE OF
GOOD PEACE £1.25
SCEND OF THE SEA £1.25
HUNTER-KILLER £1.25
A GRUE OF ICE £1.25
A TWIST OF SAND £1.35
A RAVEL OF WATERS £1.50

FONTANA PAPERBACKS

# Fontana Paperbacks

Fontana is a leading paperback publisher of fiction and non-fiction, with authors ranging from Alistair MacLean, Agatha Christie and Desmond Bagley to Solzhenitsyn and Pasternak, from Gerald Durrell and Joy Adamson to the famous Modern Masters series.

In addition to a wide-ranging collection of internationally popular writers of fiction, Fontana also has an outstanding reputation for history, natural history, military history, psychology, psychiatry, politics, economics, religion and the social sciences.

All Fontana books are available at your bookshop or newsagent; or can be ordered direct. Just fill in the form and list the titles you want.

FONTANA BOOKS, Cash Sales Department, G.P.O. Box 29, Douglas, Isle of Man, British Isles. Please send purchase price, plus 8p per book. Customers outside the U.K. send purchase price, plus 10p per book. Cheque, postal or money order. No currency.

NAME (Block letters)

ADDRESS